The Brotherhood

Book One

Templar Steel

By

K. M. Ashman

Published by
Silverback Books Ltd

Copyright K M Ashman 2018

All rights are reserved. No part of this publication may be reproduced, stored, or transmitted in any form or by any means, without prior written permission of the copyright owner.

All characters depicted within this publication are fictitious and any resemblance to any real persons living or dead is entirely coincidental.

Also by K. M. Ashman

The India Sommers Mysteries
The Dead Virgins
The Treasures of Suleiman
The Mummies of the Reich
The Tomb Builders

The Roman Chronicles
The Fall of Britannia
The Rise of Caratacus
The Wrath of Boudicca

The Medieval Sagas
Blood of the Cross
In Shadows of Kings
Sword of Liberty
Ring of Steel

The Blood of Kings
A Land Divided
A Wounded Realm
Rebellion's Forge
The Warrior Princess
The Blade Bearer

Individual Novels
Savage Eden
The Last Citadel
Vampire

The Brotherhood
Templar Steel

Audio Books
A Land Divided
A Wounded Realm
Rebellion's Forge
The Warrior Princess
The Blade Bearer
Blood of the Cross
The Last Citadel

MAP OF THE HOLY LAND CIRCA 1177

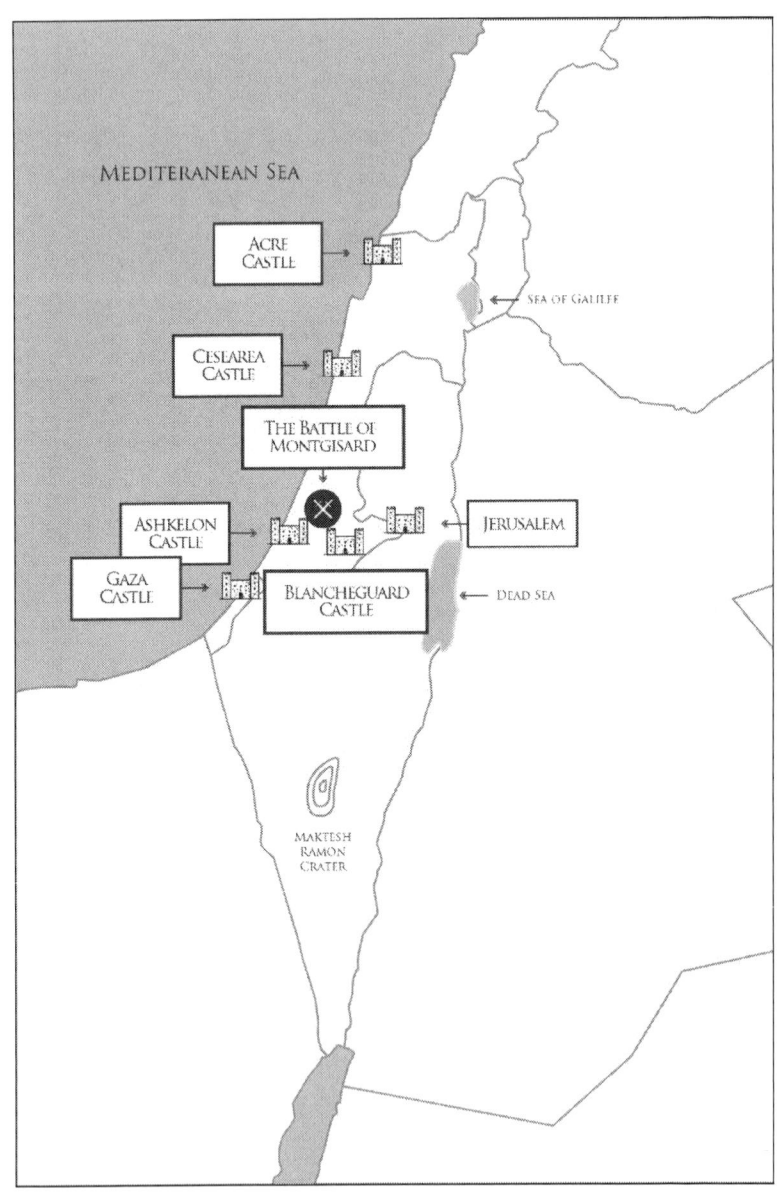

CHARACTER LIST

ARISTOCRACY
Baldwin IV - King of Jerusalem
Almaric - Baldwin's father
Agnes of Courtenay – Almaric's first wife
Maria Comnena – Almaric's second wife
Raynald of Châtillon – Lord of Oultrejordain

CLERGY
William of Tyre – Catholic prelate (and Baldwin's teacher)
The Bishop of Bethlehem – Protector of the Cross of Jerusalem

CHRISTIAN FORCES
Eudes de St. Amand – 8th Grand Master of the Knights Templar
Brother Tristan - Marshal of the Templar Order
Brother Valmont of Lyon - Seneschal of the Templar Order
Jakelin de Mailly - French Templar Knight
Richard of Kent – English Templar Knight
Benedict of York – English Templar Knight
Gerald of Jerusalem – English Knight
Robert of Essex - English Knight
Thomas Cronin - Sergeant at Arms
Simon Callow - Sergeant at Arms
James Hunter - Scout
Bedouin Squire – Hassan Malouf

MUSLIM FORCES
Salah ad-Din - Saladin – Sultan of Egypt and Syria
Shirkuh ad-Din - Saladin's General
Farrukh-Shah – Saladin's nephew
Taqi ad-Din - Ayyubid commander at Montgisard

Prologue

In November 1095, Pope Urban the Second addressed a large gathering of French clergy and noblemen at the Council of Clermont in Auvergne, France.

In his speech, he referred to the terrible unrest across the country and reminded the nobles of their holy duty to rule their provinces with an even hand. In particular, they were to ensure the protection of the clergy at all levels and restore justice and public order to the people.

Those present acknowledged and supported the Pope's direction and it wasn't long before he cleverly turned their attention to the main issue on his mind, suggesting that once righteousness had been restored, it could be used in God's service to support the Christians in the east, who were suffering terrible atrocities at the hands of the Turks.

He went on to report that untold numbers of Christians had either been killed or captured by the Saracens in the east, with many being tortured to death or sold into slavery. Churches were being desecrated and the kingdom of God was being devastated. The audience was horrified and listened intently as he went on to recount terrible stories of the rape and murder of Christian women amongst other unspeakable atrocities.

Pope Urban went on to entreat everyone present to spread the message widely, persuading people of all stations to rise in anger at the treatment of the Christians and engage in a holy war to defend God's people. He went on to preach that brothers who had fought brothers could now unite under one banner, and those who had led a life of crime could become righteous once more in the service of God's army. Furthermore, he promised that all who died in such a war would receive full absolution from whatever sins they had committed throughout their lifetime, guaranteeing them entry through the gates of heaven.

The effect of Pope Urban's speech was immediate, and word spread far and wide. For the next few months, his clergy spread the message throughout Europe and soon, tens of thousands of people ranging from the highest echelons of the aristocracy to the humblest of peasants pledged to aid the Christians of the Holy Land.

Eventually, four separate crusader armies were recruited, assembling sometime just after November 1096 outside the walls of Constantinople and after making their holy vows, crossed the Bosporus in early 1097.

After enduring terrible hardship and fighting in many brutal battles, the soldiers of the first crusade finally reached the gates of Jerusalem in July 1099. However, due to the terrible state of their forces and vastly reduced numbers, the rumours that a relieving Turk army was already on its way forced their commanders to act quickly and they decided to take the city rather than lay siege to seek its surrender. Consequently, they attacked immediately, and on the 15th July 1099, Jerusalem fell to the crusaders.

Led by Raymond of Toulouse and Godfrey of Bouillon, the victors rampaged through the city slaughtering anyone they could find, even killing those who surrendered or who hid away in mosques and synagogues. Thousands died, and the streets ran with blood but by the time the Crusaders had finished, Jerusalem was entirely in the hands of the Christian army.

The victory was overwhelming yet despite being offered the kingship, Raymond of Toulouse refused. At first, Godfrey of Bouillon also refused the honour stating that Christ himself only wore a crown of thorns but finally he accepted the governance of Jerusalem, though only accepting the title of Advocate of the Holy Sepulchre.

The following year Godfrey struggled to expand his influence so after immense political pressure from the Archbishop of Pisa amongst others, stood aside to allow his own brother Baldwin of Bouillon to be crowned king on Christmas day AD 1100. The first crusade had been successful and at last, vast parts of the Holy Land was in Christian hands.

For the next decade or so, the number of pilgrimages from the west hugely increased. However, the journey was fraught with danger and many travellers were attacked and killed en-route in retribution for what the Muslims saw as nothing more than a sacrilegious invasion of their homeland.

Finally, in 1119, an Italian nobleman, along with eight other knights formed an alliance with the stated ambition of protecting pilgrims on their journey to the holy places of Jerusalem and approached the new king, (also called Baldwin) to seek recognition and a place to base themselves. Baldwin II subsequently allowed the knights to set up their headquarters in the Aqsa Mosque on the Temple Mount within the city walls.

The new order needed a name and as the Mosque was also known as *'Templum Solomonis,'* they became known as *'The Poor Fellow-Soldiers of Christ and of the Temple of Solomon.'*

This title soon become shortened and within a few years, the order became famous across the Christian world as a body of fearless knights who fought to protect pilgrims in the name of the lord.

The order of the Knights Templar had been born.

Chapter One

The Mediterranean Sea
October 12th
AD-1177

Jakelin de Mailly stood on the forecastle of the galley, feeling the familiar desert wind on his face as it blew from the shores of the Holy Land somewhere over the horizon. At his side, stood the ship's Captain, a surly man more interested in dock-women and gambling than the ideals of Christian men, but he was a master mariner and his reputation sailed before him like a ship in favourable winds.

'Another few hours,' said the Captain, ignoring the knight's higher station, 'and you will see the towers of Acre rise like serpents from the sea.'

'And not a minute too soon,' said Jakelin. 'Our horses need to feel solid ground beneath their hooves before they wither away.'

'We have lost neither beast or man on this voyage,' replied the Captain, 'I promised safe passage and have delivered on my word.'

'Just get us to Acre,' said Jakelin, 'you will receive your purse upon landfall.' The Templar Knight walked to the rail and peered forward, seeking the land that he would soon be calling home.

'We should be there by noon,' continued the Captain, following the knight, 'but disembarkation may yet be a few days away as there are so many ships to unload. I heard that Phillip of Flanders landed a huge fleet in Acre only a few weeks ago.'

'It seems so,' replied Jakelin, his gaze never leaving the horizon, 'it is rumoured that he brought an army to join with the Byzantines in the fight against the Ayyubid.'

The Captain stared at the impressive knight with interest. Templars were famous throughout the Christian world, but this was the first time he had ever seen one up close. Like the other knights in his order, Jakelin was heavily bearded yet kept the hair on his head cut close to his scalp. His muscular frame bore witness to the countless hours spent on the training field, and he carried an air of invincibility about him like the heaviest of cloaks. A trait common to all such men familiar with the trials of war.

The captain found the monastic order strange and secretive, as did many men, and the fact that he had been requested to divert his ship to pick up three from Southampton only added to the intrigue. Every Templar knight came with three Destriers and an equipment chest. In addition, each had a company of two sergeants with two more horses, and a hired squire of common stock with his own mount and pack mule. In all, there were only three knights aboard the ship, but the space needed was the equivalent to at least twenty ordinary men at arms.

'So, have you come to fight the Saracens?' he ventured.

'We have come to join our brothers in protecting those pilgrims who seek the holy places,' replied the knight, 'and if that means conflict with the Saracens then so be it.' He turned away, once more gazing toward the east.

'What awaits you in Acre?' asked the Captain, determined to engage in conversation with the strange man while he still had the chance.

'Once we disembark,' said the knight, 'our Grand Master will direct us onwards as required.'

'Ah, the famous Eudes de St Amand,' said the Captain. 'I have heard he is a very impressive man.'

'I think he would be disturbed to be described as such,' said Jakelin, 'for reputation raises us above our station.'

'Nevertheless, he is known across the Outremer as a great warrior and has fought in many battles. Such a man deserves respect.' He paused and stared at the knight again. The three Templars and their entourage kept their own company and occupied the lower deck at the stern of the ship. They asked for no favour or any extra rations that their station may well expect, preferring instead to share the crew's humble fayre and were first to volunteer when any aid was needed to fix a problem or stand a watch. Any spare time was spent in prayer or solitary contemplation, such was their humility.

'These are dangerous times, Sir knight,' continued the Captain, 'and I have heard that Saladin is preparing a great army in Egypt. You may have come to protect pilgrims, but I suspect you could be fighting Saracens before the year is out.'

'You seem to hear a lot of things,' said Jakelin without taking his gaze from the horizon, 'why don't you just concentrate on getting us there.'

'Forgive my interest, Sir Knight,' said the Captain, 'it is just that your order intrigues me. You proclaim poverty yet are better equipped than any other men I have ever carried on my ships. It is said you spend most of your time in prayer yet fight like demons when the need arises and seek nothing in return except absolution from your chaplains at the end of each day. Humility is a great thing but surely all men have a need for something?'

'To live in the service of the Lord is reward enough,' said Jakelin, 'now, if you don't mind, I wish to be alone with my thoughts and with God.'

With a grunt, the Captain turned away to resume his duties, knowing full well that to press the warrior monk further was pointless.

Jakelin de Mailly placed his hands on the rail and breathed in the salty sea air. All around him was nothing but emptiness, a vast lonely space where the swell of the Mediterranean mimicked the rolling, desolate deserts of the Holy Land, the place he had once called home. Each vista was as beautiful as the other, yet both equally as deadly.

The sound of the rhythmic waves breaking upon the ship's bows seeped into his consciousness, easing his troubled mind, but even as he allowed himself a rare moment of relaxation, he knew the Captain had been correct. War was coming and if Saladin carried out his threat to invade Jerusalem, the strength of the Templars would be needed now more than ever.

He had no fear of battle for if he was to fall, then it would be in God's service, but even as the thought crossed his mind, his hand crept to the hilt of the sword hanging from his belt.

The weapon was like an old friend and comfortably heavy, a reminder that even with God on their side, there was one thing more than any other that would keep him and his comrades alive in the dangerous days ahead, Templar steel.

Chapter Two

The Port of Acre
October 12th
AD-1177

Hassan Malouf stood on the dock, cradling a tray of figs as he watched the ships unload. The sight never failed to amaze him and though he had been born an Arab, he longed to one day see the far-off lands that these wonderful people came from. Hassan was fourteen years old, the son of a Bedouin trader but had been indoctrinated into the Christian faith by the priests of Acre after being found injured in the desert a few years earlier.

The port was a hive of activity. Six ships lay at anchor at any one time and as each finished unloading, they were replaced by one of the many others waiting their turn outside the harbour walls. Lines of soldiers, each carrying their own equipment made their way carefully down swaying gangplanks and hustled into ranks on the quayside, berated on all sides by belligerent sergeants. Half-naked slaves grafted in the heat of the midday sun, passing countless boxes of supplies down to the waiting carts while others waited to restock the ships with barrels of fresh water and crates of supplies for the journey back.

Most of the ships carried men at arms from across Europe but others had a humbler cargo, pilgrims desperate to reach Jerusalem and though most of the street urchins made these the target of their attention, Hassan was interested in a completely different type of person, the type that filled his nights with dreams of chivalry and adventure. As the last ship of the day approached, Hassan jumped up from the empty crate where he had sat for most of the day and picked up his tray of figs. He brushed away the flies and made his way quickly over to where the dock workers were preparing to accept the mooring ropes.

For the next half hour, he watched as the ship was made safe and the slaves started to unload the cargo from the forward ramps. To the rear, a wider gangway allowed horses, long starved of meaningful exercise to be led nervously down to the quay, followed by two dozen knights adorned with surcoats displaying their individual coats of arms. Each man was bedecked in chainmail and carried a sword almost as tall as himself, but though their presence caught the eye of everyone near, he hoped there would be others, far more impressive. The last of the knights finally disembarked to take possession of their horses on the dock and when they were all finally assembled, rode away towards the city and the courtly welcome they knew awaited their arrival.

Gradually, as the sun settled near the horizon, the dock started to empty, and Hassan was about to give up when a noise from the ship made him pause. He looked up and saw a man staring down at him from the prow of the ship, a formidable bearded warrior clad in a black surcoat emblazed with a red cross. The man looked around the empty dock and as Hassan watched, another led a horse down to the quay before tying it to a hitching rail near a storehouse. Another five warriors, each dressed the same as the first followed him down accompanied by three young boys leading pack mules piled high with equipment.

For a few moments, Hassan stared, almost forgetting the reason he was there but finally he plucked up the courage and walked along the dock to speak to them. One of the squires turned towards him as he approached.

'Stay back,' said the squire as he neared, 'my masters have no need of your wares.'

'You waste your time,' said another squire to his comrade, 'he probably doesn't understand you.'

'You,' shouted the first boy again, 'be gone.' He pointed along the wharf, indicating what he wanted Hassan to do. 'Quickly now, before you get a beating.'

'There will be no beating today,' said one of the men in black. 'Show humility, master Tobias, the boy is probably hungry.'

The squire bit his tongue but stepped back from the strange boy. Master Cronin was one of the Templar sergeants and as such, his word was law to all the squires who served them and the knights alike.

Cronin was an experienced fighter and had worked his way up the ranks in King Henry's army back in England before electing to join the Templars. As he was not born of noble stock, he could never assume the white mantle as worn by the senior knights, but this didn't mean he was any less part of the sacred order. His surcoat was black and emblazoned with the same red cross, and during battle his role, along with his fellow sergeants, was to form a unit of light cavalry, following up any Templars' main charge to fight alongside them in any close quarter fighting. Unlike the main knights who favoured fuller beards, Cronin kept his facial hair short and neatly trimmed. His strong build evidenced an upbringing of hard graft on his family's farm while his weathered face displayed a military confidence born of many years fighting for his king.

As the squires turned away, to everyone's surprise, Hassan spoke up, addressing them in perfect English.

'My lords,' he said nervously, 'I neither beg for alms nor seek to sell you any wares. My sole purpose is to greet you as a fellow Christian and to offer refreshment after your arduous journey.' He lifted the tray of figs for them to see. 'Freshly picked today by my own hands.'

Everyone stared in astonishment. Hassan was dressed in a white linen thawb and his skin was the colour of horse chestnuts. His jet-black hair and facial features clearly indicated he was native to the Holy Land, yet he spoke English as clear as any man they knew.

'My name is Hassan Malouf,' he continued nervously. 'Please, eat your fill. I also have a flask of the sweetest water for you to quench your thirst.'

'You speak very good English, Hassan,' said Cronin stepping forward and taking a fig from the tray. 'Who is it that taught you our language?'

'My lord,' interjected one of the squires before Hassan could reply, 'wait. The fruit may be poisoned.'

Cronin looked down at the fig and back up at Hassan, staring deep into the boy's eyes.

'Is the fruit good, Hassan?' he asked quietly.

'My lord, it is from the best fig tree in Acre. If you wish, I will eat it myself.'

Cronin paused before popping it into his own mouth and chewing quietly. All the time his eyes not leaving those of the Bedouin boy.

'Delicious,' he said finally. 'Thank you. You said you have fresh water?'

'I do,' said the boy, 'drawn this very day from the cleanest well in Acre.'

'Then bring it to me, Hassan, for the water on the ship is warm and foul of taste.'

Hassan placed the tray of figs on an upturned crate and ran back to the shadows before returning with a large goatskin of water. He handed Cronin a leather cup and loosened the drawstring around the neck of the water skin before filling the cup to the brim.

'Would you like me to taste it for you, my lord,' he asked, seeing the sergeant's momentary pause.

'Do you need to?' asked Cronin.

'No, my lord.'

'Then, in that case, I will trust you again.' He lifted the cup and drained it in one go, leaving his head tilted back as he savoured the freshness of clean water for the first time in weeks.

'Well?' asked one of the other sergeants, 'does he speak truly?'

'Aye he does,' said Cronin. 'The water is as pure as an angel's tears.'

The rest of the men walked over to share the fruit and the water and chatted quietly as they waited for their masters to appear.

'So,' said Cronin eventually, 'do you have an answer to my question?'

'Your question, my lord?' asked Hassan.

'Aye. How is it that you speak our language? Are you not a Saracen?'

'Nay, my lord,' said the boy, 'my father was a Bedouin and my family made the deserts their home. Until I was ten years old, we traded amongst the pilgrims but alas we were set upon by a Mamluk raiding party and my father was killed. I would have shared his fate, but my mother hid me amongst the rocks and held me down, so I did not run to his aid. When they were gone, we sought others of our tribe, but she had been wounded in the attack and died in the night. I buried them both with my bare hands and wandered for days but I had no horse and no water so surely would have perished had not Father Clement found me on the road and brought me to Acre. Here he taught me in the ways of our lord Jesus Christ and had me baptized as a Christian. It was he who taught me your language.'

'And you speak it very well,' said Cronin. 'So, was it this Father Clement who sent these gifts you bear?'

'No, my lord. The gifts are mine. I hope they are to your liking.'

'They are,' said Cronin, 'but we must pay you. What is the cost?'

'I will accept no coin, my lord,' said Hassan, 'for I only wish to serve.'

'Serve?' asked one of the other sergeants, 'in what manner?'

'I have seen many men such as you pass this way,' said Hassan, 'and have learned that your squires are not noble born but hired. Every night I pray to God that one day I will be blessed with such a position.'

'You wish to be a squire?' asked the sergeant.

'I seek no such elevated title, my lord,' said Hassan, 'only to serve you on your travels and prove my allegiance.'

'He could be a spy,' said one of the squires looking the Bedouin boy up and down with suspicion. 'Send him away.'

'Hassan,' said Cronin, 'to be a squire is more than just preparing food and drink. There are weapons to maintain, horses to look after and clothing to clean. The life is hard and often dangerous. Many ride to war with their masters and some die on the field of battle. We are honoured by your request but alas, we cannot offer you a position.'

'My lord,' said Hassan, 'My background is lowly and my culture, Bedouin. However, God has shown me in a dream that my fate is to serve the men of the red cross and I will seek out that path until the day I die. When you lie down your head this very night, I will sleep beneath the walls of the castle and wait in case you call.'

'Hassan,' said Cronin, 'your pledge pays you merit but we have everything we need so I bid you go about your life as best you can. Now, you should be gone for our masters' approach.'

The sergeant turned away and Hassan looked up at the ship as the men he wanted to serve more than anything in life appeared on the deck, and though he had known what to expect, his mouth opened in awe at the majestic sight.

Three warriors, each clad in a mantle of pure white emblazoned with a blood-red cross, led their chargers slowly down the gangplank to join the sergeants. To Hassan, they were giants, huge men whose stature was enhanced by the gambesons and heavy hauberks they each wore beneath their cloaks. Fierce looking swords hung from their belts, and coifs of chain mail were pulled back from their heads to rest heavy upon their shoulders.

The horses were no less impressive, magnificent destriers draped with heavy white caparisons, also emblazoned with the red cross. Bedrolls lay strapped to the saddles along with huge, kite-shaped shields, spiked maces, and the full-faced helmets each knight would wear if they should ride into battle.

The sergeants fell quiet as the knights approached across the dock.

'Brother Cronin,' said one as he approached, 'I trust we are ready to move.'

'We are, my lord,' said Cronin. 'I have made arrangements with the Captain to have the rest of the horses brought to the castle in the morning along with the lances and equipment chests. In the meantime, we have everything we need.'

'Good,' said the knight, 'then let us be away. I am keen to see us within the walls before dark.'

Cronin nodded and turned to the rest of the men.

'Mount up,' he said, 'and follow me.'

Hassan saw an opportunity and walked out of the shadows.

'My lord,' he called, 'if you are going to the castle, allow me to show you the way.'

'I can find my own way, boy,' said Cronin, climbing up onto his horse, 'the castle walls dominate the skyline.'

'Aye, but the alleyways are full of cutthroats and beggars not fit to set eyes upon men such as you. Let me show you an easier road.'

Before the sergeant could reply Hassan turned and ran fifty paces along the dock to stand at the entrance of a side street.

'This way, my lord,' he shouted pointing up the narrow alleyway, 'it is the best road in Acre.'

'It seems you have found a disciple there,' said the second sergeant riding up to join Cronin, 'and yet we have been in Acre less than an hour.'

'He seems harmless enough,' said Cronin, 'come on, let's get moving.' He spurred his horse to follow Hassan along the dock and as the sun set, they headed from the harbour and up through the backstreets to the imposing castle above.

Chapter Three

Acre Castle
October 12th
AD 1177

At the city walls, the newly arrived Templars approached the gate tower, watched in silence by the beggars of the street as they passed. Two pike bearers guarded the approach and despite the knight's impressive appearance, eyed them with a half-hidden air of disdain.

'I see the latest monks have arrived,' said one quietly, 'it looks like we can all now safely sleep in our beds.'

'Thank heavens for that,' said the second guard, recognising the sarcasm, 'all those nasty barbarians out there have been giving me nightmares, so we are fortunate we have someone to chase the bad men away.'

Cronin and the rest of the sergeants ignored the jibe and kept riding under the imposing arch into the castle. Behind them came the three Templars followed by the squires.

'You be careful now,' said one of the guards quietly as they passed, 'we wouldn't want to get those nice white cloaks dirty now, would we?'

Their laughter faded away as the last of the knights reined in his horse and turned to face them. The guard swallowed hard as he realised his jibe had been overheard. To insult a knight of any order was punishable by flogging and he cursed silently at his mistake.

'My lord,' stammered the second guard, 'we meant no offence. Please pardon our impertinence.'

The knight rode his horse slowly back along the paved roadway until he was level with the first soldier. For a moment he paused before slowly and methodically removing his gauntlets.

'My lord,' gasped the guard, knowing that the knight was well within his rights to demand redress, 'please, I am just a humble soldier and know no better. My mouth speaks before I know it and I can only beg forgiveness.'

The knight stared in silence for a moment before reaching out his hand to offer the gauntlets to the guard.

'Take these,' he said, 'I see yours are threadbare.'

The guard looked up at the imposing knight in shock. He had been expecting a beating but instead, was being offered a gift.

'My lord,' he stuttered, 'I do not understand.'

'Take them,' said the knight, 'you have the greater need.'

'But I bore you insult. Why would you reward me so?'

'Your words bear me no pain, my friend,' said the knight, 'but the nights can get cold and I would not see you suffer.'

The guard lifted his hand nervously and took the gauntlets from the Templar knight, half expecting it to be a trick but when no sudden blow was forthcoming, he looked up again, his face lined with gratitude and astonishment.

'Go with the lord,' said the knight before the guard could speak and turned his horse away to follow the sergeants into the castle.

As the squires followed them in, the guard with the new gauntlets reached out and grabbed one of the bridles.

'Boy,' he said, 'who was that man?'

'That was Jakelin de Mailly,' said the squire, 'and a finer knight never stepped foot in the Holy Land.'

'But why did he give me the gauntlets?'

'I don't know,' said the boy, 'but perhaps it is true what they say.'

'And what is that?'

'That the Templars truly are selected by God himself.'

Without another word he urged his horse forward and followed his masters into the city of Acre.

Hassan led the newcomers along the narrow streets, finally stopping outside an archway into a courtyard.

'You will find your comrades in the far hall,' said Hassan pointing across to a building. 'I am not allowed to go any further.'

'You have been a great help, Hassan,' said Cronin, 'but I have no coin with which to make payment.'

'To be of service is payment enough,' said Hassan. He pointed to a dark doorway in a building opposite the archway. 'That is the house of Milam the trader. I work for him in the markets and he allows me to sleep in the corner of his cellar. If there is anything you need, please send for me.'

'Thank you, Hassan,' said Cronin and led the column of riders under the archway into the cobblestoned courtyard.

At the far end, everyone dismounted, and the three Templar knights walked over to an imposing oak door set into thick stone walls. One stepped forward and drawing his knife from his belt, knocked the door hard three times with the hilt.

A few moments later, they heard a bolt being slid back and a servant peered out into the gloom. He looked up at the three knights and after mumbling a greeting, stepped aside, inviting them to enter.

The noise from within was subdued considering the number of men present but as the first knight stepped over the threshold, the conversation died away completely, leaving the hall in silence.

The room held three lines of trestle tables and on each side sat a mixture of men wearing either the white or black surcoats of the Templar order over thin linen undershirts. At the far end, one arose from his seat and strode down between the tables to greet the newcomers.

'Sir Richard of Kent, I presume?' said the imposing man as he approached. 'You are here at last.'

'My Lord Amand,' said the first knight, dropping to one knee as he recognised the Grand Master of his order, 'it is my honour to be here.'

'Please, get to your feet,' said the Grand Master, 'we are all brothers here. My sincere apologies for not greeting you at the harbour, I was told your ship was berthing on the morrow.'

'That was the plan,' said Richard, 'but we took advantage of a delay amongst those ships still anchored outside the harbour walls and instructed the Captain to seek moorings. I hope you are not inconvenienced.'

'Not at all,' said Amand. 'Are your companions with you?'

'Indeed they are,' said Richard, 'and wait with the horses outside.'

'My lord,' said one of the sergeants getting to his feet at a nearby table, 'Allow me to arrange the stabling while our comrades are introduced.'

Amand nodded and the sergeant left the hall as the Grand Master turned back to address the other two knights at Richard's side.

'If the despatches I received from England are correct, then you must be Jakelin de Mailly and Benedict of York. Welcome to the Holy Land.'

Both men bowed slightly in acknowledgement as the other knights in the hall slapped their hands on the tables in welcome.

'Please,' said Amand, as the noise abated, 'divest yourselves of your cloaks and armour and find a seat amongst your brethren. Our fayre is simple but adequate. Once you have eaten we will find quarters for you and your men and on the morrow, brief you on the current situation.'

The door behind them opened as Cronin and his fellow sergeants filed in to join their masters, and as the hall erupted into the welcoming banging of tables once more, they knew they were at last amongst those who made up the heart of their holy order.

The newest arrival of Templar knights and their entourage had arrived.

Chapter Four

The Citadel of Jerusalem
October 28th
AD 1177

William of Tyre walked along the candlelit corridor toward the king's chambers, his feet echoing in the gloom. The armed guards paid him little heed, aware that this journey was carried out every night without fail.

Outside the night was dark and cold, but the flickering light from dozens of watchfires sent dancing shadows onto the stone walls of the castle as the guards along the parapets struggled to keep warm in the chilly easterly wind.

He walked up to the open doors and paused as the waiting servant turned to announce his arrival.

'Your grace, William of Tyre is here.'

'Let him come,' said a voice and William strode into the king's chamber.

At the far end, King Baldwin IV stood with his back to the door, his upper body naked in the gloom. Servants busied themselves about him, dipping cloths into bowls of scented water and gently washing down his torso.

'I will be but a moment,' he said, his voice echoing off the carved panels fixed to the stone citadel walls, please take a seat.' Despite being only sixteen years old, Baldwin's voice was strong and authoritative, an important trait that served him well when dealing with those who saw his age as a potential weakness.

William looked over to the king's chair, a beautiful upholstered piece of furniture brought from the city of Genoa. Before it, a humble wooden stool had been put in place ready to receive visitors. He walked over and sat down, gazing upward as usual at the beautiful frescoes painted on the ceilings and walls. For a few moments, he forgot his burdens and marvelled at the craftsmanship needed to produce such wondrous things.

'Enough,' said the king behind him, sending the servants scurrying away, towel me dry and bring me a shirt.'

William got to his feet and waited patiently, his eyes fixed on the throne before him as he waited for Baldwin to appear. It was an unusual requirement when meeting a monarch, but one that Baldwin insisted on.

As he waited, two physicians scurried through the door, each carrying a tray. The first held ointments and balms while the other bore a sharp knife, a bowl, a pile of small linen towels and a small blue bottle. Both men paused at a side table to set out the equipment before approaching the king and bowing their heads in respect.

'Your Grace,' said one, 'it is good to see you are out of your bed today. We have brought your medicines and as you haven't been bled for a few days, I suggest we take the opportunity to balance the humors.'

'A stuck pig has not been bled more than me,' said the king, 'so, for now, I will keep what little I have left.' He looked over at the blue bottle on the table. 'What is that poison you have brought me?'

'Your Grace,' said the man, 'only this morning we heard from a priest who has come all the way from London and he swears that honey laced with gold balances the humors and the purity can cleanse the body of black bile. He says it has cured many back in England.'

'Really?' sneered Baldwin. 'Name them.'

'I have no names, my lord,' stuttered the physician, 'but the messenger is well versed in the ways of medicine. Surely it is worth a try?'

'I have had enough of your alchemy for today,' replied the king, 'everyone leave. I need to speak to my advisors.'

'Your Grace,' said the first physician, 'we still need to apply the bandages. '

'I said get out,' said the king and take your concoctions with you.

The shocked physicians collected their equipment and hurried out leaving Baldwin alone with William and one room servant.

'You,' snapped Baldwin to the servant, 'go after them. Tell them to furnish you with poppy juice and bring it back forthwith.'

William took a deep breath as he heard Baldwin's footsteps behind him. The unequal sound of the king's footfall signalled the presence of a weaker leg and though the air in the room was heavy with incense, there was still the faintest smell of putrescence lingering in the background.

'I should have them hung,' said Baldwin, walking over to the throne, 'they are supposed to be the best physicians in Christendom and I endure endless hours trying their potions and ointments, yet here I am, worsening by the day.' He walked around to the front of William and stopped to face him square on, causing the prelate to swallow hard, transfixed by the grotesque features of King Baldwin IV.

'Well, William,' he said, his breath slightly rasping, 'how do I look today.'

The Prelate stared at the king, trying not to take too deep a breath due to the stench coming from the sores on the young man's face. When Baldwin had been a boy, William had been the first one to recognise that his inability to feel pain upon his flesh was a common sign of leprosy but had never suspected the disease would affect him so badly.

The left side of the king's face hung down as if heavily laden and part of his nose was missing skin, exposing the sensitive flesh beneath. His upper lip curled up, exposing some of his teeth, yellowed through disease and one eye was half closed.

The opposite side of Baldwin's face was intact though covered with sores and William knew that despite all the attention bestowed upon the monarch by the best physicians they could find, the disease was getting worse.

'Well,' said the king again, 'am I not handsome?'

'It is not a description I would have used,' answered William eventually, 'but God judges a man by his heart, not his appearance.'

'A clever retort as usual,' said the young king and pointed to an item of clothing hanging from a peg on the wall.

'Give me my shirt?' he said and waited as the prelate retrieved the garment.

'Finest silk,' said William, feeling the fabric, 'since when have you been attracted to the trappings of wealth?'

'The value of a silk shirt to me lies only in its lack of weight,' said Baldwin, gingerly pulling it over his head. 'Linen lies heavy on the sores and sticks to the raw flesh like a second skin.'

'Does it ever ease?'

'There are good days and bad days,' said Baldwin, carefully lowering himself into his chair, 'today is one of the latter.'

'Shall I pour you a drink?'

'That would be good. Join me.'

The prelate poured red wine into two silver goblets and handed one over before sitting on the stool.

'It seems strange to me,' he said, after taking a sip, 'that one of the symptoms of your disease is lack of feeling in the flesh yet here you are in pain.'

'Just one of the many curses of this affliction,' said Baldwin sinking back into his chair. 'Cut my flesh with a knife and there is nothing, yet the open sores laying less than a hand's width away burn like the fires of hell.' He took a mouthful of his own wine, careful that none spilled due to his deformities. 'So,' he continued eventually, the goblet now held in two hands, 'do you have any updates for me?'

'Indeed,' said William, placing his own goblet on the table. 'I fear the rumours are true and the Byzantium ships have already weighed anchor. Even as we speak, they are headed back across the sea to their home ports. The alliance that Phillip championed as the saviour of the Outremer has faltered before it even had time to make landfall.'

'I always suspected it was a fragile arrangement,' said Baldwin. 'My cousin is well known for making promises of gold but delivering results of copper.'

'Yet you still offered him the regency of Jerusalem.'

Baldwin looked up at the prelate with mild surprise in his eyes.

'It seems your spies are truly adept at bringing you even the most private of information,' he said.

'Not as hard a task as you would imagine,' said William. 'The man himself was quite verbose about the offer, and indeed his refusal to accept.'

'And your opinion on this matter?'

'I have to admit I was surprised,' replied William. 'Phillip has not been in the Holy Land for even a month, so I would have thought that he lacks the political knowledge to bear such a responsibility.'

'This disease will kill me sooner rather than later,' said Baldwin, 'and the burden of leadership weighs heavily upon my shoulders. I yearn to pass it on to someone whose lineage is unchallengeable and as Phillip is my cousin, I considered him to be a solid choice. Still, it matters not, he turned down the offer, declaring he was a pilgrim first and foremost without coveting any title or position.'

'Forgive me my scepticism, your grace,' said William, 'but in the short time I have known the man, I believe he carries his piety around him like an easily discarded cloak.'

'A harsh judgement,' said Baldwin,' but one that perhaps is closer to the truth than I care to believe.'

'So, what are your intentions now?'

'I'm not sure. With my strength deteriorating I need a Regent as soon as possible but my choices are limited.'

'Can I make a suggestion, your grace?' asked William after a few moments silence.

'That is your role, William,' said Baldwin, 'speak freely.'

'Have you considered Raynald of Châtillon?'

'Ah, the Lord of Oultrejordain,' said Baldwin. 'I was wondering when his name would arise.'

'Is he not an obvious choice?' asked William. 'Not only does he have an impressive pedigree, but his loyalty is absolute and his prowess on the field of battle second to none. The fifteen years he spent as a prisoner of Nur ad-Din in Aleppo has hardened his heart and his pledge to protect Christian interests is absolute.

'Agreed, but his exploits may yet be a weight around our necks. He is so hated by Saladin, it may become a hindrance if we should ever need to talk terms.'

'With respect, your grace, I would suggest that the reputation of one man will not influence the mind of a Sultan. Besides, I think that he is exactly the sort of leader you need, at least until you can find someone more suitable.'

'My mother speaks very highly of him,' said Baldwin, 'though I suspect that Phillip of Alsace will be outraged.'

'The lady Agnes is a very astute woman, your grace, you would do well to heed her counsel. With regards to Phillip, I would suggest that he has had his chance, so his opinion is not even a consideration.'

'I need a man capable of diplomacy, William,' replied the king. 'This is not just about Jerusalem, Tyre and Acre, we need to keep the kingdom united to maintain strength in the face of diversity. Someone who can rally Antioch, Edessa, and Tripoli to our aid at a moment's notice should the need arise.'

'Worry about diplomacy when the time comes,' said William. 'At this moment you need the sort of strength that someone like Raynald can bring. He may not be ideal, but we can waste no more time. Even as we speak, Saladin watches us like a vulture at a dying horse and we cannot display even the slightest weakness.'

Baldwin sighed deeply and stared into his goblet.

'As usual, your counsel is balanced,' he said eventually, 'and I tire easily from the constant political maneuvering by representatives from all sides. What matters now is that I consolidate our forces and send Saladin a clear message.'

'A message?' asked William.

'Aye, that as long as I have even a single breath left in this diseased body, I will not cede a single league of the Holy Land.' He paused and looked at the man who had taught and advised him his entire life. 'Send for Raynald, William, let me judge the man in person.'

Chapter Five

The Citadel of Jerusalem
October 29th
AD 1177

The following morning, the young king sat on an ornately carved mahogany seat in the receiving chamber within the citadel. Alongside him stood William of Tyre and a scribe to record the events. In front of him stood Sir Raynald of Châtillon, one of the most experienced and battle-hardened knights in the Holy Land.

'Sir Raynald,' said Baldwin eventually, 'I suspect you know why I have summoned you here?'

'If my sources are correct, your grace, then I suspect it is to offer me the regency of Jerusalem.'

'Your sources are very astute,' said the king, 'but before we discuss the issue, you should know that I offered the position to Phillip of Alsace before you.'

'I am aware of this.' said Raynald.

'And it does not bother you?'

'The matters of court do not interest me,' said Raynald, 'what matters is men on the ground with blades in their hands and fire in their bellies.'

Baldwin stared at the man before him. Raynald's reputation was well known right across the crusader states. The second son of a French noble, he had arrived in Jerusalem thirty years previously and had fought in the king's army as a mercenary. Since then he had worked his through the ranks and eventually became the Prince of Antioch through marriage before being captured by Nur ad-Din of the Seljuk empire and thrown in jail. The fact that he had survived his confinement was surprising enough but to come back after fifteen years' incarceration was almost a miracle in itself.

'Tell me,' said Baldwin. 'How did you manage to survive your captivity?'

'With faith and fortitude,' said Raynald. 'Each morning I awoke with only one thought on my mind, that God had seen fit to spare me so that one day I could return to the fight.'

'Your reputation is far from savoury,' said the king. 'Why should I appoint you as Regent?'

'I am a fighting man, your grace, and with respect, you sent for me, not the other way around. As such, I do not feel the need to justify the position offered.'

Baldwin bristled at the response but held his tongue. Raynald was certainly a man of few words and he was rude in his manner, but there was something about him that drew admiration from the king.

'Your grace,' continued Raynald, 'can I speak freely?'

'You may,' said the king and sat back in his chair.

'With respect,' said Raynald, 'every moment we joust with words is a moment that Saladin takes a step closer. I did not seek this position nor this audience and though I am honoured to be in your presence, there are more pressing matters to attend.'

'Such as?'

'Preparing the army to defend Jerusalem against Saladin.'

'But Saladin is in Egypt.'

'At the moment, yes but how much longer do you think he will stay there now the threat from the Byzantine fleet has diminished? He has an army over ten thousand strong at his command and it grows by the day.'

Baldwin glanced at William at his side.

'Is this true?'

'It is true that Saladin has amassed an army to defend Egypt, your grace but whether he intends to march north is another question.'

'Of course he will come north,' sneered Raynald, 'he has the biggest army seen for many years and sees us as fractured. The only question is when?'

'And you think that he will attack Jerusalem?'

'Wouldn't you?' asked Raynald.

An awkward silence fell in the room as Baldwin considered the revelations.

'If this is indeed the case,' continued the king eventually, 'what would you have me do to resolve the situation?'

'If I were in charge,' said Raynald, 'I would send your army to Gaza. From there they can watch the southern border and as soon as Saladin as much as breathes in our direction we can mobilise our men to cut him off.'

'The army is in the north,' said Baldwin, 'laying siege to the city of Harim as we speak. To recall them now will negate any advantage we have gained and leave the city in the hands of the

Seljuqs. I swore to my father before he died that one day I would return it to Christian governance.'

'Your grace,' said Raynald, 'I would ask yourself this. What is more important to you? A troublesome outpost already in the hands of the Seljuqs or Jerusalem itself?'

'You declare a devilish consequence, Sir Raynald,' interjected William, 'and I am not sure if it is not intended to further your own ambitions.'

'And what ambitions would you be referring to?' asked Raynald turning to face the prelate.

'Your love of death and mayhem are well known. Perhaps you see this as an ideal opportunity to further such activities?'

'I am not afraid to wreak the Lord's vengeance on unbelievers, that much is true,' replied Raynald, 'but to even suggest that such things are done for pleasure or personal gain is an accusation below a man of the cloth.'

'You misunderstand me,' said William calmly. 'I only point out the perceptions that others may make. Do not mistake my caution with concern, for indeed, it was I that championed your appointment in the first place.'

'If I was to recall the army,' said Baldwin, interrupting the pending argument, 'how long would it take to get back here?'

'By the time the message reached Harim, your grace,' said William, 'and allowing for the siege to be lifted, perhaps two months.'

Baldwin stood up and walked around the room, deep in thought. Both William and Raynald waited patiently in silence. Finally, the king returned and sat back in his chair.

'I have considered this situation and though I am not convinced about the severity of the threat, I am not willing to risk Jerusalem. Therefore, my decision is this. Our army will stay in Harim, at least for the time being. If we get confirmation that Saladin has started riding north, then we will send for them immediately. In the meantime, we will petition Eudes de St. Amand to send what Templars he has at his command to reinforce the garrison at Gaza along with a detachment of turcopoles. That way, if the Ayyubid come then at least we can slow their progress while my army returns to defend Jerusalem.'

He looked between the two men, receiving slight bows of the head from both in acknowledgement.

'In addition,' continued the king, staring directly at Raynald, 'I will appoint you as Regent of the kingdom and of the armies. You are tasked with defending Jerusalem at all costs.'

Raynald again bowed his head, this time in gratitude.

'Your grace,' he said, 'you have my solemn oath that I will carry out this task, even unto my death.'

'So be it,' said Baldwin, 'leave it with William to arrange the formalities. For now, you are dismissed. Report back to me in three days with a plan of action.'

'Of course, your grace,' said Raynald and turned to leave the room.

After he had left, the young king turned to look at William.

'Well?' he asked. 'You have opinions on all things, declare what you are thinking.'

'I confess I do not like him,' replied William, 'but in the circumstances, I believe he is the right man for the role.'

'As do I,' said Baldwin and turned to the scribe. 'Before you document what went on here today, I want you to draft a message to Eudes de St Amand in Acre. Tell him that he is needed in Gaza, he and every Templar knight he can muster.'

Chapter Six

**Acre Castle
November 3rd
AD 1177**

Eudes de St. Amand strode into the Templar hall and waited as the subdued talk fell away. There were almost seventy men present in all, thirty Templar Knights, sixty sergeants, and the few clergy dedicated to the spiritual welfare of the order waiting to see why they had been summoned. Those who looked after the administration and business of the order were stationed in other quarters but this morning, the briefing was for the main members only.

'Brothers,' he said eventually, 'I trust you slept well and have broken your fast. I have summoned you here to brief you on the current situation.' He started to walk through the gathered men, talking as he went.

'As you may be aware, Count Phillip of Alsace and his army recently sailed here to Acre with intending to join forces with King Baldwin and lead a campaign south into Egypt to extinguish the threat from the Ayyubid. He also made an arrangement with the Byzantine empire to launch a simultaneous naval attack on Egypt's fleet. Some of you may have even seen the waiting ships out in the bay, over one hundred and fifty war galleys full of armed warriors waiting to take the fight to Saladin.' He paused and looked around the room before continuing. 'However, that alliance no longer exists. What is more, it seems that Phillip has fallen out of favour with the king and has now ridden north with his army to campaign alongside the principality of Antioch.'

A murmur of surprise rippled around the room and he waited for a few moments before lifting his hand for silence.

'I know,' he said loudly, 'that this may come as a shock to most but if I am to speak truthfully, many of us long suspected such a thing would happen as there has always been a suspicion that Phillip sought more than a peaceful border with Egypt, with some even suggesting that personal advancement and wealth was his main driving force.'

'So where does that leave us?' asked a voice from the back. 'Were we not to join this crusade southward?'

The Grand Master paused and filled a wooden tankard with fresh water from a goatskin before taking a few sips and continuing.

'Indeed we were,' he said eventually, 'for there was talk of a great alliance, everyone committed to destroying the Ayyubid once and for all. However, in anticipation of our attack, it seems that Saladin has amassed a huge army to protect his borders, over ten thousand mounted warriors ready to protect Egypt. If the attack had gone ahead as planned I have no doubt that we would have emerged victorious but now the alliance has failed, it leaves us in a precarious position.'

'Is Jerusalem at risk of attack the Ayyubid army?' asked Richard of Kent.

'That is the concern,' answered the Grand Master. 'Saladin now has the largest Saracen army anyone has seen in years and he is too astute a commander to let it disband while the blood races hot in their veins. It is only a matter of time before he hears that the alliance has faltered and when he does, the king fears he will take advantage.'

'So, you think they may ride north from Egypt?' asked Sir Richard.

'Aye, we do and that means Jerusalem itself could be under threat.'

Another murmur of unease spread through the hall.

'So, do we ride to reinforce the holy city?' asked one of the other Templars.

'No,' replied the master, 'King Baldwin wants to wait until the threat is confirmed before recalling his army from Harim but in the meantime has asked us to ride south to Gaza. There we will join with others of our order and muster a sizeable force able to react to any movement into Jerusalem by the Ayyubid.'

'How many brothers are already stationed there?'

'Twenty knights in all,' said Amand, 'and approximately two hundred other men at arms. There is nothing saying Saladin will actually come, but if they do, our role will be to disrupt their advance, delaying them until King Baldwin can deploy his army in confrontation.'

The hall fell silent again as each man contemplated the size of the task before them.

'So,' continued the Grand Master, 'use today to gather and secure your equipment for tomorrow we ride to Gazza. We will head south along the coast and resupply at the castles in Caesarea, Jaffa, Ibelin and Ashkelon. Each is separated by no more than a few day's riding allowing for good weather and there are several waterholes en route. We will bear full arms and have been allocated a unit of two hundred Turcopoles for the journey.'

'Are you expecting trouble on the way?' asked one of the knights.

'We should always be prepared for trouble,' said the Grand Master, 'don't forget, the Saracens see the Outremer as their lands and look upon us as the invaders. As such we are always under threat. So, are there any more questions?'

He looked around the room. Every man there was highly trained and experienced in the ways of war. He knew that he need not outline the details of what was expected of them for even if the worst should happen and they were engaged by an enemy, their constant training and vast experience meant everyone would know exactly what to do at a moment's notice.

'Good,' he continued when nothing was forthcoming, 'in that case, use this day to prepare. I have sent for your squires and they will be here shortly. Have them ready your horses before first light on the morrow and before we ride out, we will gather in the church to thank God for his blessings.'

The men broke into conversation as the Grandmaster and his two sergeants strode out of the hall. When he was gone, Sir Richard of Kent walked over to the two knights he had befriended on the ship over the previous few weeks.

'Well it looks like we have arrived not a moment too soon,' he said sitting on the table.

'The sooner the better as far as I am concerned,' said Sir Benedict, leaning back in his chair, 'I came to the brotherhood to rid the Holy Lands of the heathen so am happy to meet them wherever and whenever they see fit. My sword is hungry for Saracen blood.'

'Brave words for a man who has never faced a Saracen blade,' said Jakelin de Mailly. 'I suggest you reserve judgement until you actually face one in battle lest you are humbled before you get chance to do God's work.'

'And I suppose you have?' asked Benedict.

'Not as a Templar, but I served as a young knight in the forces of King Almaric seven years ago.'

'You have been out here before?' asked Sir Richard with surprise, 'why did you not say previously?'

'It is not a time that I am proud of,' said Jakelin. 'We were young men, full of bravado and the surety our position as knights brought. We sought honour and chivalry yet were no more than paid men directing our swords at whomever the king pointed.'

'Mercenaries?' suggested Benedict.

'Aye. When first I accepted the role, I thought I would be doing God's will but soon found that Almaric was like so many before him, putting self-gain before the needs of the pilgrims.'

'So, you joined the brotherhood?'

'Eventually yes. First, I had to travel back to my home town to seek absolution for my sins. I entered the monastery at Mont St Michel and spent three years as a monk before seeking permission to join the Knights Templar. I took the final vows six months ago and here I am again.'

'So, have you fought the Saracens?' asked Benedict.

'I have,' said Jakelin, 'usually in skirmishes out in the desert and once in a pitched battle.'

'And the very fact you are here amongst us suggests that you were victorious?'

'We were,' said Jakelin. 'It was a bloody fight, and many fell but the day was ours.'

'What are they like?' asked Benedict.

'Very skilled,' said Jakelin, 'and fearless in the fray. Many carry curved scimitars sharp enough to cleave an unarmoured man in half. Their horses are smaller yet hardier than ours and very mobile.'

'Yet they are not our equals.' suggested Benedict.

'One on one, the skills are probably balanced,' said Jakelin, 'but it is the quality of our armour and tactics that gives us the advantage. There is little plate armour amongst the Saracens for they prefer cuirasses of leather or chainmail.'

'Why?'

'The reasoning is sounder than you may think,' said Jakelin. 'The lack of plate armour offers them more flexibility on horseback. This means they can ride amongst their enemies with the maximum of mobility. It is a good practise in the mayhem of open battle but against a solid knightly charge or at close quarters the tactic is rendered useless.'

'So, what exactly was your role under King Almaric?' asked Benedict.

'We rode as enforcers,' said Jakelin. 'The king used us as a display of strength against anyone who dared argue against his decrees. The mere sight of a hundred fully armoured knights riding through their villages was usually enough incentive for most to bend the knee but as is often the case, the younger men sometimes saw fit to resist and it was they who paid the ultimate price.'

'You killed civilians?' asked Richard.

'We did, and like I said, it is not a thing that brings me pride.'

'Still,' said Benedict, 'the very fact you spent so much time here is an asset indeed. Your experience will be invaluable.'

'My lords,' called a voice from the doorway before Jakelin could reply, 'your squires have arrived outside and await your instruction.'

'We will talk more of this another time, Jakelin,' said Benedict as everyone turned to leave, 'for I would learn all there is to know.'

Outside the courtyard Hassan peered around the gate pillar, straining to see what was happening. All day the place had been a hive of activity as knights and squires alike prepared their equipment and horses and he was desperate to learn what was happening.

The past few days had been exciting for Hassan for although at first he had been ignored by those he had met on the docks, his persistence had finally paid dividends and recently they had softened their stance towards him. Even the squires had become friendlier and as his knowledge of the city and the traders became more apparent, he was beginning to be seen as an asset to those who lived within the Templar quarters. Often, he was sent on errands for the knights, in particular carrying messages to other orders within the city walls. Other times he was asked to simply report on the comings and goings as more ships arrived at the docks but usually, it was sourcing and supplying fresh meat and ale for the squires, a task requiring trust and secrecy in case their Templar masters found out and issued admonishments for their weakness.

Hassan climbed up onto a cross-rail of the open gate and strained to see above the heads of the many men in the courtyard.

'Master Tobias, over here,' he called, waving at one of the squires. 'Please, I would talk with you.'

When it became obvious the squire had not heard him Hassan called out again, but it was fruitless. The noise in the busy courtyard was just too much and his voice was being drowned out. As he tried again, one of the gate guards walked over and dragged him from the rail.

'Enough of your clamour, boy,' he said, 'these men have God's work to prepare and have no time for beggars.'

'I am no beggar, sir,' said Hassan, 'and need to talk to my friends.'

'They are no friends of you or I,' said the guard, 'now get back to your hovel else I will give you a beating you will never forget.' He pushed Hassan away from the gate, sending him sprawling into the dusty road.

For a few moments, Hassan just lay there, his mind racing. He knew he had the favour of the Templar sergeants, especially Cronin, but if they were to leave Acre now, all the trust and respect he had garnered so carefully over the past few weeks would be for nought. Frustrated, he got to his feet, knowing full well he would have to do something drastic. He walked away, stopping in the doorway opposite to watch the comings and goings into the courtyard. Within the hour he had a plan and though it meant he could get into serious trouble, he knew it was his only chance.

He walked quickly away from the gates and waited at the corner of the narrow street. Ever since dawn, carts of supplies had been taken into the courtyard to be loaded onto the Templar supply wagons and he knew if he could just hide on the back of one of the carts, he could get past the gate guards and into the compound.

It wasn't long before three men walked towards him, each leading a mule drawing a cart of various supplies for the garrison. Recognising his chance, Hassan ran down the road and approached a young boy begging on the corner of the street.

'Haquim,' he said quickly, 'I have a task for you. If you do as I say, I will give you this blade to sell in the market. It will bring a fine price.' He produced a knife from the folds of his thawb and showed it to the younger boy.

'What do I have to do?' asked the beggar, standing up.

'Not much, just distract the last cart master as he passes.' He nodded toward the approaching carts.

'Are you going to steal from his wagon?'

'No, but you should worry not. Just distract him for a few moments and this knife is yours.'

Haquim nodded and Hassan handed over the blade.

'Do not let me down or I will seek you out,' he said and ran back across the narrow lane to hide in a doorway.

Moments later, the first two carts passed but as the third approached, the beggar ran out into the road and collided with the cart master leading the mule.

'Watch where you are going,' roared the man as Haquim fell to the ground, crying out in feigned agony, 'are you a simpleton?'

'My ankle is broken', cried Haquim, reaching for his foot, 'may Allah have mercy on me.'

'You are not hurt,' growled the man looking around, 'do you think me a fool? This is nothing more than a trick to rob me.' Realising what was happening, he turned and ran to the back of the cart, checking amongst the goods to see nothing had been taken. Satisfied that any attempt at theft had been foiled, he returned to the front, determined to give the boy a beating, but there was no sign of him. He looked up and down the street and considered asking some of the other beggars where the boy had gone, but soon realised it would be pointless, the rogues looked after their own and there would be none that would give up a fellow thief. Realising the gates to the Templar courtyard was only a hundred paces away, he urged his mule forward once again. The quicker he delivered his goods the quicker he could get back to his farm outside the city walls.

Squire Tobias knelt on the floor of the courtyard, rolling up his waxed blanket before tying it tightly with leather laces. His master's equipment was already packed and ready to be stowed on the carts later that evening so all he had to do now was finish preparing the few possessions he owned, the bedroll, an eating pot with a knife and spoon, a waterskin, a leather jack and a heavy cape. These he had brought with him from England and though it wasn't much, the Templars provided anything else he needed while he campaigned with them and he wanted for little.

Unlike other squires in England, he was not noble born or had aspirations to be a knight but had been recruited as a paid servant due to his knowledge of horses having grown up on a horse farm near one of the Templar churches. His wage was meagre, and he would not receive a penny until he returned to England, but it meant that should he survive the coming campaigns, he would return home in three years and have enough money to start a life of his own.

He pulled tighter on the straps as dozens of men milled around the courtyard, each focussed on preparing for the following day's march. For a second he thought he heard someone faintly call his name and he looked up, but seeing nobody, continued with his task.

'*Squire Tobias,*' came the whisper again, and this time he saw Hassan hiding behind a stack of water barrels.

For a moment he stared in shock. As he was not directly employed by the order, Hassan was forbidden to enter the courtyard and could be severely punished. He considered ignoring him but when Hassan called out again, he knew he had to do something. Leaving his bedroll unfinished, Tobias got to his feet and walked quickly over to the barrels, dropping down beside the Bedouin.

'Hassan,' he whispered, 'what are you doing here? You could be whipped. How did you even get past the guards on the gate?'

'I hid beneath a cart,' said Hassan. 'I know it is not allowed but I needed to talk to you.'

'I don't have the time,' said Tobias. 'We are moving out in the morning and I have much to do.'

'It is this that concerns me. Where is it that you go?'

'I cannot say,' said Tobias looking around, 'for to do so invites punishment. Why do you ask?'

'Only because wherever it is that you go, then that is also my path.'

'Hassan,' said Tobias, 'we have discussed this. You have been useful to me and the brothers, but this is where it must end. Go home before it is too late.'

'But my destiny is with the men of the red cross,' said Hassan, grabbing the squire's arm. 'God told me in a dream.'

'Hassan, there is nothing I can do,' replied Tobias, 'now please, be gone before we both get in trouble.'

Without waiting for a reply, Tobias got to his feet and returned to his task. The last thing he needed right now was a beating and to be seen talking to a trespasser within the Templar compound could result in severe punishment from one of the chaplains. He finished tying the bedroll and got to his feet before glancing back toward the water barrels. With relief, he saw that Hassan was gone and with luck, would already be back through the gates. He turned to walk over to the equipment wagon but before he could take another step, an angry voice roared out across the courtyard.

'You boy, hold there!'

Tobias turned around to see two of the guards striding across the courtyard to where Hassan was cowering under a cart. One of the soldiers lowered his lance and pointed it at the boy.

'Stay right where you are,' he growled, 'or I swear I will stick you like a pig.'

'I saw him earlier trying to sneak in,' said the second guard. 'He must be spying on behalf of the Saracens. Throw him in the jail and the Marshal will have him hung at first light.'

'No,' gasped Hassan, 'it is not true. I am a Christian and only seek to serve.' He scuttled from beneath the cart to run toward the gate but had not reached halfway before one of the other soldiers fell upon him, dragging him to the floor.

'Hold him tight,' shouted the guard running over, 'he'll not escape us this time.'

'Master Tobias,' shouted Hassan, 'please tell them I am no spy.'

Despite the plea, Tobias watched in silence. His heart felt sorry for the boy, but Hassan had been warned many times so only had himself to blame. He turned away to continue his own tasks, confident that it was none of his business and if Hassan really was as innocent as he claimed to be, then the Marshal would show leniency and let him go free.

The following morning, Tobias waited with his horse and mule, both loaded with stores for the forthcoming journey. All around him, the courtyard was busy with horses and carts as the column prepared to leave for Gaza.

Eventually, the church door opened and Eudes de St Amand led the brotherhood out into the early morning air. As they dispersed to their mounts, Cronin walked through the throng to address the squires.

'Is everything as it should be?' he asked.

'Aye, my lord,' came the reply from two of the boys but Tobias remained silent.

'You did not reply, Tobias' said Cronin, 'are you not ready?'

'My tasks are fulfilled,' said Tobias, 'but my conscience lays as heavy upon me as a pack upon a mule.'

'What is it you have done?' asked Cronin.

'It is not what I have done,' said Tobias looking up at the Sergeant, 'but that which I did not do.'

'You make no sense, Tobias, share what concerns you, so I can be the judge.'

'My Lord,' said Tobias, 'I may not be of noble stock yet every day I live my life amongst those who serve the cross and I see clearly the way that we should all live our lives. I often think that one day I may aspire to wear the red cross, even as a Sergeant, yet the first time I had a chance to do something noble, I shied away like a coward.'

'Tell me,' said Cronin.

'My lord, yesterday, Hassan came to find out where we were going and to beg passage in our service.'

'He came into the courtyard?'

'Aye, he did, and was arrested as a spy by two of the castle guards. He declared his innocence and called upon me as a witness, yet I maintained my silence lest I too was punished. Now I fear he is to be hung for a crime he did not commit.'

Cronin. stared at the squire, his mind working furiously.

'Where is he now?'

'I heard them say he was being thrown into the jail and would appear before the Marshal this very morn.'

'And do you know where this place is?'

'Aye, my lord, I took a message there on behalf of the Grand Master not two days since.'

'Then come, lead the way.'

'Cronin,' said another sergeant who had overheard the conversation. 'We are close to leaving. You should seek permission.'

'There is no time,' said Cronin. 'I will be within the sound of the bells as is our sworn oath and will return as quickly as I can. If you leave before I return, I will catch you up on the trail.'

'On your own head be it,' said the other sergeant and watched as Cronin followed Tobias out of the courtyard gates.

'It is only three streets away,' gasped Tobias as he ran, 'we are almost there.'

Moments later they reached a small square full of people gathered to witness the daily executions. In the centre stood a wooden scaffold with a noose hanging from a gibbet and on the floor to one side lay three bodies already wrapped in shrouds.

Frantically Tobias looked around, hoping against hope that Hassan was not amongst them and gasped in relief when he saw the boy in a queue of four men, each waiting to be executed.

'My lord Sergeant,' he gasped, 'look.'

Cronin spied Hassan and his heart sunk as it became clear the boy had received a severe beating. Tobias started to head in his direction, but Cronin stayed still, looking around the rest of the crowd.

'My lord,' said Tobias, coming back to the sergeant, 'what are you waiting for? We have to seek the Marshal and declare Hassan's innocence.'

'There is no time,' said Cronin. 'He has already delivered his verdict and could be anywhere. By the time we find him, it will be too late.'

'Then what are we to do?'

'Look around you, Tobias,' said Cronin, 'do you see the men who arrested him?'

Tobias scanned the crowd.

'No, my lord.'

'They have to be here,' said Cronin, 'the law says the accuser must witness the execution. Look again.'

Tobias climbed up on a box and searched the rest of the square.

There,' he said suddenly, pointing to the far wall, 'he drinks ale with his comrade.'

'I see him,' said Cronin. 'Come with me.' The sergeant forced his way through the throng as the cheering crowd and the sound of the trap door slamming open behind him told him another man had been hung.

'You there,' he said approaching the guards, 'I hear you are the accuser of the Bedouin boy.'

'I am,' said one of the men standing up, 'what's it to you?'

'He is innocent of all charges,' said Cronin, 'and is as Christian as you or I.'

'Are you blind?' laughed the second man standing up alongside his comrade. 'He is as brown as your sword belt and wears heathen garb. He is surely a Saracen spy and we will receive a bounty for his capture.'

'The boy's skin colour does not reflect his guilt nor his faith,' said Cronin. 'There are thousands of good Christians in Jerusalem, some blacker than the darkest night, as well you know.'

'Yes, but none of them were hiding in the Templar courtyard, were they? You should be thanking us, not serving admonishment for we probably saved Templar blood with our watchfulness.'

'You say he wore a thawb,' said Cronin.

'Aye, so what if he did?'

'Then ask yourself this. If he was truly a spy, why would he wear such garb when he is deep amongst his enemies, especially when he was in a forbidden place? Surely that would be the last thing he would wear?'

The guard stared at the sergeant for a moment, before glancing at his comrade.

'Perhaps he is an imbecile,' said the second soldier with a shrug, 'it is not our place to judge. We told the Marshal and it was he who passed sentence. Now be on your way and let us be.'

The trapdoor crashed again as another man died behind them.

'You look like good men,' said Cronin, 'and I doubt you would let an innocent die. I swear to you, that boy is not a spy and I entreat you to withdraw your testimony.'

'What?' gasped the guard. 'Are you stupid? The bounty alone is worth a month's wages for both of us and even if you are right, which I don't think you are, it would be a great folly for either of us to recant our statement. Not just because of the money but we could be punished by the Marshal for wasting his time.'

'A mere flogging, nothing more.'

'Says the man whose skin will not be cut with the lash. No, it is too late, my friend. The boy dies.'

Cronin stared at the two guards. Their smirks told him they would not budge so finally he knew he had to resort to desperate action.

'How much?' he asked.

'How much what?' replied the guard.

'How much will it cost for you to recant your statement?'

'Why do you even ask such a thing?' replied the guard. 'It is well known that Templars are forbidden to carry money, whether knight or sergeant and even if you did, the cost would be beyond you.'

'We will see,' said Cronin and turned to walk away.

'My lord,' hissed Tobias, 'what are you doing? We have no money.'

'Wait here,' replied Cronin and walked around the corner away from the eyes of the crowd. When he was sure he was alone he drew his knife and cut a small slit in the bottom of his surcoat before placing his fingers inside and retrieving a coin.'

He returned to the men, noticing on the way that there was only one more condemned man waiting to be hung in front of Hassan.

'Listen,' he said, 'if you recant your testimony, here and now, in front of the crowd, I will make you a rich man.'

'And how do you intend to do that?' asked the guard.

'With this,' said Cronin and held out his open hand.

The two soldiers looked down and Tobias gasped in shock. In the centre of Cronin's palm was a solid gold denier.

'Where would you get such a thing?' gasped the guard looking up, 'the order is supposed to be poor.'

'The origin is no business of yours,' said Cronin, 'but if you save that boy, the coin is yours and we will say no more about it.'

The soldier looked at his comrade. The coin was worth ten times as much as the bounty and could easily be sold in the narrow streets of Acre for smaller denominations.

Cronin looked over his shoulder as Hassan was led up onto the scaffold.

'Make your mind up,' he said, 'for in a moment, the offer will be withdrawn.'

The guard looked at his comrade and after receiving a nod of agreement, stepped forward to call across the square.

'My lord, hold the execution.'

The steward on the platform looked over with surprise.

'Who demands this action,' he said loudly, 'and on what grounds?'

'My lord,' said the soldier making his way through the crowd, 'my name is Oswald and I am a sergeant in the king's army. It was I who accused this boy but as a true Christian soul, I cannot stand by and watch an innocent man die.'

'If you are his accuser, what makes you change your mind and proclaim him innocent? Was he not caught spying in the compound of the Templars?'

'Somebody was, my lord,' said the soldier, 'but I cannot with clear conscience swear that it was the one who stands before you with a rope around his neck.'

'Do you mean there has been a mistake?'

'I believe so, my lord. This boy does not look familiar and I fear the real spy escaped in the confusion. I beg mercy on his behalf and withdraw my accusation.'

For a few moments, silence fell in the square as the steward consulted his colleagues. 'If this is the case,' he continued eventually, 'you do realise that you will have to answer for your actions before Marshall's office and explain why you have wasted his time?'

'Aye I do, my lord but better that than see an innocent child die.'

The crowd broke into argument, some in agreement for the boy's release while most called for the hanging to continue.

'My lord,' said one of the clerics, seeing his hesitation, 'the soldier only said he was unsure, so we could indeed have the right boy. Surely it is better to let him hang as an innocent than risk allowing a Saracen spy to live amongst us. Who knows what ill he could bring upon our heads? The judgement has already been made, I advise continuing with the execution.'

The steward looked around the crowd uneasily, unsure how to proceed. Either way, he was well within his rights to release a condemned man, but the crowd expected that justice was seen to be done.

Realising the decision lay on a knife edge, Cronin stepped forward and made his way over to the scaffold.

'My lord,' he said, 'My name is Cronin and I am a Templar sergeant. May I speak?'

'Of course,' said the steward, recognising the emblem on Cronin's tunic, 'your order has my respect and I welcome your counsel.'

'My lord, I do not know if this boy is a spy or not, but I can speak for the honesty I have witnessed him display since I arrived here in Acre a few weeks ago. He declares he is a Christian and I believe him on that matter. He has also served the order without fail, even though we shunned his first approaches. If he dies here today, then there is a risk that you hang an innocent man.'

'Yes,' interrupted the cleric at the steward's side, 'but if we release him, and he is indeed a Saracen, then he is free to continue Satan's work amongst us.'

'Then let me take him,' said Cronin, 'I will set him to work amongst our servants and make sure his hands bleed from the effort. The brothers of the order will watch him like a hawk and if we suspect he is what you say he is, I swear I will cut him down with my own blade.'

The steward stared down at the sergeant and then at Hassan as the crowd again erupted into argument. Finally, he held up his hand for silence.

'In the absence of the marshal,' he said, 'I am empowered to make a decision on his behalf. This boy was accused of being a spy but without testimony supporting the accusation, I cannot be certain he is guilty as charged. Therefore, I have no other option but to release him. However, as there is still doubt, I place him into the custody of the Templars as suggested.'

Most of the crowd erupted into anger again and as the proceedings came to an end, Tobias jumped up onto the scaffold to untie Hassan' hands.

'My lord,' whispered Hassan as he was led down from the scaffold, 'I knew you would come. God is truly great.'

'Don't thank us yet, Hassan,' said Cronin, 'we still have to get you out of here.'

He threw the boy over his shoulder and as Squire Tobias forced a path through the crowd before them, made his way back to the Templar compound.

Chapter Seven

Blancheguarde Castle
November 4th
AD 1177

Thirty leagues to the south of Acre, the outpost of Blancheguarde Castle was settling down for the evening. It had remained in Christian hands since being built by King Fulk of Jerusalem thirty-five years earlier, but the ever-present threat of those who resented the occupation meant the men who patrolled the castle walls had to stay alert at all times. Despite the overwhelming heat of the days, the nights were bone chillingly cold and the flames of the many watchfires along the defences brought welcome warmth to the guards on duty.

Darkness fell, and the quietness of the night was only interrupted by the occasional barking of scavenging dogs as they vied for whatever they could find in the dirty streets of the ramshackle village beneath the fortifications.

In the countryside on the far side of the village, three men crept along a goat path, shielded from the guards above by the tangled undergrowth of an untended field. Their black thawbs and turbans made them almost invisible in the darkness and every hundred paces or so, they paused to squat down in the shadows, recording the strength of the defenders and the location of their watchfires on a roll of parchment. For the rest of the night they continued their circumnavigation until eventually, as the first light of dawn crept over the eastern hills, they returned to their horses hidden in a patch of scrubland.

Farrukh-shah, one of those who had carried out the survey, mounted his horse and stared back toward the castle. The task had been monotonous, but he knew the information was of vital importance. Similar tasks were being carried out on other Christian fortifications and though none had yet been singled out for an attack, the details they collectively gathered would help his uncle make his final decision.

For too long the kingdom of Jerusalem and the surrounding territories had been in the hands of the unbelievers and he knew that if they were to succeed in their ultimate quest to drive the invaders back across the western sea, they would first have to take any Christian fortresses lying on or near the main Ayyubid supply routes from Egypt.

Farrukh-shah had waited many years for these glorious days to arrive, and as a young man had been frustrated as Muslim killed Muslim amongst the many tribes of Egypt and Syria. Those whose ancestors had walked the holy pathways for thousands of years had spilled each other's blood in futile attempts at dominance over their brothers whilst all the while, Christians spread through the Holy Land like a plague of locusts. But now, at last, the powerful Ayyubid dynasty had unified the many Arab tribes against a common enemy and had declared war on those who had invaded their lands.

Farrukh-Shah turned his horse to ride away from the castle. The location was impressive and the fortifications sound, but he had no doubt it would fall. For as sure as the sun rose each morning, Saladin would lead them to victory, and this time there would be no turning back.

Sixty Leagues south, Saladin sat amongst a pile of silken cushions on the carpet of his campaign tent alongside two of his most senior generals. On his right sat Shirkuh, a huge Mamluk warrior who had fought his way up through the slave army's ranks to earn a place at the Sultan's side, while on the left sat his nephew, Taqi Adin, the sovereign of Mesopotamia in the east and a very astute tactician.

The tent was slowly emptying. The celebratory feast had ended and now the dozen concubines who had entertained them with excellent lute playing and exquisite singing had left to return to their own guarded tents elsewhere in the sprawling Ayyubid encampment.

Saladin nodded almost imperceptibly to one of the several servants still standing near the doorway and the slave glided over the sumptuous carpet to retrieve a pitcher of freshly squeezed fruit juice, still cool from being stored beneath a waterfall in a nearby stream. He filled three silver goblets and took them over to a table situated alongside one wall of the tent before retreating to his place alongside the other slaves. Another brought over a small casket and retrieved several scoops of crushed ice, an expensive luxury brought from the specially built ice pits in the high mountains far to the east.

'Come,' said Saladin to his generals as he got to his feet. 'The evening has been pleasant but there are important matters to discuss.'

He walked over to the table and picked up a goblet of fruit juice as he stared down at the exquisitely drawn map before him. The other two men joined him, also examining the document to see if there had been any alterations since the last time they had been in the tent.

'Our patrols have reported many interesting things these last few days,' said Saladin, picking up an ornamental dagger from the table. 'Especially here at the mound of Al-Safiya.' He pointed at a tiny picture of a castle with the point of the knife.

'The Christians maintain a fortress there,' he said, 'and call it Blancheguarde after the whiteness of the rocks upon which it sits.'

'I know this place,' said Taqi, 'and have passed it many times.'

'As have I,' said Shirkuh, 'it overlooks the road from Ashkelon to Jerusalem and holds a garrison of knights who have taken it upon themselves to guard the Christian pilgrims who travel from the southern ports. It is far from Jerusalem and of little consequence.'

'I do not agree,' said Saladin, 'its location proves a hinderance to our ambition.'

'But our route goes well away from the pilgrim road. We agreed as such when first making our plans in Egypt.'

'I know,' said Saladin, 'and I remain true to our intentions, but it has occurred to me that the amount of time it takes for our supply caravans to reach us overland from Egypt could be halved if we were to use our ships to bring them to the port of Ashkelon and then onward from there to our armies.'

'Agreed,' said Shirkuh, 'but Ashkelon is in Christian hands so in order to use the port we would first have to take the city.'

'Understood,' said Saladin, 'but with the number of men at our disposal, it would only be a matter of days before the walls fell. Once inside, any counter attack by Baldwin could easily be repelled. Our spies report his strength is less than a tenth of ours so he would be hesitant to engage us upon an open field, let alone try to besiege a walled city.'

'What about Gaza? It lies only thirty leagues south and holds a garrison of Templar Knights. They can be at Ashkelon within a day and disrupt any siege before it had any effect.'

'My scouts tell me the garrison has few horsemen and even less infantry. It is not a significant risk.'

'So, Jerusalem remains our true target?'

'In time, yes,' said Saladin,' but if we were to take Ashkelon first, it would make the task far easier in the long term.'

'Tell us what you want us to do,' said Shirkuh, 'and it will be done.'

'I think we need to plan two campaigns,' said Saladin. 'The first will be to besiege Gaza, and the second will be to take Ashkelon.'

'But I thought you said Gaza was not a risk?'

'I do not believe it is, but if we were to lay siege to it, not only would it keep the Templars within busy but also focus King Baldwin's attention on something we are not really interested in.'

'A feint?' asked Taqi, his eyes widening in admiration.

'Yes,' replied Saladin. 'Let them think that Gaza is our target and react accordingly and whilst they are chasing shadows, we will take Ashkelon.'

'It is a bold plan,' said Taqi, 'and not without merit. Let us discuss the tactics.'

Saladin turned to the slaves at the doorway to the tent.

'Bring a platter of sweetmeats and refresh the pitcher,' he said, 'and then you may retire for the night.'

The servants did as they were told and as they disappeared out of the tent, Shakur looked at the sultan quizzically.

'It is not like you to dismiss your servants so quickly, my lord,' he said. 'Who will serve our needs?'

'We will serve ourselves,' said Saladin, 'for there were far too many ears within this tent.'

Shirkuh glanced at Taqi with confusion before turning to face the Sultan again.

'My lord,' he said, 'forgive me but you seem to be suggesting there may be a spy amongst them. If that is the case, let me know and I will tear out his eyes and tongue with my own bare hands.'

'If that is your suspicion,' added Taqi, 'kill them all and I will furnish you with slaves from my own household by dawn. Trusted men who would slit their own throats at my behest.'

'There will be no killing,' said Saladin, 'and yes, there is one amongst them who has a loose tongue. He is known to have dealings with the Christians via a trader who furnishes our army with grain. But for the moment it is important he remains alive and well.'

Both men gasped at the revelation and Saladin could see the growing anger in their eyes.

'You are allowing a serpent to slither amongst us,' said Shirkuh.' He has seen our maps and heard our plans. What else has he heard that may cost Ayyubid lives?'

'He hears what I want him to hear,' said Saladin, 'and that way I have a bearing on what the Christians do.'

Both men stared at the Saladin for a few moments before Taqi smiled, realising the significance of the Sultan's words.

'So, my lord,' he said, his voice a lot calmer, 'are you telling us that everything we just discussed is actually a ruse to set our enemy upon the wrong path?'

'On the contrary, I think we should put these things in place with all haste. That way they will see there is truth in the spy's words and react accordingly. However, it will be a fruitless campaign and while they explore blind alleyways, we can concentrate on the real prize. *Jerusalem!*'

Chapter Eight

**North of Caesarea Castle
November 6th
AD 1177**

  Cronin sat alongside Simon Callow outside a tent alongside the road to Caesarea. They had been in the saddle for two days since leaving Acre, and though the ride had been relatively trouble-free, the rough ground had been hard on the supply carts and they had made poor time. Consequently, the column had to spend an unforeseen extra night under the stars before they reached the first of their destinations on their march to Gaza.
  Both men shared a bowl to eat their evening meal of vegetable stew, each taking it in turns to spoon the nutritious food into their mouths or break a chunk from a loaf to dip into the accompanying broth.
  Cronin chewed quietly, staring across the fertile farmland to the coastline less than a league distant. He removed the stopper from his water bottle and drank deeply to wash down his supper.
  'The food is better than we received in Acre', said his comrade, wiping the bowl clean with his last chunk of bread. 'Perhaps campaigning in the Holy Land may not be as bad as we have been told after all.'
  'I would hesitate to judge after only a few days,' said Cronin, 'the coastal road is well farmed and food easily available. I suggest we just enjoy it while we can.'
  'Have you ever been to Caesarea?' asked Callow, reaching for his own bottle.
  'I have not,' said Cronin. 'You?'
  'No, but I hear it is a very beautiful place abundant with greenery from the river that runs through it. I have also heard it said that they have fountains fed directly from underground springs, water that is used to feed the fruit trees within the castle walls.'
  'I would not pay too much heed to the hearsay of lay servants,' said Cronin, 'I have often found their claims to fall somewhat short of the truth.'

'I agree, but this was told to me by a trader in Acre with no reason to lie. He says it is amongst the finest cities in the Holy Land.'

'We will find out soon enough,' said Cronin.

Callow took a drink before tossing the water skin into the tent and picking up a sheathed knife laying beside him. He reached into the pocket on his linen shirt to withdraw a small whetstone and after spitting on the surface, started carefully sharpening the blade.

'It will be cold again tonight,' said Cronin eventually, looking up at the sky. 'There is no blanket of cloud to keep in the heat.'

'We are certainly a race hard to please,' replied Callow, focussing on the knife, 'we moan about the heat of the day and then again at the cold of the night. If only the Holy Land could maintain the temperatures found at dusk, then perhaps we could die happy men.'

Silence fell as Cronin watched the sun dip toward the horizon. Behind them, the evening was alive with the sounds of the camp as men saw to their kit and squires looked after the horses. Further back, the brother knights stayed in a separate circle of tents at the centre of the marching camp, each looking after their own needs and spending time in quiet contemplation.

'Master Cronin,' came a voice and the Sergeant looked up to see a lay servant standing a few paces away.

'I am he,' he replied.

'My lord, you have been summoned to attend the Marshal at once.'

'Did he say why?'

'The Marshal does not share such things with the likes of me,' said the servant, 'he just asked that you come immediately.'

'Thank you,' said, Cronin getting to his feet, 'please tell him I am on my way.'

The servant ran off as Cronin ducked inside the tent to retrieve his surcoat and belt. To attend an audience with one of the senior Templars incorrectly dressed invited punishment.

'I wonder what he wants?' said Callow as his comrade re-emerged.

'I'll find out soon enough,' replied Cronin fastening his belt around his waist. 'If I am away for any time, could you see that my horse is watered before you retire?'

'Of course,' said Callow and watched as his fellow sergeant walked toward the centre of the camp.

A few moments later, Cronin stood outside a circular tent, waiting for permission to enter. The tent itself was large and bedecked with the flag of the Templars. Several other similar tents were pitched around the clearing, each one the overnight quarters of the Templar Knights.

'Enter,' said a voice and Cronin ducked through the flap to see two brothers sat at a table. Though he knew one was the Marshal, he had never seen the other before.

'My lords,' he said with a slight bow, 'I am Sergeant Cronin. You summoned me?'

'We did,' said the Marshal. 'Please, come in. '

Cronin approached and faced the two men.

'Brother Cronin,' said the Marshal, 'this is Brother Valmont of Lyon. He is headed to Gaza to take up the position of Seneschal due to the untimely death of the current incumbent.'

'Greetings,' said Cronin with a slight nod. 'I did not have the pleasure of meeting you in Acre.'

'No,' replied Valmont, 'I only arrived from Damascus on the day the column rode out so, by the time I sorted out my affairs, you had a day's start on me.'

'Yet you have caught us up. You must have ridden hard.'

'God was with me, so here I am.'

'Brother Cronin,' said the Marshal, 'I have just heard some disturbing news and would bid you shed some light on the accusation.'

'If I can,' said Cronin.

'I have been told that on the morning we marched from Acre, you left the compound to help free a convicted spy from justice. Is this true?'

'It is true that I helped the boy to freedom,' said Cronin, 'but as far as I am aware, he is no spy.'

'And how do you know this?'

'Because we have had dealings with him over the last month and he has been proven trustworthy.'

'Yet you cannot be sure?'

'I cannot,' said Cronin. 'However, we watch him with a keen eye.'

'He is here amongst us?' asked Valmont with surprise

'He is my lord, he has been given a role preparing food amongst the lay servants. He works for his keep and is reported to be a hard worker.'

'That he may be,' said the Marshal, 'but what concerns me is that you left your post during mobilisation without the express permission of the Grand Master. Surely you are aware of your responsibilities to the order?'

'I am my lord,' replied Cronin, 'but you were all otherwise engaged and as I was aware that an innocent boy was about to die, I decided to do what I could to see justice applied.'

'Surely that was none of your business. Your role is to serve your master.'

'My lord,' said Cronin, 'I confess I left my post and will gladly take any punishment awarded but, in my defence, I could not stand by and see an innocent Christian boy hung for a crime he did not commit.'

'Wait,' said the Seneschal, 'you say this boy is a Christian?'

'He is, my lord. He is Bedouin born but was baptised into our faith by a priest of Acre.'

The knight looked across at the Marshal with surprise.

'Brother Tristan,' he said, 'I am aggrieved and ashamed that we have a Christian soul working amongst the slaves without as much as giving him a chance to explain. Surely there are other tasks he could be doing more suitable?'

'This is the first I have heard of it,' said the Marshal, 'and I will investigate further. However, it does not change the fact that Brother Cronin absented himself from his post without permission.'

'It is a point well made,' said the Seneschal, and turned back to the sergeant. 'Brother Cronin, I'm sure that you understand that discipline is of the utmost importance in any organisation, but especially during a deployment in a hostile land. Indeed, if this had been one of our brother knights who had done such a thing, the order would have had no other option than to administer a heavy punishment, such is the seriousness of the accusation. However, we note that you have only just arrived from England and have perhaps not had time to fully understand our ways. Do you have anything to say in your defence?'

'My lord,' said the sergeant, 'I have already admitted my guilt, but could it not be said that my actions did not stray far from your own oaths in the Holy Land, that is to defend the humble wherever they are unable to defend themselves? It may not have been on the field of battle or the caravan routes to Damascus, but nowhere have I seen a decree that says we only help those outside of our city walls.'

The Seneschal nodded in acknowledgement and turned to the Marshall.

'He makes a good point. There are many things to consider so perhaps we should adjourn this hearing to make our judgement.'

'I agree,' said the Marshal, turning to face the sergeant, 'you may leave but report back here at dawn. We recognise the intention was honourable, but the charge is serious enough to warrant a penance.'

'Of course, my lord,' said Cronin and turned to leave the tent.

When he was gone, Brother Valmont got to his feet and walked over to pick at the platter of dates laying on another table near the tent entrance.

'So, what do you think?' he asked over his shoulder.

'I think his intention was admirable,' replied Brother Tristan, 'but to allow him to go unpunished sends out a signal that absenting themselves from their posts is acceptable, and that we cannot allow. I suppose we refer him to the Grand Master.'

'We could but I think that may result in a flogging and to inflict such a thing so early in a campaign, especially for the crime of rescuing a fellow Christian, will raise an unease amongst our men. No, perhaps we need to be more lateral in our thinking.'

'What do you mean?'

'I hear he comes with good references from England?'

'Aye, he does. He fought in France under King Henry and acquitted himself well. He is an honourable man.'

'In that case, his punishment should befit the crime and allow him to redeem himself.'

'Do you have something in mind?'

'Aye, I do,' said the Seneschal, 'and if truth be told it couldn't have come at a more opportune time.'

The following morning the camp was busy with most of the tents already struck ready for the day's march to Caesarea. Lay servants set about piling them onto the carts and the squires fed the horses before sorting them out with caparisons, saddles and bridles.

At the centre of the camp, Cronin waited patiently outside the command tent alongside his horse. Both were fully equipped and ready for the march.

'Brother Cronin,' said the Marshal appearing from the direction of the corrals, 'please, step inside.'

'The two men ducked into the tent and found the Seneschal sat at the table looking over one of the maps.

'Ah, there you are,' he said as they entered. He walked from behind the table and into the centre of the tent. 'Brother Cronin' he continued, 'we have had time to consider your crime and I know that despite your honourable intentions, you accept it was an error to leave your post without express permission from one of the brother knights. Consequently, we are obliged to administer a penance. Ordinarily, a period of confinement within one of the churches to contemplate your actions would be in order but as we are setting out on a campaign, to divest ourselves of an experienced man such as yourself could be a self-inflicted wound so we have come up with an alternative.'

'Like I said, my lord,' said the sergeant, 'my conscience is clear, and I will gladly accept any penance.'

'Good. In that case, there is a task that I would have you carry out in our name. I have in my possession a package intended for the king in Jerusalem. I was going to take them there myself but, in the circumstances, I think it is far better that I stay with the column, especially as there is a risk of Saladin moving his forces out of Egypt. Can I trust you to be the bearer of this package to the king?'

'Of course, my lord,' said Cronin, 'but my knowledge of the Holy Land is limited and the road to Jerusalem is unknown to me.'

'You will be furnished with a map,' said the Seneschal, 'and enough supplies for five days. In addition, you will be accompanied by the boy you freed in Acre.'

'Why him?' asked the sergeant, surprised.

'There are a few reasons,' said the knight, 'the first is that we are still unconvinced he does not spy for the Saracens so despite his proclamation of being a Christian, perhaps it would be better for him not to march amongst us, at least until we know for certain. The second reason is that, if, as you attest, he is Bedouin born then his knowledge of this land will aid you in your task. Take him with you and use his knowledge to shorten your journey.'

'Understood,' said the sergeant.

'You will also report to the king that as requested, we are headed to Gaza to reinforce the garrison there. However, our numbers are few and we will need reinforcements as soon as his army returns from Harim.'

'And what is it you would have me do, assuming a successful completion of this task?'

'Wait until the next column leaves Jerusalem and join their ranks. When you get to Gaza, seek me out and your penance will be regarded as spent.'

'A generous outcome,' said Cronin 'and I accept your judgement.'

The knight reached down and produced a satchel from beneath the table, handing it over to the sergeant.

'This package is from the Pope himself and intended for the king alone. Guard it with your life.'

'Of course, my lord,' said the sergeant. 'Anything else?'

'No, that is it. However, you must realise that a task such as this for someone riding alone is not without danger. Two men can ride faster than many and it is hoped the boy will know the hidden ways amongst the hills where our carts cannot go.'

'I understand,' said Cronin. 'We will be away as soon as the boy is horsed and equipped.'

'Thank you, Brother Cronin,' said the Seneschal, 'and may God go with you.'

Chapter Nine

North of Caesarea Castle
November 7th
AD 1177

Cronin looked at the distant trail of dust in the wake of the column as it headed south toward Caesarea. All around him, the remains of the overnight camp littered the scrubland and some of the night fires still smouldered in the rapidly warming morning air. For a few moments he considered covering the ashes with sand to leave no indication as to the number of men on the road but soon realised it would take far too long and besides, a column the size of that headed toward Gaza could easily be seen at distance so any attempt at subterfuge was a false endeavour.

A few yards away stood Hassan, securing the last of the supplies on the back of his own horse. When he was done he walked over to the sergeant.

'I am ready, my lord,' he said, 'but I do not understand. Why have we been expelled from the caravan?'

'We have not been expelled, Hassan,' said Cronin, looking down at the boy's still bruised face, 'we are to undertake a task on behalf of the Grand Master.'

'And what would this task be?' asked Hassan.

Cronin was about to answer but paused, realising that despite his own beliefs, there was still a chance that Hassan could actually be relaying information to the Saracens.

'The detail is not important,' he said eventually, 'but we need to get to Jerusalem. Do you know the way?'

'The road is well trodden,' said Hassan, 'and easily followed but we could have stayed with the column as far as Ibelin before turning inland.'

'I am not talking about the traders' route, Hassan, we will be headed across country as straight as an arrow. I know there are many hidden paths used by your people and trust that you will be able to lead the way.'

'I know of some,' said Hassan, 'but the hills are also filled with bandits and horsemen loyal to Saladin. To go that way would see our heads being struck from our shoulders before the sun sets.'

'We will be careful,' said Cronin, 'but that is the route we must take.'

Hassan looked around at his own horse and then at the one belonging to the sergeant.

'My lord,' he said, 'I will go wherever you order me to go, but first there are things we must do.'

'Like what?'

'We need to lose most of the equipment our horses carry.'

'Why?'

'The way is hard with little water. The mountain path is difficult, and I fear that to be weighed down as they are, we would lose the horses before we got half way.'

'We need those stores,' said Cronin, 'and there is little we could leave behind.'

'Please, my lord,' said Hassan. 'If you would have me lead the way, I humbly entreat you to trust me. At least half of this baggage must go if we are to head inland, otherwise, we are dead men before we start.'

Cronin stared at the strange boy. To get rid of any equipment went against everything he had learned during many years of warfare, but these were strange lands and he knew he would have to adapt quickly if he was to learn.

'In that case,' he said eventually, 'I will cede to your local knowledge. What is it you suggest we remove?'

'The tent is unnecessary weight,' said Hassan, 'as is your horse blanket. We can sleep beneath the stars. I would also suggest that you leave your armour, but I suspect you will decline.'

'My chainmail goes with me,' said Cronin, 'but the tent and caparison can go. What else?'

'Most of the food,' said Hassan, 'and half of the water. I will feed us from the hills and there are water holes hidden amongst the wadis know only to the locals. We will drink from them.'

'I'm not happy leaving our food and water, Hassan,' said the sergeant, 'it places us at the mercy of the landscape. What if the water holes are dry?'

'Then we will find another, but all this weight will tire the horses out. Either we do this, or we must seek an easier road.'

'So be it,' said Cronin eventually and helped Hassan unload the animals.

Within half an hour he looked again at the horses. Now he had just the one water skin and one satchel of dried food as well as his heavy cloak and his weapons, along with his shield and chainmail.

Hassan carried extra water and food as well as his own cloak and a cooking pot but carried no weapons except for his skinning knife.

'Now we are ready, Master Cronin,' said Hassan. 'Let the horses drink their fill before we leave for we will only have what we carry until tomorrow night.'

I hope you know what you are doing, Hassan,' said Cronin, pouring some of the excess water into a leather bucket.

'Trust me, Master Cronin,' replied Hassan with a smile, 'you are going into my homeland now. I will look after you.'

Ten minutes later, they left the camp and headed inland towards the distant mountains. The sun was rising quickly and the further they went, the hotter it became. By mid-afternoon they had left the fertile coastal plains behind and had started climbing into the hills. The cool sea breeze had long gone and soon, the glare of the sun combined with the heat reflecting off the barren scrubland became overwhelming.

'We will need to rest soon, Master Cronin,' called Hassan from behind. 'To push hard in this sun is the action of madmen.'

'We have no time to rest, Hassan,' said the sergeant, 'we have to reach Jerusalem as quickly as we can.'

'If you drive this hard, the horses will not even reach the mountains,' said Hassan.

Cronin reined in his horse and looked down at his own linen shirt. It was black with sweat and he was desperate to get out of the sun.

'We will stop for a short while,' he said, 'but then we press on. Find us a suitable place.'

'There,' said Hassan, pointing at an olive tree tucked beneath a nearby ridgeline.

Cronin followed the boy over and dismounted before collapsing against the tree trunk and removing his shirt. Hassan slid from his own horse and set about removing the saddle.

'What are you doing?' asked Cronin, 'surely we will rest moments only.'

'My lord,' said Hassan, 'the horses also need to cool down. This way they will see us through to Jerusalem. This afternoon, when the sun weakens we will make good ground and make up for the time we steal now. In the meantime, you should rest.'

The sergeant watched as Hassan continued to strip the horses of all the equipment before pouring some of the precious water into the cooking pot.

'Steady, girl.' said Hassan soothingly as one of the horses almost tipped the pot in its eagerness to drink, 'there is enough to go around, I promise.'

When both animals had been watered, Hassan tied a loose rope around their front legs as a hobble and allowed them to wander.

'I thought you said they needed to stay cool,' said Cronin as the young man sat down beside him. 'Why do you not keep them in the shade?'

'They are hardy,' said Hassan, 'and are used to the heat but there is some sweet grass and herbs on this hillside. If it gets too hot they will seek shade. Trust me, Master Cronin, horses are very clever.'

'You seem to know them well,' said Cronin.

'I do. Those and camels. My father bred both and sold them in the markets across Syria and Egypt.'

'And which do you prefer?'

'Horses are good for the trading roads and the cities,' said Hassan, 'also for battle. Camels will carry you twice as far with half the amount of water across the worst of the deserts, so my choice will vary depending on the need.'

'So, which would you prefer for this journey?'

'Today,' said Hassan with a sigh, 'I wish the horses were camels.'

The sun was already dropping toward the horizon when Cronin awoke to find Hassan standing over him with one of the water skins and a bowl half full of food.

'It is time to go, Master Cronin,' said Hassan as the sergeant squinted to make him out against the dipping sun. 'We only have a few hours, but the path is good from here and we can make the Judean mountains by nightfall.'

'What have you got there?' asked Cronin, sitting up.

'Dried goat and freshly picked herbs,' said Hassan. 'The meat is salty, so you can drink deeply but tomorrow, we will drink sparingly. The herbs should be kept in the mouth as long as possible. They will give moisture and a refreshing taste.' He placed the water skin and food bowl on the floor. 'The horses are already packed,' he continued, 'so we can move as soon as you are able.'

Cronin pulled on his boots and realised he had slept longer than he had wanted. The afternoon air was silent, and in the distance, he could see a small fleet of fishing boats heading out from some unseen harbour. He reached out and took the goat meat from the bowl. It was hard and like Hassan had said, very salty but to have any meat at all was a bonus. The brothers in the order rationed themselves to meat only three times a week and whilst the sergeants were in attendance, they shared the restriction. He swigged at the water skin to help break down the meat in his mouth before standing up and donning his shirt.

'The path ahead is safe, master Cronin,' said Hassan leading the sergeant's horse over to him, 'so you will not need your armour, but I have placed your cloak over the front of your saddle as it will get colder as we climb into the hills.'

'Hassan,' said Cronin as he reached over to remove his hauberk from behind his saddle, 'I may bow to your knowledge in surviving this land but in matters of armour and warfare, allow me to be the judge.' He pulled the chainmail shirt over his head and secured his sword belt around his waist before mounting his horse. 'Ready when you are, Hassan,' he said eventually, 'let us be gone.'

A few minutes later, the boy led the way up a goat track to head for the mountains rising in the distance.

Back down on the coastal road, two men dressed in thawbs and black turbans rode slowly through the site where the Templar column had spent the previous night, each peering down to the ground. Finally, one stopped to dismount and watched by his comrade, knelt down to examine a set of hoof prints leading from the camp. Satisfied he had found what he was looking for he got back to his feet and mounted his horse.

'That way,' he said pointing to the far hills, 'and let us make haste for there may yet be reward in this thankless task.'

Without another word, they spurred their horses and rode hard toward the distant mountains, following in the footsteps of Cronin and Hassan.

Chapter Ten

The Citadel of Jerusalem
November 8th
AD 1177

Baldwin lay on his bed, sleeping fitfully. The silken pillows beneath his head were already soaked with a potent mixture of sweat and pus from what was left of his rotting nose. One of his servants sat at a nearby table, waiting in silence for him to wake up so he could provide fresh bed linen, a task often needed to be carried out several times a night to keep the king as clean as possible.

Midnight had long gone and though the servant knew that to fall asleep invited a terrible punishment, his eyes started to droop, and he pinched himself hard to stay awake.

Outside the chambers, two guards stood silently, each wearing a sheathed sword as sworn protectors of the king's person. Another servant sat further down the candlelit corridor, always available to run errands should Baldwin need anything.

The corridor was silent and one of the guards sighed deeply, knowing that the fourth bell would soon be sounding. When it did, his relief would arrive, and he could go back to the barracks to grab what sleep he could before morning muster.

A faint, unexpected sound made them both turn and look down the long corridor. The sound of a door slamming in the distance made a welcome break from the endless hours of silence but as they listened, they realised the voices were coming closer and the people responsible were either very angry or very upset.

The door at the end of the corridor flung open and both guards became instantly alert as they recognised Raynald of Châtillon striding towards them, along with William of Tyre

'I need to see the king,' barked Raynald, without breaking his stride, 'I have news he needs to hear.'

'My lord,' said one of the guards, 'we have orders that he is not to be disturbed. Can your business not wait until morning?'

'No, it cannot. Instruct his servants to awaken him straight away.'

'My lord,' said the first guard, 'with respect, the king has been unwell, and he specifically ordered he was not to be disturbed this night.'

'I understand you are carrying out your orders,' replied Raynald, 'but this is a matter of war. Have him awoken and I will take the responsibility.'

The guard glanced at the prelate standing alongside Raynald. He was well known to the garrison whilst Raynald was a relative newcomer.

'Do as he asks, sergeant,' said William, 'his concerns are valid.'

The guard nodded and turned to knock on the door. A few moments later the bed servant peered around the edge and the sergeant relayed the message.

'Well?' said Raynald.

'Now we wait,' said the guard, as the door closed again.

Almost ten minutes later the door opened again, though this time the servant held it wide open in invitation.

'The king will see you now,' he said and stood aside as they marched into the room.

Inside the bed chamber, only the remains of a fire in the hearth lit the darkness along with a few candles placed in niches around the wall. William breathed shallowly as they entered for the king was currently suffering a fresh bout of infection, an occurrence that seemed to flare up more often as the leprosy got worse. Several incense burners swung gently on their chains, freshly lit to cover the sickly smell of the king's illness permeating the room

Baldwin was sitting in a chair near the fire with one of the bed covers over his lap. Alongside him, the bedroom servant poured warm water from a pot into a silver bowl before soaking a linen pad and gently dabbing the scented water onto the king's face.

'Your grace,' said Raynald with a bow of the head, 'please forgive our intrusion but we have grave news direct from within Saladin's camp itself.'

'Come closer,' said Baldwin, his voice weak and tired.

Both men approached to within a few paces though even at this proximity, it was hard to make out the king's face as the chair had been carefully placed as not to be illuminated by the light of the flames.

'Continue,' said Baldwin when they were just a few paces away.

'Your grace,' said William, 'this evening a man called Fariq bin Malouf, a Bedouin trader of silks throughout the Holy Land, arrived at court and begged audience. He has brought important information relating to the plans of Saladin.'

'Why would a Bedouin trader come to Jerusalem with information about Saladin?'

'The Bedouin are no friends of Saladin,' said William, 'and this man believes he will be well compensated for the information he brings.'

'And you came straight here to tell me of this man?'

'No, your grace, I first reported to the Regent, and it was he who has recommended that you need to hear it yourself, such is its importance.'

'So, what is this information that is so important you drag me from my sleep?'

'Your grace,' said Raynald, 'according to this man, Saladin is mobilising his army to advance northward in the next few days.'

'I hear such stories ten times a day,' said Baldwin, 'why should I pay this one any credence?'

'Your grace,' replied William, 'I know such rumours are as abundant as olives upon a tree, but it is not the words of the trader that gives them credence, it is their source.'

'Which is?'

'They are from a man who has been in our employ for many months amongst the ranks of the Sultan. His information has been found to be trustworthy on many occasions and I have no doubt that it is he that sends the message.'

'So, what is this message exactly?' asked Baldwin taking a sip from a nearby goblet containing warmed, watered wine.

'Your grace,' said Raynald, 'it would seem that even as we speak, Saladin is gathering his horsemen to attack Gaza. Once he has the city under siege his plans are then to secure the port of Ashkelon.'

'Why would he want Ashkelon, it is of little tactical importance?'

'With respect,' said Raynald, 'the port is able to berth many ships and Saladin could land a great fleet there should he wish. If he advances on Jerusalem, he could use Ashkelon to resupply his armies.'

Baldwin's eyes opened wider at the explanation. Ashkelon lay far inside the area controlled by Jerusalem and to have it in the hands of the Saracens would be a serious risk to the stability of the region.

'I accept the strategic value would be of benefit to the Ayyubid,' he replied after a few moments, 'but surely Saladin must know we would immediately make every effort to take it back?'

'Perhaps so,' said Raynald, 'but once in enemy hands, it would take a great effort to retake Ashkelon, especially as it could be resupplied by sea during any siege. Even if we were successful, the time and cost would be significant and that can only help Saladin's long-term plans.'

'What is our strength in Ashkelon and Gaza?' asked Baldwin.

'Ashkelon is poorly manned and though our forces are better in Gaza, they will be no match for the numbers Saladin is reported to field.'

'Did you not send for the Templars of Acre as I requested?'

'Aye, your grace, I did,' said Raynald, 'they should be there in a matter of days but still, I fear that their numbers will add little to the overall strength of the garrison. We should send for the army in Harim immediately and order them to ride for Gaza with all haste.'

'To recall them now would destroy all advantage gained in the siege of Harim. Are we sure your messenger tells the truth?'

'There is no guarantee,' said William, 'only that he has never let me down before.'

'Your grace,' interjected Raynald, 'with respect, if Saladin takes Gaza and Ashkelon, Jerusalem itself is at risk. Can I suggest that Harim is a minor problem when compared with the possible consequences of an attack on the holy city itself.'

'We should send out patrols and verify this report as soon as we can.'

'Your grace,' said Raynald, 'there is no time. If this information is correct, then we must act now. Not only should we send for the army but also muster however many men we have available and ride to Gaza immediately.'

'To what end?'

'To cut off Saladin's advance before he has a chance to gain momentum. If we combine all our forces from Gaza and all our outlying castles I believe we can hold him until the main army arrives.'

'What say you?' asked Baldwin turning to the prelate.

'Your grace,' interjected Raynald again before William could respond, 'with respect, these are matters of war, not religion. Allow me to advise you accordingly.'

'William of Tyre has been my teacher and advisor for many years,' said Baldwin, 'and I trust his judgement. We will hear what he has to say.'

Raynald fell quiet as William took a deep breath and thought for a moment.

'Your grace,' he said eventually, 'ordinarily I would advise parley with anyone who threatens war. To lose even one man in any conflict is one too many. However, I know the source of this information is as trustworthy as it can be and if the facts are as reported, I fear it is already too late to seek agreement.'

'So, your counsel is?' replied the king.

'Your grace,' said William, 'my commitment is to God and my king in that order. In my heart, I know that the spirit of one and the person of the other lies within these city walls. If they were to fall, then the things that I hold so dear to my soul are at risk, and that I cannot countenance. Therefore, though I am a man of peace, my counsel is that you should take advice from someone who is the opposite.' He turned slowly and stared at the man beside him. 'Master Raynald has spent a lifetime fighting the Saracens,' he continued, 'and if it is his advice that we ride south, then I am in no position to caution otherwise.'

Raynald nodded slightly to the prelate in recognition of the unexpected acknowledgement and turned back to face the king.

'The urgency is real, your grace,' said Raynald, 'just say the word and I will assemble every man able to carry a sword and prepare for the ride south. With God on our side, we can be a barrier to the Saracens until the reinforcements arrive.'

'I accept your advice, Sir Raynald,' said Baldwin eventually, 'but with one condition, that I will ride alongside you and the men.'

'Your grace,' said William, aghast at the suggestion, 'you are in no fit state to ride, let alone lead a campaign. I must advise that you stay here in Jerusalem to oversee the defences. Let Master Raynald do what it is necessary.'

'You should listen to him, your grace,' said Raynald. 'We will be riding hard and there will be little time to rest.'

'I may be ill,' said Baldwin, 'but I am still king. If Jerusalem is at risk, then it is my place to be at the head of those who race to defend her. Tell my personal guard to prepare to ride alongside me.'

'But…,' started William

'Enough,' interrupted the king, 'my decision is made. Have the Bishop of Bethlehem prepare the true cross, we will campaign under its glory.'

Both men stared at the king in silence. Although they both knew it was a foolish idea, they also knew that once Baldwin had made up his mind there was no way to change it.

'Well?' asked the king, breaking the silence.

'As you wish, your grace,' said William, and bowed his head in deference.

'Sir Raynald?' said the king turning to face the knight.

'If this is your wish, then so be it,' said Raynald.

'Good. Make the arrangements, we will ride at dawn the day after tomorrow. Now be gone for I need to dress my afflictions.'

'Of course,' said William and both men turned to leave. Outside they both walked down the corridor away from the king's chambers.

'Why did you do that?' asked Raynald eventually.

'Do what?' asked William.

'Give me your endorsement. It is no secret that my methods are distasteful to you.'

'Indeed they are,' said William, 'but my worries are for Jerusalem and the king. I may be a man of God but even he saw fit to smite his enemies. I just agree that if war is unavoidable, then you are the right man to lead it.'

'So, you recognise my prowess in such matters?'

William paused before a junction in the corridor.

'Do not fool yourself, Sir Raynald,' he said eventually, 'I have no admiration for the things you do. Let's just say that out in the desert, snakes are often killed by bigger snakes. Now if you will excuse me, I have many things to prepare. Goodnight, Sir Raynald.'

Without waiting for an answer, he turned away and headed deeper into the citadel. If the king was going to lead the army under the true cross, there was much to prepare.

Chapter Eleven

**North West of Jerusalem City
November 9th
AD 1177**

    Cronin lay wrapped in his cloak under an overhanging rock on the face of a barren hill. Up above the crystal-clear night sky was filled with an untold number of stars but the new moon meant the only light of any consequence came from the dying embers of the fire Hassan had lit to keep away the night's chill.
    With only a few hours left until dawn, the sky was at its darkest and both the sergeant and the boy slept deeply, both exhausted after the hard ride they had endured across the plains and up into the mountains the previous day.
    Down on the path below, their horses' ears twitched nervously. They had heard something on the lower hill and their eyes were wide, seeking out who or what was approaching in the darkness.
    Cronin's eyelids opened slowly, and he stared at the dying fire, momentarily confused as to where he was. Moments earlier he had been sat before a roaring fire in a tavern in Chester, drinking ale with the many dead comrades with whom he had shared his life over the years, but now, he was shivering in the darkness, wondering what had woken him up. Slowly his senses returned, and he blinked rapidly, desperately trying to adjust his vision. For a few seconds he just sat there, controlling his breathing as he listened intently, trying again to pick up the noise that had interrupted his dream.
    At first, there was nothing but then it came again, the quiet nickering of one of the horses down on the path.
    Cronin remained still, listening for anything more worrying and was about to close his eyes again when something touched his arm and he spun his head around in fear.
    'Shhh,' whispered Hassan, holding his finger up to his lips in warning. *'Someone is coming.'*
    Cronin took a few breaths, gathering his senses before pushing his cloak aside and reaching for the sword belt laying beside him.

'I heard a voice down in the valley,' continued Hassan quietly, as Cronin threw sand on the remains of the fire, 'they will pass on this very path within minutes.'

'Fetch the horses,' said Cronin getting to his feet, 'we need to get out of here while we still can.'

'My lord,' said Hassan, looking around, 'the path is dark and to rush will result in injury. Whoever is there will know these mountains better than us and will quickly catch us up.'

'We cannot stay here, Hassan,' said Cronin, picking up his cloak, 'we know not who we face.'

'I agree,' said Hassan, 'but there is another direction.'

'Where?'

'Up there,' said Hassan, pointing upwards. 'The hill is steep but if we hurry, we can lose ourselves amongst the scrub. Hopefully, they will pass us by.'

Cronin thought for a moment before nodding his agreement.

'So be it, but hurry.'

Hassan ran down the slope and grabbed the horses before leading them back up to where Cronin had gathered the last of their belongings. Within moments, they were scrambling up the dusty hill and soon found themselves winding their way between the sparse scrub.

'My lord,' said Hassan, 'we need to hide. Our trail will not be seen in the dark, but noise carries a long way.'

'At least we have some room to manoeuvre up here if it comes to a fight,' said Cronin. 'We need to find somewhere we can defend.'

They led their horses across a clearing and into a deep thicket before tying them to a tree.

'You stay here,' said Cronin, 'I'll go back and watch the path. If they come, I'll hold them off as long as I can, but you must ride on to Jerusalem and deliver the satchel. Understand?'

'Yes, my lord,' said Hassan and watched as Cronin unsheathed his sword before making his way back towards the edge of the thicket.

Moments later the sergeant was standing behind a tree, peering back down the hill.

His heart rate slowed, and he focussed his thoughts on what might happen in the coming few hours. He was an experienced soldier and feared no man, but darkness was a great leveller and he did not know the strength of those who followed.

The silence of the night was almost overwhelming and for several minutes he could hear nothing except the sounds of the insects in the darkness. Gradually his nervousness started to ease, and he began to hope that they had escaped discovery, but just as he was about to return to the horses, a poorly disguised cough whispered through the trees to his front. Again, his heart raced, and he adjusted his grip on the hilt of his sword as he peered into the night.

Suddenly a movement to his left made him spin around in alarm and he raised his sword, holding it back at the last instant when he saw it was Hassan.

'What are you doing here?' he hissed. 'I told you to stay back.'

'I have come to help,' said Hassan quietly, holding up his skinning knife.

Cronin was about to admonish the boy when another cough came from the lower slopes and they both ducked back behind the cover of the trees.

'See anything?' whispered Cronin, eventually.

'No, my lord,' said Hassan.

For the next hour or so, they waited, expecting someone to emerge from the darkness until finally, the faint tendrils of light started creeping into the eastern sky. The night had been tense, but apart from the earlier two coughs, they had heard nothing more from the lower slopes.

'My lord,' said the boy quietly, 'I think they have gone but I should go and see while there is still enough darkness to cover my approach.'

'I'll come with you,' said Cronin.

'With respect, my lord,' said Hassan, 'your footfall is heavy and will be easily heard. I can get much closer on my own.'

Cronin nodded and watched as Hassan made his way around the clearing and down the slope to the path.

Fifteen minutes later the boy returned and ran across to the sergeant.

'My lord,' he said, 'they have gone.'

'Are you sure?'

'Yes, my lord. It seems there were two riders and they stopped to water their horses only before going on their way. I do not think they knew we were here.'

'In that case,' said Cronin, 'let us also be on our way.'

They walked back through the trees towards the horses but as they approached, Hassan stopped dead in his tracks, staring at a footprint in the sand at his feet.

'What is it?' asked Cronin.

'Someone else has been here,' said Hassan looking around nervously, 'they must have come up a different route.'

'The horses,' gasped Cronin and broke into a run, heading to where they had left their mounts.

'They're still here,' he said with relief seeing them still standing near the tree. 'But the bridles have been cut.'

'My lord, the water and food has gone,' said Hassan from his own horse, 'while we were watching the path they have robbed us of everything we need.'

'My chainmail and shield have also gone,' started Cronin but stopped suddenly as he realised something even more important was missing, the satchel.

'Oh no,' he groaned, looking around, hoping to see it somewhere on the floor nearby, 'the messages from the pope have gone.'

'The messages were from the pope?' gasped Hassan.

'Aye, they were,' said Cronin, 'and now they are in the hands of the Saracens. If they reach the eyes of Saladin it could cost the lives of thousands of Christians.'

'My lord,' said Hassan, 'it may not be as bad as you think. If these men were only brigands, then they may not see the value in such things and discard them on the road.'

'If that was the case,' said Cronin,' why take them in the first place?'

Hassan didn't answer, knowing that the sergeant was correct.

'What I don't understand,' continued Cronin, 'is why they left us the horses.'

'Perhaps they thought it would make too much noise to get them down the hill,' said Hassan, 'so only took what they could carry.'

'Whatever the reason,' said Cronin sheathing his sword, 'we need to catch them up and get the satchel back.'

'My lord,' said Hassan, 'whoever they were, they know these hills and will be expecting us to follow. To do so puts us at great risk.'

'It matters not,' said Cronin. 'I was given a task on behalf of his holiness the pope himself and was found wanting. I will regain that satchel or die in the trying.'

'Then I will come with you.'

'Good,' said Cronin, 'I will need your skills if I am to stand any chance of finding the men responsible. Now come, we need to repair these bridles as quickly as we can and get after them.'

Half an hour later, they led the horses back down onto the path and climbed up into the saddles.

'I reckon they've got a couple of hours start on us,' said Cronin, 'so if we ride hard we may catch them up before dark.'

'We should not be too eager to close them down,' said Hassan, 'at least not while it is light. Do not forget they are expecting us to follow so will see us easily from any high ground. I suggest we keep them within our reach but wait until the circumstances favour us in other ways before we make any attempt at regaining your messages.'

'Time is limited, Hassan,' said Cronin, 'so we will ride as hard as we can. If, as you say, there are only two then I will take my chances with my sword.'

'So be it,' said Hassan and turned his horse to head back the way they had ridden the previous day.

'Where are you going?' asked Cronin. 'Surely they headed further into the mountains.'

'No, my lord,' said Hassan, 'the tracks show they went back the way they came.'

'But that doesn't make any sense.'

'Sense or not,' said Hassan, 'it is the way it is.'

'In that case,' said Cronin, 'we must make haste. Those messages cannot reach anyone who has the ear of Saladin.'

Chapter Twelve

**Southwest of Jerusalem
November 11th
AD 1177**

    The sun was heading for the horizon when Cronin and Hassan finally closed in on the men who had stolen the satchel. For the past two days they had followed at a distance, always careful to make sure they were not riding into an ambush.

    'They are close,' said Hassan eventually, reining in his horse. 'We should leave the animals here and proceed with care in case they lay in wait.'

    Cronin agreed and dismounted before tying his horse to a tree. Together he and Hassan followed the path up to the ridgeline, crawling the last few yards until they looked down into a wadi. For a few minutes, both stared through the undergrowth before Hassan pointed to a wisp of smoke rising amongst the olive trees.

    'There,' he said, 'there is probably water amongst the rocks, so it is likely they have made a camp for the night. To have made a fire means they do not think they are being followed.'

    'In that case, we have the advantage,' said Cronin, 'and I must take the opportunity while I can.'

    'Not yet,' said Hassan, 'they will still be alert from the ride. I will go forward alone and seek a route to reach them without discovery, and later, when their bellies are full they will be an easier foe.'

    'So be it,' said Cronin and watched the boy slip over the crest of the hill, keeping low amongst the undergrowth.

    For the next hour or so he waited for Hassan to return but just as he was contemplating going to find him, a noise to his rear caused him to turn in surprise. The boy was back.

    'I was getting worried,' said Cronin when they returned to the horses. 'You were gone longer than expected.'

    'The path is harder than I thought,' said Hassan, 'and we would be exposed if we were to continue the same way. However, I found another that takes us straight into the heart of their camp.'

    'Did you get close?'

    'I did, my lord. There are indeed only two of them, each with a horse.'

'Did you see any of our possessions?'

'No, but they have pitched a tent near a stream, so I suspect our things are within. This also means that they intend to stay here for at least one night so we can make our plans.'

'Tell me about the path.'

'It is steeper than the first but well hidden from their eyes and you can get within a few paces of their tent without discovery.'

'You have done well,' said Cronin. 'For now, we will gather our strength and see to the horses. As soon as the sun starts to set you will lead me into the camp.'

'If this is your desire,' said Hassan and his head lowered to look at the floor.

'Hassan,' said Cronin, after a few moments silence, 'worry not. This is God's work and he will be with us at every step. If we fail, then it will be his will.'

'Do you believe there is a heaven, my lord,' asked Hassan, looking up.

'I do. It is a fact preached by the pope himself but surely as a Christian, you also believe such a thing?'

'I have been taught such things,' said Hassan, 'but death has always been a distant thought. Now it could be upon me I find myself wondering if God has a place in heaven for someone such as I.'

'You are a good person, Hassan,' said Cronin, 'and when your time comes, your pure heart will grant you entry.'

'Perhaps my heart is not as pure as you believe,' said Hassan, 'for I have done things in my life that makes me a bad person.'

'None amongst us is as pure as we could have been, Hassan,' said Cronin, 'but we have a forgiving God. He sees all but needs you to ask forgiveness in your prayers. Before we attack their camp tonight, we will pray together.'

Hassan nodded silently but still looked troubled.

'Come,' said Cronin, 'let us see to the horses and get some rest. One way or the other, today will soon be behind us.'

An hour later, Hassan crouched low and led the way down a tiny crevice. Behind him came Cronin, carrying his sheathed sword in his hand so as not to knock it on the rocks as he scrambled down to the wadi floor. The sky was dark and as they reached the bottom, the sergeant called a stop as their eyes adjusted to the gloom.

'Which way now?' he asked quietly.

'There,' replied Hassan quietly and pointed across to the looming shadow of the cliff opposite with his skinning knife. 'They have made camp against the rocks.'

'Put your knife away, Hassan,' said Cronin, 'this is not your fight.'

'I don't understand,' said Hassan, 'you may need me.'

'What I need of you, Hassan,' said Cronin, 'is the completion of a task far more important than fighting.'

'What task is this?'

'When we get to their camp, I will call out and demand they return our property. I expect they will brace for a fight but whatever they do, I want you to get into the tent while they are distracted and find the satchel. When you do, get back to the horses and ride for Jerusalem with all haste. When you get there, head for the citadel and beg audience with the king.'

'But what about you?'

'I will follow you but do not wait for the outcome. I may fall and if so, you will have little time before they follow.'

'But my lord, this is not why I came. I wanted to serve, not run at the first sign of trouble.'

'You are not running, Hassan, you will be continuing our mission. Do this and I swear, that if I survive, I will petition the Seneschal himself for your appointment as a squire.'

Hassan stared at Cronin and took a deep breath before finally nodding his agreement.

'Good,' said Cronin, drawing his sword from the Scabbard, 'now hide amongst the shadows and as soon as you hear my voice, get to the tent.'

Twenty leagues to the south west, the Templar column continued along the trading route close to the Mediterranean coastline. The previous night they had rested in Caesarea Castle but had ridden hard all day to make as much ground as they could before it got dark. At their head rode the Marshal along with the Seneschal, each heavily robed in their white surcoats emblazoned with the red cross of their order. Behind them came the rest of the Templar knights along with the sergeants and the supply column.

Following reports of increased activity in the area, the turcopoles had been deployed along the high ground to the east to provide early warning of any surprise attack.

A few riders behind the Seneschal, Benedict of York rode up alongside Jakelin de Mailly and offered him his water skin.

'Drink?' he said.

'Thank you,' said Jakelin and took a few mouthfuls of the warm water before handing it back.

'So, what do you think?' asked Benedict, replacing the stopper in his water skin.

'About what?' asked Jakelin.

'This situation. If the castellan back in Caesarea is to be believed, there are roaming bands of Saracens from here all the way down to Gaza.'

'There have always been brigands,' said Jakelin, 'the news does not surprise me.'

'Aye, but his information suggests these were more than brigands, and that they may be loyal to Saladin himself. Why would they be so far north?'

'Your guess is as good as mine,' said Jakelin, 'but let us not forget, in the Sultan's eyes, *we* are the invaders, and this is *his* country. As such, his people are free to roam as they will.'

'If that is the case, why do they not attack?'

'Our column is strong, brother Benedict,' said Jakelin looking back over his shoulder at the long line of knights and sergeants, and it would take a strong force to provide any real threat. Such enemy strength would be well reported before they got anywhere near.'

'So, you think the reports are untrue?'

'Not at all, I have no doubt that we are watched every step of the way and that Saladin is kept well aware of anything we do from Gaza to Damascus.'

'I have seen nothing to suggest we are being watched,' said Benedict, looking around. 'Surely the turcopoles would notice if there was any such activity on the higher ground.'

'Saladin has no need of patrols,' said Jakelin, 'every man we pass on the road whether they be shepherd, goatherd or farmer, counts our numbers. All Saladin's men have to do is come out of hiding after we have passed to collect the information.'

As he spoke, the column passed a goatherd on the side of the road and Benedict stared down at him with quizzical eyes.

'What I do not understand,' he said eventually, 'is why do we allow them to carry on unhindered? Surely it would be better to take them into custody until we reach our destination?'

'And how would that work?' asked Jakelin. 'We would have to imprison every man woman and child we passed and even then, there would be countless others who watch from the shadows. No, it is best that we do what we do and allow Saladin his small victories. By the time he receives any reports we are already leagues away, so the damage is limited.'

'Do you think he will come north?' asked Benedict after a few moments.

'He makes no secret of his ambition to retake Jerusalem,' replied Jakelin, 'so my only surprise is that he hasn't done it sooner.'

Benedict was about to respond when the order to halt came from the front and each knight automatically turned their horses outward in a pre-drilled defensive manoeuvre. One of the sergeants rode back along the column, relaying the Seneschal's orders to the column.

'We have reached the wadi,' he shouted as he rode, 'we are to stop here and set up camp. See to the horses and rest while you can but be prepared to set out again at first light.'

Relieved to be stopping after a long day's march, the column made their way down into the wadi. The Templar knights assumed a position of defence in all directions while the rest of the column slaked their thirst and only when everyone was finished did they allow themselves to approach the water hole.

Benedict knelt and filled his own water skin as his horse drunk deeply beside him. When done, he led his mount to the area designated for the knights. One of his sergeants was removing the tack from his own horse and a squire already had the makings of a camp fire in place to keep the worst of the night's cold away.

'The tents stay on the carts tonight, my lord,' said the squire, 'upon the orders of the Seneschal. Tonight, we sleep within our cloaks.'

Benedict nodded and turned to the sergeant.

'Brother Callow, how fared your horse today?'

'She is fine,' said the sergeant, patting the horse on the neck, 'but hungry.'

Benedict looked up and saw two squires struggling down the path carrying a sack of oats between them.

'She will be fed soon enough,' said the knight and turned to see to his own horse.

'My lord,' said Callow, 'we have not had much chance to talk these past two days. I would ask what has become of Brother Cronin.'

'I truly do not know the detail,' replied the knight over his shoulder, 'and have only been told he has been sent to Jerusalem on an errand for the Seneschal.'

'But surely to send one man across these lands alone invites trouble.'

'I do not question the motives of my betters,' said Benedict, 'they have their reasons.' He turned and carried his saddle over to a nearby rock before walking back to face the sergeant. 'You two spent a lot of time in each other's company on the ship, do you know him well?'

'Aye, we fought alongside each other many times back in England under the banner of Henry. He is a good soldier and a close friend. A few days ago, he was summoned to appear before the Seneschal to receive a penance for saving a Bedouin boy, but I have not seen him since.'

'I promise I know no more detail, brother Callow,' said the knight, 'but if he is as good as you say, then I'm sure he will be fine.'

'I hope so,' said the sergeant, 'for he is too good a man to die alone in a strange country.'

Back in the mountains, Cronin crouched low and made his way towards the brigand camp. Up in front, he could see the glow of a fire reflecting off the rocky walls of the wadi. Slowly he crept through the last of the undergrowth before finally getting a clear view of the camp site. For a few seconds, he stared in confusion. The clearing held a fire but there was no sign of a tent or any horses. Confused, he stepped backwards before turning to retrace his steps but as he did, his eyes opened wide with shock.

Standing in his way was a giant of a man wielding a club but before Cronin could react, the man lashed out and smashed him across the head sending him crashing to the ground.

Semi-conscious, the sergeant tried to get to his feet but collapsed again as the waves of pain swept through his head. His vision blurred, and he looked up at his attacker, now standing alongside a second man wielding a sword.

Hardly able to move, Cronin fully expected to die. Silently he cursed himself for not taking more care to avoid such an ambush, but he had been so focused on retrieving the satchel, his usual thoroughness had been found wanting.

The sergeant knew there was nothing he could do, and he braced to receive the killing blow. A movement behind the men caught his eye and hope stirred anew in his breast as he saw Hassan slowly walking up behind the two attackers. For a few seconds he tensed his body, determined to do what little he could to help when the boy attacked, but as Hassan approached, the first man turned around, speaking to the young Bedouin in his own language.

Cronin stared in horror as the man put his arm around Hassan's shoulder and turned back to grin at the injured sergeant still prone on the floor.

'Hassan,' groaned Cronin, realising what had happened, 'what have you done?'

'My lord,' said Hassan, 'please forgive me but I had no choice.'

'You betrayed me,' gasped Cronin as any hope faded away, 'and you betrayed your faith. May God forgive you.'

'My lord,' said Hassan, his voice cracking, 'you must understand…' but it was too late, the Templar sergeant had slipped into unconsciousness.

Chapter Thirteen

**Southwest of Jerusalem
November 11th
AD 1177**

On the other side of the mountains, another column made camp for the night. Under the command of King Baldwin IV and Raynald of Chatillon, three hundred and fifty Christian knights, two thousand Turcopoles, five hundred archers and over three thousand infantry had marched out of Jerusalem intent on thwarting Saladin's designs on Ashkelon. For the past two days they had headed south, a strong force capable of thwarting any attack short of a full-scale army and now lay camped on a small hillside less than two days away from Castle Blancheguarde, an important fortress on their way to the coastal city.

At the centre of the camp lay the king's tent, a structure much larger and more decorative than any of the others. Inside, Baldwin sat on an ornate chair holding counsel with his officers and senior knights. Alongside him, as usual, was Raynald and William of Tyre.

'Sir knights,' said Baldwin, wincing as a servant applied a cool poultice of mashed Aloe and Comfrey to the king's lower arms, 'it has been a long day and I will release you to your duties soon enough, but we are in receipt of fresh information. A few hours ago, our patrols reported seeing at least three parties of Saracens within a day's ride of here. Each was over a dozen strong and seemed content in watching us pass.'

'Were they engaged?' asked Sir Gerald, one of the Jerusalem knights.

'Each time our patrols approached, the enemy turned and rode away. Our men pursued as long as they could, but they dispersed amongst the hills and it was impossible to follow further.'

'A hundred men here and there are hardly a threat,' said Sir Gerald.

'Maybe not, but it is an indication that Saladin is indeed testing our resolve and roams much further north than he has for a long time. However, this is in itself is not why I brought you here. Our same patrols have reported signs of a larger body of men in the lands between Bathsheba and Ashkelon.'

'How many?' asked Gerald.

'The numbers are unknown as none have been seen directly, but there are many tracks and signs of old campfires, each hidden beneath the sand as to remain unseen. In addition, villages report groups of armed men taking livestock and crops in the night.'

'With respect, my lord,' said Sir Gerald, 'this does not sound like an invasion force led by Saladin. I have campaigned against this man many times and always he has been well supplied. Even when forced to take from the villages, he has always paid recompense. These actions sound like the activities of brigands, nothing more.'

'Ordinarily, I would agree,' said Baldwin, 'but consider this. If Saladin was nearby and wanted to keep his presence secret, would he not resort to such measures in an effort to remain hidden? Could it not be that he or those that ride in his name are actively seeking recruits to his cause and are forced to steal in the night to remain invisible to our allies?'

'Possibly, but why are we so eager to dismiss the theory that it is no more than brigandry?'

'Because of the scale,' interjected Raynald. 'The further we go south the more destitute are the villages we pass. There is hardly one that does not report a great loss to the thieves of the night and that says to me that somewhere out there, there is a body of men that need feeding without recourse to a supply line.'

'It's possible,' said Gerald, 'but without anyone actually seeing these men with our own eyes I would remain a sceptic.'

'And you would be right to do so,' said Baldwin, 'but we cannot just head straight to Ashkelon while there is a risk of a Saracen army within striking distance somewhere to the east. If we leave these reports untended then we invite an ambush further down the road. We need certainty and that is why I have asked you all here.' He looked around the tent. 'I seek a volunteer to ride into the Judean Mountains with a body of men and follow the tracks our patrols have found. The task is of observation only and he is to report back to me with absolute details as to whether or not there is a risk from the east.'

Several men stepped forward, each volunteering their services, but it was Gerald that caught the king's gaze.

'Sir Gerald,' said Baldwin, 'despite your scepticism, I know your report will be accepted by all as true. I am happy to bestow the responsibilities upon your shoulders.'

'Thank you, my king,' said Gerald with a nod of the head. 'I have to admit that I find the task somewhat unnecessary but to ride free from the constraints of the snail our column has become excites me.'

A murmur of laughter rippled around the tent. The slow pace of the column frustrated everyone, but it was important they stayed with the supply wagons, despite the importance of reaching Ashkelon.

'You are free to ride as fast as you like,' said the king, 'indeed, speed is of the essence but in addition, there is a need for caution. The priority here is the gaining of accurate information so unless you are forced to defend yourselves, you are forbidden to undertake any sort of conflict as every sword will be needed in the defence of Ashkelon. Is that clear?'

'It is, my lord,' said Gerald with a slight nod of the head.

'Good. In that case, select twenty knights and fifty turcopoles. In the morning, the scouts will lead you back to where the Saracens were last seen. See what you can find but return no later than tomorrow night. In the meantime, the rest of the column will continue on to Blancheguarde.'

'I understand, my lord,' said Gerald. 'If there is nothing else, I shall assemble my men immediately.'

'Indeed,' said the king.

As Gerald turned to leave a younger man stepped forward and spoke up.

'My lord, may I join Sir Gerald on his quest?'

The king turned to look at the knight. Robert of Essex was new to Jerusalem and though he was inexperienced, he came with a good pedigree and it was no secret that he was keen to see action to prove his worth.

'Sir Robert,' said the king, 'Sir Gerald needs no second from within this tent. His choices will be made from the other ranks.'

'I understand, my lord,' said Robert, 'but I beg leave to serve alongside him. I have been here for six months and have scarcely left Jerusalem. I am confident I have the skills of any man but have not had the opportunity to wield my blade in anger.'

'Did you not just hear me say that this was a task of information gathering only?'

'Aye, my lord, I did. But such a task always involves risk and I would happily stand alongside Sir Gerald in the case of any attack.'

'Your bravery is not and never has been at question, Sir Robert,' said Baldwin, 'and indeed, if you have half the skills of your father, then your sword arm will one day become one of Jerusalem's greatest assets. However, I recognise the fervour in your heart and if Sir Gerald is happy, then you may ride with him as his second.'

All heads turned to face the first knight, still standing in the doorway.

'Well,' continued the king, addressing the older knight, 'what do you say?'

'I say this,' said Gerald after a pause, 'why is he still standing there like a maid waiting to dance when there are horses to prepare?'

A grin appeared on the young man's face and he strode across the tent to duck outside, even forgetting to acknowledge the king.

'Forgive him,' my lord, laughed Gerald, 'it is nought but the exuberance of youth.'

'Travel well,' said the king. 'We will rest the column at Blancheguarde and will wait there for five days only. After that, we will continue to Ashkelon without you.'

'Aye, my lord,' said Gerald and after bowing again to the king, left the tent.

The following morning, Sir Gerald led a patrol of sixty men away from the camp and into the hills. With them went the two scouts who had seen the signs of the Saracens the previous day. They rode hard along the sun-baked ground until finally the scouts reined in their horses and waited for the column to catch them up.

'Is this the place?' asked Gerald, coming to a halt alongside one of the scouts.

'Aye, my lord,' said the rider, 'yesterday there was a large Saracen patrol on the ridge ahead. When we approached they disappeared like the morning mist.'

'Not even Saracens can disappear without leaving a trail,' said Gerald. 'See what you can find.'

The scouts rode on, their eyes focussed on the ground and had hardly gone a few hundred paces when again they reined in their mounts.

'There,' said one, pointing at a patch of softer ground to the side of the path, 'I reckon about a hundred horses passed this way less than a few hours ago.'

Gerald turned to address his men.

'From here on in,' he announced, 'we will assume we are being watched and will stay alert for any attack. Keep your shields to hand and unfasten the ties on your scabbards.'

All the men adjusted their equipment and a few minutes later, the scouts led them further into the hills.

Chapter Fourteen

Southwest of Jerusalem
November 12th
AD 1177

Cronin groaned as he regained consciousness. Binds around his wrists cut into his flesh, as did those around his ankles but apart from the pain in his head and an overwhelming thirst, he was relatively unscathed.

He lay motionless in the dust for a few moments, allowing his head to clear before struggling to sit up and lean against a rock at his back. Slowly he looked around. The sun was high and a few paces away, two Arabs sat cross legged near a stream, each taking it in turns to pick meat from the carcass of a hare cooking over a fire. On a nearby rock, he could see Hassan, eating alone.

As the full memory of how Hassan had betrayed him finally came flooding back, Cronin struggled to control his anger. Many people had warned him that the boy could have been a spy, but he had ignored them all, choosing instead to believe his own judgement. Now he cursed himself for not having listened to them.

Despite his anger, Cronin realised that as long as he was breathing, he had a chance of escape. Slowly he forced himself to calm down and knew that if he was to stand any chance of getting out of the situation alive, he had to control his ire and keep a clear head.

'Hassan,' he said eventually, his throat gravelly from his severe thirst.

The boy looked over and immediately his face fell. Fear appeared in his eyes and he glanced between the sergeant and his captors.

'Hassan,' croaked Cronin again, 'come closer.'

'What do you want? asked Hassan.

'Just a drink,' said Cronin, 'please, I have a great thirst.'

The boy hesitated but eventually got to his feet before picking up a water skin and walking over.

'Do not try anything foolish,' he said as he neared, 'those two will cut you down in a heartbeat.'

'What could I do?' asked Cronin. 'My feet and hands are bound.'

Hassan loosened the ties around the folded neck of the goatskin and walked slowly closer.

Cronin adjusted his position the best he could and tilted his head back as the boy poured the warm water into his mouth. He swallowed greedily, not knowing if or when he would get another chance and it was only when Hassan stopped pouring did he look up at his betrayer.

Hassan swallowed heavily and broke the sergeant's gaze before turning to walk away.

'Hassan, wait,' said Cronin, 'I need to understand.'

'I have nothing to say to you,' said Hassan without turning, 'what is done is done.'

'Please, said Cronin, just a moment, that's all I ask. You owe me that much at least.'

Hassan turned and after a few moments lifted his head to stare directly into the sergeant's eyes.

'Why did you do it, Hassan,' asked Cronin, 'why did you betray me?'

'These men are my people,' said Hassan, his voice heavy with regret, 'I had no choice.'

'They are Bedouin?'

'Yes.'

'But I thought they were our allies. Why have they done this?'

'They are Bedouin born but owe no allegiance to any tribe.'

'So, they are bandits?'

Hassan nodded silently.

'I don't understand,' said Cronin, 'you are a good person, Hassan. Why do you associate yourself with such men?'

'I have my reasons, master Cronin,' said Hassan, 'and one day, God alone will be my judge.'

Before Cronin could reply, Hassan turned and walked back to his rock but even though the conversation had come to an abrupt end, the sergeant had already learned enough to give him the slightest glimmer of hope. One, the boy had called him master so still had a measure of respect for him, but more importantly, he had referred to God, which meant he still considered himself Christian.

Ten leagues away, Gerald followed the two scouts deeper into the mountains but the longer the day went on, the more nervous he became. He looked up at the steep sides of the ravine to their front.

'I don't like this,' he said to the young knight riding at his side. 'This is perfect ground for an ambush.'

'We have riders on our flanks,' said Sir Robert,' and I'm sure they will provide more than enough warning of anyone near enough to try any attack.'

'We will go an hour more,' said Gerald,' and then return to the column.'

Slowly the patrol continued into the ravine, the sound of their horses' hooves echoing amongst the rocks but within a few minutes, they came to a halt as the walls narrowed to form a bottleneck.

'This is as far as we go,' said Gerald. 'To press further invites an attack.'

'It seems like it widens out on the other side,' said Robert, standing up in his stirrups. 'To come so far and stop at this juncture makes no sense.'

'I will not risk our men,' said Gerald. 'Remember what the king said, our blades will be needed at Ashkelon.'

'Then at least send the scouts ahead,' said Robert. 'Then we can truthfully report that we came as far as we could and saw as much as we can.'

One of the scouts twisted in his saddle to face Gerald.

'My lord, I am happy to proceed alone. Allow me to test the passage and report back.'

Gerald nodded and watched as the man rode slowly forward, scanning the high walls of the ravine as he went.

As they waited, the second scout dismounted and walked back and forth across the ravine floor, his head down as he examined the tracks.

'Is there a problem?' asked Gerald, breaking the silence.

'I don't think so,' said the scout, 'the signs show many horses passed this way just a few hours ago.'

'Yet you look concerned?'

'There is something wrong,' said the scout, 'but I cannot be sure. '

Up ahead the first scout emerged from the bottle neck into a much wider part of the ravine. The ground was flat and but only continued a few hundred paces before dropping away over a cliff edge. Slowly he looked around, carefully scanning every possible hiding place, searching for any sign of an ambush until finally, satisfied he was alone, he turned to send the signal back to the patrol.

'My lord,' said one of the knights behind Gerald, 'the way is clear.'

Gerald looked up to see the scout waving on the far side of the ravine. He was about to give the order to advance when the second scout spoke up from the dusty ground to one side.

'My lord, you should see this.'

'What is it?'

'These tracks, something is wrong.'

Gerald glanced at Robert.

'Hold the men here,' he said, 'I will return in a moment. He dismounted and walked over to the scout. 'Show me.'

'These are the tracks of the men we have been following,' said the scout, 'as you can see, there are many horses, possibly up to a hundred, but look here.' He crouched down to point at a single hoof mark. 'This track is not as deep and is rough around the edges. The horse has obviously thrown a shoe.'

'Continue,' said Gerald.

The scout got to his feet and walked a few paces away.

'This horse has also thrown a shoe,' he said, on the same leg as the first one.'

'Coincidence?' suggested Gerald.

'I thought so at first,' said the scout, 'but the more I look, the more I find. If these tracks are to be believed, there are at least six horses that have lost one shoe, each on the rear hind leg, and they are just the ones I have found so far. I'm sure if I keep looking I will find more.'

'But that doesn't make sense. How could several horses all lose the same shoe?'

'They wouldn't,' said the scout, 'which can mean only one thing.'

Gerald stared at the scout as they came to the same conclusion.

'It's the same horse,' he said quietly.

The scout nodded and looked back down the path they had ridden up earlier.

'The riders we have been tracking,' he said, 'have doubled back several times to leave a trail that makes the group look much larger than it actually is. They must have known we were following.'

'But why do that?'

'They must have wanted us to believe that they were still ahead of us when all the while...'

Gerald's face fell at the implication. If the group ahead was much smaller than they had thought then that could mean only one thing, the main force was now behind them.

He turned suddenly to order the men to assume a defensive position but before he could speak, someone shouted out from the column.

'My lord, there's something happening up ahead!"

On the far side of the narrow ravine, the first scout turned his horse to stare at the ravine walls. Only seconds earlier they had seemed silent and devoid of life but as he watched with horror, dozens of archers stood up from behind the rocks, each aiming their bows toward him. Desperately he turned his horse to re-join the patrol, but it was too late and before he could ride, his horse fell from beneath him, cut down by a hail of arrows. The scout landed heavily but was unhurt and he scrambled quickly to his feet to run back toward his comrades but had gone only a few paces when a single arrow pierced his leg and sent him crashing to the ground.

His cry of pain echoed around the ravine and as his horrified comrades watched on, he tried desperately to crawl to safety.

Gerald thought furiously. Although one of his men was wounded, he had to consider the whole patrol. To ride further into the ravine was a huge risk as he had no idea how many Saracens were hidden amongst the rocks, yet to retreat meant leaving one man to die and the rest of them facing an unknown threat further back down the ravine. Quickly deciding it was better to face the enemy on known ground, he decided to turn and ride hard back down the way they had come, knowing it was imperative that as many as possible returned to Baldwin to fight for Ashkelon.

He turned to give the order but before he could speak, Sir Robert, enraged at seeing one of their men wounded just a hundred paces to their front, drew his sword and raised it in the air.

'Men of Jerusalem,' he roared, *'advaaance.'*

Without hesitation the young knight spurred his horse forward and galloped through the ravine, closely followed by the patrol.

Gerald stared in horror, knowing that the inexperienced man was probably leading the patrol into a trap.

'No,' he shouted, *'hold that command.'*

Some of the men heard the knight and reined in their horses but it was too late, by far the majority were already following Sir Robert through the narrow ravine.

Gerald ran to his horse and climbed into the saddle,

'My lord,' shouted one of the men, 'what are your orders?'

Gerald looked around desperately. Only twenty men remained and if he was to withdraw now they could be cut down by the Saracens waiting somewhere further back down the valley, but to follow the inexperienced knight through the ravine meant he was probably riding into an ambush. Knowing he had no choice but to help the young man, he drew his own sword.

'Present shields,' he roared, *'advaaance.'*

Within moments the remainder of the column thundered through the ravine... *straight into a storm of Saracen arrows.*

Back in the brigand camp, Cronin watched as his two captors finished their meal and laid back in the shade to rest while the sun was at its highest. Occasionally one looked over to make sure he was not attempting to release himself from his bonds.

'Any chance of some food?' asked Cronin eventually, catching the glance. He lifted his bound hands and pointed into his mouth to emphasise the point. 'Food,' he said again.' I need to eat.'

The man talked to his comrade briefly before getting to his feet and walking back to the fire to remove the carcass from the spit above the fire. For a moment Cronin thought he was going to get fed but his optimism was short lived as the man returned to his place in the shade and sat back down, picking nonchalantly at the meat still on the bone while staring at the prisoner.

'Hassan,' called Cronin, getting the boy's attention, 'ask him if I can have some food.'

'There is no need,' said Hassan.

'Why not?'

'Because I understand you well enough, Kafir,' interrupted the man, 'and you will eat when the rest of us have had our fill, no sooner.'

'How do you speak our language?' asked Cronin, surprised.

'I spent a long time as a slave to your people in Jerusalem,' said the man, 'and would be there still if I had sat back and blamed Allah for my predicament, as did those who toiled alongside me. Instead, I learned the language and used it to plan my escape from servitude.'

'Yet here you are, cast away from your own people as a brigand.'

'It is better than the cells of the citadel,' said the man, 'out here I am free to live or die according to my own judgement, unlike you.'

'Do you mean to kill me?' asked Cronin.

'Not I,' said the man, 'for you are too valuable alive but I doubt your new masters will make your life so comfortable.'

'And who may that be.'

'Saladin has placed a good price on any Templar knight brought to his camp alive. You are such a man, yes?'

'I am no knight,' said Cronin.

'Maybe not, but you bear the same blood cross upon your tunic. Titles bestowed upon men by other men mean little, but the fact that you shared the same quarters as the Templars gives you value.'

'I see our mutual friend has been very talkative,' said Cronin, glancing toward Hassan, 'what else do you know about me?'

'Not much, except you are a formidable fighter and need to be watched with the eye of a hawk.'

'You waste your time taking me to Saladin,' said Cronin, 'for I know little. I arrived in the Holy Land only a few weeks ago and have not been involved in any tactical planning. The fact that I was out here at all shows you that I hold little sway in the order.'

'I will let Saladin's people decide what you do or do not know,' replied the brigand. 'They have ways of getting men to tell the truth.'

'Even a tortured man cannot repeat that which he does not know.'

'That is not my concern.' The Bedouin turned his head to speak to his comrade before throwing the remains of the hare over to land in Cronin's lap. 'Eat,' he said, and the sergeant lifted the carcass to his mouth to strip it of what remained of its meat.

He chewed quickly, all the time watching his two captors. The older of the two seemed to know no English but the one who had given him the food was more talkative. Again, Cronin knew it was to his advantage that the man was happy to talk as the more he found out, the better chance he had to escape.

The afternoon dragged on yet to Cronin's surprise, they seemed in no hurry to leave the makeshift camp.

'Can I have some more water,' he asked eventually.

The younger man brought the water skin and waited as the sergeant again drank his fill.

'Should we not be going?' asked Cronin when he had slaked his thirst. 'I would think that Saladin would be a bad man to be kept waiting.'

'Do not be in such a rush to die, Kafir,' said the Bedouin. 'This life is short enough.'

'What is your name?' asked Cronin.

'Why is that your concern?'

'I am just being courteous. To address a man, especially in his own lands without knowing his name is a rudeness that does not sit well with me.'

'You Franks have a strange concept of decency,' said the Bedouin, 'you think to talk without knowing a man's name is an insult, yet are happy to kill indiscriminately in a land where you do not belong.'

'Respect costs nothing,' said Cronin, 'but if you would rather I do not know, then that is fine with me.'

'Your western tongue would not wrap itself around my full name,' said the man. He nodded toward Hassan. 'He calls me Mehedi, it will suffice.'

'And your friend?' Cronin nodded toward the second Bedouin watching the exchange from alongside the fire.

'Mustapha. A man who helped me after I escaped from Jerusalem.

'Does he also speak English?'

'He does not.'

'But he is not kin?'

Mehedi paused and stared at Cronin with interest.

'I see what you are trying to do, Kafir,' he said, 'but it will not work.'

'And what would that be?'

'You explore the possibilities of turning me against my comrade, but it is a fruitless ambition. You are the enemy of these lands and are responsible for my time spent in slavery. I would slit your throat in an instant should Mustapha command it.'

'Again, I meant no insult,' said Cronin.

Mehedi got to his feet.

'The presence of your people in my country is offence enough,' said Mehedi, 'so I lose no sleep over anything you have to say. Just know that tomorrow your life gets a lot worse.' He turned away and walked over to where the horses were tied to a tree.

Cronin turned his head and saw Hassan staring at him, having heard the conversation between the two men.

'Well, asked Cronin, have you prayed yet, Hassan?'

'Prayed for what?' asked the Bedouin boy.

'For forgiveness,' replied Cronin and without waiting for a reply, turned away to lay on his side, his back deliberately turned to the boy who had betrayed him.

Chapter Fifteen

The Ravine
November 12th
AD 1177

'Shields,' roared Gerald galloping out from the tight ravine, 'try to pin down their archers.'

Immediately the horsemen raced towards the rocks, their skill in horsemanship and archery coming to the fore. Within moments the deadly hail of enemy arrows dwindled drastically.

Gerald looked around at the damage already done. Almost a dozen men and horses lay dead or dying in the dust and he swore to himself when he realised that Sir Robert was amongst the fallen.

'Some of you do what you can for the wounded,' he shouted, 'the rest of you, dismount and follow me.'

He leapt from his horse and ran towards the enemy's position, holding up his shield against the few arrows still falling around him. The counter barrage from his own turcopoles meant he and his men quickly reached the enemy position and they clambered over the smaller rubble to reach their attackers, their hearts raging after being caught out in such a cowardly manner.

One of the hidden Saracens ran out from behind a boulder and with a roar, launched himself down onto Sir Gerald, his scimitar smashing against the knight's raised shield.

Gerald ducked to the side, absorbing the impact and his attacker fell to the ground, knocking his head against a boulder. Immediately the knight spun around and thrust his sword down into the Saracen's chest. He ran on, and though other attackers burst from their hiding places to engage the knights, their lighter equipment meant they were no match and Gerald's men hacked them down with impunity.

Within a few minutes, the main threat was broken and only a few men remained hidden amongst the higher rocks.

'Archers,' he shouted, 'keep their heads down. The rest of you, collect what arrows you can from the field. We may need them on the return journey.'

With his men busy, the knight returned to where Sir Robert was being tended by one of the sergeants.

'How bad is it?' he asked, removing his helmet

'I took an arrow to my arm,' said Robert, grimacing, 'but my horse was killed immediately and trapped me beneath it when it fell.'

'It's a typical tactic,' said Gerald. 'Can you walk?'

'I don't know yet,' said Robert, grimacing again as the sergeant tightened a makeshift bandage around his arm, 'help me up.'

Gerald grabbed Robert under the arms and helped him to his feet.

'It's not good,' continued Robert, trying to place some weight on his injured foot, 'but I don't think its broken.'

'Find him a horse,' said Gerald, looking around, 'what about the others?'

'Seven dead, eight wounded and another three who probably won't see the day out,' said the sergeant. 'We've also lost ten horses with another six beyond help.'

Gerald sighed heavily. It was a huge loss, especially as now their return would be severely hindered by trying to care for the wounded.

'Right,' he said, 'this is what we are going to do. Kill the horses that won't make it back and place all our wounded on whatever horses remain. Double up where necessary.'

'What about our dead?'

'We have no time to dig graves,' said Gerald. 'I'm worried there may be a Saracen force behind us and I don't want to be here when they catch us up.'

'My lord,' said a voice and Gerald turned to see the surviving scout walking over.

'What is it?'

'My lord, I took the liberty of trying to find a way out of here other than the way we came.'

'And?'

'There is none, this ravine ends at a cliff edge a few hundred paces away.'

'Is there no way down?'

'No, my lord, the only way out is the way we came.'

'But that makes no sense,' said Sir Robert. 'If what you say is true and their main force doubled back, why would they allow their own archers to be trapped in this place. Surely they would have known about the cliff?'

'The numbers of archers hidden amongst the rocks was actually very low,' said Gerald, 'and had no realistic chance of defeating a well-trained force. It's almost as if they were used to lure us here....' His eyes widened as he realised what was happening and his head turned suddenly.

'Men of Jerusalem,' he roared, *'close in...'* but already he knew it was too late and watched in despair as hundreds of Saracen horsemen galloped through the ravine behind them, roaring their battle cries as they bore down on the dismounted patrol.

The Saracen lancers crashed into the Christian forces and dozens of Gerald's comrades fell at the first pass. Gerald was hit but his shield took the brunt of the impact and he fell to the ground with only a flesh wound to his side. Taken by surprise, the mounted turcopoles were slow to respond and most of their horses were cut down from beneath them. Frantically they used the last of their arrows against the rampaging enemy cavalry but to little effect and after suffering terrible casualties, what was left of the patrol huddled together, their shields presented outward offering a semblance of protection against the enemy arrows.

Gerald staggered to his feet and looked around to see the damage done. Within moments he realised they were heavily outnumbered with even more lancers pouring through the narrow ravine, closely followed by hundreds of infantry. Soon he and his men were completely surrounded.'

'Oh, sweet Jesus,' whispered one of the men at his side, 'we have no chance. We need to surrender.'

'There will be no surrender,' said Gerald. 'Saladin's torturers will make every man here willingly scream what they know before slitting our throats and leaving our bodies for the buzzards.'

Before anyone could say any more, a solitary Saracen rider rode out from the enemy cavalry and toward the group of surrounded men.

'Men of Francia,' he called, 'I am Shirkuh ad-Dun, General in the armies of the great An-Nasir, Salah ad-Din, Yusuf ibn Ayyub. Exalted sultan of Syria and Egypt. Who speaks for you?'

'I do,' said Gerald, stepping forward, 'what do you want?'

'I demand your surrender,' said the Saracen, 'and vow that if you do, then there will be no more deaths.'

'And will we be allowed to leave as free men?'

'Alas no, that but at least you will be alive.'

'And what would become of us?'

'You will be my prisoners and taken to a place far away from here.'

'To rot in a Saracen dungeon?'

'I have no say in the place of incarceration but is it not better than being impaled on a lance? Perhaps one day you would be ransomed and returned to your families.'

'I know men who have spent time in a Saracen dungeon,' replied Gerald, 'and they say it was a fate worse than hell itself.'

'If what you say is true, then it is obvious they survived to tell the tale,' replied Shirkuh ad-dun. 'Do not make the mistake of spurning this gift of Saladin for it is your only hope of life.'

Gerald turned to the scout at his side.

'You say the cliff is impassable.'

'It is.'

'How severe is the drop?'

'It falls away for about the height of four men. After that, the slope is less severe and is covered with brush.'

'Could a man survive the fall?'

'If God is with him.'

'Then that is our exit,' said Gerald.

'You can't expect us to jump off a cliff,' hissed Robert. 'I would rather die here at the end of a lance than have my body smashed upon on the rocks. At least that would be an honourable death.'

'Death is death,' said Gerald and turned away to address the mounted Saracen.

'I need to talk with my men,' he said, 'give me some time to consider your terms.'

'What is there to discuss?' asked Shirkuh. 'You are trapped here. The only choice is life or death.'

'A few minutes,' said Gerald, 'that's all I ask.'

Shirkuh paused for a moment before answering.

'A hundred heartbeats,' he said eventually, 'then I will hear your answer. Use them wisely, Kafir.' He turned his horse and re-joined his lancers at the far end of the plateau.

Gerald turned to his men.

'Listen to me,' he said urgently, 'you heard what he had to say. To surrender means torture and a short life in a stinking jail, yet to fight against such odds invites certain death.'

'God is on our side,' growled a voice, 'and our lives will be dearly sold. I say let them come.' Several others added their agreement.

'I respect your valour,' said Gerald, 'but to die needlessly is a sin. We cannot prevail by staying here and we cannot retreat, but there is another way.' He pointed toward where the Saracen lancers were reforming for a second assault. 'Beyond them, there is a cliff edge that drops away to a slope leading to the plains. If we can get there we can risk the fall and use the cover to make our way back to the king's column. It is impassable to horses but at least some of us may survive to fight at Ashkelon.

'What about the wounded?' asked another knight. 'Surely we cannot leave them here?'

'We have no other option,' said Gerald, 'they would not survive the fall and would hold up those of us who make it. We can only hope the Saracens have enough humanity to treat them well.'

'You ask us to run from conflict,' said the knight, 'yet my code forbids such a thing.'

'I ask only that you remember your oath to your king,' said Gerald, 'and he needs us to fight under the true cross. Don't forget, Jerusalem itself is at risk and that is far more important than fleeting glory and a bloody death.'

'I will not flee,' said the knight eventually. 'I will stay and fight.'

Gerald turned to the other men.

'Who else chooses death before loyalty?'

Another five stepped forward, much to Gerald's annoyance. They were good men and would be needed at Ashkelon.

'Is there nothing I can say to change your minds?'

'I will die before I flee,' said one and the others banged their swords against their shields in a sign of assent.

'In that case, I ask a boon,' said Gerald. 'In a moment, their cavalry will attack again, and I ask that you form the first line of defence. If you can disrupt their advance for even a moment, we have a chance to break through to the cliff. Will you do that?'

'Aye,' came the reply.

'And I will lead them,' said Robert stepping forward.

'You should come with me,' said Gerald, 'the king will expect it.'

'I will remain and lead those who sacrifice themselves in the greater cause,' said Robert, 'it was my misjudgement that got us into this mess, so it is the least I can do.'

'You will not survive,' said Gerald.

'My decision is made,' said Robert. 'I stay behind.'

'So be it,' said Gerald and turned to the remainder of his men.

'Look to your weapons, my friends, and prepare to fight for your lives.'

Shirkuh ad-Dun looked over at the surrounded Christians in the centre of the plateau. His comrade rode up and reined in his horse beside him.

'It looks like your offer was not accepted,' he said, watching as a group of heavily armoured knights emerged from the group to present a shield wall facing the Saracens.

'Then their commander is a foolish man,' replied Shirkuh ad-Dun, 'and they will die where they stand.'

'Does not Salah ad-Dun want them taken alive?'

'He does but at minimal cost. Their capture would have been a great prize but there will be others of equal value.'

'Shall I give the order for our archers to cut them down?'

'No, their heavy armour and shields will protect them against most of our arrows. Wait until their position has been broken by our lancers and then send in the foot soldiers.' He lifted his lance so it was visible to all the Saracen cavalry.

'Ayyubid,' he roared, *'for Salah ad-Din, advance.'*

'Allahu Akbar,' roared the mounted warriors, and moments later, over a hundred horses thundered across the arid plateau towards the Christian position.

'Here they come,' roared Gerald, raising his sword into the air, 'in the name of God Almighty, *advance.'*

Led by Robert of Essex and the other six knights who had sworn to fight to the death, every able man in Gerald's patrol raced forward to engage the charging lancers head on. The tactic was totally unexpected by the Saracens, and as the two groups collided, the first of the heavily armoured knights dropped low to avoid the enemy lances, swinging their heavy swords to smash through the legs of the horses. Men and beasts fell to the floor and Gerald's knights fell upon them, cutting them apart with swords and axes. Some of the Saracen cavalry ploughed in amongst Gerald's men but without the advantage of speed, their impact was minimal, and they were soon hauled to the ground and killed without mercy.

The initial contact had been brutal and three of the knights fighting alongside Sir Robert were now on the floor, either dead or dying with lances sticking out of their chests. Others had also fallen but Gerald knew they could not pause to offer any help.

'Keep going,' he roared and with renewed effort, they raced toward the cliff edge where only moments earlier, the Saracen lancers had mustered for an attack. They reached the edge and Gerald peered over, his heart sinking as he realised the drop was just too far for any man to survive.

'My lord,' shouted the scout, 'over here.'

Gerald looked over and saw the part of the cliff face nearest the scout was covered with scrub. It wasn't much but he knew it would aid a descent.

'Lancers to the fore,' shouted Gerald, 'the rest of you, shield wall.'

His remaining knights turned to face the enemy now on the far side of the plateau as their comrades started to lower themselves over the cliff. The Saracen commander, knowing he would be unable to launch a mounted attack so close to the edge, ordered his foot soldiers to form up to fight the Christians at close quarter.

'Hurry,' shouted one of Gerald's men, 'they are coming.'

The last of the turcopoles disappeared from sight and he finally ordered the last of his knights to follow them down before turning to see Sir Robert and three other knights still standing and facing the enemy.

'Sir Robert,' he shouted, 'come there is still time.'

'I told you,' replied the young knight, 'I am staying here with these men.'

'There is no need to stay,' shouted Gerald, 'there is enough time to save everyone. Get down the cliff.'

'No,' shouted Robert, *'and if you delay any longer you will die alongside me.'* He turned around and faced the knight. 'Be gone, my lord, and tell my father I died with God's name on my lips.'

'I gave you an order,' roared Gerald but it was of no use. As he watched, Sir Robert and the other two knights turned to face the enemy and after making the sign of the cross upon their chests, ran towards the Saracen infantry.

Seconds later, they smashed into the Saracen horde, cutting the enemy down with every swipe of their swords but despite their bravery, the three men were soon overwhelmed and disappeared from sight, paying the ultimate price for loyalty and honour.

Knowing there was no more he could do, Sir Gerald lowered himself over the edge.

Hundreds of Saracens raced across the plateau, but it was too late, most of Gerald's men were already headed into the tangled brush on the steep slopes below and were soon lost to sight amongst the undergrowth.

As he fell, Gerald grasped for purchase at a sapling, but it came away by the roots and he fell the last few feet to the dusty slopes before rolling uncontrollably down the hill to smash against an olive tree, his body motionless amongst others who had not survived the fall.

Up above the Saracen foot soldiers gathered at the edge of the plateau, waiting for the order to pursue but it did not come. Shirkuh ad-Dun forced himself to the fore and peered down at the scattered bodies below.

'Shall we follow?' asked one of his men.

'We will risk no more time pursuing cowards,' said Shirkuh ad-Dun 'for if this is the mettle of the men who deem to defend Jerusalem then there is nothing for us to fear.'

'Some may survive.'

'If they do, so be it. The story they carry to their king will be how they were forced to flee like frightened children. It will sow fear in the Christian's hearts.'

He turned away and walked back across the battlefield. More than two dozen of his own men had fallen but the Christian casualties were far higher and many still lay moaning in the dust.

'See to our wounded,' he said, 'and bury the dead.'

'What about the Christians?' asked one of his men.

'Take those who will survive as slaves but slit the throats of any who are already on the road to death.'

The crowd of warriors stood aside as two foot soldiers dragged a beaten man across to cast him at the feet of the general.

'This one still lives,' said the warrior, 'and will fetch a good ransom.'

Shirkuh placed his boot beneath the chin of the man and lifted his head so he could look into the prisoner's eyes.

''You are a knight,' said Shirkuh. 'And fought well. What is your name?'

'I will not allow my family name to be sullied by allowing it to be spoken by your stinking mouth,' spat Robert.

'Careful, sir knight,' said Shirkuh, 'you may be worth a ransom, but your next words could be your last.' He turned to the two men holding the prisoner. 'Stand him up.'

Once on his feet, Robert straightened up as best as he could and stared into the Saracen's eyes.

'There is no need for you to die, Christian,' said Shirkuh, 'the day is done and you are my prisoner.'

'The day is not done,' gasped Sir Robert, his left hand clutching at a wound in his side. 'Return my sword and I will fight every man here or are you all cowards?'

Shirkuh smirked.

'I have heard such things many times from young men with more bravery than sense,' he said. 'To die needlessly is not a good thing, Christian. Cease your foolish words and accept your fate is now in my hands.' He turned to the two men. 'Take him away.'

'What are you afraid of, Saracen?' shouted Sir Robert over his shoulder, 'is it because you don't want your men to see the strength of Almighty God over your false Prophet?'

'Wait,' demanded Shirkuh, holding up his hand, and the two captors stopped in their tracks turning their prisoner to face him.

The Saracen leader walked over to stand less than half a pace from the young knight, his breath heavy in Robert's face.

'I have met many of your knights, Christian,' he said quietly, staring into Robert's eyes, 'both in battle and in parley. Most have been honourable, a few were braggarts, a minority were insolent. You, unfortunately, are amongst the latter.'

'Then fight me like a man,' gasped Sir Robert.

'You know you cannot win, 'said Shirkuh, 'so your false bravery is nothing more than a way to seek an honourable death.

Such things are earned not gifted, and to resort to such desperate means to achieve something that is not yours by right is proof you deserve no such thing.'

Without warning his hand drew a curved knife from his belt and dragged it across Robert's throat, opening it up like a second mouth.

The two men holding the knight released his hands and he fell to his knees, his eyes wide with fear, hands clutching uselessly at his wound.

'Honour is for the honourable,' said Shirkuh as the young man started to choke on his own blood, 'remember this as you die little better than a common slave.'

Chapter Sixteen.

The Brigand Camp
November 13th
AD 1177

Cronin slept fitfully. His wrists and ankles were still tied and though he had tried for hours to loosen his bonds, they remained as tight as ever. Finally, he had fallen asleep, his dreams filled with the many horrors he had seen on battlefields across England and France and he jumped in his sleep many times, haunted by memories no man should bear. Suddenly a hand covered his mouth and his eyes flew open in fear as he saw the flash of a knife within inches of his throat.

'*Shhh,*' hissed Hassan, and lowered the blade to cut through the binds around Cronin's wrists. 'They are asleep,' continued the boy, cutting the rope around the sergeant's feet, 'and you have little time. Take your horse and get as far away as you can. Do not stop or rest until you are safe amongst friends for they will surely follow.'

'Why are you setting me free?' whispered Cronin. 'I don't understand.'

'I made a mistake,' said Hassan, 'and thought I could benefit by betraying your trust. I was wrong and if I allow you to die there will be no forgiveness by God for my deeds.'

'Did they pay you?' asked Cronin rubbing his wrists to regain circulation.

'No, my lord, they threatened to kill my mother and sister if I did not do as they say.'

'But I thought your family were dead?'

'I lied,' said Hassan, 'another sin on my list of many.'

'Where are your family?'

'Held in the hills not far from here. Once you have gone. I will head there with all haste and try to set them free.'

'Are they guarded?'

'I know not but I must try. As soon as these men know I have betrayed them they will come after you, so I have some time but after that, they will kill my family. Now go while you still can.'

Cronin looked over at the sleeping men. He wanted to flee with every bone in his body but knew there was something he had to do.

'Hassan,' he said, 'the satchel with the documents from the pope, where is it?'

'Forget such things, my lord,' said Hassan, looking nervously over his shoulder, 'they are nothing and will cost you your life.'

'I was entrusted with God's work,' said Cronin, 'and cannot leave without trying to retrieve that which is lost.'

'Listen to me,' hissed Hassan grabbing the sergeant's arm, 'the satchel has gone along with all the scrolls within. They used them to fuel the fire and now only a trinket remains.'

'What trinket?'

'A silver necklace with a cross of gold and gemstones. They want me to sell it in the backstreets of Acre and give them the proceeds.'

'I was not told of any such necklace,' said Cronin.

'Nevertheless, Mustapha has it secured in his purse for safekeeping.'

'Then I should retrieve it.'

'You are not listening to me,' gasped Hassan. 'These men are skilled in the ways of murder and will cut you down without thinking should they wake. You must get away from here while you can. Do not die for a bauble.'

Cronin thought for a few moments before getting gingerly to his feet.

'Your horse and sword are waiting on the far side of those trees,' continued Hassan, pointing into the darkness. 'Head westward until you reach the coast road then ask any farmer the directions to the nearest fortress. With God's help, you should make it by nightfall tomorrow.'

'What about you?'

'I will stay here and wake them just before dawn. I will say you escaped in the night and offer to track you down but will lead them astray until noon. After that, I will follow your trail to prove my worth.'

'And if they don't believe you?'

'Then I will be dead before the sun appears over the olive trees. Be gone, master Cronin, dawn is fast approaching.'

The sergeant paused a moment. He knew that Hassan was risking his life to set him free but as it was the boy's fault he had been taken prisoner in the first place, it was a concern not of his making.

'I hope you find your family, Hassan,' he said eventually, 'and I will pray for your soul. 'But this matter is not over.' Without another word, he disappeared into the night, determined to be as far away as he could by dawn.

Hassan sat against the tree waiting for the sun to rise. He was tempted to run but knew the men would simply kill his family in retribution. Eventually, as the first orange hues appeared over the eastern mountains, he could wait no longer. Gingerly he lifted a rock and after hesitating for almost a minute, smashed it as hard as he dared against the side of his head.

The pain was overwhelming, and he fell sideways to the ground, his hand pressed against the wound as he gasped in pain. He was still conscious but as the blood seeped through his fingers, he knew that it was bad and just hoped he had done no lasting damage.

With his head throbbing, he lay still, afraid to move and though he had every intention of waking the two men with claims of being attacked, he gradually slipped into unconsciousness.

An hour or so later, Hassan was dragged back to reality with a kick to the ribs and Mustapha's angry voice echoing around the camp.

'Wake up,' shouted the old Arab, 'you have let the prisoner escape.'

Hassan groaned and tried to sit up. The pain in his head had spread down his neck and as Mustapha continued to berate him, he leaned forward and threw up into the sand.

'Mustapha,' snapped Mehedi, 'enough. Can't you see he has been injured?'

'If he had stayed awake,' snarled Mustapha, 'then perhaps the Frank would not have caught him unawares.'

'You do not know that for certain,' said Mehedi, 'let him explain.'

'I was not asleep,' groaned Hassan, taking some comfort in the fact that at least that part was not a lie.

'So, he just escaped his bonds and caught you unawares,' sneered Mustapha, 'why do I find that hard to believe?'

Mehedi crouched down and moved Hassan's blood sodden hair aside to examine the wound. It was as long as two knuckles and surrounded by an angry bruise.

'The boy is lucky to be alive,' he said, 'I have seen stronger men die from less.'

'Just get him on his feet,' said Mustapha, 'we'll need him to help us track the Christian.'

'I need to stitch the wound,' said Mehedi.

'Make haste,' growled Mustapha, 'and I'll get the horses ready. When I am done, we ride, whether he is bleeding or not.' He walked away as Mehedi turned back to the boy.

'He is not happy, Hassan, and you should take care not to anger him further. I have seen him slit a man's throat for a simple insult. Can you stand?'

Hassan nodded and Mehedi helped him walk over to the stream.

'Sit down,' said Mehedi, 'and I will get the thread. That wound is as wide as the gorge itself.'

For the next ten minutes or so, Mehedi did what he could for the boy and by the time Mustapha rode back into the camp leading the other two horses, they were ready to ride.

'Do not think I am happy with this situation, boy,' he said, 'your incompetence may have just cost me a purse of silver. Find the Christian and I might allow you to live but if he escapes, then you will be bound upon an ant hill, along with your family. Now ride out, I want him caught by nightfall.'

For several hours, Hassan led the two bandits westward, following the trail left by Cronin's horse. At first, he pretended his head was fuzzy from the injury and tried to lead them away from the true path but as the ground became more open, he knew he could delay no longer. Mustapha was already suspicious, and he had ridden his luck as long as he could.

'Enough,' called Mustapha, as they reached a stream just before midday, 'we will rest the horses here and refill the water skins.'

Hassan slipped from his saddle and knelt at the side of the stream to scoop water over his head, cooling his whole body down from the effects of the afternoon sun. He tilted his head back and breathed deeply. At some point, he would have to flee the two bandits and ride as hard as he could to where he knew his mother and sister were being held captive but so far, the opportunity had failed to materialise. He took another drink but as he got to his feet, his eyes widened in shock as a noose settled on his shoulders and he was jerked backwards to fall upon the floor, his fingers clutching desperately at his throat as he was dragged along the floor by the older Arab.

'What are you doing?' gasped Mehedi.

'I am doing what I should have done back in the camp,' growled Mustapha throwing one end of the rope over a branch of an olive tree, 'killing someone who is a traitor to his own people.' He pulled on the rope, hauling Hassan to his feet before tying the loose end around the pommel on his horse.

'Stop,' shouted Mehedi, as Hassan struggled to breath. 'He has done nothing to deserve this.'

Mustapha spun around and stared at his comrade.

'You must be blind as well as stupid,' growled the older man, 'did you really believe his lies about what happened?'

'Why would I doubt him? You saw the injury on his head, he was attacked.'

'You believe what you will but before you defend him, explain how it can be that a man with his hands and feet tightly bound, somehow managed to crawl freely amongst us, steal a knife and then proceed to cut his binds without making as much as a sound. Then, use a rock to hit his guard yet leave his two captors alive? If you believe that, Mehedi then you are a bigger fool than I took you for.'

'Do not call me a fool,' said Mehedi, 'I have told you before.'

'Or what?' shouted Mustapha, spinning around and drawing his sword. He strode forward and placed the point of his blade against his comrade's throat. 'Don't forget it was I who found you dying in the desert, Mehedi, you were as weak as a kitten hidden away amongst the ruins waiting to die. If it wasn't for me you would be dead or at the least, toiling as a slave for the Christians.'

'I know I am indebted to you,' said Mehedi, 'but that does not mean I should not speak out when I think you are wrong.'

'Why am I wrong? Even you can now see the Christian was helped by this traitor. Why should I let him live?'

'We need him to track the prisoner,' said Mehedi.

'He was useful when the ground was hard,' said Mustapha, 'but out here, even my old eyes can pick up the trail. Your life is mine, Mehedi, and my actions, right or wrong demands loyalty. Declare it or draw your blade, there is no other way.' He took a few paces back and lowered his sword to his side, waiting for Mehedi to make a move.

Mehedi stared into the older man's eyes. What he said was true, he owed him his life and, in their culture, that was a debt he would carry to the grave.

'Well?' said Mustapha, 'what is it to be.'

'I cede to your leadership,' said Mehedi eventually, 'and acknowledge the debt between us.'

'Good,' said Mustapha eventually and sheathed his sword. 'Now prove it.'

'How?' asked Mehedi.

'Mount the horse and ride it over to the stream.'

Mehedi looked at the horse and then over to Hassan, still struggling to breathe as he stood on the tips of his toes to ease the pressure around his neck. To ride the horse away meant the boy would be drawn slowly up amongst the branches to choke to death. It was a horrible way to die.

'I will gladly kill him if that is your wish,' said Mehedi, 'but let it be by my blade. That way it will be a quick kill.'

'Mount the horse, Mehedi,' said Mustapha menacingly, 'or our alliance ends here with one of us dead.'

Mehedi looked at the struggling boy once again and swallowed hard. He had killed men before but for some reason, his heart railed against seeing this boy die a slow and horrible death.

'Well,' said Mustapha, 'what are you waiting for?'

Knowing he had little other option, Mehedi walked over and mounted the horse.

'Please,' gasped Hassan from beneath the tree, *'don't do this.'*

'You should have thought about the consequences before you decided to betray your own countrymen,' said Mustapha. 'Now you will die the death you deserve knowing that your family will suffer the same fate in a few days.'

'No,' gasped Hassan, 'the crime is mine alone. Please let them live.'

'Too late,' said Mustapha and turned to his comrade. *'Ride.'*

Mehedi took a deep breath and after a moment's pause, urged the horse forward, drawing Hassan's struggling body up amongst the branches of the Olive tree.

Chapter Seventeen

The Judaean Mountains
November 13th
AD 1177

Gerald struggled back to consciousness. Someone was dabbing a wet cloth on his forehead and he opened his eyes to see the scout looking down upon him through a bruised face.

'You look bad,' said the knight eventually.

'You don't look so good yourself,' said the scout. 'Keep still, there are still thorns embedded in your face from the fall.'

Sir Gerald waited as the scout did the best he could.

'We need a physician's tools to get the rest,' he said eventually. 'Some are beneath the skin and short of using my blade, are beyond my reach.'

'They will wait,' said Gerald, pushing himself up into a sitting position and looking around. They were surrounded by heavy scrub and he could see more men being tended by their comrades amongst the bushes. 'Where are we?'

'About a league from the cliff,' said the scout. 'We are safe here for the time being.'

'Did they follow?'

'Not as far as we are aware, but we have sentries out, just in case.'

'How did I get here?'

'We carried you, along with several others.'

'How many survived?'

'There are seven of us still able to fight, eight including you.'

'Any knights?'

The scout shook his head.

'None, my lord. Those that survived the fight died in the fall or are lost somewhere upon the plain. We have men looking for them but without sounding a rallying horn, there is no way to find them.'

'Eight is more than I could have hoped,' said Gerald, struggling to his feet. 'What is your name?'

'James Hunter, my lord. My family have served many noble families over the years tracking deer and boar in the forests of England.'

'A noble trade. How are you here?'

'The foolishness of youth,' said Hunter. 'I saw my peers marching off to join King Henry's army and was caught up in the fervour. I joined them and my skills as a tracker soon saw me being employed as a scout.'

'That does not explain why you are in the Holy Land and not England.'

Hunter paused and stared at the knight, wondering if he should tell the truth.

'You hesitate,' said Gerald, 'so I assume your tale is one of shame?'

'I killed a man,' said Hunter suddenly, 'yet I do not regret my actions. He had forced himself on a young girl, no more than a child really, and I set about him with my fists. During the fight, he drew a knife and I used it against him, piercing his heart with his own blade.'

'I see no crime in such an action.'

'Nor did I at the time yet the sheriff thought differently.'

'Did the girl back up your version of the events?'

'Aye, she did, and indeed there was another witness, but it turned out the rapist was the sheriff's nephew, so I could expect no justice.'

'So, you ran?'

'I fled to the nearest port and worked my passage on the first ship I could find. When I got to Acre, I sought work as a mercenary, the only order that would take on men at arms without asking too many questions. Again, my skills found me employment as a scout and here I am, lost in the desert with a knight who's face looks like a pincushion, yet has the power to have me hung as a murderer.'

'I don't think that is going to be an issue,' said Gerald.' You have already proven your worth and if we get out of this situation alive, perhaps I can petition the king to grant you a pardon.'

'Which king?' asked Hunter, 'for the pardon of Baldwin holds no sway in England.'

'You wish to return?'

'Aye, one day. I hope to go home and pick up what I so foolishly left.'

'A mantra repeated by many men I believe,' said the knight. 'Anyway, enough talk. Let us see who is left and who is able. The quicker we get back to Baldwin's column the better.'

Several leagues away, King Baldwin and his entourage approached the imposing castle of Blancheguarde. The fortress sat high upon a hill with sheer walls that dropped to a rocky escarpment. The only approach was across a deep ditch excavated to provide the stone blocks that made up impressive defensive walls.

As they neared, they could see men running along the battlements, taking up defensive positions at the castelades, not because they had mistaken the column for the enemy, but to pay him the respect he was due as king of Jerusalem.

'It looks like they have seen your banner,' said William riding at his side. 'I suspect the castellan will make every effort to ease your pain.'

'A warm bath will do wonders for my sores, William,' said Baldwin,' but will not be the salve for the worry in my heart.'

'My lord,' said William, 'God has gifted us with free will to do what we can in this life but ultimately, only he can see what lies ahead. I believe you have done everything you can within your power to put a halt to Saladin's ambition so allow your heart to ease. What will be, will be.'

'I agree with the prelate, my lord,' said Sir Raynald from his horse on the far side of the king. 'We are almost four thousand strong and can probably rely on the same number from in and around Ashkelon that will heed our call if needed.'

'I have every faith in our men,' said Baldwin, 'but let us not forget that our spies report that Saladin fields over ten thousand warriors.'

'This is true.' said Raynald, 'but there are other factors to consider. First of all, the standard of each and every one of our men is far higher than any Saladin can field. In a pitched battle, our strengths come to the fore and they cannot withstand a close quarter charge. All we need to do is buy ourselves some time until our army arrives from the north and I see no reason not to sleep soundly at night.'

'I hope you are right,' said the king as they neared the slope leading up to Blancheguarde's magnificent gates, 'for if we engage them and are found wanting, then there is nobody between Saladin and Jerusalem.'

All three men fell silent as they crossed the wooden bridge and as their column waited on the plains below, rode between the gate towers to enter the castle.

Inside, a Templar knight strode across the courtyard to greet the king. His tabard was pure white emblazoned with a blood red cross and a heavy sword hung from his side.

'Your grace,' said the knight as he neared, 'welcome to Blancheguarde.'

'Sir Redwood,' said the king looking down from his horse, 'it has been a long time.'

'Indeed it has,' said Sir Redwood. 'The last time we met, you were yet a boy and I served under your father in Jerusalem.'

'Five years is a long time,' replied the king, 'and it was before you joined the Templar order. I only wish you had stayed to serve under me.'

'Your father treated me as a brother,' said Sir Redwood, 'and when he died I grieved as if he was my own blood. But his death freed me to follow my true calling and I enlisted with the brotherhood to do God's work.'

'And are you happy?'

'Happiness is not a goal we seek,' said Redwood, 'but my soul is at peace and if I am to die wearing the red cross, then I do so knowing it is truly God's will.'

The king nodded and turned to introduce his entourage.

'This is William of Tyre and my regent, Sir Raynald of Chatillon. They are to be treated as well as I while we are here.'

'Both are known to me,' said Redwood with a nod, 'and will be well quartered.' He turned to indicate the man at his side. 'This is my second in command. He will ensure your needs are met while you are here but if we fall short in your expectations then please seek me out.'

'Thank you,' said the king. 'Now, if you don't mind we are tired and hungry. I trust you can accommodate us?'

'Of course,' said Redwood. 'Leave your horses here and come to the main hall. We have refreshments waiting. While you dine, I have arranged fresh food and water to be taken out to your men. They can camp below the castle walls and tonight I will provide the necessary sentries to allow them a good night's rest.'

'Will you not be joining us?'

'Alas it is a day of fasting for us, but God will provide any sustenance we need.'

Baldwin nodded and gingerly removed his aching feet from his stirrups. Two courtiers ran forward with a set of wooden steps and placed them beside the king's horse before helping him dismount and walking beside him and Sir Redwood to a nearby doorway.

'He seems to have everything under control,' said Raynald when they had disappeared into the hall.

'So he should,' said William. 'He has had over two days' notice.'

Raynald turned to look at the prelate.

'You sent word that the king was on his way?'

'Aye,' said William. 'Is that a problem?'

'You risked the messenger being caught and the king's plans being known to those loyal to Saladin. We could have been caught in the open.'

'Did you not say only a few hours ago that you feared nobody, such is our strength?'

'Words designed to soothe the king's mind only,' said Raynald, 'as well you know. Come, let's see what this fellow has provided in the way of food and wine.' He dismounted and handed over the reins to one of the many waiting grooms before making his way over to the hall, closely followed by William.

Below the castle walls, the rest of the column unloaded the carts and pack mules. Sergeants strode back and forth amongst the many men issuing their commands and soon a village of tents started to sprout up. In amongst them, prisoners built the fires needed to cook the huge amounts of food needed to keep an army fed and young boys made countless journeys from the supply wagons to the cooking areas. While the camp was being sorted out, the mounted knights rode around the perimeter, ensuring they were victim of no surprise attacks but eventually a mounted column emerged from the castle to take over the responsibility and those that had travelled from Jerusalem handed their horses over to their squires before divesting themselves of their armour and heading towards their allocated tents.

Back in the castle, Baldwin sat upon an ornate chair as his servants carefully removed his riding clothes. Underneath the heavy outer fabrics, the lighter silk underclothes had protected most of his skin from the worst of the desert dust, but where the sores were worse, the bandages were sodden with blood and pus. Gingerly his physicians removed the wraps and washed his body before applying the usual Comfrey and Aloe poultices.

'It feels particularly bad today,' said the king wincing as one of the physicians pulled away some rotting skin at the edge of one of the wounds.

'The heat of the sun and the stress of the road has done you no favours,' said the physician, 'you would have been better advised to stay in Jerusalem.'

'We have had this conversation,' said the king, 'my place is here with my men. Just patch me up as best you can and pray this will soon be over.'

'After I have cleaned the infections,'' replied the physician, 'I'll prepare some hemlock to ease the pain. While you are eating, I'll arrange hot water for a bath and check your quarters are adequate.'

'A clean bed and an end to my pain, albeit temporary is all I desire,' said the king.

The physicians finished what they were doing, and dressed in a clean robe, Baldwin walked slowly across the hall to join the rest of his entourage standing near a table laden with food.

'My king,' said Sir Raynald as he approached, 'I trust you are feeling more comfortable.'

'As good as can be expected,' said Baldwin, lowering himself into a chair, 'please, do not stand on ceremony. Eat your fill and relax. We have a few days to recuperate before ploughing on to Ashkelon.'

The men approached the table and started filling trenchers with a variety of food.

'My lord,' said one of the servants, 'would you let me bring you a platter?'

'No need,' said a voice and both men turned to see William of Tyre carrying a bowl filled with boiled goat and onions in a gravy sauce.

'Thank you,' said the king, his eyes widening with surprise at the sight of his favourite meal, 'this is a luxury even I did not expect.'

'There is also some chilled wine when you are ready,' said William, settling on a chair next to the king. 'Sir Redwood stores jugs deep in a cavern beneath the castle where the dampness mimics the coolness of winter.'

'I am impressed,' said Baldwin lifting the spoon gingerly to his mouth. He sipped the warm gravy carefully to check the temperature before closing his eyes with pleasure at the delicious richness.

'This stew is sublime,' he said eventually 'and bearing in mind the Templars are an order that preaches abstinence in most things, it is my great fortune that Sir Redwood happened to provide such a delight.'

'A coincidence indeed,' said William glancing over to Raynald. 'I shall arrange fresh fruits to be finely chopped and bring them when you are ready.'

The king nodded as he gently bit down on a piece of tender goat meat and William walked over to join Raynald at the table, leaving the king in the hands of his personal servants.

'How fares he?' Asked Raynald.

'As well as can be expected,' said William. 'These journeys always take it out of him and I just wish he had stayed behind.'

'I pressed such a thing upon him, but he would not listen.'

'Sometimes he can be as stubborn as a mule.' He turned to look at the weather worn features of the infamous knight. Raynald's reputation for brutality was well known but though the prelate loathed what he stood for, he knew the Regent was loyal and not afraid to defend the king with his life.

'Your comments outside have me worried,' he said. 'I thought we had nothing to fear from Saladin, such was our strength.'

'Shelve your fears, priest,' said Raynald, 'and worry only about garnering as much of God's grace as you can. '

'I pray constantly,' said William, 'but worry it will not be enough.'

'I would expect no less,' said Raynald picking up a slice of mutton on the end of his knife, 'but there may be something more practical that you could do that will aid our campaign, should the need arise.'

'And that is?'

'Convince the king to issue an Arriere-ban.'

William paused and stared at the knight.

'Is the situation really that serious that such a thing is necessary?'

'In war, you can never have too many forces,' said Raynald, 'and a general call to arms would mean our military strength could increase tenfold.'

'It would also mean castles would be stripped of their garrisons, farms being left untended and families torn apart as fathers and sons leave to answer the king's call.'

'All better than allowing Baldwin and the true cross to fall at the feet of the Ayyubid,' said Raynald.

'Even if I can persuade him, what is to say they will muster in time for any battle? Surely by the time word gets out there will be little time for anyone to get to Ashkelon.'

'Ten thousand men will be a gift from God,' said Raynald, 'but if even one man joins us as a result of the Arriere-ban, then that is one more sword to fight the Saracens. Hopefully they won't be needed but I am nothing if not experienced in war and believe this is a necessary step.'

William sighed heavily. What had started out as a mere rumour only days earlier had escalated to a point where all-out war was almost inevitable, and he knew only too well that no matter who emerged victorious, hundreds if not thousands of men would die, on both sides.

'Are you sure about this?' he asked eventually.

'As sure as the sun rises in the east,' said Raynald. 'So, can I count on your support?'

'Aye,' said William, 'you can, but may God preserve us.'

'Leave God to do what God does best,' said Raynald, slapping William on his shoulders, 'but in the meantime, there is food to eat and that wine is not going to drink itself. Come, let's see if we can do it justice.'

Several leagues away, Hunter led Sir Gerald and what was left of his patrol westward from the scene of the ambush. The going was slow, as many of the men had suffered wounds in the battle or carried injuries after their retreat from the escarpment, but gradually they realised that they were not being followed and spirits rose.

'Do you know where we are?' asked Sir Gerald, walking alongside the scout.

'Not exactly,' replied Hunter, 'though I recognise those mountains to the north-west. If I am correct then we will be back in friendly territory in a few days and with a bit of luck, may be able to secure some horses to get back to the king.'

'My lord,' called a voice, 'the men beg a respite.'

Gerald nodded and pointed to a copse of leafy trees.

'We will rest there a while,' he said. 'See to our injuries and share what water we have but drink sparingly, we know not when we will find another source.'

The stragglers made their way over to the shade and collapsed on the ground as Gerald lowered himself to sit alongside the scout.

'So, he said, 'What did you make of it back there?'

'The ambush?'

'Aye.'

'I thought it was very cleverly planned out and designed to get as many as possible to surrender.'

'I agree,' said the knight, 'but why do that when they had us so outnumbered? They could easily have killed every one of us with minimal casualties.'

'Sometimes, my lord,' said Hunter, 'our perceptions of Saladin are blurred by stories of brutality that gather intensity the more they are repeated. I have heard tales of chivalry being retold as savagery depending on the teller and on how much ale has passed across the table.'

'Where is the honour in doing such a thing?'

'For a foot soldier whose lot it is to die in a foreign land, the opportunity to regale a listener with tales of bravery against a savage foe garners more free ale than stories of peace and parley. Alas, it is often the way that the more brutal the story, the more likely it is to be remembered by the listener and it is these tales that colour our perceptions.'

'So, you believed that Saracen when he said we would be imprisoned and not tortured?'

'Ordinarily yes,' said the scout, 'but there is a doubt.'

'And that is?'

'The fact that Saladin is definitely bracing for war against Jerusalem. To do so will involve a huge mobilisation of men and to march into a kingdom as heavily armed as we are, means he needs information and plenty of it.'

'So, our capture would have been a source of that information.'

'Possibly, that and the fact that the Saracen force was by far the largest I have seen this far north since I have been here.'

'Do you think Saladin has already left Egypt?'

'Aye, I do. There can be no other explanation.'

'In that case,' said Gerald getting to his feet, 'there is no more time to waste. The king needs to know as soon as possible.'

Chapter Eighteen

The Judean Mountains
November 13th
AD 1177

Hassan's eyes bulged, and he clawed desperately at the noose around his neck as he was drawn up amongst the branches of the tree. His legs kicked wildly, and his bladder emptied in fear as realised he was about to die. His lungs strained to draw even the slightest amount of air, but it was no use and as he slowly choked to death, his eyes rolled back, and he slipped into unconsciousness.

Mehedi reined in the horse and looked over his shoulder, his heart sinking as he watched the boy struggling.

'It is nothing more than he deserves,' said Mustapha, but before Mehedi could reply, he caught a movement from the corner of his eye and spun around to see Cronin charging from the bushes, sword in hand.

Immediately he reached for his own blade but was shocked when the sergeant ran straight past to cut through the rope, sending Hassan's body crashing to the floor.

With a roar of his own Mustapha drew his scimitar and charged toward Cronin but the impetus was with the Christian and as Mustapha raised his sword, Cronin ducked low to swing his sword up beneath the Bedouin's chin, carving the front half of his face clean away from his skull.

The brigand dropped to the floor, his body twitching as he died, and Cronin spun around, knowing there was still a threat to his rear. For a few moments, he and Mehedi faced each other, their eyes locked as they each contemplated their next moves but before the sergeant could resume the attack, the Bedouin pulled on the reins of his horse and raced away from the bloody scene as fast as he could.

Cronin ran over to Hassan's body and loosened the knot around the boy's throat, searching desperately for any sign of life. For a few seconds there was nothing, and it seemed he was too late, but suddenly the boy gasped and drew in a large lungful of air.

'Thank the lord,' said Cronin and helped the boy up into a sitting position. For the next few moments, he waited as Hassan's breathing returned to normal before retrieving a water skin from the remaining horse.

'Here,' he said, 'try and drink a little.'

Hassan sipped at the water before pushing it away and staring at the sergeant.

'You came back,' he gasped.

'I had to,' replied Cronin, 'my conscience allowed no other option.'

'But I betrayed you.'

'You also saved my life and that is the greater debt.'

'I will be your slave for evermore,' said Hassan.

'I don't think that will be necessary,' said Cronin, 'though I would appreciate you answering some questions.'

'It is within my power to provide the answers then that is what I will do.'

'Come,' said Cronin, 'first of all let's get you cleaned up. Wash in the stream while I check the other one is not planning to circle back and attack us unawares.'

'I think he is not as brave as Mustapha,' said Hassan, 'and is probably far from here already.'

'I'd rather not take the risk,' said Cronin pulling the boy to his feet, 'sort yourself out and we'll talk in a while.'

While Hassan washed himself and his soiled clothes in the stream, Cronin mounted his horse and followed Mehedi's tracks for half a league eastward before satisfying himself the brigand had not circled around to attack them. By the time he got back to the stream, Hassan had lit a small fire and had a pot of water suspended over the flames.

'You have been busy,' said Cronin, dismounting, 'what have you there?'

'Oats and dried meat,' said Hassan, 'from his food pouch.' He nodded toward the body of the dead man who was now covered with a blanket.

'He will have to be buried,' said Cronin and looked toward the pot. 'How long will that be?'

'A while yet. The meat has to soften.'

'I'll dig the grave. Call me when it is done.'

He walked over to Mustapha's body but without the tools to dig in the sun-hardened sand, resorted to covering the corpse with a pile of rocks. Finally, with the last stone in place, he washed his hands in the stream and returned to the fire.

'The food is done,' said Hassan and ladled some of the thick stew into a wooden bowl before adding a handful of dried dates from a leather pouch.

Quietly they both ate until eventually, Cronin took a long drink from a water skin and turned his attention on Hassan.

'So,' he said, 'we need to talk.'

'I know,' said Hassan. 'This is a terrible thing I have caused but will do everything in my power to make it right.'

'First of all,' said Cronin, 'I need to know why you did what you did. I thought you were desperate to become a squire. Indeed, I risked a lot by standing up for you yet still you betrayed me. Why was that?'

'The answer is simple,' said Hassan. 'When my father was killed by brigands, they took me, my mother and sister prisoner. When I was old enough, they placed me on a road well-travelled by western pilgrims and I was instructed to become a part of Christian life. I was to learn all I could and was told that one day, I would be called upon to relay what I knew back to those who held my family prisoner. A few months ago, I was contacted and told to infiltrate the Christian army.'

'So, your story about wanting to be a squire was untrue?'

'Oh no, my lord, it was and still is my utmost desire. At first, I resisted the Christian ways but soon I fell under God's spell and when I was baptised by father Clement, it was the happiest day of my life. After that, I became transfixed by the many different orders of knights travelling through Acre and soon knew it was a life I needed to share. In particular, the Templar's creed was a draw to me and I yearn to wear the blood cross, in any capacity I can.'

'Yet still, you betrayed us?'

'I had no other option. Mustapha said he would slay my family if I did not do as he said. Somehow he found out I was to accompany you to Jerusalem and must have guessed you would be carrying information valuable to Saladin.'

'You said last night that the satchel had been burned. Is that true?'

'Yes. When they saw the jewelled cross, they lost interest in the documents and used them to fuel the fire. Their intention was to sell you to Saladin's men and sell the cross in the streets of Acre.'

'Where is the cross now?'

'I know not. I searched Mustapha's body when you were gone but it is not there so must be still in the saddlebags of his horse.'

'Which is the one his friend used to flee?'

'Yes.'

Cronin fell silent for a few moments, absorbing everything he had just learned. The fact that the documents had been destroyed was devastating but if he could retrieve the cross, then at least he could partly fulfil his task. However, he could not ignore that Hassan's family was now at risk of retribution so had to consider every option that lay open to him.

'Hassan,' he said eventually, 'do you know where your family is being held?'

'I think so.'

'And could this be the place where Mehedi is headed?'

'He rides in the opposite direction, but I believe he will return there if only to hurt my family.'

'Then our course of action is clear. We will ride there with all haste. Hopefully, we will arrive before him and set about securing your family's release. After that, you will lead them to safety while I seek out Mehedi.'

'Why would you do this for me?' asked Hassan. 'Especially after what I did to you?'

'Because,' said Cronin, 'it is the only thing I *can* do. Now let's get the horses sorted, we have a hard ride ahead of us.'

Chapter Nineteen

The Judean Mountains
November 15th
AD 1177

Cronin and Hassan had ridden south east for two days. On occasion, they were forced to hide away from patrols of men riding under no banner, but Hassan was sure they were Ayyubid and the two Christians ensured they stayed well hidden from sight.

'How far now?' asked Cronin, sipping from a water skin.

'Those hills to the front mark the edge of the Negev Desert,' said Hassan, 'and if I am correct, my family are there.'

'Why do you have doubts? Did you not live there with them?'

'I did but many years have passed, and their captors are nomads. This time of year, they should be back in this place.'

'Well there is only one way to find out,' said Cronin replacing the water skin onto his saddle, 'and that is to take a look for ourselves.' He urged his horse forward and headed for the distant hills.

Hassan followed him and soon took the lead, taking the smaller paths amongst the scrub away from the main paths. For the rest of the day, they headed uphill until eventually, Hassan reined in his horse amongst some huge boulders.

'From here we must walk,' he said. 'It's not far.'

'The last time we did this, you led me into a trap,' said Cronin.

'I swear in the name of our lord Jesus himself that this is not such a thing,' said Hassan.

'I will trust you, Hassan,' said Cronin, 'and anyway, this time I will not be caught out so easily.' He tapped the handle of his sword. 'Come, let's go.'

Leaving the two horses hobbled amongst the rocks they made their way through a series of small gulleys before Hassan dropped to his belly and crawled forward to look down into a cleft amongst the cliffs. Cronin joined him.

Down below, the rocky floor of a small ravine was filled with the obvious signs of having once been an encampment. Circles of rocks indicated old fire places and the remains of long unused tents lay tangled amongst the sparse bushes that clung to the few areas of soil. Overall the place was silent, and it became obvious to the two watchers that the camp had long been abandoned.

Hassan stared his heart heavy with despair. With the camp empty, it could only mean his family's captors had moved on and he had no idea where he could find them. His head dropped, and he closed his eyes, saying a silent prayer, beseeching God to look after his mother and sister but a moment later, he felt Cronin nudge his arm and he looked up to see the sergeant pointing towards one side of the valley.

Hassan followed his stare and his heart missed a beat, for there, at the tiny entrance of a cave stood a young woman holding a baby.

'Do you know her?' whispered Cronin.

Hassan nodded but couldn't speak. It was his sister.

Despite his desperation to call out, he remained silent, knowing there could still be those around who could do her harm. As they watched another woman emerged from the cave and carried a leather bucket over to a pool of water amongst the rocks.

'It is my mother,' whispered Hassan through his tears, 'God is truly merciful.'

'I see no others,' said Cronin, 'and that camp hasn't been used for a long time. Perhaps Mustapha's men moved on and abandoned your women to survive alone.'

'No,' said Hassan. 'Women are important to such men, and when they move camp, they are taken along. Something else has happened here.'

'Come,' said Cronin, 'let's get down there.'

Carefully they made their way down the rocky slope, remaining hidden as long as possible until they were level with the two women, albeit a few hundred paces distant.

'I have to go to them,' said Hassan, standing up but was immediately pulled down by Cronin.

'Wait,' hissed the sergeant, 'look.'

He pointed to the far side of the valley and Hassan could see a man leading his horse down from the hill beyond.

'It's Mehedi,' said the boy after a few moments, 'he has come to hurt my family.' He rose to his feet but again was pulled down by Cronin.

'Wait,' said Cronin, 'if he sees you he may turn and run again.'

'I care not for whether the man lives or dies,' spat Hassan, 'only that my family are safe.'

'Just give me a moment,' said Cronin. 'I doubt very much that he is going to ride all this way just to kill them immediately. Let's see what he does.'

In the distance, Mehedi walked carefully down the rocky path, looking around him in bewilderment. It was obvious he had not expected it to be deserted.

'I smell death,' said Cronin as Mehedi drew closer, 'yet see no corpses. Something has happened here and even your friend there is surprised his comrades are missing.'

'My mother has seen him,' whispered Hassan urgently and watched as she ducked low and led her daughter back into the cave.

'Come on,' said Cronin, 'follow me.'

'Where are we going?' replied Hassan.

'I think we can get behind him without being seen,' said Cronin, 'and that path is the only way out for a horse. Stay low.'

They crouched down and ran from boulder to boulder until eventually, they were on the far side of the valley, blocking off Mehedi's only means of escape.

'Now we have the advantage,' said Cronin drawing his sword.

Hassan drew his knife and together they stood up and walked silently toward the unsuspecting brigand.

Cronin managed to get within twenty paces before Mehedi realised he was there. The Bedouin spun around and drew his blade, gasping in surprise when he saw the Templar sergeant standing alongside Hassan. For a moment there was silence as his eyes met Cronin's and his fingers flexed nervously on the hilt of his sword as he silently weighed up his options.

'You are a resourceful man, Christian,' he said eventually, 'and it seems you are determined to fight me.'

'I do not want to fight you,' said Cronin, 'but will do so if you do not cede to my demands.'

'And what demands are these?' asked the Bedouin. 'You have the boy. I have nothing else of value.'

'I want the release of this boy's family,' said Cronin, 'and I want the return of the property you stole from me.'

'His family?' said Mehedi with surprise. 'I am not their captor, Christian. It was Mustapha who took them hostage years ago and yes they were once here but look around you, they are long gone.'

'On the contrary, they seem to be the only ones alive in this place.' He turned and nodded to Hassan. 'Go and bring them out.'

The boy sheathed his blade and ran across to the cave, leaving Cronin and Mehedi warily watching each other across the rocky floor.

'If what you say is true,' said Mehedi, 'then why do you ask for that which you already have?'

'Because I want to make it clear that when we ride away from this place, you will have no more interest in the boy or his family. What is done is done but from this day on, you will give him no more thought. Swear this and I promise you will live, but if I suspect you are lying, then the vultures of this place will tonight sleep with heavy stomachs.'

'I cannot do that,' said Mehedi but before the sergeant could answer, Hassan emerged from the cave along with his mother, sister and a young boy of about ten years old. His sister carried a baby and Hassan shepherded them towards one side of the valley away from Mehedi and Cronin.

'As you can see, Christian, they are as alive as you or I. Now let us live our own lives.'

'You are also in possession something that does not belong to you,' said Cronin, 'and I want it back.'

'If you refer to the bag,' said Mehedi, 'it has gone, used to feed the fire. Ask your little slave there,' He nodded towards Hassan, 'he saw us do it.'

'I know the parchments are gone,' said Cronin, 'but there was a pendant, a cross of gold encrusted with jewels. That cross belongs to the pope himself and was a gift to King Baldwin. I want it back.'

'I saw no such cross.'

'You lie,' said Hassan walking across from the rocks, 'I saw you place it around your neck and share laughter with Mustapha as you discussed the price it would bring.

Mehedi turned his head slowly and stared at the boy. His voice lowered, menacingly.

'I think Mustapha was right,' he said, 'and we should have killed you sooner.' He returned his gaze to Cronin, his scimitar hanging loosely at his side.

'So, there was a cross, but Mustapha did not entrust it to me, he kept it about his person, and that, my friend, is the truth.'

'I searched his body before I buried him,' said Cronin, 'it was not there.'

'Then he must have kept it in his saddlebag,' said Mehedi and his voice trailed away as he realised it was Mustapha's horse he had been riding since he fled the scene of the fight. He turned to stare at the horse at his side, frustrated that all this time he may have been riding with a fortune close to hand but had never realised.

'Check it,' said Cronin pointing at the saddlebag, 'and don't try anything stupid. If you try to escape I will cut your horse's legs from beneath you as you pass.'

Mehedi untied the laces on the leather bag fastened to the pommel of the saddle. He looked inside and after moving some of the eating implements inside, saw a silken pouch nestled amongst a handful of dried dates. Gently he drew it out and looked up at the sergeant.

'Open it,' said Cronin.

Mehedi unwrapped the silk and lifted the necklace up by the chain. Cronin withheld a gasp at the cross's beauty and Hassan's family murmured amongst themselves.

As it spun slowly on the end of the chain, the sun reflected off the jewels, causing everyone to stare in silence at its magnificence.

'Hand it over,' said Cronin eventually, but Mehedi's gaze did not leave the magnificent pendant, entranced by its beauty.

'I said hand it over,' said Cronin and this time the Bedouin raised his head to stare at the sergeant. Cronin could see the Arab's manner had changed and there was a dangerous look in his eyes.

'Don't do anything stupid, Mehedi,' warned Cronin. 'This does not belong to either of us and is not worth dying for.'

'If a life away from hunger and slavery is not worth dying for, then what is?' asked Mehedi. 'The Christians in Acre covet such things and with the money this will bring I can buy my own camels and set up a trading caravan.' He nodded towards the women. 'They can also benefit, even the boy if he so wishes. Go back whence you came, Christian and leave us to our lives.'

'What foolishness is this?' asked Cronin. 'These women were prisoners, forced to do your bidding yet you claim they will live alongside you. The sun has boiled your head, Mehedi and we waste time. Hand it over.'

Mehedi glanced over at the women again and then back at Cronin.

'You still have no idea, do you?' he said eventually. 'You people come here from your cold countries across the sea and deem to judge our way of life. You know nothing about us yet decide what is normal and what is not.' He nodded towards the women. 'They are alone and will not survive a month without a man at their side. These are difficult times and brigands abound so to have a man to look after them, with enough money to make them respected all along the trading routes is a temptation few will ignore.'

'Yet you killed her husband.'

'I was not with Mustapha on that day so carry no blame but there is another reason they will come.'

'And that is?'

Mehedi turned and shouted something in his own language.

For a moment nobody moved but eventually, the younger woman moved away from Hassan and walked over to stand beside Mehedi.

'This is foolishness,' shouted Cronin. 'Hassan, what is going on?'

Hassan turned to his mother, talking furiously in their own language. It became obvious they were arguing and despite the woman crying, she and the little boy walked over to join Mehedi and the young woman.

'I don't understand,' said Cronin, 'why would they do this?'

'Because,' said Hassan slowly, his face heavy with resignation, 'the baby is his.' He looked up at Cronin. 'They have no other choice, my lord, our ways demand the baby and mother stays with the father.'

'She is his wife?' gasped Cronin.

'No, my lord, not yet. He forced himself upon her and fathered the child.'

'But that is rape. Surely she holds no obligations to him.'

'She does not but he has fed them over the past two years and protected them from others who would do them harm. She feels that despite the circumstances, her place is at his side.'

'But what about your mother?'

'She is the grandmother and her life is to nurture the children. She will not leave the baby. Besides, where would she go?'

'She could come with us.'

'To Acre? Have you seen the old women within the city walls? Once proud women who rode the spice trails with their tribes now rot away begging for the driest of crusts from those who would rather see them dead. No, my lord, my mother would rather die amongst the desert hills than live amongst the stone streets of a diseased city.'

'You see, Christian,' said Mehedi, 'nothing in this world is as clear as you would like. If I give you the cross, then you will be condemning these women and children to a life of poverty. Take it from my dead body and the outcome will be the same. But ride away from here emptyhanded and they will live a good and worthy life. Is that not the way of true followers of your God?'

'You raped that woman and tried to kill her brother,' snarled Cronin, 'yet now proclaim a righteous stance and wish to become their protector. What sort of man does this?'

'I do not claim righteousness, Christian,' said Mehedi, 'only sensibility. Moments ago, I was a poor man with a life of brigandry in front of me.' He held up the cross and let it spin in the sun again. 'Now, I am rich with the beginnings of a family at my side. The only thing that stands before me is a misguided Frank who does not belong here in the first place.' His voice lowered, and he lifted his scimitar to point toward the sergeant.

'Now tell me it is not worth dying for.'

The valley fell silent as Cronin weighed up his options. He was confident he could better the man in a fight, but the consequences were not so clear. If Mehedi was even close to telling the truth, then to return the cross to the king meant that the two women and two children before him faced a very uncertain future. He turned to Hassan.

'Does he lie,' he asked.

'I know not the truth of his intentions,' said Hassan, 'but it is true that my mother and sister will not live long without a protector,' he looked up at the sergeant, 'whether that be brigand or knight.'

'If I allow him to keep that cross,' said Cronin, 'then I cannot return to Jerusalem and will be thrown out of the Templar order.'

'The king may not know it was on its way?'

'Not yet, but the pope would be expecting acknowledgement sooner or later and when it does not arrive, he will seek an explanation. It will be only a matter of months before the truth will be found out.'

'But it is not your fault.'

'I was the one tasked with taking it to Jerusalem, the responsibility is mine.'

'So, what are you going to do?'

'I don't know,' said Cronin and turned to stare again at Mehedi.

'I am growing a thirst, Christian,' said the Arab, 'and need to bring this to an end. Leave and we both win, pursue your quest by fighting me and we both lose, whatever the outcome.'

Cronin slowly lowered his sword to his side and took a deep breath.

'You have me cornered, Mehedi,' he said, 'as you well know. If I let you keep the cross and cede the path do I have your oath you will treat these people well.'

'With money to my name, there is no need to do otherwise, Christian, so if you want my oath, you have it.'

'There is one more thing,' said Cronin. 'If I allow you to take the cross, then in return I want information. What do you know about Saladin?'

Mehedi stared between the sergeant and the boy, thinking carefully before answering.

'I am Bedouin,' he said eventually, 'and no ally of the Ayyubid, but if you expect me to share the sultan's plans, then you are talking to the wrong person. I know nothing of such things.'

'Surely a man such as yourself hears rumours?'

'I hear many things,' said Mehedi, 'some I can repeat, some I will carry to my grave. You seem like a sensible man, Christian and I'm sure that if you were in my place you would feel the same.'

'But if you owe no allegiance to the Ayyubid so why not share what you know?'

'Saladin may not be my ally, but we share a dream that one day our lands will be free from the scourge of your people and I will not betray any man who may bring that situation about.'

'So, you do know something?'

'I have stated my case, Christian,' said Mehedi, 'so now you must make your choice. Do we fight, or do we act like civilised men?'

Cronin considered pushing the man more but could see Mehedi was resolute. Finally, he sighed and replaced his sword in its scabbard.

'You are a clever man, Mehedi,' he said, 'I'll give you that. I came here seeking a cross, a family, information and your head. I leave with you still in possession of all four. The king of Jerusalem could do worse than to have you amongst his advisors for I think Saladin would surrender within weeks, such would be his frustration.'

'You compliment me,' said Mehedi, returning his own blade into his belt. 'Now, if we both agree not to slaughter each other, perhaps there is time to eat.'

Cronin stared again at Mehedi. Moments earlier he would have cleaved open his head without remorse but now, somehow, he was considering sharing a meal.

'My lord,' pleaded Hassan, 'is it not good to share food?'

'So be it,' said Cronin eventually, still facing Mehedi, 'but know this, my sword will be at my side at all times. If there is trickery, then my blade will not falter.'

'Is there not now a truce between us, Christian?' asked Mehedi holding his hands out as if in welcome.

'One as fragile as a bird's wing,' said Cronin.

'Then let us not talk of war,' said Mehedi. He turned to the women at his side and spoke in his own language. The older woman took the baby while the younger walked off towards the cave.

'There is meat and herbs in the pot,' continued Mehedi, turning back to face Cronin, 'as soon as it has been warmed up, you will join us.'

An hour or so later, Cronin sat across the fire from Mehedi, both men eying the other with interest. Alongside Cronin sat Hassan while his sister and mother busied themselves with the food and water.

'So, this was your home?' asked Cronin eventually.

'It was. Most of the people here were the destitute and those without tribes. Our numbers grew as your people ate up more land until there were too many mouths to feed. Some of us turned to…well lets just say we did what we had to do to survive.'

'You preyed upon the pilgrims that sought access to the holy places. Poor people who knew only peace.'

'Hungry men do not discriminate between rich or poor. Only whether the caravan carries enough food to keep their children from starving.'

'A noble explanation,' said Cronin accepting a bowl of soup from the older woman, 'yet I hear the soldiers of Jerusalem are often tasked with burying the bodies of pilgrims slaughtered at the hands of men such as you.'

'You listen to too many stories, my friend,' said Mehedi, accepting his own bowl of soup. 'We rarely killed any who shared their food, only those who sought their blades.'

'In defence of what was theirs.'

'It is a difficult life, Christian. Ownership is temporary, whether bread, horses, castles or life itself. We hold them for only the fleetest of moments.'

'Your clever tongue can convince a man that day is night,' said Cronin, 'so I will argue no more.' He dipped some flatbread into the soup to retrieve a chunk of tender goat flesh. 'So where are your people now?' he continued, after he swallowed the meat.

'Dead,' said Mehedi abruptly. 'Slaughtered by men who came in the night. They spared nobody, but the women managed to hide away.'

Cronin stopped eating and looked at Mehedi. The Arab's focus had not left his bowl and he ate heartily as if he had just discussed the mere death of a sheep.

'Where are the bodies?' he asked eventually.

'Do you not smell them on the air?' said Mehedi. 'The women dragged them to a hole amongst the rocks and threw them in to avoid disease, but it was a task poorly done. Tomorrow I will cover them with soil and say a prayer for their souls.'

'How many were there?' asked Cronin.

'About fifty including the children,' said Mehedi. 'They stood no chance.'

'Was it Saladin's men who did the killing?'

'What does it matter?' asked Mehedi looking up. 'Death is death and the shape of the sword that conveys it does not matter to the child who stands in its way.'

The two men fell quiet again as they finished their meal. Finally, Mehedi got to his feet.

'It has been a long day, Christian,' he said, 'and I look forward to closing my eyes. Am I to be assured you will not come as an assassin while I sleep?'

'You have my word,' said Cronin, 'and we will be gone before the sun clears the hills tomorrow morning.'

'In that case, I wish you well,' said Mehedi. 'Perhaps one day we will meet again.'

'It is unlikely,' said Cronin, 'but if we do, I hope it is with the peace that we now share.'

'As do I,' said Mehedi and after a nod of acknowledgement, followed the two women into the cave.

'So, what do we do now?' asked Hassan when he was gone.

'You can stay if you wish,' said Cronin. 'Your family is here, and I believe that Mehedi may turn out to be a good man. Perhaps it is time for you to return to your own people.'

'My place is with you,' said Hassan. 'I am a Christian now and if you will have me, I will travel at your side until the day I too can wear the cross.'

'I fear association with me will only hinder you in that hope,' said Cronin. 'I was given an important task yet failed to carry it through. My incompetence will mean I will be cast out of the order and probably imprisoned. You would do well to find a different path.'

'What will be, will be,' said Hassan spreading out his cloak on the floor near the fire, 'but until then, my place is with you.'

'Are you sure?' asked Cronin.

'As sure as those stars are in the sky,' said Hassan.

Cronin laid back on his own cloak and stared up. The last few days had been hard, and he had tried everything he could to see out his task, but he had fallen short and now had no other option than to return to the column and face the consequences. Despite his troubled mind, his exhaustion meant he soon fell asleep and the camp fell into silence.

The following morning, Cronin and Hassan rose before dawn and had already mounted their horses when Mehedi emerged from the cave along with the older woman.

'Christian,' he said, making Cronin turn in his saddle to face him. 'I have been thinking. Yesterday's bargain was the right outcome, yet I am aware that it was weighted in my favour.' He paused as he considered what he was about to say. 'I cannot give you the answers you seek but if you travel east into the Negev desert, you will find a place called the Makhtesh Ramon. I have heard that there may be enlightenment there. Now, I have said too much so will bid you a fair journey. Travel well, Christian.'

Before Cronin could respond, Mehedi disappeared back into the cave.

'Makhtesh Ramon?' said Cronin to Hassan, 'have you heard of this place?'

'It is amongst the high hills just inside the Negev desert,' replied the boy. 'I have never been up there but have been told there is no water and once the heat of the sun reaches the rocks, it is trapped there forever. It is a bad place and no man goes there.'

'Do you know where it is?'

'I do but surely it is not your intent to go there?'

'I don't see why not,' said Cronin, 'besides, what have I got to lose?'

'Your life?' suggested Hassan.

'That seems to be already cursed,' said Cronin, 'so whatever the outcome, it can get no worse. Lead the way, Hassan, take me to the Makhtesh Ramon.'

Chapter Twenty

Castle Blancheguarde
November 16th
AD 1177

'Your grace,' said Sir Redwood getting to his feet as King Baldwin walked across the great hall, 'You look so much better than when you arrived.'

'Your hospitality has been a great relief to me,' said Baldwin, 'for the journey so far has been far harder than I expected. Alas, this disease takes more of a toll the older I get but now it is time for us to leave.'

The knight looked at the young king. Baldwin was badly affected by the leprosy but his inner strength and determination meant he often carried on when others would falter.

'Your supply wagons have been refilled with as much as we can spare,' said Redwood, 'I only wish you would allow my garrison to ride alongside you.'

'Your generosity is noted,' said the king, 'but Blancheguarde's position here is of vital strategic importance. If we were to leave it unguarded and it fell to Saladin, the road to Jerusalem would be left wide open. Your place is here and if the Ayyubid should reach this far, your task is to hold them back as long as you can until the army returns from the north.'

'I understand,' said Redwood, 'and worry not. Not a single Saracen will pass this way as long as there is a single breath left in my body.'

'I hope it doesn't come to that,' said the king, 'but your pledge does you credit.' He turned and looked around the hall. 'I was expecting to find Sir Raynald here,' he said, 'do you know his whereabouts?'

'I do, my lord,' said a voice and both men turned to see William of Tyre entering the room.

'William,' said the king, 'is everything ready for us to leave?'

'It is,' said the prelate, 'and the wagons have already broken camp. That is why Raynald is absent. There was a report of Saracens on the road and he took a patrol out to ensure the way is safe.'

'Why was I not consulted?'

'You were sleeping, my lord, and I advised the Regent not to wake you. Your sleep these past few days has been sparse.'

The king nodded. It was indeed true that rest had been hard to find but the previous night he had slipped into a refreshing darkness that had lasted until halfway through the morning and he felt like a renewed man.

'Your concern is acknowledged,' said Baldwin, 'but I should have been consulted on such a thing.'

'My apologies,' said the prelate with a nod, 'I thought it was the better option but in future, I will, of course, consult you on all matters.'

'Thank you,' said the king. 'Now, if we are to wait until the Regent returns, perhaps I have time to break my fast.'

'I will arrange something immediately,' said Sir Redwood and beckoned a servant from a nearby doorway. 'Arrange a platter of hot meats and fresh bread for the king,' he said, 'and have it brought up immediately. In addition, bring some watered wine and a jug of honey.'

'Of course, my lord,' said the servant and ran out of the hall to the kitchens.

If you will excuse me,' said Redwood, 'I have some business to attend but will be back within the hour.'

'You carry on,' said the king, 'for I expect we will still be here when you return.'

'My lord,' said William when he was gone, 'perhaps we can use this time to discuss the issue that I raised a few days ago?'

'I assume you refer to the Arrier Ban?'

'I do,' said William. 'Have you given it any more thought?'

'I have,' said the king walking over to sink into the upholstered chair placed there for his sole use.

'And your decision?'

'To call an entire nation to war is a serious move, William, and once issued, it is a difficult summons to retract.'

'I realise this,' said the prelate, 'and believe me, it goes against everything I believe in, but Sir Raynald's arguments have convinced me it is the right thing to do.'

'You have said yourself that the Regent's tendency is to seek conflict for little reason and though I trust his judgement, I worry that this may be a request solely made in order to flex his sword arm across the south.'

'I'm sure not even Raynald would counsel war without good reason,' said William, 'for it risks raising the ire of every tribe across the Outremer, an alliance that we cannot contemplate.'

'Yet is that not the risk we run should we issue an Arriereban?'

'My lord,' said William. 'The army is still in the north, and we can muster no more than four thousand men at best. Despite their undoubted skills, the estimated strength of Saladin's forces is in excess of ten thousand and I fear we are risking a defeat that could easily be avoided.'

'The estimated strength of Saladin's army is the result of rumours only. We have no exact knowledge and no sightings of him or his men. To call the whole of Jerusalem to war on such weak hearsay is a move that needs certainty.'

'But why? Is it not better to have the men ready and not needed?'

'And how do we feed such an army? It is hard enough to keep our own men in food and water so if tens of thousands more flood southward, our supply lines would collapse under the strain. I will not sentence my people to starvation on the strength of rumours.'

William sighed and nodded in deference. He had tried his best, but he knew when the king had his mind set, there was little he could do to change it.

Several leagues south, Raynald led a patrol of thirty knights along the road, seeking any sign of the Saracens reported by the scouts. So far there had been nothing and as the sun reached its highest, they stopped to water their mounts. Some of the squires carried heavy water skins amongst the horses, pouring it into leather buckets as the knights talked amongst themselves.

'These false sightings wear me down,' said one of the knights, 'and I yearn to unsheathe my sword.'

'A shared sentiment, Sir Warwick,' said Raynald, 'yet we cannot fight what we cannot see.' He took a long draft of water from his own gourd before replacing the stopper and looking around. 'This is a harsh land,' he said yet we seek to secure it in God's name so must take every obstacle before us in our stride.'

Warwick's eyes widened as he stared over the Regent's shoulder and his hand sought the hilt of his sword.

'We have company,' he said.

Raynald turned to see a rider galloping up the rocky path towards them.

'It's one of ours,' he said, 'stand down.'

The scout reined in his horse, kicking up a cloud of dust.

'My lord,' he said, 'there is an enemy encampment hidden in a valley just over the next hill.'

'Saracens?' asked Raynald.

'Aye. I saw about fifty tents along with many camels and horses.'

'Could it not be just a trading column?' asked Warwick.

'If they were traders,' interjected Raynald, 'then why hide away amongst the hills instead of making their camp alongside the road?' He turned to the rest of his men. 'Mount up and secure your equipment. It seems our luck has just changed.'

Without response, every man turned away to prepare their equipment and within a few minutes, sat upon their horses, each bearing lances adorned with pennants bearing their individual colours. Raynald turned to Warwick.

'There will be no time for strategies or adjustment. I want this to be an effective strike, so we fall upon them with unbridled commitment.'

'I understand,' said Warwick, tightening his sword belt.

Raynald turned to the scout.

'Take us as close as you can without being seen.'

'Aye, my lord,' said the scout and turned to ride back the way he had come, closely followed by the column of fully armed knights.

Twenty minutes later, Raynald lay on the ground peering down into a shallow valley. Below him was the encampment. His eyes moved rapidly as he took in the strength of the enemy and his heart raced as he saw many horses tethered within a makeshift paddock. Good horses were hard to come by as most either had to be bought from the men who travelled the trading routes or had to be brought from Europe, a long and dangerous journey that caused many to die on the way.

'It looks like we have caught them unawares,' said Raynald quietly, 'and will use it to our advantage.'

He crawled backwards before getting to his feet and running back to the patrol waiting nervously fifty paces below the ridge.

'God is with us,' he announced climbing into his saddle. 'On the other side of this ridge, the enemy relaxes as if they own the whole of the Holy Land. We will form up and give them no chance to reach their horses or prepare a defensive position.' He spun his horse around to face his men.

'Be aware,' he continued, 'every man on the other side of this ridge is capable of killing you or one of your comrades. If they escape, there could come a time when our failure means a friend could die at the end of a Saracen lance. There are also women amongst them but let not this fact affect your resolve. Every woman lives to bear the children that will grow up to hate our faith and every child is indoctrinated into a way of life contrary to the teachings of our Lord. Though it may leave a sour taste in your mouth, now is not the time to doubt your commitment to God's cause. We are on our way to stop a heathen army from advancing upon Jerusalem and cannot afford to carry prisoners so there will be no quarter.'

'For anybody, my lord?' asked a voice.

'There will be no quarter,' repeated Raynald slowly, making his point clear, 'is that clear?'

A murmur of assent rippled around his men.

'Good,' said Raynald. 'Upon my command, we will fall upon them like a storm.' He donned his helmet and lifted his visor before turning his horse and riding slowly up to the crest of the slope, finally halting to allow his men to spread out either side of him. When everyone was in place, he lifted his lance out of its holder and couched it under his arm before wrapping the horse's reins around the pommel of the saddle and drawing his sword.

'*Men of Jerusalem*', he called, '*in God's name, advance.*'

The traders down in the valley never had a chance. Many were resting in their tents, taking shelter from the heat of the midday sun while women and children went about their business outside, blissfully unaware of the devastation about to befall them.

A child called out to his mother and as she looked up, her face fell as she saw the column of knights charging down the slopes into the valley. For a few seconds, she stared in shock before her scream of terror echoed around the camp.

Panic erupted everywhere. Women raced to pick up their crying children, desperate to get out of the way and men stumbled out of the tents, many half-dressed but bearing whatever blades they kept to hand. With no time to think, they had little option but to face their attackers, desperate to protect their terrified families.

'Here they come,' roared Raynald over the sound of his charging cavalry, *'no prisoners.'*

The knights dug their spurs even deeper into their horses' flanks and lowered their lances to take aim at whoever stood before them. Seconds later they crashed into the camp and though some of the defenders managed to dodge the initial impact, the second rank caught them off guard and they were cut down mercilessly by heavy swords wielded by battle hardened men.

More Arabs poured from the tents and ran to help their comrades, but the impetus was with the knights and the initial tight ranks broke to ride freely amongst the panicking defenders. People ran everywhere, desperate to escape the carnage and Raynald ordered half his men to dismount, seeking the even greater advantage their superior experience and heavy armour would bring to the fight.

In pairs they strode through the camp, their visors raised as they smashed their heavy, two-handed swords into unprotected flesh. Blood and bone flew through the air and though some of the defenders managed to reach their attackers, the knights' chainmail protected them from all but the most well-aimed of thrusts. Men fought everywhere but it was one sided and it took only minutes for the attackers to finish off the brave, but totally unprepared Bedouin traders.

Soon there was nobody left to fight and as some of the mounted knights pursued those who had tried to flee, Raynald turned back to the men on foot. Many stood where they were, breathing heavily from the effort of their bloody task, their bodies soaked with sweat and limbs aching from the exertion.

The Regent was about to finally sheath his sword when a young boy carrying a blade far too big for him charged from behind a tent and swung at the knight's legs.

'My Lord,' shouted one of the knights, *'look out.'*

Instinctively, the Raynald turned and swung his own sword in a wide arc, slicing into the boy's neck, sending his young head tumbling into the sand.

The knight stared at the boy's body. He couldn't have been more than ten years old and wouldn't have made any dent in his armour even if had he been allowed to hack until dark, but it was an assault nevertheless, and one that had to be dealt with. He turned to look at his men.

'I told you they were dangerous,' he shouted, 'and there lies the proof.' He paused as he saw the hesitation in their eyes. '*Well*', he roared after a few moments, *'our job is yet half done.'*

Encouraged by their leader, the men, still affected with the blood rage of war, turned their attention on the women and children still scattered through the camp, hacking them apart without mercy. Screams of terror were soon replaced with howls of pain and despair as Raynald's men ran amok, and under the heat of the midday sun, the Jerusalem knights slaughtered every single member of the Arab caravan.

A few hours later the patrol once again formed up on the ridge above the valley and looked down at what remained of the camp. Everything had been piled into one enormous bonfire and clouds of black smoke billowed into the afternoon sky. Even from their position on the ridge they could smell the stench of burning flesh but though there was some unease about the way they had wiped out the entire caravan. Raynald had assured them that it was God's work and no matter how young their victims, the fact that they wouldn't grow up to attack Christian pilgrims meant that the knights would be forgiven their sins when they eventually reached the gates of heaven.

The regent himself was silent as they watched the flames burn higher. He knew many of his men would privately question the need to kill women and children, but he suffered no such qualms. The fifteen years he had spent in prison at the hands of these people was a heavy burden and even if he lived for a hundred years, he could never kill enough to settle the score. Slowly he sheathed his sword and turned his horse away to head back towards Castle Blancheguarde. His men followed behind, each leading one of the valuable captured horses but though usually after any victory there was celebration, this time there was silence. Somehow, they knew that now first blood had been drawn, it was nothing to what lay before them.

The following day, King Baldwin's column paused on the road south as he, William of Tyre and Sir Raynald rode slowly through the remains of the enemy camp. All around lay the bodies of the dead men, already beginning to rot in the desert sun.

The king lifted the back of his gloved hand to his nose, trying to block what he could of the stench.

'I count thirty-seven bodies,' said William eventually. 'A goodly result considering your men suffered only minor wounds.'

'We caught them unawares,' said Raynald, 'and our prowess saw us through. It was a brutal fight.'

'I thought your report said you burned the bodies,' said William.

'Only the women and children. If we had added all the men, the pyre would have burnt out before consuming the corpses.'

'I would suggest that it would have been easier to not kill them in the first place,' said William.

'In battle there is little time for such niceties,' said Raynald. 'Every hand able to wield a blade is a potential enemy and in the heat of the moment, we have no time to make considered judgements.'

'Did this hand wield a blade?' asked the king, kicking at the ash at the edge of the still smouldering fire.

Raynald and William looked down and saw the tiny burned remains of a baby's hand. The prelate looked up at the knight with undisguised contempt.

'Well?' he said. 'What risk did this infant present to a fully armoured knight of Jerusalem?'

'Do not deem to judge me, priest,' snarled Raynald, 'it is I who face the swords and arrows on a daily basis while you hide behind the silks and incense of the church. Don the armour and join me in the fray for one day only and I will gladly accept your judgement but until then, keep your condescending opinions to yourself.'

'Yet he has a point,' said the king quietly.

'My lord,' said Raynald. 'You made me Regent to press war against your enemies in your name. This is what we have done. My men should be lauded as great warriors, yet I see the look of disdain in your eyes and hear the sharp criticism from a man who represents the very faith which I have sworn to fight and die to defend. If you want a man of peace, then strip me of my title for this is what I do, this is what I am. I hold no regrets and will gladly face God's judgement when the day comes.'

'There is no need for that,' said the king, 'and I accept that in war, such things happen. Tell your men I am grateful for their actions and will celebrate their victory alongside them as soon as is possible. Now leave us with our thoughts.'

The knight nodded and walked back through the camp towards the waiting column.

'You do know this was nothing more than a trading caravan,' said William eventually, 'and offered no risk to our men?'

'I know,' said the king quietly, 'yet my hands are tied in this matter. To berate the man tasked with leading my armies will only sow discontent and that cannot be countenanced.'

'So, he is to be allowed to get away with it?'

'It is a time of war, my friend,' said the king, 'and I'm sure there will be many such sights before we enjoy the peace of our beds again.'

'You do know that there will likely be retribution?'

'I do, and that is what concerns me most. Yet the answer has already been suggested to me and my thoughts are now clear on the matter.'

'What do you mean?' asked William.

'The first blood has already stained the sand, William, and the news will spread with the desert winds. Those not already against us will likely join the forces of Saladin to get revenge so we have to make sure we are prepared as best as we can be.'

'And how do we do that?' asked William.

'By carrying out your suggestion.' He looked up at the priest. 'This is a damage that cannot be undone,' he said, 'and there will be a heavy price to be paid.' He paused as the weight of his next words sunk in. 'I have changed my mind, William, and despite my misgivings, I will issue the Arriere-ban.'

Chapter Twenty-One

Gaza
November 16th
AD 1177

The column of Templars and Turcopoles rode wearily through the crowded streets of Gaza. Their surcoats were dirty from sweat and the dust of the road and the horses plodded heavily through tiredness. The journey had been harder than expected, especially as they had to bypass the city of Ashkelon on the way and the Seneschal knew his men needed to rest.

'There it is, Brother Tristan,' he said with a sigh, looking up at the walls of the small castle on a hill at the heart of the city, 'our new home for the foreseeable future.'

'Not the biggest I have seen,' replied the Marshal at his side, 'which makes me worry about how we are to defend it. The walls alone don't seem able to withstand any major siege.'

'Our role is not so much the defence of the castle,' replied the Seneschal, 'but to use it as a base from which to operate. It is owned by our order and as such is dedicated to our needs.'

'I thought we were to defend Gaza?'

The Seneschal looked around at the sprawling town. Although there was a wall surrounding Gaza itself, it was poorly built, and he knew it wouldn't last a day should it be attacked.

'Alas,' he said, 'I feel that even with our best efforts, this place is indefensible. Seven years ago, Saladin attacked Gaza and while Miles of Clancy cowered behind the castle walls, the Ayyubid slaughtered everyone within the town.'

'Why did they not seek refuge in the castle,' asked the Marshal.

'Because, Brother Tristan,' said the Seneschal, 'our esteemed predecessor refused them access and watched from the towers as the streets ran with blood. That is a situation that will not be repeated while we are here.'

'I still don't understand why Saladin covets this place,'' said Tristan, there are so many others along the coast that would be of a better value strategically.'

'There are minds greater than ours who believe this place is the gateway to the north,' said the Seneschal, 'and as such we are tasked to keeping it safe until the king decides what to do to about Saladin. Any army of the size needed to attack Jerusalem will need to pass within ten leagues of here, so we are to act as a barrier should they come.'

'We cannot stop an army,' said Tristan.

'We do not have to,' Just slow them up using shock tactics and using Gaza as a base.'

'They may not come at all.'

'Perhaps not but there are enough spies at Baldwin's disposal that suggest otherwise.'

The sound of their horses' hooves changed as they crossed the wooden bridge leading up to the castle gates and the whole column filed slowly inside. Soon the small courtyard was filled with tired men and exhausted horses.

'Master Seneschal,' said a knight striding towards him from the keep. 'You and your men are expected. Welcome to Gaza.'

Brother Valmont looked at the knight. He knew that to judge was a sin, but he couldn't help but notice how pristine his clothing was in comparison to the filth of his own men. He looked up at the dozen Templars staring down from the parapets, each bedecked in their pure white cloaks emblazoned with the blood red cross.

'You must be Brother Harold,' said the Seneschal, returning his attention to the man bidding him welcome.

'I am,' said the knight, 'castellan of Gaza.'

'Castellan?' mused the Seneschal. 'The title infers ownership and I recoil from anything that suggests governance over those less fortunate than ourselves.'

'My apologies, my lord,' said the knight, 'the term was a slip of the tongue and of course, Gaza castle is occupied in the name of the order. I used the term loosely as my role is to ensure this place is managed as best as it can be under the circumstances.' He waited as the Seneschal and Marshal dismounted and brushed the dust from their surcoats. 'So,' he continued eventually, 'how was the road, did you have any trouble?'

'None that meant we needed to draw blades,' replied the Marshal, 'but it was harder than expected and the men need respite.'

'They will be well looked after,' said Brother Harold, 'as will you. Please, come this way and I will find you something to drink.'

'Just point us toward the chapel, Brother Harold,' said the Seneschal, 'we would first give thanks for our safe arrival. After that, I will meet you in the hall and expect to be fully briefed on the situation. Please ensure you have all the information to hand.'

'Of course,' said the castellan, nodding his head in deference. 'The chapel is built in to the walls in the north east corner. Alas, it is big enough for twenty men only, but we could arrange a service for all your men in the hall later this evening.'

'Do that,' said the Seneschal and turned away to find the chapel, closely followed by the Marshal

----

An hour later, both Templar officers stood at a table in the main hall alongside Brother Harold and the castle steward.

'My lords,' said the castellan, 'this is Master Robert, a trader from Bristol who made this place his home many years ago. He was granted the role when Miles of Clancy was murdered a few years ago.'

'You were here when he was killed?' asked the Seneschal with interest looking at the steward.

'I was, my lord. I worked as his treasurer at the time but after he died, the Grand Master recognised my skills and made me the castle steward. This place and the staff herein are at your complete disposal.'

'Thank you,' said the Seneschal, 'so let's start with my men. Where will they be quartered?'

'There are some rooms available within the castle walls,' said the steward, 'and more within the keep. In addition, we have the two halls and the chapel. It will be crowded but I believe we can house everyone without the need of tents.'

The Seneschal nodded his approval.

'And the horses?'

'They will be stabled just outside the castle walls but can be brought inside with a moment's notice. There is plenty of fodder and the grooms are the best available.'

'Stores?' asked Brother Valmont.

'The granary is full, and the cellars are stocked with barrels of salted fish, dates and dried mutton. Fresh vegetables are bought from the markets every other day as are eggs and fruit as required. I have no worries regarding feeding your men but of course, that could change if Saladin isolates the city.'

'That is a concern,' said the Seneschal, 'so I suggest increasing our stores of dried food wherever possible. This posting will be hard enough as it is, so we do not need the worry of starvation should it come to a siege. What about water?'

'We benefit from our own well,' said the steward, 'though I think we may struggle to service your column as it is limited in what it can provide. We store what we can in barrels, but thirst would be a concern should we be besieged.'

'Again,' said the Seneschal, 'increase the storage. Bring in barrels of water from elsewhere if needs be. Stack them wherever there is space.'

'Like I said, my lord, space is limited. We would have to stack them outside in the sun.'

'Then so be it. A thirsty man does not judge water by its temperature, but by its availability.'

The steward nodded and waited as the Seneschal turned to the Castellan.

'So, Brother Harold. Tell me about the garrison.'

'We have twenty knights, my lord, all Templars, and fifty lancers. We also have fifty archers and a hundred foot-soldiers. Our arrow supplies are healthy and our horses well-tended. We patrol the city walls every day at dawn and dusk and have local shepherds acting as our eyes out in the hills. So far there are no reports of any Saracen activity.'

'Place permanent sentry posts a hundred paces apart along the city walls,' said the Seneschal, 'closer if they cannot see each other from their positions and increase the patrols to every hour. From tomorrow, I want our own men out in the hills watching the approaches from the south and east. I will not entrust the safety of Jerusalem to the opinion of a shepherd.'

'With respect, my lord,' said Brother Harold nervously, 'I do not have that sort of strength available.'

'After a night's rest,' replied the Seneschal, 'our own men will reinforce your garrison. We will patrol the surrounding hills and increase our presence in the town. No doubt the place will be infested with Saladin's spies, but I want them to see we are strong and confident. I want him to think that Gaza is a formidable obstacle in his path.'

'Will that not increase the risk of an assault where previously there may have been none?'

'Possibly, but every day Saladin hesitates means King Baldwin has a chance to consolidate his armies. Like I said, our task is one of delay and containment and if we are successful, then with God's will we may avoid a war.'

For the next hour or so, the four men discussed strategies and tactics until finally the castellan and steward left the room to make the arrangements. When they had gone, Brother Valmont poured two goblets of watered wine and handed one to the Marshal.

'Well,' he said, 'what do you make of him?'

'He seems competent enough. His administration of this place is impressive, yet I wonder about his skills in the field. There is a fatness about him that suggests a life overly luxurious and I have no time for self-indulgence. In the coming months we will need men as hard as steel, toughened by life in the saddle and adept with sword in hand. I feel that at this moment in time, Brother Harold falls somewhat short. I just hope his men are more suitable.'

'I share your concerns,' said the Seneschal, 'so perhaps you can reintroduce them to the reason they serve in our order.'

'What do you suggest?'

'Task them with the harder roles. Include them in our patrols of the eastern mountains and when they are stood down, arrange sword practice until they are equal to our own men in skill at arms. I need warriors, not lords and though it should not be needed, I feel they need reminding.'

'Leave it to me,' said the Marshal

In the east, Cronin and Hassan led their horses along a mountain path. The sun beat down relentlessly and they knew they should seek shade, but the rocky slopes held no trees or heavy brush to provide shelter.

'How much further?' asked Cronin eventually.

'Hassan looked up at the ridge still several hours away.

'We should be there by nightfall,' said Hassan, 'though I still think we should turn back.'

'Our journey is almost done,' said Cronin, 'we will see it through.'

'I do not understand why you are so determined to see this place,' said Hassan. 'Mehedi could have been playing games with you and sends you to your death.'

'Because I have no other quest to pursue, so before I return to meet my fate at the hands of my betters, I will see this place for myself and if there is nothing there, we will make our way back.'

'You live a dangerous life, my lord,' sighed Hassan, 'and so far, God has been merciful. I just hope he is also patient.'

The two continued climbing the hill before stopping just below the crest near an outcrop of enormous rocks. After watering the horses, they collapsed into the shade and removed their jerkins to take advantage of the slight breeze.

Cronin took a drink from his flask before looking up at the sky.

'It is almost dark,' he said, 'and we will need to make a camp.' He looked around the rocks. 'This place is as good as any, we will stay here tonight.'

'I will see if I can find some wood for the fire, said Hassan.' He got to his feet and walked out onto the hill as Cronin took another drink from his flask.

The sergeant stared westward, back over the foothills of the Negev desert to the mountains they had crossed only a few days earlier. Beyond those were the much more fertile lands that stretched down the coast from Antioch to the borders of Egypt. Life was certainly a lot easier there and he longed to head back to sit in the shade of a leafy tree or drink clear water from a running stream, but first he had to settle his mind about the Makhtesh Ramon. The boy had been right and Mehedi could well have sent him on a fool's errand, but something ate at his insides, and even if it led to nought, at least he would return to the column with his conscience clear. Slowly his eyelids grew heavy and within moments, his chin fell to his chest as he slept the sleep of the exhausted.

It seemed like it had been only minutes when the sound of Hassan's nagging voice dragged him from his troubled dreams, an urgent demand couched in a nervous whisper.

'Master Cronin, wake up.'

He opened his eyes suddenly. No matter how deep the sleep, the path he had chosen as a man of war meant his nerves were always alert for danger and his mind needed no second invitation to return to full consciousness

'What is it? he asked as is hand automatically sought the hilt of his sword.

'You need to come with me,' said Hassan. 'There is something you should see.'

Cronin looked around and realising there was no immediate danger, reached for his water bottle. Hassan waited patiently as the sergeant drank sparingly, fully aware that they were down to their last water skin.

'Tell me what concerns you, Hassan,' he said turning back to the boy.

'Master,' replied Hassan, 'there is no explaining to be done. You need to see for yourself.'

Cronin sighed and got to his feet.

'Lead the way,' he said and within moments was scrambling up a steep slope towards the top of the hill. As he went he realised the sky seemed slightly lighter, despite it being the depths of the night and deep inside, his stomach turned at the implications.

'Hassan,' he whispered, drawing the boy's attention. 'Is that a natural thing?' He pointed upward to the illuminated clouds.

'No, my lord,' replied the boy. 'It is not.'

Cronin swallowed hard and continued the climb to the top of the slope. Finally, they reached level ground and lowered themselves down to crawl the last few yards to where the ridge dropped away.

Despite the darkness, far below he could see an immense valley that disappeared leagues into the distance with no sign of ending. As it was the middle of the night, he should have been able to see nothing but to Cronin's astonishment, the entire place was illuminated by thousands of camp fires, lighting the place up as if it was beneath the brightest moon.

Row after row of tents disappeared into the distance and amongst them, he could see dozens of roped corrals, filled with horses and camels. Other compounds contained sheep and goats and even at this hour, he could see lines of slaves carrying sacks of food or fuel between the camp fires, the whole place as busy as if it had been the middle of the day.

Saracen warriors walked everywhere, and as he watched, several columns containing dozens of riders appeared from the depths of the enormous camp to ride up the well-trodden paths that would take them from the hiding place and out into the countryside leading to the coast.

Hassan crawled up beside him and stared down into the camp.

'What is this place?' whispered Cronin.

'My lord,' said Hassan, 'it is the Maktesh Ramon, the very place you wished to see. Normally there is nothing here but sand and the bones of those foolish enough to come here, but as you can see, it has been populated by those below.'

'Do these hills surround this place on all sides? asked Cronin, looking around.

'Yes, but there is no water or shelter, so few men ever come here. They must bring what they need from the nearest river which is many, many leagues away. It is a terrible place to make a camp.'

'I disagree,' said Cronin. 'It is a fantastic place to make a camp, especially if you want an army to remain hidden. I suspect they replenish their water skins at night and with these hills shielding the light of their fires from interested eyes, they are able to hide from everyone except the most lost of men. The question is, who are they and what are they doing here?'

'Is it not obvious?' asked Hassan.

'Why would it be obvious? This country seems to be populated by more tribes than I can recall, and I see no colours or banners. Can you tell who they are?'

'Aye, my lord, I can,' replied Hassan. 'There is only one tribe who can muster such a force and have the resources to keep them fed and watered and that is the Ayyubid.'

Cronin's head snapped around to stare at Hassan.

'You must be mistaken. Every briefing I have attended reports that Saladin builds himself an army deep within the borders of Egypt.'

'I am not mistaken, my lord,' said Hassan. 'The layout of the camp, the warriors' clothing, the way they ride. Everything is as the Ayyubid do. These are Saladin's people.'

Cronin turned to stare again at the camp. Again, he focussed on the many corals of horses, and this time also noticed the racks of spears standing outside each tent. Whoever they were, they were certainly highly mobile and well-armed.

'This is one of the largest armies I have ever seen camped in the field, Hassan,' he said soberly, 'and if you are right, they have already left Egypt and are mustering for an advance northward. I need to get to Gaza and let the Grand Master know.'

'Why would he be in Gaza?' asked Hassan.

Cronin turned to face the boy, realising his role as a servant in the rear echelons of the column from Acre meant he probably knew very little about the political situation. For a few moments, the familiar feelings of mistrust swept over him and he hesitated to expand on the Templars' mission.

Hassan noticed his hesitation and his head lowered.

'My lord,' he said, 'forgive me my impertinence. I overstepped my station and I know I have a long way to go to regain your trust.'

'Hassan,' said Cronin eventually. 'I know I still exhibit wariness, but such traits often keep men at arms alive longer in times of war. However, whatever your true alliance, I do not believe you are a spy of Saladin.' He paused, staring at the boy again, wondering whether to tell him the full truth. Finally, he realised that if he was to gain the full benefit of the Bedouin's undoubted knowledge then he had to trust him.

'Listen,' he said. 'When we left Acre, our column was tasked with reaching Gaza as soon as possible to reinforce the city there. Saladin was reported as building an army in Egypt with the intention of marching northward along the coast. Our task there was to defend the road north and hold him up as long as possible until the king managed to muster his forces and come south to reinforce the city. If this is indeed Saladin's army, then Gaza and Ashkelon are already in great danger and the Grand Master must be informed as soon as possible.

Hassan's brows knitted in confusion.

'What's the matter?' asked Cronin. 'Can you not see the urgency?'

'My lord,' said Hassan, 'I think you misunderstand. If this is Saladin, then he is not interested in Gaza.'

'Why not?'

'For it lays many leagues to the south west. To reach this place he has had to come inland a long way and then travel north, far further than Gaza, to one of the most inhospitable places in the Negev desert. Why would he come so far and suffer so much hardship only to turn south again to take a small city such as Gaza? Surely he has bigger things on his mind?'

Cronin stared at Hassan, his mind working furiously. What the boy said made a lot of sense but every piece of intelligence they had heard on the trip south from Acre suggested that Saladin intended to advance north along the coast road to take advantage of the supply routes, both by land and sea.

He looked again down into the valley, absorbing the vastness of the forces amassed there. Even if the boy was wrong, and the coastal cities were indeed the target, the overwhelming numbers were certainly in excess of those needed to achieve victory.

'We have to find out more,' he said.

'How?'

'We have to go down there.'

Hassan's face fell. To go so close to an Ayyubid camp invited almost certain capture.

'My lord,' he said eventually. 'If we were to climb down this hill we would not get halfway without being discovered.'

'I have no choice, Hassan,' said Cronin, 'we need to find out more.'

'If it is unavoidable, then let it be me who goes,' replied the boy. 'I am as agile as a mountain goat, whilst you, my lord, often bears the traits of a camel amongst the rocks and will be heard at a thousand paces.'

Cronin looked at the boy, knowing that he made perfect sense. His own muscular frame and unfamiliarity with the terrain meant he often stumbled along the hidden paths whilst the boy still had the lightness and flexibility of youth.

'I will not be caught,' continued Hassan, 'and will be back before dawn.'

'And if you are caught?'

'I will say I am a goatherd looking for my flock. If I am not back by the time the sun rises, you must flee from this place as fast as you can and seek the safety of one of your castles.'

'It sounds like our roles have been reversed,' said Cronin, 'and it is now you who is the master and me the squire.'

'I am no squire, my lord,' said Hassan, 'just your humble servant.'

Cronin realised he had no other option. To approach the camp risked almost certain capture for little reward. Besides, he could not speak any of the eastern languages whereas the boy could understand most dialects of Arabic.

'Be careful,' he said eventually' and be back by dawn. I cannot wait any longer. This information is too important not to reach the ears of the Grand Master.'

'I understand,' said Hassan. 'What is it that you wish me to find out?'

'Anything you can,' said Cronin, 'who they are, their strengths, their weaponry, any knowledge is useful, but in particular, any clue as to what their true intentions are.'

Hassan swallowed hard, realising just how difficult his task was going to be.

'Be careful, Hassan,' said Cronin, 'and take no risks. I need you back here to lead the way back over the mountains.'

'I will be as silent as a desert spider,' said Hassan. 'Now I must go for there is little time left before the sun returns.'

Cronin watched the boy disappear into the darkness before turning his attention back on the camp below. There was little he could do now except wait.

Hassan crept down the hillside and onto the dusty floor of the valley. The nearest tents were several hundred paces away and there was sparse vegetation for cover, but he knew he had to get as close as he could. Seeing no sentries, he crouched low and ran as quickly as he could across the desert floor, finally stopping alongside the nearest tent.

His heart raced, and he could hear the snores of several men inside. Eventually, he caught his breath and peered around the side of the tent. This part of the camp was quieter with few fires lit but as he watched, a spear wielding sentry walked past, causing Hassan to duck back in the shadows.

He swallowed hard but knowing there was little time, got to his feet and ran to the next tent. Again, he was met with the sound of sleeping men and he cursed silently, knowing that if he was to learn anything, he had to get close to someone who was awake. He looked up and a few rows away could see the glow of a large fire and the shapes of several men sat around it.

It was dangerous but talking men often had loose tongues and he knew that was where he had to go. After checking for sentries again, he got to his feet and ran towards the fire, flitting between the tents and using their shadows for cover. A few moments later he lay flat on the ground with only one shelter between him and the fire. Outside the tent, he could see a rack of spears and a water skin hanging from a tripod. He crawled forward until there was only open space between him and the men around the fire but though they were all talking amongst themselves, he struggled to hear any of the detail. Frustrated he lay in the shadows, wondering what else he could do but as he watched, a boy of a similar age, dressed only in a loincloth and sandals, walked directly up to the men bearing a platter of bread.

The men each took a loaf before one waved him away and they continued their conversation.

An idea formed in Hassan's mind and deciding to act before he could change his mind, he immediately discarded his thawb and got to his feet. Taking a deep breath, he lifted the water skin from the tripod and stepped out of the shadows, heading straight toward the Saracen warriors.

Unbeknownst to Hassan, only a few hundred paces away, Saladin himself walked through the same camp accompanied by Taqi ad-Din. Before and behind them walked a hundred Mamluk bodyguards, ensuring nobody approached within twenty paces of the Sultan and as they passed, anyone seeing Saladin immediately fell to their knees, kissing the ground, murmuring salutations as he passed.

'It has been a demanding day,' said Saladin as they walked. 'What this place gives with one hand, it takes with another.'

'You have truly endowed us with a massive advantage,' said Taqi, 'to muster such an army under the noses of the Christians is a feat worthy of the greatest of men.'

'Yet it is all I can do to keep them fed and watered,' said Saladin. 'The quicker we can leave this place the better it will be.'

'Our scouts report that the Franks have taken the bait,' said Taqi, 'and already fortify the cities of Gaza and Ashkelon. A few more days and they will be chasing shadows in the south while we seek the greater prize.'

'How do my armies fare?'

'We have over a thousand men roaming the coastal plains from Acre down to the borders of Egypt. Each patrol ensures that they are seen or at least leave evidence behind them wherever they go. They create the illusion that we are scouting the lands ready to invade from the south. Even the villages abound with rumours that your attack on the coastal cities is imminent.'

'In that case, perhaps we should increase the illusion.'

'In what way?'

'Send a force to attack Gaza. Task them with placing the city under siege to strengthen the idea it is there that my focus lays.'

'How many men, my lord?'

'Five thousand only.'

'A force that small will not bring down Gaza, my lord.'

'I know, and that is not their purpose. It is one of containment and harassment only. While the Christians skirmish with our men, our main army can leave this place without risking being discovered by roaming patrols. By the time news of our advance reaches the Christian King, the streets of Jerusalem will already be swarming with our men.'

'So, are we to start the advance soon?'

'To wait much longer risks Baldwin's army arriving from the north. Tell our warriors to prepare. The time is upon us.'

'It is a plan worthy of greatness,' said Taqi.

'Now leave me,' said Saladin. 'I wish to be alone with my thoughts.'

'As you wish, my lord,' said Taqi, and stopped to allow the Sultan to continue alone.

Near the edge of the camp, Hassan walked towards the fire. He knew he risked everything for if all the slaves were known to these men then he would immediately be identified as an outsider and taken prisoner. As he approached he started to hear the conversation and was relieved to hear they were talking in a dialect he could understand.

'The thing is,' said one of the men to his comrades as Hassan approached, 'they are indeed a formidable foe when their ranks are closed, and they charge as one, but once they have been dispersed they are no better than you or I.'

'You misunderstand my meaning,' said his comrade. 'What I am saying is what they lose in mobility by wearing such heavy armour is gained by the protection it serves. I have seen their knights continuing to fight with many arrows hanging from their gambesons for our arrows have not penetrated through to their flesh. Would we not also benefit from such protection?'

'The Sultan's knights wear chainmail,' said a third man, 'why would we as lancers need such encumberment?'

The conversation went on as Hassan reached the men. The nearest turned to stare at him and Hassan's blood ran cold.

'Did I not just send you away?' he snarled. 'Be gone.'

'I thought you may be thirsty,' said Hassan holding up the waterskin.

'We need no water,' said the man, 'now leave us alone.'

'Wait,' said the second man. 'I will take some.'

Hassan walked over and gave the man the leather cup hanging from the waterskin. His hands shook, and he overfilled the cup, pouring just as much onto the floor.

'Be careful,' shouted the man and slapped Hassan across the face, sending him crashing to the ground, spilling even more.

'Are you an imbecile?' shouted the warrior, 'water is hard enough to come by and you waste it as if we are camped near a river.' He lashed out with his boot, kicking Hassan in the ribs.

'Leave him be,' said one of the other men, 'he is just a boy.'

'He is a slave and should know better,' said the first man. 'Perhaps I should remind him of his position here. He walked over to a nearby pile of brushwood and retrieved a thin branch before walking back to the fire swishing it through the air like a sword.'

'On your knees,' he shouted, and Hassan looked up with fear.

'I said on your knees,' shouted the man again and Hassan shuffled into an upright position.

'I reckon you wasted about ten cups of water,' said the warrior, 'so your punishment will match the crime, one blow for each cup.' Without warning he lashed out with the switch, cutting deep into the bare flesh on Hassan's back, sending the boy gasping in pain to the floor.

'Get up,' snarled the man, 'or I will double the number of blows.'

Hassan raised himself to his knees and grimaced as he waited for the second blow. Again the switch flew through the air, cutting into Hassan's flesh.

'That's better,' said the man as Hassan struggled to stay on his knees, 'now let's get this done.' A third strike sent Hassan collapsing to the ground again, raising the warrior's ire.

'I told you to stay up,' he shouted, and he lashed out with his boot, kicking Hassan in the ribs again.

Hassan knew he had to do something or he would probably die right there but with ten men watching the beating unfold, he knew he was powerless. He closed his eyes and prayed silently, tensing for the next blow but before it landed, a voice called out from between the tents, temporarily ending his torture.

'Shareef, what goes on here?'

The warrior immediately dropped the cane and fell to his knees, his forehead touching the ground.

'My lord Taqi ad-Din,' he said, lifting his upper body up and touching his hand to his heart and lips, 'As-Salamu-Alaykum.'

'Wa-Alaykum-Salaam,' replied the commander, 'get to your feet.'

Shareef stood up and faced his commanding officer.

'Tell me why you are beating this boy,' said Taqi.

'My lord, he wasted water, so I administered a punishment.'

'How much water?'

'Ten cups.'

'And how many lashes have you given him?'

'Three of ten, my lord.'

'Three is adequate. Let him seek aid for his wounds. Our slaves need to be strong and healthy to serve us well, not injured for petty mistakes.'

'As you wish, my lord,' said Shareef.

'The rest of you,' said Taqi turning to see the rest of the men still bowing towards him by the fire, 'get some sleep for tomorrow we strike camp and there will be little rest until we reach Jerusalem. Pass the word to all in your unit.'

'As you wish, my lord,' came the replies.

Taqi turned and walked away, leaving Shareef and his men staring after him.

'It looks like Saladin has committed to the attack,' said one.

'And not a minute too soon,' said Shareef. 'Every second the Franks stay in Jerusalem stains it even more. I look forward to the day we hang them all from the city walls.'

'As do I,' said the first man, 'but we should do as the commander says and get some rest. Tomorrow we will be busy preparing the horses and weapons.

Each got to their feet and dispersed back to their tents but Shareef turned, deciding to give the slave one more kick before he left, but he was too late, Hassan had gone.

Dawn was almost breaking when Hassan stumbled back into their makeshift camp, collapsing into the sergeant's arms with exhaustion.

'Hassan,' gasped Cronin, 'what have they done to you?'

'Nothing more than a beating,' said Hassan weakly, 'our Lord Jesus suffered more. I just need some rest.'

Cronin saw the blood seeping through the boy's thawb and lifted it up tom see the injuries.

'It looks painful,' he said but the wounds have not penetrated past your flesh.' He reached for the water skin and drizzled it on Hassan's back to clear away the dust. You will need Aloe on that, but we have none. We'll have to find some on the way back. Can you ride?'

'I can,' said Hassan, donning his thawb again, 'but first I have news.'

'What did you learn?'

'My lord, I do not believe Saladin makes Gaza or Ashkelon his target. I heard only mention of Jerusalem. Twice it was said, and the army below is preparing to leave.'

Cronin's face fell, and he looked at Hassan with a look of horror on his face.

'Master,' said Hassan, 'what is it?'

The sergeant dropped to his knees and smoothed out a large piece of dusty ground before using his knife to draw an image representing a crude map of the Holy Land.

'Hassan,' he said, dragging his knife in the dust, 'if this is the sea and these lines represent the mountains. Show me where we are in relation to Gaza.'

Hassan lowered himself gingerly to his knees and taking the knife, drew an elongated oval shape on the eastern side of the mountains.

'This is the Maktesh Ramon,' he said, 'and this is where we are now.' He drew a cross on the western edge of the oval.

'Show me Gaza,' said Cronin.

Hassan put a stone alongside the sea at the lower edge of the map.

'And Ashkelon?'

Hassan put another stone bit further up the coast from Gaza.

'So, we are approximately in line with Ashkelon?'

'We are my lord. If Gaza is Saladin's target, he would have to cross the mountains and then head south west back down the coast towards Egypt.

'Where is Jerusalem?' asked Cronin and watched as Hassan placed a larger stone on the drawing to depict the holy city.

Cronin fell silent and stared in horror. If Hassan's map was anywhere near to scale, the distance to Jerusalem from Saladin's camp was less than the distance to Gaza.

'He has tricked us all,' he said eventually. His designs on Gaza are no more than a ruse designed to draw our forces south, so he can get behind them and campaign unhindered northward.' He looked up at Hassan with concern in his eyes. 'He's going straight for Jerusalem and there is nothing we can do to stop him.'

'My lord,' said Hassan, staring at Cronin's worried face. 'I see you bear great concern.'

'Indeed I do,' said Cronin. 'Even if we head back now, Saladin's army will be right on our heels. Jerusalem needs time to muster her defences and even if we get there in time, I am a single soldier unknown to the king with an unlikely tale of imminent invasion.'

'But you are a soldier of the Templar order. Does that not carry any importance?'

'If I was a knight, perhaps but don't forget, I am new to this country and have already lost a precious package from the pope himself. What credibility can I offer and besides, even if I get an audience with the king, stories of Saladin's imminent invasion are as common as English raindrops. Who is to say that I will be believed?'

'But I heard them with my own ears.'

'To them, you are no more than an Arab boy and unlikely to believed.'

'Would it help if the tale was to come from a Templar knight?'

'Aye it would, but most are in Gaza under the command of the Grand Master. By the time we got there, and his messengers rode for Jerusalem it would be too late.'

'But are there not Templars at Blancheguarde Castle?'

'I believe so, but again it is out of the way and we do not have the time. By the time we reach Blancheguarde Saladin will be at the gates of Jerusalem.'

'My lord, there is something you do not understand,' said Hassan picking up the knife again, 'let me show you.'

Cronin looked down to the map and waited as Hassan again drew in the dust.

'This is Blancheguarde castle,' said Hassan, scratching a cross on the makeshift map, 'three day's ride northwest. It guards the trading route to Jerusalem so if Saladin wishes to advance, he has to pass that way.'

'I don't understand,' said Cronin, 'why would the Ayyubid first go towards the coast before heading north. Surely the direct route will be three times as quick?'

'Because that way lies the western edge of the Negev desert and it will be too difficult for even Saladin to cross.'

'But your people do it all the time.'

'Yes, but they travel in small groups and pull no carts. Saladin leads a huge army and they would be weighed down just by the weight of water needed to survive. By the time he got anywhere near Jerusalem his army would be vastly diminished.'

'So, they have to cross the same mountains as us and then head north past Beersheba towards Blancheguarde?'

'Yes, my lord. There is no other way.'

Cronin thought furiously. Even though he was new to the Holy Land he knew that Blancheguarde was populated by a garrison of Templars who would provide a serious obstacle for the Saracens. In addition, if he could reach the castle ahead of Saladin, he was far more likely to be believed by whoever was in command and any messages for the king borne onward to Jerusalem would carry much more credence, allowing the city to prepare the defences.

'I hope you are correct in this,' said Cronin eventually, 'for if so, we may have the slightest of chances to slow the Ayyubid down.'

'I can only say what my own mind tells me, my lord, I may be wrong.'

'We will trust you are not,' said Cronin, 'and must head for Blancheguarde with all haste.'

'I will have the horses saddled as soon as I can', said the boy, getting to his feet. 'Once we are down from this hill, I will seek the quicker paths. We should be in the far mountains by nightfall tomorrow.'

'Then that is what we will do,' replied Cronin, 'but first, we must find some Aloe for your wounds.'

Chapter Twenty-Two

Ashkelon
November 17th
AD 1177

King Baldwin sat in a wooden tub filled with lukewarm water. His head laid back against the rim and his eyes were closed, enjoying the momentary silence and fleeting release from pain.

He and his column of knights had been as Ashkelon for two days after a harder than expected journey from Blancheguarde. The rigours of the road had been telling and as well as the pain from his affliction, his body now also bore the uncompromising aches of horseback travel.

William had pressed him to use the litter they had borne from Jerusalem in anticipation of this exact circumstance, but Baldwin had been stubborn stating that if his armies were marching to war, he would lead them, not be carried by them. He knew the decision had been the right one and that the men respected his determination but by the time they had reached Ashkelon, he ached in every part of his body and collapsed onto his bed exhausted, unwashed and wracked with pain.

Since then the close attention from his physicians including the application of Aloe poultices and liberal doses of poppy milk had eased his pain and at last, he could think clearly about the situation unfolding about them.

He sighed deeply, taking in the aroma of the scented oils in the water and of the incense wafting around the room, carried on the late afternoon breeze blowing gently through the open shutters in his quarters. Outside, a bird sang to the sinking sun and for a few moments, Baldwin could almost imagine that he had no worldly worries, no courtly intrigue, no incurable disease, and no imminent war with the Ayyubid.

The last thought brought his mind crashing back to reality. His brow furrowed as the thought of Saladin filled his consciousness. Since arriving at Ashkelon there had been increasing reports of Ayyubid scouting parties ranging through the countryside with some being spotted no more than a few leagues from Ashkelon itself but on each occasion, they had withdrawn rather than engage any of his own forces sent out to confront them. Their continued presence reinforced the intelligence Baldwin had received, stating that Ashkelon was Saladin's true objective so, despite the temptation to ride out with a larger force to hunt the enemy down, he knew the bulk of his men had to remain garrisoned at the sea port until the main army arrived from the north.

Realising that he could waste no more time on the luxury the bath afforded, he beckoned the two servants to help him out of the tub and donned a cool silken wrap before walking over to the window and staring out over the city. Outside he could see the red clay roof tiles of the jumbled town beneath the castle walls and out into the port where several ships lay at anchor, waiting their turn to unload the stores brought from further up the coast.

The port was one of the largest and busiest on the coast and it was no wonder that it was so coveted by Saladin. From here, he could easily keep his army supplied on any campaign against Jerusalem.

A knock came on the door and one of the servants looked toward the king, receiving a nod of authorisation in return. The boy slid back the bolt and William of Tyre walked into the room, before approaching the king.

'Your Grace,' he said, bowing slightly in acknowledgement, 'you are on your feet again, and if I may be so bold, looking much refreshed.'

'Thank you, William, 'said the king, 'I indeed feel much better and for the first time in an age, the pain is manageable.'

'Then let us hope that God continues to grant you such a boon and you remain so for as long as possible.'

'I would suggest my relative comfort it is the poppy's work, rather than any holy intervention,' said the king, 'but I will accept any intervention offered. Wine?'

The prelate nodded silently, deciding to ignore the king's throwaway dismissal of the lord's power, putting it down to tiredness and theological ignorance. Besides, he was the king and could say whatever he wanted.

One of the two servants poured two goblets of watered wine and placed them on the table while the second brought over a bunch of grapes. The king and prelate sat at the table as the servants set about emptying the tub.

'So,' said Baldwin, after sipping from his glass, 'as I have been entombed between these walls these past few days, perhaps you can brief me as to the current situation. My men must think me the most neglectful monarch to ever rule Jerusalem.'

'Nobody begrudges you the time needed to recover,' said William, 'and they hold you in high esteem for your leadership. Worry not about their thoughts, only about your health.'

'And the coming war.'

'Raynald sees to it that our army, such as it is, remains alert and well prepared. The city is well stocked to survive a siege and we have already arranged for extra supplies to come by sea. Everything is advancing as well as we could have hoped. Also, we have just today received some very good news. That is the reason I am here.'

'Good news is in short supply. Pray share.'

'The Lord of Edessa has sent word to say he is on his way with almost a thousand men from Acre and Arsuf. He will be here in a few days.'

'Lord Joscelin is a good man,' said Baldwin. 'I knew I could rely on him.'

'That's not all.' said William, 'the Arriere-ban is taking effect and men at arms are already drifting in to answer the call to arms.'

'How many?

'Only a couple of hundred at the moment but we have received messages from several other lords who muster their men as we speak including Balian of Ibelin and Reginald of Sidon. If Saladin holds back for even a few more days, then I think our ranks will swell considerably.'

'And the main army?'

'Already on their way but it will be a while until they arrive. However, judging by the way the word has already spread, we may soon have enough men to hold Saladin back until they get here.'

'Let's hope you are correct,' said the king, leaning forward to retrieve a grape from the platter.

'Here, let me,' said William, stretching out from his own chair.

'No,' snapped Baldwin, sending the prelate back into his chair in shock. He stared at William of Tyre with undisguised anger until eventually the look softened and he took several grapes before sitting back in his chair.

Silently, William watched the king eat, waiting until he had finished before speaking up.

'My lord, I meant no insult,' he said, 'my intentions were only to help.'

'When the day comes I cannot even feed myself, Master William,' said the king, 'then I will not be fit to wear the crown of Jerusalem and I hope I have the courage to throw myself off the nearest tower.'

'You don't mean that, your Grace,' said William.

'Don't I?' asked Baldwin. 'I may have lived only sixteen years, yet I have the responsibilities, body and pains of a man five times that age. Every day is a struggle, but I endeavour to act as a king should. One day, I suspect I will no longer have the strength for that fight and it seems to me the peace of death will be a very attractive option rather than wait to rot in my own skin.'

'To kill yourself is a sin,' said the prelate quietly.

'It may be,' said the king staring at his friend, 'but does not God forgive the sins of anyone who fights in his name?'

'Yes but…'

'Then I should have nothing to worry about. My term as king may not be great but every moment is dedicated to increasing God's glory and ensuring Jerusalem is protected for his pilgrims to come to worship where his son gave up his life. If that is not enough to garner forgiveness for one simple sin, then I do not know what is.'

William decided not to anger the king further by arguing the point, choosing instead to pray for forgiveness on his behalf later that night.

'What about Gaza?' said the king eventually, almost as if the previous confrontation had never happened.

'Eudes de St. Amand and his Templars should be there by now. They have been ordered to substantially increase the city's defences and actively patrol the lands between Gaza and the eastern mountains. If Saladin comes, they will be the first ones to know and will send us a warning in plenty of time. Like I said, everything is being done that can be done. The final piece of the jigsaw will be the arrival of Jerusalem's army but that is out of our hands.'

'In that case,' said Baldwin getting to his feet, 'you may leave. Ask the knights that rode with us from Jerusalem to assemble in the great hall an hour from now. I would share bread with them and give them thanks for their loyalty so far.'

'I'm sure they will be honoured, my king,' said William and after bowing slightly, turned to leave the room.

'Oh, one more thing,' said Baldwin. 'Is there any news of the patrol we sent eastward before we reached Blancheguarde?'

'Nothing yet, my lord,' said William, 'and if truth be told, it causes great concern amongst Sir Gerald's peers.'

'As it does I,' said Baldwin. 'He is one of my best knights and for him to go missing bodes ill. Let me know immediately if he returns or there is any news of his fate.'

'I will, your Grace,' said William, 'and in the meantime, I will pray for God's protection over you.'

'You do that,' said the king quietly, and popped another grape into his mouth as he watched the prelate retire from the room.

In the mountains east of Ashkelon, Cronin and Hassan walked carefully up a winding path, deep in a narrow rocky ravine full of twisted trees starved of water yet hanging onto life. The shadows grew longer as the sun disappeared over the rim of the canyon and Cronin knew they would have to stop for the night or risk breaking one of the horse's ankles in the darkness.

'It's no good, Hassan,' he said eventually, 'we are going to have to make camp. See if you can find somewhere safe away from the track.'

'It has been harder going than I expected, Master Cronin,' said Hassan. 'I have not used this route before but know it to be the quickest.'

'At least we haven't come across any of Saladin's men, 'said Cronin. 'Perhaps we yet have some time. '

The boy carried on until he saw a break in the brush and disappeared for a few moments before reappearing and beckoning the sergeant onward.

'Over here,' he said, 'there is a clearing against the rocks.'

Cronin followed him in. The space was small but just enough to hold them and the horses.

'It's not much,' he said, 'but it'll do.

They set about removing the saddles and making as much room as they could, cutting away some of the thornier branches for the horses to stand freely.

'How much water do we have left?' asked Cronin.

'A quarter of a skin,' said Hassan, 'and what we have left in our gourds. But we can help to quench our thirst from these. He hacked at a nearby cactus and prized away a chunk of the fleshy pulp before lifting it to his mouth and sucking at the moisture.

'It doesn't taste good,' he said, 'but water is water.'

Cronin cut some of the plant and followed suit. The liquid was bitter, but it moistened his mouth enough to make a difference.

'It is better than nothing,' he said, 'are there more of these plants on our route?'

'They are sparse but easily found,' said Hassan.

'When do you think we will find a stream or well?'

'Once we clear the mountains, there will be water on the far side. By noon tomorrow, we should be able to drink our fill.'

'In that case, use what is left to water the horses,' said Cronin. 'We will manage with this plant and what we have left in our gourds, but they have nothing, and we need them alive if we are to reach Blancheguarde in time.'

'As you wish,' said Hassan and carefully shared the last of the water in the goatskin between the two horses. When he was done, he tied them to a tree and sat down against a rock opposite Cronin.

'My lord,' he said, 'you should eat.' He threw a small piece of dried beef over to the sergeant and sat back against the rock.

Cronin, caught the precious food, realising how hungry he was but as he began to chew, he stopped and looked up at the boy sat opposite.

'Where's yours?' he asked eventually.

'I am not hungry,' said Hassan.

Cronin stared at the boy with suspicion.

'Show me,' he said.

'Show you what, my lord?'

'Your share of the beef.'

'There is no need,' said Hassan. 'I am just not hungry.'

'Show me the food, Hassan,' said Cronin.

The boy didn't move and did not answer.

'You can't can you,' said Cronin, 'because this is the last of it. He held up the strip of beef in his hand.

'It is the last, my lord,' said Hassan, 'but it matters not, for like I said, I am not hungry.'

The sergeant looked down at the meat and snapped it in half before throwing a piece back over to the boy.

'We are in this together, Hassan,' he said, 'if I eat, you eat, it is as simple as that.'

'You are a kind master, my lord,' said Hassan with a grin and bit off a piece of the meat with enthusiasm.

'We need to leave as soon as we are able to see the way,' said Cronin eventually.

'I will prepare the horses and awaken you before dawn,' said Hassan before turning on his side with his thawb wrapped tightly around him.

To Cronin's surprise, the boy was asleep almost immediately and he sat in the darkness contemplating everything that had happened in the past few days. To lose the package from the pope had been a disaster but compared to the potential consequences of not warning Jerusalem of the proximity of Saladin's army in time, it was an irrelevance not even considering. The thought of the long ride to Castle Blancheguarde the following day was daunting but there was no other option. The Holy Land itself could be at risk.

Gradually his eyes fell heavy and though he had intended to stay awake as long as possible, he was soon fast asleep, oblivious to the world around him.

The following morning saw Cronin and Hassan cross over the mountains and start the descent on the other side. The night had passed uneventfully, and they had made good ground in the relative coolness of the morning air.

By midday, they could see the foothills stretching out toward the sea in the distance, but Cronin knew the task was only half done. The mountains had been hard but at least there had been cover from prying eyes. Now they were headed for the lowlands and if they were to make good time, they had to use the well-trodden roads between the many towns and villages, hopefully without drawing the attention of any of Saladin's roaming patrols.

'My lord,' said Hassan, 'look over there.'

Cronin followed the boy's pointing finger but saw no more than a line of green leaved trees, stretching down the hill like a line of busy ants.

'What am I looking at?' he asked eventually.

'Water,' said Hassan with a grin and without waiting for a reply, turned off the path. Cronin followed and soon they were walking beneath the boughs of leafy olive trees, but as much as he searched, he could see no stream.

'Where is the water, Hassan,' he asked eventually.

'It is here, said Hassan, we just need to find it.'

'And how are we supposed to do that?'

By trusting those who have better noses than us,' said Hassan. He turned and removed his horse's bridle before giving her a gentle tap on the rump, watching as it trotted off beneath the trees.

'Hassan,' said Cronin, 'be careful she does not gallop off, we need her to get to Blancheguarde. One horse won't carry us both.'

'I know horses and they are just as thirsty as us. The difference is, if there is water, they will smell it. Come, we should go where she leads.'

Without another word, Hassan followed the horse, heading back up the hill beneath the shade of the trees.

'Are you sure about this, Hassan?' asked Cronin, struggling to keep up. 'We are wasting valuable time so perhaps we should seek water further down.'

'Or we could fill our bottles there,' said Hassan with a grin and pointed to where his horse was already drinking deeply from a pool near a rocky outcrop.

'Now that's a clever horse,' said Cronin approvingly.

'I told you, Master Cronin, they can smell water from afar.' He walked over and patted the animal on the haunches. 'She is a good girl, yes?'

The sergeant was about to speak when he stopped dead in his tracks, staring in shock towards the bushes at the far side of the spring.

There, amongst the tangled undergrowth was an Arab archer, and he had an arrow aimed straight at Cronin's heart.

Chapter Twenty-Three

The Western Mountains
November 18th
AD 1177

Hassan dropped to his knees and dipped his head into the clear water, completely unaware of the drama unfolding behind him.

'It is cold and sweet, Master Cronin,' he gasped, lifting his head and pushing his long black hair back from his face, 'better than the choicest wine in Christendom.'

When there was no answer, he turned to look back, his face falling as he saw the archer training his bow on the sergeant. He looked rapidly between the two, realising that it must seem to Cronin that he had once more been led into a trap.

'My lord,' gasped Hassan, 'I had no idea he was here. This is not of my doing.'

'Don't move,' said Cronin slowly, 'keep very, very still.'

He stared at the archer, his heart racing as he sought a way out of his predicament. If he ducked and rolled and the first arrow missed, perhaps he could cover the ground before the man had a chance to reload. With no other options available, his hand reached for his knife, but the archer drew back his drawstring even further to emphasise the menace. Cronin swallowed hard, unsure what to do. To risk an attack seemed like the only option and even if he was wounded or killed, at least Hassan may survive to continue with the message for the king.

'Hassan,' he said quietly, 'in a moment I am going to rush him. As soon as he releases his arrow, whether I am hit or not, you must grab my horse and ride as hard as you can for Blancheguarde.'

'No, my lord,' gasped Hassan, 'you must be the one to warn Jerusalem. Let it be me who takes the arrow.'

'*No Hassan,*' snapped Cronin, 'you will do as I say. Hopefully, I can delay him long enough for you to escape. After that, the fate of Jerusalem is in your hands.'

'My lord,' gasped Hassan again, 'please...'

'The decision is made, Hassan,' said Cronin, 'move on my command. *Ready...?*'

'I wouldn't do that if I was you,' said a voice in English and Cronin spun around to see two dishevelled European soldiers standing a few paces behind him, along with another two archers, each with arrows already notched into their bowstrings.'

Cronin gasped with surprise and stared at the men. His hand fell away from his belt and he stood there in silence, unsure of who they were or where they had come from.

'Unsheathe your knife,' said the man, 'and throw it to the ground.'

'What?' gasped Cronin, 'why do you want me to do that? Are we not comrades in a foreign land?'

'I have no idea who or what you are,' said the man. 'For all I know you could be a brigand or even a Saracen sympathiser.'

'Are you mad?' asked Cronin. 'Do I look like a Saracen? Am I not talking in the king's English?'

'I can take no risks,' said the man, 'just do as I say. There will be time enough to find out who you really are when you are unarmed.'

'And unable to defend myself.'

'Look around you, stranger. If I wanted to kill you, you would be already dead. Now lose the knife.'

Cronin looked around in frustration and he knew there was nothing he could do. With a curse he removed his knife from his belt and threw it on the ground.

'Now get down on your knees,' said the man.

'Why?' asked Cronin. 'I am no longer any danger to you. Just tell me who you are and what you want.'

'On your knees,' said the man, the quicker you comply, the sooner we can sort this out.'

Cronin dropped to his knees as another two men dragged Hassan over, throwing him to the ground besides the sergeant.

'Right,' said the man, as the archers lowered their bows. 'Let's get something straight. We are going to talk, and we are going to be completely honest with each other. However, if I feel at any moment that you are lying, then you will be dead in a heartbeat. Understood?'

'You make yourself very clear,' said Cronin, 'but how am I to know you are not a brigand yourself, using trickery to extract information and sell it to the Saracens?'

The stranger paused before reaching inside the neck of his tunic and retrieving a cross on a leather string.

'This is the symbol of our lord,' he said, 'and I swear on the body of Christ himself that I am a Christian, and as such seek only truth, honour and justice in his name.'

'You are a knight?' asked Cronin.

'I am,' said the man, 'and these are my men, or what is left of them.'

'What happened to your command?'

'We were on a patrol and were ambushed by the Saracens. We few are the only ones who escaped and seek a path back to our king.'

'What is your name?' asked Cronin.

'I am Sir Gerald of Jerusalem,' came the reply, 'and I ride under the banner of King Baldwin the Fourth.'

The revelation took Cronin by surprise. Whoever these men were, to find them so far off the beaten track, and in such a dishevelled state was a shock.'

'So,' said Gerald, 'tell me your tale first, stranger, for it is I who holds the advantage.'

Cronin paused, still uncertain whether to believe the man as his filthy appearance and the fact he was accompanied by Turkish archers suggested otherwise. However, realising he was in no position to argue, proceeded to recount everything that had happened to him since arriving in the Holy Land. When he had finished he sat back and returned his captor's stare. If the man was lying, then his fate was sealed.

Gerald stared back at Cronin. The tale was fanciful yet there was a truth about the man, evident in both the way that he spoke and the manner of his address.

'So, you claim you are Templar,' he said eventually.

'Not a knight,' said Cronin, 'a sergeant at arms. However, we serve the same order. The circumstances I have recounted separated me from my brothers, so I need to get to get to Blancheguarde Castle as soon as possible to raise the alarm.'

Gerald paused again before walking over and retrieving Cronin's knife from the dust. He walked back and extended an arm to help the sergeant to his feet.

'I believe you, Tom Cronin,' he said, handing back the knife, 'and will do everything in my power to help for we share the same concerns. I too fear Saladin is about to push northward though I have to admit, I did not realise he was already north of Gaza.'

'Not only is he here,' said Cronin, 'but is already on the move. I fear he is only a day or so behind us.'

'Then there is no time to waste but I have a question. Why is it that you head for Blancheguarde? Surely you should be riding to Ashkelon?'

'Why would I go to Ashkelon? The king needs to know, and he is in Jerusalem.'

Gerald stared again before responding.

'Of course,' he said eventually, 'you would not know what has happened in your absence. The king rode out from Jerusalem to reinforce Ashkelon after receiving intelligence that Saladin's threats to Gaza were no more than a feint. By now, with God's grace, he is already safely ensconced behind the city walls.'

'But if that is the case, who defends Jerusalem?'

'A holding garrison only. The main army is still in the north and every other available man has ridden south to join the king.'

'That means,' said Cronin, 'that Jerusalem is at the mercy of Saladin. We have to let them know.'

Gerald thought furiously, his mind spinning at the implications.

'I agree,' he said eventually, one of us needs to get to Ashkelon as soon as possible. You are the only ones with horses so your mission to Blancheguarde must be forfeited to ensure Baldwin is alerted as soon as possible.'

'Blancheguarde is the only well garrisoned castle between Saladin and Jerusalem. Is it not important that they too are warned?'

'Aye it is, but Baldwin needs to know Saladin is on his way so he can divert what forces he has against him. That must take priority over Blancheguarde, so you have to ride to Ashkelon. We will follow as quickly as we are able.'

Cronin stared at the knight, knowing that what he was about to say involved huge risk.

'No,' he said eventually. 'It must be you who tells the king. If I went, he would waste too much time asserting my identity and even then he may not believe me. If you go, he can mobilise his men within hours.'

'But I have no horses.'

'Then take ours. Like you said, it is a matter of priorities.'
'And what about you?'
'We will continue to head for Blancheguarde on foot. They are my brethren and are more likely to believe my tale. Besides. it is closer and if the remainder of your men join us, we have every chance of making it alive. If we do, we will alert them to the risk and have them stand to the defences.'

Gerald looked at Cronin, knowing he was right. God had seen fit to provide them with an opportunity and it had to be seized. He held out his hand and grasped Cronin's forearm in respect.

'You are a good man, Tom Cronin,' he said. 'With God's grace, your selfless service will see us prevail in the struggle against Saladin and if we do, make no mistake, the king will know of your role in all this.'

'Just promise me one thing,' said Cronin. 'If you make it to Ashkelon, waste not a second in sending a message to Gaza. There is a strong Templar garrison there and something tells me the king is going to need every sword he can muster.'

'Consider it done,' said Gerald.

'My lord,' said Hassan quietly after Gerald had turned away to brief his men, 'are we to give up the horses?'

'We are, Hassan,' said Cronin, 'but it is for the greater good.'

'Then I will see them watered well and fed whatever I can find. They will not let your comrades down.'

'I'm sure they won't, Hassan,' said Cronin, 'but make haste for our own journey to Blancheguarde still lays before us.'

An hour later, the men were ready to leave. Gerald of Jerusalem and Hunter were to take the horses and ride to Ashkelon while Cronin, Hassan and the rest of the men would walk to Blancheguarde Castle.

'We will waste no more time,' said Gerald, leading his horse over to Cronin. 'With God's speed, we should be there no later than tomorrow morning. If we are, I will send back a patrol to find you.'

'You just worry about alerting the king,' said Cronin.

Gerald was about to respond when one of the sentries came running down from the ridge, his face ashen with fear.

'My lord,' he gasped in broken English, 'we must leave this place with all haste.'

'Why, asked Gerald, 'what is it you have seen?'

'My lord, I have just challenged a goat farmer who is hurrying this way with his flock. He says a great army is on the march from the Maktesh Ramon and are headed this way.'

'Saladin has broken camp,' said Cronin urgently, turning to Gerald, 'and is heading west. You have to get to Ashkelon and warn the king.'

'My lord,' interrupted the sentry, 'there is more. He says he saw an even greater army heading across the mountains towards Al-Safiya.'

'Al-Safiya is the gateway to Jerusalem,' said Gerald, 'with only Blancheguarde to protect the road. Saladin must intend engaging Baldwin in Ashkelon while the main threat rides north unopposed.

'You need to be gone,' said Cronin. 'Ride like the wind, Sir Gerald, we will try to warn Blancheguarde in time.'

'With God's will, we will talk again soon,' said Gerald and without another word, turned his horse to ride down the slope.'

Chapter Twenty-Four

**Gaza Castle
November 18th
AD 1177**

'*Brother Harold,*' roared Sir Valmont, striding through the main hall and casting his gloves onto the table, 'attend me.'

The castellan appeared from a side door and scuttled across to stand before the Seneschal. The column from Acre had only been in Gaza for a few days but the whole garrison had been shook-up at the commander's overpowering authority.

'My lord,' said Harold, casting a stripped chicken bone to a lurking dog and wiping his hands on the sides of his surcoat, 'I thought you were out on patrol.'

'I was,' said Sir Valmont, 'but have a task that needs addressing.' He glanced at the dog scurrying away with his prize. 'I must have lost track of time,' he mused sarcastically, 'for I have surely missed the bell for the evening meal.'

Harold looked at the dog and his face reddened with embarrassment.

'Oh that,' he said awkwardly, 'it was a mere morsel I assure you. I have just returned from a rigorous drill session with the Marshal and needed to eat.'

'I would imagine your comrades also feel the pangs of hunger,' said the Seneschal, 'did you share your treat with them?'

'My lord,' he stuttered, 'it was just…'

'I know what it was,' interrupted the Seneschal, 'it was displaying weakness while your brothers around you remain true to their oaths. Tonight, you will take your evening meal to one of the beggars outside of the castle walls and watch over him while he eats.'

'Yes, my lord,' said Harold, his head hanging in shame.

'Stand up straight,' ordered the Seneschal, 'and act like the knight you purport to be. Now, tell me, who of the men still in the castle is your best?'

'That would be brother Lyon,' said the castellan. 'He is a master swordsman, fearless and is true to his vows.' His voice lowered. 'Unlike me.'

'Enough of the self-pity, Brother Harold,' said the Seneschal. 'Serve the penance and move on. Now, where can I find Brother Lyon?'

'I believe he is in the armoury,' said the castellan, 'he broke his lance this morning on the training field.'

The Seneschal left the hall and strode across the courtyard to the armoury. Ducking inside he immediately saw a tall man with a shock of red hair stood by the racks of lances, accompanied by the much shorter, and much fatter armourer.

'Brother Lyon,' he said, walking across to the two men.

'Master Valmont', replied the knight with a slight nod of deference, 'what can I do for you?'

The Seneschal looked at the armourer who immediately turned and left the room. Short of issuing the weaponry, he had no place in the company of knights.

'I have a task for you,' said the Seneschal turning back to face his brother knight. 'As you know the Grand Master rode back to Ashkelon yesterday for a briefing with the king. On the way, he passed a caravan of pilgrims headed this way and has sent a message back for us to ride out and escort them in. The coastal road should be free of brigands but in the circumstances, it may be prudent to afford them suitable protection. I want you to bring them back here.'

'Aye, my lord,' said Brother Lyon. 'How many of our men shall I take?'

Twenty lancers should be ample,' said the Seneschal, 'though I need all our brother Templars to remain here. Are you comfortable with this?'

'As long as they can fight, then I have no issue with whom I share the task.'

'I expected no less,' said the Seneschal. 'If you leave within the hour you should be back by midday tomorrow.'

'Of course, my lord,' said the knight.

Brother Valmont nodded and left the armoury before heading for the southern tower and climbing the stone staircase. At the top, he walked out onto the battlements and over to the two sentries posted there, mercenaries recruited from the many soldiers who hired out their sword arms across the Holy Land. He looked out over the city and towards the southern plains. The land stretched away as far as the eye could see and he knew that somewhere out there, the most feared Saracen leader in a generation was making his plans against them.

'Have you seen anything?' he asked eventually.

'Not yet, my lord,' said one of the soldiers, 'only the usual comings and goings of the locals going about their business.'

'Half of those locals are likely to be Saracen sympathisers,' said Brother Valmont, 'and their business is spying on Saladin's behalf.'

'They have us disadvantaged in that respect,' said the soldier.

'Aye they do, but it is we who are incumbent in this fortress and it is for them to dislodge us. That evens the fight. Keep your eyes peeled and let one of us know the moment you see anything out of the ordinary.'

'Of course, my lord,' said the soldier and turned back to his post as the Seneschal left the watch tower.

'There is an air of arrogance about them that makes me feel uneasy,' he said when the knight had left.

'The Templars?'

'Aye. They strut about as if they own the whole of the Holy Land.'

'That may be so,' said his comrade, 'but when it comes to a fight, I know who I would prefer alongside me, the men who bear the cross of St George upon their chest.'

Several leagues north, in the coastal fortress of Ashkelon, King Baldwin held court for his lords and knights. The hall was packed with many men, each bearing their different coats of arms emblazoned upon their tunics, and the flags of Jerusalem hung from the walls and rafters. Amongst them all were the Outremer lords, Joscelin III of Edessa, Balian of Ibelin and Reginald of Sidon, while representing the Templars was Eudes de St. Amand, the Grand Master of the order.

The noise in the hall suddenly fell away as a herald announced the arrival of the king and everyone fell silent, bowing their heads in respect as Baldwin entered, dressed in a chainmail hauberk and a surcoat bearing the colours of Jerusalem. Behind him came William of Tyre.

He climbed up onto the platform and approached the war throne, ignoring the offered hand from William and turned to address the men who would be fighting on behalf of Christianity itself.

'Gentlemen,' he said, 'thank you for assembling here. I know you have a thousand tasks to address and time is precious, but I thought it important that we are all briefed on the current situation. As you can see, we have several new faces amongst us and their arrival is most welcome.' He paused, breathing deeply. Even to speak uninterrupted for so little time was an effort and he mentally cursed his affliction. This was a time to display strength and confidence, not weakness and doubt.

'Everyone in this room,' he continued eventually, 'is here because of your leadership and abilities in battle. It is to you that I entrust the fight against the Ayyubid and though I am your king, I am not vain enough to claim better knowledge of war than any man here. Consequently, I have appointed Raynald of Chatillon as my Regent and commander of Jerusalem's armies. It is to Sir Raynald that I now cede the platform to speak on my behalf.' He sat down on the throne and waited as the regent climbed up the steps to address the gathering.

'My fellow lords,' he said, 'esteemed knights. I will keep you for as little time as possible but there is much to discuss. First of all, I will address the main question on everybody's minds. Where is Saladin?' He looked around the room before continuing. 'The true answer is that we just don't know.'

A murmur of disquiet rippled throughout the hall.

'We are aware of the many sightings of his patrols all across the Outremer,' he continued, 'but they remain elusive and despite our spies reaching all the way into Egypt, even into the heart of Cairo itself, we cannot find out the location of his army.'

'Ten thousand men would be hard to hide,' said one of the knights.

'Aye, they would and that is what is such a worry. Until we know where they are, it is hard to make detailed plans to confront them.'

'Perhaps they are on a fleet of ships out at sea,' said another knight, 'and waiting for an opportune moment to launch an attack.'

'Possibly,' said Raynald, 'but we have spies in all the Egyptian ports and such a fleet would have been noticed.'

'Could it be that he has not actually assembled an army,' said another voice, 'and we have mustered here on a fool's errand?'

'Again it is a possibility,' said Raynald, 'but the intelligence we have managed to collect so far suggests otherwise. We have it on good authority that somewhere out there, Saladin has over ten thousand men waiting to fall on Ashkelon.'

'I thought Gaza was the target,' said Lord Reginald from the back. 'The call to arms said there was evidence that the Saracens targeted the city's port.'

'The message was not quite correct,' said Raynald, 'and I apologise if you were misled but we had to ensure that Saladin thought we had fallen for his ruse, should the messages had been intercepted.'

'What ruse?'

'A few weeks ago, we received news that Saladin was to attack Gaza. This has caused concern and we reacted accordingly but subsequently, we found out the assault would be nothing more than a feint to lure our forces south, enabling Saladin to attack his real target, Ashkelon.'

This time a murmur of surprise rippled around the room until Raynald held up his hand for silence.

'I know this comes as a shock to most of you,' he said, 'but you can see why we had to be seen to play his game. If he had found out we knew the truth of his plans then his strategies would have changed, and we would have been chasing shadows from dawn till dusk. This way, by the time the attack comes we should have assembled enough men within Ashkelon to more than match his army and our response will be deadly.'

'I thought you said he had ten thousand men,' said one of the knights, 'yet in my estimation we brought only five thousand from Jerusalem.'

'At the moment yes, but don't forget, between them, Lords Joscelin, Balian, and Reginald have added another three thousand to our roll. Their men will be here by noon tomorrow. In addition, hundreds more flood in on a daily basis in response to the Arriereban. I estimate that within the week, we will be able to field just as many men as Saladin.'

'My lord Raynald,' said a voice from the back, 'I have a question.'

Everyone turned to see the imposing figure of Eudes de St Amand standing slightly apart from the other men. His stature and heavily bearded face contributed to his already impressive presence and despite the heat, he still wore the heavy woollen cloak and surcoat of the Templar order.

'Grand Master Amand,' said Raynald, 'welcome to Ashkelon. I hear you have ridden from Gaza especially for this briefing and your attendance is much appreciated.'

Amand nodded his acknowledgement before continuing.

'My question is this,' he said. 'You state that Ashkelon is Saladin's true target and that Gaza will be just a feint, but if that is the case, why have you tasked my order with providing a garrison there? I have fifty Templar knights and over five hundred men at arms wasting their days patrolling the lowlands in anticipation of an attack that may never come. Surely we would be better utilised in the defence of Ashkelon?'

'There are two reasons,' said Raynald. 'The first is that Gaza, whether the main target or not, has sea ports of its own and they must be denied to the Ayyubid. Granted they are smaller than those at Ashkelon but any coastal gateway to Jerusalem must stay out of Saracen hands. You will defend them at all costs.'

'And the second reason?' asked Amand.

When the Ayyubid come they will have to come northward along the coastal plain. That means you will be aware of their approach long before us and can send us suitable warning. Even if they should decide to bypass Gaza and head straight here, you will be well placed to disrupt their advance using your castle as a base. Besides, we need a strong garrison at Gaza to ensure Saladin thinks we have fallen for his ruse.'

'Understood,' said Amand, 'but I must say that I think the strategy flawed. My men are the best there are when it comes to battle. To act as nothing more than bait is frankly an affront to myself and our order.'

Heads turned to stare at the Grand Master at the claim. The Templar's prowess in battle was well known but to have it flaunted before comrades in arms as better than any others was little short of insulting.

'Grand Master Amand,' interrupted Reginald of Sidon, 'I suggest that when it comes to prayer and abstinence then you probably have no peers, but please allow us the smallest of dignities to believe that when it comes to killing Saracens, our sword arms are just as capable as yours.'

The sarcastic remark drew sniggers from some of the men but Amand chose to ignore the barbed comments, choosing instead to stare at Raynald in anticipation of an answer.

'My Lords,' said Raynald, raising his hand, 'let there be no argument between comrades. Each man here is as capable as the other and will be recognised as such.' He turned to look at the Templar. 'Grand Master Amand,' he continued, 'I recognise your concern but to you falls the greater responsibility. Gaza is a target in itself and like I said earlier, must be defended at all costs.'

'At all costs?' Asked Amand.

'Aye.'

'Even if that cost is Jerusalem itself?'

The room erupted into argument at the claim and it took several moments to quieten down at the demand of Raynald.

'My lord Amand,' he said eventually, his voice raised, and words clipped showing his annoyance. 'Your attendance here is most welcome and we need the knights of your order if we are to succeed, but this strategy has been worked out by the king himself and his closest advisors. Please do us the honour of accepting our judgement and carrying out the role assigned to you.'

'My lord Raynald,' said Amand. 'There has been no suggestion from me that we would do otherwise, and we will fight to the last man in God's name, but if we cannot offer constructive comment on strategies that we may perceive as being flawed then what was the purpose of this gathering?'

'You were all summoned to share what intelligence we have and to learn the plan for defending Ashkelon when the fight comes,' said Raynald, 'but I say again, this has been endorsed by the king and I respectfully request you carry your orders out to the best of your abilities.'

'In that case,' said Amand, 'my role in this affair is clear and my purpose here at Ashkelon unnecessary. With the king's permission, I will withdraw and head back to Gaza.'

Everyone's head turned to Baldwin who had been silent throughout the whole exchange.

'You are free to leave, Grand Master Amand,' said the king eventually, 'and go with my endorsement carried in your heart. The success of this war could rely on your defence at Gaza and the continued excellence of the men under your command.'

Amand nodded his head in acknowledgement.

'Thank you, my king,' he said, 'and may God look over you.' Without another word, he turned to leave the hall.

When he was gone, many men started muttering amongst themselves, critical of the Grand Master's arrogance.

'Please,' said Raynald, holding up his hand, 'there is no need for concern. Debate is healthy and as for the Templars, we all know they are almost a law unto themselves. However, Gaza can be in no better hands. Now, we need to discuss the roles of each of you in the coming fight.'

As the briefing continued, William leaned over and whispered discreetly in the king's ear.

'You were surprisingly lenient with the Grand Master, my king,' he said, 'I thought he was exceedingly rude and to walk out in such a manner displays an arrogance unheard of.'

'On the contrary,' said Baldwin. 'The Templars have rightly earned their reputation as formidable knights and do not need to impress anyone with tales of bravado or engage in needless conversation. Amand was concise and absolutely clear about his concerns. To admonish him over something as petty as courtly manners when a war is imminent would have been churlish of me and whatever you or Raynald think about their arrogance, make no mistake, we need them fully committed to our cause if we are to have any chance of emerging victorious.'

Chapter Twenty-Five

The Coastal Road
November 19th
AD 1177

Grand Master Amand and his patrol of ten Templar knights and fifty Turcopoles rode slowly along the coastal road toward Gaza.

After leaving the briefing the previous afternoon, Amand had taken the opportunity to seek extra supplies for the garrison at Gaza and spent the rest of the day dealing with traders for everything from food and water to arrows and bandages. Despite their formidable reputation in war and the secrecy in which they ran their affairs, there was no hiding the fact that they were excellent business men and there was often a clamour to trade with them whenever the opportunity arose.

Consequently, there was no shortage of takers for the Grand Master's promissory notes and by the time he had finished, six ships full of supplies had been ordered to sail for Gaza as soon as possible. By the time his business had finished, night time had fallen, and the Templars had spent the night within the walls of Ashkelon Castle before setting out at first light the following morning.

Alongside Amand was Jakelin de Mailly, the French knight who had arrived in the Holy Land only weeks earlier. His previous experience under the command of King Almaric had quickly become apparent and he had soon been recruited to the Grand Master's bodyguard.

'So, Brother Jakelin,' said Amand as they rode, 'are you regretting your decision to return here from France?'

'There are no regrets, my lord,' said Jakelin, 'the last time I was here, I wanted to leave with every fibre of my being, yet the moment I stepped upon the ship headed for France, I regretted my decision. And besides, there is no greater glory than to fight and perchance to die in the name of God.'

'I know what you mean,' said Amand, his gaze constantly scanning the horizon for any sign of trouble, 'this place is like an itch you can't scratch, and God's work is certainly an addiction.'

'Can I be so bold as to ask the outcome of the briefing, my lord?' asked Jakelin.

'There is nothing new to report,' said Amand, 'our role remains the same as it was before we left Gaza. To defend the city and use it as a base from which we can lead sorties against Saladin when he comes north.'

'So, they did not listen to your petition for us to join the forces at Ashkelon?'

'They did not, but fear not, Brother Jakelin, I suspect you will once more be carrying out God's work before too many days have passed.'

The two men fell silent again as they rode. The ground rose slightly before them and as they reached the top, both reined in their horses sharply, staring at the devastation before them. Amand raised his fist in the air and immediately the rest of the Templars rode up alongside him, their shields already in position in response to the signal.

Down below, spread out on either side of the road, were dozens of dead bodies. Their clothing identified them as European and it was clear from the debris and burned carts, it had been a pilgrim caravan headed for one of the coastal towns.'

'Turcopoles, secure the flanks,' shouted Amand, looking around urgently. 'Templars, spread out, *advance.*'

As the mounted archers rode outward to either side, Amand and his fellow knights urged their horses slowly down the hill. As they approached they could see the bodies included men women and children, each horribly mutilated.

Across the battle site also lay the bodies of those tasked with protecting the caravan, western soldiers, still wearing their heavy chain mail and helmets, their weapons laying beside them where they had fallen. Many of the civilians had several arrows sticking out of their bodies suggesting they had been used as little more than target practise while most of the soldiers had been killed by lances or swords, victims of an overwhelming force.

Jakelin de Mailly and the Grand Master dismounted and walked amongst the bodies looking for any survivors, but it was soon obvious there would be none. The attack had been thorough, and no mercy shown. Suddenly, Jakelin stopped and leaned down to examine a corpse before standing up and turning back to face the Grand Master.

'My lord, I know this man, he is a foot soldier from Acre and I believe joined our ranks as an infantryman before we left for Gaza a few weeks ago.'

'Are you sure?'

Jakelin bent down again and removed one of the gauntlets from the dead man before standing up and turning back to the Grand Master.

'Aye, I am sure,' he said holding up the gauntlet. 'I gave him these when I first arrived in Acre. These men are ours.'

'They must have been sent out to escort this caravan after we left Gaza,' said Amand. 'Alas, they must have run into one of the Saracen patrols and have been found wanting.'

'My lord,' shouted one of the other Templars from behind one of the upturned carts, 'over here.'

Amand and Jakelin walked around the cart, gasping aloud when they saw a body pinned to the base with arrows through his wrists and ankles, spread eagled as if in mockery of a crucifixion. But it was not the manner of the man's death that caused their horror, nor was it the note pinned to the man's chest with a dagger through the heart, it was the fact that the victim was a knight, and he wore the garb of the Templars.

'Who is he?' asked Jakelin eventually.

'It's Brother Lyon,' said Amand, 'one of those stationed at Gaza. A good man and a fearful fighter. Whoever did this to him would have paid a terrible price before he fell.'

'There is much blood,' said Jakelin looking around, 'and not all of it Christian. They must have taken their own casualties with them.' He walked over to withdraw the knife holding the parchment from the dead knight's chest.

'What does it say?' asked Amand.

'Allahu Akbar,' said Jakelin before crumpling up the parchment and throwing it to one side. 'I don't understand,' he continued eventually, 'this is not how Saladin works. Yes, he is ruthless in battle but to mutilate his victims is not a trait I recognise.'

'Nevertheless, the message is clear,' said Amand, 'and to have it delivered like this so close to Gaza can mean only one thing.' He looked nervously around the horizon. 'Cut him down, we will take him back for burial.'

'What about the others, my lord?' asked one of the nearby knights.

'There is no time to dig so many graves so lay them together and cover them with rocks. When this thing is over we will come back and bury them but until then, we will pray for their souls.'

Jakelin made the sign of the cross upon his chest before helping one of the others take Brother Lyon's body from the wagon and laying it gently on the floor.

The men hurriedly gathered the corpses before covering them with sand and rocks. Somebody fashioned a rudimentary cross and hurriedly drove it into the ground. Whoever had committed this atrocity was still somewhere close by and they had to make it back to Gaza before dark.

Amand removed his helmet and said a short prayer before everyone remounted and with Sir Lyon's body draped over one of the pack horse's backs, turned southward.

Up on the watchtower of Gaza castle, the new watch sat against the battlements, already bored with the uneventful duties that came with sentry duty. Lazily they threw dice between them, unconcerned that they should be watching the approaches to the city instead of engaging in games of chance behind the castle walls.

'You are surely looked over by angels,' said Simon Willow as his comrade threw another pair of sixes, 'unless those dice are weighted.' His eyes narrowed as the thought developed further. 'You are not cheating me, are you?' he continued suspiciously.

'Me?' replied the second guard, never. 'Honest John, that's what they call me.'

'Rotten John, more like,' said his comrade.

'Call me what you like but it doesn't change the fact that you now owe me three rations of ale.'

'I always pay my debts,' said Simon, 'and anyway, I hear the next ships to come from Cyprus are laden with wine and ale and we will be allowed to purchase extra rations against our next pay.'

'If you believe that then you will believe anything,' said John. 'These Templars abstain from almost everything and if you think they are going to let us get drunk in their own castle then you are stupider than I thought.'

'I must be stupid,' said Simon, 'for I volunteered to come out here, thinking the food was good, the women beautiful and the rivers ran with wine. What did I find? It's hotter that the devil's furnace, the food is shite and the women non-existent. Even the ale, when there is any, is as warm as a whore's bed and tastes of horse piss. Oh, to be back in England.'

'I'm not so sure about that,' said the second guard. 'I never had much luck with the ladies and spent so much money in the taverns I ran up a debt only the king himself could ever hope to repay. If I went back now I'd have my neck stretched by the sheriff as soon as I stepped foot on the dock.'

Simon got to his feet.

'Where are you going?' asked John.

'I need a piss,' came the reply and he climbed up amongst the castellations to urinate over the castle walls, laughing as the steaming stream fell down upon a couple of beggars in the street below.

'That'll teach you,' he called, as they ran from the disgusting shower. 'Take your begging bowls elsewhere.' He watched as they shook their fists up at them and finished his business before adjusting his clothing and jumping back down from the battlements. As he did, something in the distance caught his eye and he turned to stare eastward.

'That's odd,' he said.

'What is?' asked John from his place at the base of the wall.

'Something is on fire out in the desert.'

'On fire,' laughed John, taking a swig from his water bottle, 'there's nothing to burn out there except the skin of us poor English soldiers.'

'Well I know my sight is not what it used to be,' said Simon, 'but there's definitely smoke, and loads of it.'

John got to his feet with a sigh and walked over to stand beside his comrade.

'So, where's this fire?'

'There,' said Simon pointing to the horizon.

John squinted his eyes and for a few moments also thought he saw smoke, but as the seconds ticked by, he gradually realised what he was looking at.

'Oh sweet Jesus,' he said slowly, 'that's not smoke, it's dust.'

'Nah, I've been in a sand storm and that looks nothing like one. Just as well really as they are right devils and the stuff gets everywhere.'

'I didn't say it's a sand storm,' said John. 'I said it's dust, kicked up by the hooves of hundreds of horses.'

Simon lifted his hand to shield his eyes from the sun overhead.

'Oh my God,' he gasped, 'they must be…'

Before he could finish, his words were cut off by the clanging of a bell hanging on a tripod behind him and he turned to see his comrade swinging frantically on the rope.

'Stand to the garrison,' roared John as the alarm rang out across the castle, 'Saracens to the east, *thousands of 'em.*

Chapter Twenty-Six

Gaza Castle
November 19th
AD 1177

At the sound of the bells, the castle erupted into life. Men at arms poured out of every doorway and headed out of the gates to man the city walls, each one knowing their exact postings due to the constant training under the watchful eyes of the Templars. Sergeants organised their commands and servants ferried buckets of arrows from the armories to bolster those already stacked at regular intervals behind the battlements.

Up on the tower, both the Seneschal and the Marshal burst through the doors to join the two sentries at the walls.

'Where?' demanded Brother Valmont as he ran.

'There, my lord,' shouted Simon pointing to the east, 'it was me that seen em.'

Immediately, both Templar officers saw the risk and stared at the approaching army.

'I don't understand,' said Brother Tristan, 'how were we not warned of their approach, we have patrols out there.'

'Actually, we don't,' said the Seneschal, 'our men cover the southern approaches and that army comes from the north east.'

'Surely Baldwin would have seen them coming and sent word.'

'Not if they have come from over the mountains.'

'From the Western Negev? Surely that is impossible?'

'Obviously not,' said the Seneschal. 'It is the one direction where we thought we were safe from assault, but wherever their origins, they will be here soon enough.'

'What are your orders?'

The Seneschal thought for a few moments before coming to a decision.

'We cannot sit back and let them think we cower behind these walls like a mouse before a cat,' he said, 'our archers and foot soldiers will man the walls, but our knights will ride out to face them.'

'They already collect their equipment,' said Tristan. 'Are we to engage?'

'Not yet, for we are still unsure of their numbers and ten of our knights are with the Grand Master. Muster every horseman that we have and instruct them to form up outside the city walls. If nothing else, it will at least cause the enemy to pause and reconsider their tactics.'

'My lord,' said Simon, glancing over the wall, 'they are getting nearer. It looks to me that they number in the thousands. Would it not be better to let them have the city?'

'Gaza has been in Christian hands for over seventy years,' growled Valmont,' and we are not about to give it up at the mere appearance of a few horsemen. You just concern yourself with your duties and leave the tactics to those used to such things.'

'Yes, my lord,' said Simon and turned back to face outward over the wall.

Both officers left the tower, passing the dozens of archers racing to the castle battlements. Down below, grooms brought the horses from the stables and set about fitting them with the heavy caparisons that would protect them from all but the closest of arrow shots, while the foot soldiers who had been off duty raced to their stations, donning chainmail and helmets as they ran.

Brother Tristan strode out into the courtyard, tightening his sword belt and climbed up onto a barrel.

'Knights Templar,' he roared, 'assemble.'

The fourty knights still in the fortress gathered in the courtyard, each carrying their helmets while their squires ran to collect the rest of their equipment. Despite the urgency, the knights' manner was calm and confident. They formed up, awaiting their orders and when everyone was present, the Marshal raised his hand for silence.

'Brother knights,' he said, 'the day we have been waiting for has finally arrived. There are Saracens at the gates of Gaza and though their numbers are worrisome, they will not enjoy the luxury of setting up a siege unchallenged. In a few moments we will form up alongside the rest of the garrison lancers and ride out to confront them. Our role is only to face them down at this point and we will not engage unless they attack. If that happens we will meet them at full gallop before wheeling around to return to the castle. Do not engage at close combat for we are not yet at full strength and we are not yet aware of the mettle of our enemy. Our task here is the defense of Gaza and we cannot do that as corpses in the desert sand. I want everyman to come back here alive. If necessary we will hit them hard and then retreat to man the walls, but I repeat, I want no close quarter engagement. Is that clear?'

'Yes, my lord,' roared the Templars.

'Good, in that case, let us ask the lord for his blessing.'

Every knight dropped to one knee, watched from the battlements by the rest of the garrison.

'Lord. Give us the strength to do your work this day,' intoned the Marshal, 'grant us your holy blessing and should we fall short in our devotion, welcome us into your care. Amen.'

'Amen,' replied the Templars and made the sign of the cross on their heads and chests before getting to their feet.

'Your horses are waiting,' shouted the Seneschal from the side. 'Mount up and reform outside the city gates. Let's show these Saracens who it is that they dare to engage.'

A few leagues away, Eudes de St Amand and his men rode hard for the castle. Since leaving the site of the slaughtered pilgrims they had seen enemy patrols on several occasions and they knew they had to get back to Gaza as soon as possible. For two hours they pushed their horses as hard as they dared and finally crested the last hill on the road to Gaza before reining in their mounts and staring in horror.

Before them, they could see the Saracen army lined up before the city walls, a wide front of mounted warriors many ranks deep. Facing them stood a smaller yet equally formidable force, fifty fully armored lancers from the castle, fronted by the easily recognised white cloaks of the fourty Templars spearheading their defense. The two armies stayed where they were, each motionless in the afternoon sun.

'What are they doing,' asked Jakelin, 'our men are heavily outnumbered? Why do the Saracens not attack?'

'Whoever is in command of the Saracen army is an astute man,' said Amand, assessing the situation. 'To attack a well-formed defensive force is always a risk, even with numeric superiority. He risks many of his men falling in the fight, especially against armored knights and even if he was to emerge victorious, he would have gained nought for Gaza will still be in Christian hands.'

'Our numbers look scarce,' said Jakelin. 'Where are the rest of the men?'

'I suspect the Marshal has deliberately left the rest within the city walls. This stand off by the enemy is to test the opposition's resolve, nothing more. Come, let's get to the castle before the road is cut off.' They spurred their horses and galloped as hard as they could towards Gaza. Sentries on the walls saw them approach and the huge gates swung slowly inward to allow them through.

Amand rode straight up to the keep and dismounted before handing the reins of his exhausted horse to a squire and heading for the stairway up to the castle battlements.

'My lord,' called brother Valmont, 'over here.'

Amand joined the Seneschal and stared out at the stalemate in front of the city walls.

'Brief me,' he said shortly, accepting a water skin from a nearby soldier.

'They appeared a few hours ago,' said Brother Valmont, 'and formed up where they are now. Brother Tristan has led half the army out to confront them, but nobody has moved since.'

'It is a typical tactic,' said Amand. 'They will have men counting our numbers, judging the state of our horses and noting the weapons we carry. In addition, they will watch the way we maneuver to see whether we are skilled horsemen or if they can see weaknesses. I doubt if there will be any attack today, but you can wager they will be making plans as soon as we withdraw.' He looked around at the men along the walls of the castle. 'The defenses look sound,' he continued, 'what about the outer walls?'

They are manned with foot soldiers, archers and civilians,' said the Seneschal. 'We have almost two hundred well trained men ready to withstand any attack.'

'I doubt there will be one yet,' said Amand. 'To attack a fortified city with just cavalry will have as much effect as waves upon a shore.'

'The sea can erode the greatest of cliffs,' said the Seneschal.

'Aye, but only after a long siege. Look at the enemy. I estimate they have five thousand men, all mounted lancers but I see neither siege engines nor infantry. No this is an exercise in containment only and I see no reason to fear any meaningful attack until they are joined by their foot soldiers.'

'What are your orders?' asked Brother Valmont.

'Stand down half the men. Get them rested and fed but arrange regular relief along the walls. They are to remain within earshot of their posts and ready to fight at a moment's notice, but it is pointless wearing them out before a blow has been struck.'

'And our cavalry?'

'Sound the recall. They bake under the sun and again, I wish to present the Saracens with no undue advantage.'

'So be it,' said Valmont and walked away to carry out the orders.

A few minutes later, a signal horn echoed from one of the towers recalling the knights from the field and as the mounted ranks wheeled to return in close formation, Amand spoke quietly to himself.

'So far your intelligence seems to be correct, King Baldwin,' he said, 'but we are yet to see how this game plays out.'

Chapter Twenty-Seven

Ashkelon
November 20th
AD 1177

A lone rider galloped hard towards Ashkelon, stooped low over the pommel of his saddle. His horse frothed at the mouth, its eyes wide at the exertion after the demanding ride. Its flanks were specked with blood, but it bore no wounds, for the blood seeped from the arrow wound lodged in the arm of the man upon its back.

'Rider approaching,' shouted one of the guards atop the gate tower, 'he looks in trouble.'

The sergeant of the watch climbed a ladder to see what was going on before turning and bellowing across the courtyard.

'Someone send for the physician,' he roared, 'open the gates.'

Men rushed to obey the command and moments later, willing hands helped the wounded man from his exhausted horse before lowering him to the floor and sitting him against a water trough.

'Let me through,' shouted a voice and the men stepped aside, allowing the physician access to the wounded man.

'It's an arrow wound,' said one of the men, 'and a Saracen one at that.'

'I am not blind,' snapped the physician, 'now step back.'

They gave him more room as he dropped to his knees beside the victim.

'What is your name?' asked the physician.

'Geraint of Colchester, my lord,' said the man with a grimace. 'I'm a lancer in the king's army.'

How did this happen, Geraint?'

'I was on patrol with my comrades, checking out the foothills in the mountains to the east when we were ambushed by a Saracen patrol. We fought hard, my lord, I swear we did but their numbers were too many and we were overrun. A few of us escaped but the others died where they fought.'

'Where are the rest of those who escaped?'

'They were cut down as we rode. I was hit but managed to hang on.'

'So, you are alone?'

'Yes, my lord.' He grimaced as the surgeon snapped the arrow shaft to make it easier to move him.

'Right, Geraint of Colchester,' said the physician, 'we need to get this out of you. Can you walk?'

'I think so.'

'Good. Stand up and we will go to the infirmary to see what we can do.'

As the lancer got to his feet, a voice echoed across the courtyard.

'Out of the way, 'shouted Raynald of Chatillon and the sea of men rapidly parted to let the Regent through.

'What's happened here?' he demanded looking at the two men.

'It seems one of your patrols was attacked,' said the physician, 'and this lancer is the only survivor.'

'Is this true?' asked Raynald turning to the wounded man.

'Aye, my lord. We fought hard, I swear we did but there were just too many of them.'

'How many?'

'Hundreds, my lord. And I saw more amongst the foothills as I rode here. They are everywhere, like ants upon the sand.'

'Where was your patrol sent?' demanded Raynald.

'The mountains to the east, my lord. There is a wadi at the base and we headed there for water. On the way, they appeared from nowhere.'

'I know the place,' said Raynald, 'and you are sure you saw an army there?'

'Larger than I have ever served in, my lord. They flow from the mountains like water.'

Raynald turned to the physician.

'Keep him alive,' he said. 'The king may want to speak to him before this day is out.'

'Am I going to die?' gasped the lancer as the Regent walked away toward the keep, 'it's just my arm?'

'Let me worry about that,' said the physician,' taking the man's good arm, 'now let's get to the infirmary and get this arrow out of you.' He turned to the watching men. 'The rest of you, get back to your stations.'

Inside the castle walls, Raynald strode towards the king's quarters. Servants stepped aside, pushing themselves against the walls as he passed, knowing that when the Regent was in this sort of mood they risked a beating for even looking at him without reason.

'My lord,' said the guard on the door as he approached, 'the king is in audience with God.'

'Out of my way,' snarled Raynald and barged past the young soldier to walk straight into the room unannounced.

Inside, King Baldwin knelt in prayer before the prelate with his eyes closed and a bible held in his open hands. At the intrusion, both men turned their heads to stare at the Regent with undisguised anger.

'What is the meaning of this?' asked William his voice raising in anger, 'the king is at prayer. *Get out.*'

'Your Grace,' said Raynald to the king, ignoring the prelate, 'we need to talk. *Now!*'

'*I said get out,*' shouted William, 'you may be Regent but while we are in prayer this room is as sacred as any church, and you, my lord, are in danger of desecration.'

'*King Baldwin,*' shouted the Regent without moving, 'one of our patrols has been wiped out and Saladin's army is no more than ten leagues east of here. We need to assemble the war council immediately.'

William fell silent and the king struggled to his feet before placing the bible on a side table.

'How do you know this?' he asked, turning towards Raynald.

'One of our men just rode in wounded. He is the sole survivor of a patrol sent to scout the eastern mountains.'

'How could Saladin's army be in the mountains, there is nothing on the far side but the Negev.'

'Nevertheless, the lancer says he saw an army of Saracens flooding down to the plains.'

'And you believe him?'

'Why would he lie?'

'You said he is the sole survivor,' said William. 'Perhaps he exaggerates the enemy's strength to justify the defeat.'

'Even if he is,' said Raynald, 'we cannot take the risk. The possibility of Saladin crossing the mountains is not one we have countenanced before and we have to take it into consideration.'

'I agree,' said King Baldwin. 'Gather our commanders and send out a patrol to learn the truth of the lancer's claim. If his story is true, then a full attack is imminent, and we should prepare our army.'

'I'll see to it straight away,' said Raynald but as he turned to leave the room, a servant came running in, clearly distressed.

'What is this?' roared William. 'Are the king's quarters now no more than a common tavern for every man to come and go as he pleases?'

'My lords,' gasped the servant, 'terrible news. A messenger has just arrived from the south. *Gaza is under siege.'*

Less than an hour later, Baldwin's commanders gathered in the great hall and the air filled with heated conversations. Argument broke out between men and it was only when Raynald entered the room did the noise die down.

'Enough,' he shouted as he walked to the centre, holding up his hand for silence. 'You are supposed to be leaders yet exhibit the qualities of washer women.'

'Where is the king?' shouted one of the knights.

'He will be with us shortly but first, you all need to calm down.'

'Calm down?' questioned one. 'Gaza is besieged, and an army of Saracens are headed this way before we have hardly had chance to sharpen our blades. Where is the early warning the Templars were supposed to send from Gaza?'

'From what we can gather, those besieging Gaza also crossed the mountains while Amand's men watched the southern road.'

'What good was that?' shouted another knight. 'They have been bypassed and we are now likely to feel the full force of the Ayyubid without them having been challenged in the slightest.'

'I don't see your point,' said Raynald. 'Is this not the exact scenario we planned for, that Saladin sends a feint against Gaza while the main assault comes at Ashkelon? What is it that causes you so much concern? Our forces are strong, and we will have the benefit of surprise when the attack comes.'

'We expected some sort of warning,' said the knight, 'and thought that they would have at least suffered some casualties en route.'

'If you are afraid, Sir Peter, then I suggest you seek a ship away from the Holy Land at first light. There are some laying at anchor as we speak.'

A terrible silence fell in the room. To accuse another knight of cowardice was unheard of and warranted a challenge from the accused.

'My lord Raynald,' said Sir Peter eventually, his voice lowering dangerously. 'Despite your station, I would normally have no hesitation in immediately challenging you for that remark. But as there is a battle looming, I will put it behind me until we have dealt with Saladin. However, be in no doubt, if we both survive this war, then my seconds will seek you out to demand redress.'

'So be it,' said Raynald, 'but as you said, there is a fight to win so let's get on with it.' He turned to face the rest of the men. 'We will wait behind the walls of Ashkelon as long as we can, drawing the Saracens towards the city until they are fully committed. When they are no more than a few hundred paces away and their confidence is high, the knights of Jerusalem will lead the counter charge through the gates, followed by our lancers and mounted archers. The strength of our numbers will come as a shock to Saladin's generals, so it is important that we use that surprise to its greatest effect while we have the advantage.' He looked around the room.

'Our first charge must split them apart,' he continued, 'and while they are still reeling under the shock, our infantry will follow us into the fray. The role is to draw them into close combat and while they are engaged, Lord Jocelyn will lead his knights around the flanks to block off any escape routes.'

He paused again, feeling the battle lust rise in the room. They were men of war and relished the oncoming fight.

'Make no mistake,' he said, his voice rising, 'this will be a battle like no other. Saladin thinks he can drive us back into the sea but does not know the strength of our resolve. We have the forces, the equipment and the training to more than match his army but we need to ensure our men understand the need for ruthlessness.' His voice raised again. 'There can be no turning back,' he shouted, 'there can be no negotiating, there can be no surrender. All there can be is victory or death. Which is it to be?'

'Victory,' shouted the men in the room.

'Again,' shouted Raynald, drawing his sword and holding it up into the air, 'what is it to be, *Victory or death?*'

'Victory,' roared the knights and as the battle cries echoed around the rafters, Sir Raynald of Chatillon pushed his way

through the gathered knights, knowing that within a few hours he would be leading them into a battle that could decide the very future of the Holy Land itself.

Chapter Twenty-Eight

Gaza
November 20th
AD 1177

Grand Master Amand stood on the watchtower, staring at the thousands of Ayyubid warriors encircling the city. All through the night, the Saracens had made a great show of their prowess at riding, and squadron after squadron of cavalry had taken it in turns to charge up to the city walls carrying flaming torches yet wheeling their horses away before getting within range of the Christian archers. Despite this, the day had dawned with not a single arrow being loosed in anger and both armies stared across the desert at each other's positions. The Marshal joined him at the battlements and looked out at the enemy.

'No difference?' He asked.

'Only in as much as they have spread out to encircle the city, said Amand, 'and it seems their infantry arrived in the night. Essentially they have us surrounded but with the supplies we have and unlimited access to the port we can withstand such tactics indefinitely.'

'And for how long do we need to carry on this pretence?'

'As long as is needed. Baldwin needs us to play Saladin's game in order to surprise him at Ashkelon. Once the initial action has been made, there is then no longer any need for subterfuge on our part and we can put this army to the sword.'

'They still outnumber us.'

'Yes, but I have watched them for hours. Most of their number are made up of light cavalry with very few infantry. A well-drilled charge with heavy knights, followed up by our own massed infantry would tear them apart and once their ranks are split, they would scatter like the autumn leaves of England. All we need is a message from Ashkelon to say the main battle has started.'

'In that case, I'll make sure our men stay alert and can muster at a moment's notice.'

'You do that,' said Amand and turned away to leave the tower.

Further up the coast at Ashkelon, Sir Raynald paced the floor with frustration. For the past twenty-four hours, his army had waited in the streets of the city, anticipating the command to ride from the city and confront the Saracen army advancing from the east. But the expected attack had still not come. Scouts sent out to find out what was going on had reported back that the Saracens had built a camp less than five leagues away but showed no signs of advancing towards Ashkelon.

'It makes no sense,' said Raynald, 'why would they wait? Saladin must have realised he has us disadvantaged by coming over the mountains, but any gain made is lessened with every hour he holds back his men. He is too astute a commander to think otherwise.'

'Perhaps he has found out about our strength,' said the king, 'and hesitates.'

'Possibly, but if so, why is he staying where he is? If he knows the Ashkelon is too well defended, then he may as well attack Gaza with his full army. It would last no more than a day or so and at least he would have a port for his fleet to use.'

'What if we send out a messenger and seek parley?' asked William.

'To what end?' replied the king. 'The fact he has brought so many warriors from Egypt makes his intentions perfectly clear. He means to wage war upon us and no negotiation will change his mind.'

'Perhaps not, but sometimes, simply by engaging with the enemy we can learn a great deal.'

'Alternatively,' interrupted Raynald, 'we could send out patrols and actively force him into retaliation. Once blood has been spilt he would have to react.'

The door opened, and Sir Reginald entered, his face flushed from the brisk walk.

'King Baldwin,' he said with a slight bow, 'please forgive my intrusion but there have been developments.' He held up a parchment. 'This has just arrived from Arsuf. It's a request from one of our outposts asking for immediate aid. Apparently, there is a heavy increase in Saracen activity there and they are laying waste to the countryside. '

'What?' gasped Raynald, 'let me see that.'

He walked over to the knight and retrieved the note, reading it quickly before looking up.

'If this is correct, it means there is yet a third Ayyubid army to the north of us.'

'I agree,' said Sir Reginald, 'and that is why I came straight away. This situation is more complicated than we thought. The rider who brought that message says the Saracens are virtually unopposed and roam the kingdom with impunity. People are dying while we do nothing.'

'What is the estimated strength of the army by the mountains?' asked the king.

'About ten thousand, my lord,' said Raynald.

'And encircling Gaza?'

'Another five.'

'So, including these new forces, it would seem Saladin's strength far exceeds the ten thousand we credited him with.'

'It does,' said Raynald.

The king walked over to the window and stared out over the city before turning around.

'The Sultan is toying with us,' he said eventually, 'and sets about ravaging the coastal towns while we stay hidden away like corralled lambs. Every moment we stay here risks another settlement being attacked and more Christians dying. We need to do something.'

'Like what?' asked William.

'Like leaving this castle and confronting the Ayyubid,' said the king.

'My lord,' said Raynald, 'you do realise that to do so reveals our strengths so cancels any element of surprise that we may still hold?'

'I do,' said the king, 'but I will not sit back and watch our people die needlessly while we sit in defense of stone walls. Mobilize the army, Sir Raynald, and open the gates. *We are going to war.*'

Two hours later, the huge gates swung open revealing King Baldwin bedecked in his royal armour, sitting astride a magnificent warhorse at the head of the army. Beside him was Raynald of Chatillon while on his right rode William of Tyre.

Immediately behind them was the flag escort, a group of handpicked knights bearing the banners of Jerusalem and amongst them, the Bishop of Bethlehem escorting the inspiring true cross of Jerusalem, a gold encrusted artifact standing as high as three men and embedded with a tiny sliver of wood from the cross upon which Jesus died.

As the creaking of the gates fell away, King Baldwin stared out across the plains towards the distant hills and the site of the Saracen camp. Eventually, he raised his hand above his head and as the last remaining murmurs of his men fell away, summoned all his strength to issue the command.

'In the name of God,' he roared, *'advaaance.'*

A few leagues away, two men lay hidden amongst a thicket of tangled brush, watching the busy Saracen camp below. Ashkelon lay far in the distance and if they were to reach the king and warn him about the main Saracen army headed towards Jerusalem, they would have to pass the camp before committing to a long and hard gallop across the coastal plain.

'What do you think?' asked Gerald eventually.

'I don't think we will get far before being seen,' said Hunter, 'and men on fresh horses would catch us up in no time.'

'So, we wait until nightfall?'

'The ride could be too difficult in the dark and we risk disaster but to ride in the light will surely attract their attention.'

'I don't know how they got in front of us,' said Gerald, 'we had several hours advantage.'

'These people have ridden the mountain paths for generations,' said Hunter. 'It is no surprise they knew the quicker routes.'

'Wait, said Gerald, 'what's that?'

Both men squinted and stared out across the plain. In the distance, they could just about make out a huge body of men making their way from the coast.

'It looks like Baldwin is coming to confront them,' said Gerald. 'The king has fallen for Saladin's bait.'

'Then we have to let him know as soon as we can.'

'They are still too far away,' said Gerald, 'but they will have to make camp soon. Hopefully, the distance will then be achievable.'

'Perhaps if we wait until last light,' said Hunter, 'and then ride as hard as we can towards the king, we can lose them in the dark.

'It's a risk,' said Gerald, 'but the king has to know about Saladin's main army. Come, let's get some rest and see to the horses. Tonight, we ride for our lives.'

Further north, Cronin and Hassan plodded endlessly on, accompanied by the remnants of Gerald's patrol. The boy's local knowledge meant they had made better time than expected. The sun was at its highest when they finally stopped in the shade to rest. Cronin reached for his water pouch and sipped sparingly before leaning back against the trunk of the tree.

'So,' he said, 'how long now?'

'I think we will be there by dawn,' said Hassan. 'The road ahead is easier but will be better travelled. We should be careful we are not seen by Saracen patrols.'

'Then we should waste no time and be gone as soon as we can.'

'With respect, my lord,' said Hassan, 'we should wait until the sun is on the wane. That way we will use less water.'

'We do not have the time, Hassan,' said the sergeant getting to his feet. 'Saladin's armies are all around us and could march on Jerusalem at any time. Every extra moment we can give Blancheguarde to prepare could mean a Christian life is saved.'

'In that case, my lord,' said Hassan, getting to his feet, 'our path lies there.' He pointed along a high ridge heading northward. 'But we must avoid the skyline to avoid being seen.'

'We are in your hands, 'Hassan,' said Cronin, 'lead the way.'

Chapter Twenty-Nine

Gaza
November 21st
AD 1177

'*More archers to the eastern walls,*' roared Amand, '*drive them back.*'

Men jumped to the Grand Master's commands and ran along the battlements, keeping low to avoid the Saracen arrows flying from the attackers below.

'Still no sign of siege engines,' said the Seneschal appearing at his side, 'and to waste men on their futile attempts at breaching the walls with little more than ladders is stupidity.'

'On the contrary,' said Amand, it is a clever move. Saladin has committed these men to take Gaza but even though their chances are limited, they serve a higher purpose, keeping us pinned down while the main army assaults Ashkelon.'

'Aye but this is the third attack and I have already counted over a hundred Saracen bodies with only two dead on our side. It is nothing short of farcical.'

'Nevertheless, their numbers are large, and it would only take the arrival of a couple of onagers to change this siege to their advantage. We will do what is necessary to defend the walls but don't forget this, it is Ashkelon that is Saladin's true target, not Gaza.'

'Understood,' said Brother Valmont.

Out on the plains in front of Gaza, the renewed assault on the city was watched from the rear by Farrukh-shah, the Emir of Baalbek

On either side of the Emir, the majority of his mounted forces spread out encircling the city, watching the assault unfold while to his, front, five hundred archers unleashed their weapons at the battlements, attempting to keep the defenders' heads down while their newly arrived infantry attacked the walls with siege ladders.

Up above, the air filled with black smoke trails from the many fire arrows soaring over the walls, and despite the relative weakness of the assault, the air echoed with the sound of Saracen war drums and battle horns.

'Oh for the strengths of our main army,' said one of his generals from his horse alongside him, 'these walls would fall within hours.'

'Our time will come,' said Farrukh–Shah. 'You just watch those gates closely for if the Christian knights emerge, it will be your role to cut them down.'

'We outnumber them ten to one,' said the general, 'and we will not be found wanting. He looked to either side, seeing his cavalry alert and ready to ride into battle at a moment's notice. 'Any news from Ashkelon?'

'Not yet,' said Faruk-Shah, 'our men are still camped at the base of the eastern mountains. Hopefully, the Christians will take the bait and ride out to confront them soon enough and when they do, Saladin can make his move.'

'What about Taqi Ad-Din?'

'There are reports that he is laying waste to the Christian colonies all along the northern plains.'

'I thought he was to hold back his army until Baldwin was committed to the fight?'

'Saladin has allowed him to roam freely and enjoy the spoils of war for there is little resistance along the coast.'

'It seems our advance has taken the Franks by surprise,' said the general, 'and they spread themselves thinly.'

'They do. Saladin's plan is coming to fruition and while the Christians chase shadows, our main army gathers unchallenged at Al-Safiya for the final push to Jerusalem.'

To the east of Ashkelon, in the foothills of the mountains, Gerald and Hunter waited nervously for the sun to sink to the horizon. The king's army had formed a well-defended position no more than few leagues away and in response, the nearby Saracen forces were busy reforming their lines, anticipating a dawn attack.

Hunter stood amongst the undergrowth with the horses, preparing them for the final gallop towards the Christian lines. Within the hour they would divest themselves of everything they had to lighten the load and push their mounts to breaking point but with all the water gone and having eaten very little for days except what they could find amongst the desert scrub, the horses were tired and weak.

'One last push, girl,' said Hunter quietly, patting his horse on the neck, 'and I promise you can have all the fodder you can eat.'

The horse whinnied gently as if in response and though it was the last few drops he had, Hunter emptied his water bottle into the palm of his hand, sharing the meagre droplets between the two mounts. Gerald crawled back and joined the scout.

'Are they ready?' he asked quietly.

'Ready,' said Hunter, 'but whether they are able, is another thing.'

'They are subject to God's will,' said Gerald, 'as are we.'

The two men discarded their chainmail and helmets along with their surcoats and undershirts. As the sun dipped towards the horizon, they mounted their horses, dressed only in leggings and boots.

'If one falls, the other carries on,' said Gerald, 'agreed?'

'Agreed,' said Hunter.

'In that case, let's get this done.'

Both men rode their mounts slowly out onto the open slope, using the last of the undergrowth as a screen between them and the Saracen camp. They came to a halt and with the last of the light quickly fading, surveyed the ground before them. The slope fell away to a flat plain relatively empty of obstacles, but the distance to Baldwin's camp was at least three leagues.

'That looks like a wadi,' said Gerald, pointing to a cleft in the ground halfway between them and the king's camp. 'If we skirt around to the right we can maintain our speed but anyone coming from the Saracen camp will have to ride around it. It will give us a few extra minutes.' He wrapped his reins tightly around his hands. 'Do not stop, master Hunter,' he said without looking over at his comrade, 'in any circumstances. The future of Jerusalem is in our hands.'

'Then let us begin,' said Hunter, 'and may God go with us.' Both men made the sign of the cross and as one, spurred their horses into an immediate gallop down the hill... *into full view of the Saracen camp.*

Sir Raynald rode his horse slowly around the perimeter of the Christian army's temporary position. He had almost ten thousand men and horses encamped upon the open plain but knew that they were now more exposed than they had been within the walls of Ashkelon. Consequently, no tents had been erected in case of an immediate call to arms and every man knew that if any sleep was to be had that night, it would be wrapped within their cloaks. Even the king insisted on sharing their discomfort and sat below the true cross at the centre of the camp alongside the Bishop of Bethlehem and William of Tyre.

On either side of the Regent rode two fully armoured battle commanders and together they inspected the perimeter. It was going to be a long and nervous night, and as they were so close to the enemy positions, they could afford no weaknesses.

The outer perimeter of guards stood ten paces apart and encircled the whole camp, over a hundred fully armoured mounted knights facing outward, bearing lances, broadswords and maces. Behind them stood half a dozen archers and a dozen foot-soldiers, each tasked with staying fully alert and ready to fight if needed.

Fifty paces in front of the guards, a ring of bonfires created an illuminated swathe of ground where any aggressors would be seen should an attack come. The artificial light was a barrier to the rest of the countryside, beyond which none of the guards could see, so to combat the disadvantage, Raynald had deployed several listening patrols further out, their role to be as quiet as possible and give plenty of warning should they hear or see anything that may suggest an attack was imminent.

'Pass the word,' said Raynald to the knights as they rode, 'any man found sleeping on duty tonight will be summarily executed. One weak link and this chain can be torn asunder by the Saracens. Our numbers may be even, but the element of surprise, especially in the dark is worth an army in itself.'

'Yes, my lord,' said one of the knights.

'Relieve the sentries every two hours,' said Raynald, 'and make sure the rest get some sleep and food. Tomorrow this phoney war ends, and the real conflict begins.'

Ten leagues to the north, hidden away amongst the rolling hills, another ten thousand Saracens lay waiting for the final command to advance towards Jerusalem. The movement of so many men from the Maktesh Ramon without being discovered had been almost an impossible task yet they had done so successfully and the final advance past Blancheguarde castle to Jerusalem was only hours away.

Amongst them all was Salah ad-Din himself, Ayyubid Sultan of all Egypt and Syria and alongside him, his favorite General, Shirkuh ad-Dun. Both men pored over a deer-hide map of the area in the Sultan's command tent.

'So, are our armies ready to do Allah's will?' Asked Saladin.

'They are,' said Shirkuh. 'Your plan has been executed perfectly and the Christian eyes are on happenings elsewhere.' He pointed at the map. 'Faruk-Shah has the city of Gaza under siege and yet may provide us with a surprising outcome while your general, Nizam al-Mulk readies his command to engage with Baldwin at dawn.'

'And my nephew?'

'Taqi ad-Din has laid waste to all the coastal towns from Ramla to Arsuf.'

'What about the city at Lydda?'

'Destroyed, my lord. You nephew has carried out his task well and is waiting for us to join him at Al-Safiya.'

Saladin looked at the map. Al-Safiya was only five leagues south of Blancheguarde Castle and a perfect staging post for his men to assemble before making the final push north.

'Is there water there?' asked Saladin.

'There is a river, my lord,' said Shirkuh, 'and there will be rain tonight so water will not be a problem.'

'And the men have been briefed?'

'They have. At dawn, Half of Nizam al-Mulk's army will circle around to the north of Baldwin and create a wall of steel between us and them, while the other half race northward to join us and Taqi ad-Din at Al-Safiya.'

'A sizeable force,' said Saladin.

'Indeed, my lord, over twenty thousand men ready to march on Jerusalem while the Christians run in circles like mad dogs.'

'And our baggage trains?'

'They travel along the hidden paths. Five thousand camels laden with enough supplies to keep our men in the field for weeks. Another ten such trains are already on their way from Egypt and Taqi ad-Din has taken a mountain of supplies from the Christian towns along the coast. Our ships also stand ready to be loaded and will bring extra men as soon as we make a port available.'

'That will have to wait,' said Saladin. 'Jerusalem must be the only thing in our minds until our banners fly over the city. After that, we can turn our thoughts to securing a port.'

'Understood,' said Shirkuh.

'In that case,' said Saladin, 'it seems all that can be done, has been done. Tell our men they must be as silent as death for to be discovered now could see our mission fail. Our fate is now in Allah's hands.'

'Allahu Akbar,' said the general, touching his hand to his chest and lips as he bowed before the sultan.

'Allahu Akbar,' replied the Sultan and waived the general away while he remained staring at the map. Everything he had so carefully planned had come to fruition and even the Christians had played their part by falling for his deceptions. Everything now relied on the gathering of his armies at Al-Safiya before the final push north to Jerusalem

----

Chapter Thirty

The Ashkelon Plains
November 21st
AD 1177

'They've seen us,' shouted Gerald, looking over his shoulder and seeing a line of riders emerge from the Saracen camp, *'come on.'*

He dug his heels into his horse's flanks, driving it to the extremes of its endurance. Hunter rode just as hard and a cloud of dust flew high in the air behind them, but despite the head start, it was obvious the pursuers' horses were fresher and they gained ground with every second that passed.

'We are not going to make it,' shouted Hunter as the Saracens closed in, 'it's too far.'

'Keep going,' shouted Gerald, 'we're almost there.'

'I'm going to try something,' shouted Hunter, 'keep going.'

'Stay with me,' roared Gerald as Hunter veered off route, but it was too late, the scout had ridden in a circle and now galloped straight back at the Saracens.

'Hunter,' he shouted again but the scout ignored him, galloping straight back towards their pursuers. Gerald thought furiously. Kinship demanded he rode back to help Hunter but with the future of Jerusalem at stake, it was more important that the king knew the truth. He kicked his heels again and bent low over his horse's neck, urging her to one last effort, leaving the scout heading toward certain death.

Behind him, Hunter headed straight for the Saracens, drawing his sword and raising it high into the air.

'Come on,' he roared, *'here I am.'*

The effect was immediate, and the Saracens lowered their lances in response. The distance closed but seconds before they met, Hunter veered his horse to the right, galloping towards the wadi they had seen earlier.

Taken by surprise, the Saracens, reined in and wheeled their horses to pursue him before their commander realised what was happening.

'*Hold,*' he roared, 'he seeks time for his comrade to escape. Ten men go after him, the rest, continue the chase.'

The group split into two, but the momentary hesitation had given Gerald some extra valuable seconds and at last, he thought he was actually going to make it.

'*Come on,*' he shouted at his horse, '*almost there,*' but no sooner had the words left his mouth than his mount tripped and sent him crashing to the floor. For a few moments he lay there stunned, but as his senses returned, he struggled to his feet and turned to face his pursuers. His left arm lay limp at his side and blood ran down into his eyes from a wound on his scalp, but his sword arm was uninjured. He drew his blade, vowing that if he was about to die, then he would take as many as he could with him.

As the noise of the horses thundered closer, he cursed silently, not in judgement of his imminent death but because he knew that the knowledge of Saladin's true plan would die with him.

He said a silent prayer and flexed his fingers around the hilt of his sword, taking a deep breath and adjusting his stance in the sand of the desert floor, but just as the Saracen horsemen appeared out of the darkness, his prayers seemed to be answered and the attackers swerved sharply away.

Gerald was stunned but everything became clear as thirty Christian lancers thundered past him in pursuit of the fleeing Saracens. He fell to his knees, gasping in relief and just stayed there until another patrol followed the first, this time stopping alongside him.

'Who are you?' shouted the knight in charge, looking down from his warhorse.

'Sir Gerald of Jerusalem,' came the reply, 'and you need to get me to the king, urgently.'

'Are you wounded?'

'My injuries will wait, my message will not.'

'What message?'

'The true nature of Saladin's plan. Please, we are wasting time. I have to see King Baldwin.'

'Can you ride?'

'Aye,'

The knight turned to one of his men.

'Get this man back to camp,' he snapped, 'the rest of you come with me.'

'Wait,' said Gerald, 'I have a comrade still out there. The last I saw he was headed for the wadi with Saracens in pursuit.'

'If he is alive,' said the knight, 'we will find him. Now get your message back to the king.' Without another word, he spurred his horse to lead the rest of his patrol after the first and disappeared into the darkness.

The remaining lancer offered his arm down to Gerald and moments later, both men were astride his horse, riding as hard as they could back to King Baldwin's camp.

Hunter reached the wadi and raced headlong down the steep rocky slopes into the darkness below. Somehow his horse survived the descent, but the nature of the ground and the overwhelming darkness meant he knew he had to find somewhere to hide. He quickly dismounted and slapped the horse's haunches, sending it trotting further into the darkness before crawling beneath a nearby thicket of tangled scrub.

He gathered his breath and placed his sword in front of him along with his knife, swearing to himself that he would not rot in a Saracen jail.

The sound of men clambering down the slope sent fear into his heart and his hand reached for the hilt of his sword but as he braced, a voice rung out in the darkness.

'I don't know where you are, comrade,' it said in perfect English, 'but you are safe now. We are lancers in King Baldwin's army and have come to take you back.'

Hunter gasped in relief and crawled out from his hiding place. Moments later, he followed the three men back up to the rest of the patrol waiting on the wadi edge. Behind them came a fourth, leading Hunter's exhausted horse.

'You are a lucky man,' said a knight as he appeared. 'Another few moments and we would have been too late.'

'Remind me to buy you and you men enough ale to drown a horse,' said Hunter.

'I'll hold you to that,' said the knight.

'What about Sir Gerald?'

'Safe and on his way to the king.'

'Thank God,' said Hunter.

'Aye,' said the knight, 'thank him indeed, for tonight he was surely at your side.'

Back in the Christian camp, Gerald stood before King Baldwin and Sir Raynald, illuminated by a circle of Braziers. Above them all loomed the imposing silhouette of the true cross, the gold shimmering in the light from the flickering flames.

'Sir Gerald,' gasped the king, 'I thought you was dead. What miracle delivers you back here?'

'My lord,' said Gerald, 'I live by the grace of God and can only say that it was his will that paved my path here. Many did not survive.'

'How many are with you?' asked Raynald.

'Only a handful survived, they are on their way to Blancheguarde.'

'Why Blancheguarde?'

'It was the nearest place of safety.'

'Yet you rode here, risking the Saracen army?'

'There was no other choice, my lord, we only had two horses, and someone had to get the information to you.'

'What information?'

'Saladin's true intentions. This army to your front is a feint only, as is the attack on Gaza.'

'We know this,' said Raynald, 'Ashkelon is his intended prize.'

'No, my lord,' said Gerald, 'that is what he wants you to think. There is an even greater army already on its way north towards Blancheguarde. While you are fighting here in defence of Ashkelon, Saladin will be riding hard towards Jerusalem. We have to head north immediately.'

'Another Saracen army?' said Raynald. 'That's impossible. We already know of almost fifteen thousand Ayyubid warriors in the field. To take Jerusalem Saladin would need at least ten thousand more and even then, I suggest it would be an impossible task.'

'Would it?' asked the king quietly. 'With my main army in the north, and the rest of us down here chasing shadows, Jerusalem's walls are virtually undefended. If he can bypass Blancheguarde then his path is clear.'

'All he needs to do, my lord,' said Gerald, 'is place the castle under siege while the rest of his men continue north. Make no mistake, his eyes are on the greater prize.'

'And who told you this?' asked Raynald.

'A Templar sergeant. The information was overheard from warriors sat around a campfire in Saladin's camp beyond the mountains.'

'A Templar Sergeant was in an Ayyubid camp?'

'Not the sergeant, his squire. A Bedouin boy who could understand the language.' He paused as he saw a look of incredulity appear on the Regent's face. 'You have to believe me,' he continued, 'the boy is a Christian and as true as you or I.'

'You are telling us,' said Raynald eventually, his voice laden with disbelief, 'that a Bedouin boy, who probably has family in the Ayyubid's ranks, overheard a few warriors discussing Saladin's master plan around a fire, and on that basis alone, we should now march away from the battlefield to head north, leaving Ashkelon undefended?'

'I know it sounds unlikely,' said Gerald, 'but one of my men also talked to a shepherd who saw a great army heading north west in the mountains. The Templar sergeant is a good man and, on his word alone I would recommend such action, but over the past few days, I have seen massively increased Saracen activity with my own eyes. On the way here, we could hardly walk an hour without having to hide away from passing patrols or heavily laden caravans of camels and horses.'

'It is an astonishing tale,' said the king, 'and if true, changes everything.'

'Aye,' said Raynald, 'but if not and we change our course, Ashkelon and Gaza will be at the mercy of Saladin.'

'My lord Raynald,' said Gerald, 'a few days ago we were sent out on a patrol tasked with seeking intelligence about the Ayyubid. We were ambushed with many of my men slaughtered. Some escaped over a cliff, including myself and most carry wounds, or injuries from the fall. We have suffered the furnace of the desert sands and the iciness of the mountains with no food and little water, yet we have been steadfast in our service. If I did not truly believe that Jerusalem is at risk, I would not have ridden here and risked being killed by the Saracen army on the plains.'

He turned to face Baldwin.

'My king,' he continued, 'I have fulfilled the tasks you set before me and my command had been wiped out in your service, however, I do not deem to affect your will and you must do what you see fit. I cannot guarantee that my information is correct, but I will say this. Which would you rather lose, Ashkelon, or Jerusalem?'

Silence fell amongst the men as the seriousness of the situation sunk in. The king sighed deeply and closed his eyes as the men surrounding him waited for his decision with baited breath.

'Sir Gerald is correct,' he said eventually, drawing a gasp of surprise from the surrounding knights. 'We cannot be sure but if we have to wager our tactics on a single outcome, it has to be the safety of Jerusalem. Brief the men, tomorrow we march north.'

'My lord,' said Raynald, 'with respect I must disagree. The source of this information is a Bedouin boy who may have Ayyubid interests at heart. We cannot trust his word and should immediately attack the army to our front as soon as the sun rises.'

'On the contrary,' said the king, 'it comes from the mouth of a man who wears the red cross of the Templars upon his chest, and that, Sir Raynald, is good enough for me. Rally the camp, for at dawn, we ride for Jerusalem.'

Chapter Thirty-One

The Ashkelon Plains
November 22nd
AD 1177

The sun had still not crested the eastern mountains when the army lined up for the march north the following morning. Behind them lay their vast discarded camp including any tents or equipment deemed too heavy to carry into battle.

Relative silence fell upon the ten thousand men as they stared nervously northward, for far from being idle during the night, the Saracens too had been busy, and now stretched out across the Christian army's path, a barrier on the road to Jerusalem.

'It would seem Sir Gerald's words may be found to be true,' said the king, 'why else would they try to block our way?'

'Their numbers are smaller than yesterday, said Raynald, 'our scouts say many rode northward during the night.'

'Reinforcements for Saladin?'

'Aye, and if we are to thwart his plans, we need to ride after them at all speed. '

'What about the men to our front?'

'They will not withstand a direct charge but once we have breached their lines we will not turn and engage them. Instead, we will head directly on as fast as our mounts will carry us.'

'We will be harried at every step.'

'Probably, but we must not waste time fighting pawns when the main players lay to the north.'

'Understood,' said the king, 'but there is one more thing. If Saladin has another army already on the way to Jerusalem, then we will be heavily outnumbered and will need the Templars at our side. Somehow we need to get a messenger through the siege at Gaza and brief the Grand Master on the change of circumstances.'

'Your Grace,' said William, 'I have already taken the liberty of sending the message. With a bit of luck, he should be in Gaza by noon.'

'Who did you send?' asked the king, 'one of our knights?'

'No, my lord, I do not have that authority but there was one man who was not only confident he could get through without being seen, he also begged for the opportunity to do so.'

'And who was this man?'

'He is a scout, the one our men rescued from the jaws of death last night in the wadi. He goes by the name of Hunter.'

Twenty minutes later, Raynald sat astride his horse at the head of the vanguard. His unit formed a wedge of two hundred heavily armed knights intended to drive through the Saracen lines and open the road northward. Behind them came the main column led by the king's bodyguards, flanked on either side by five hundred lancers. Further out rode the mounted turcopoles who would try to disperse the disrupted Saracens forces while bringing up the rear came the archers and infantry, protected by another two thousand lancers on either side.

Raynald turned his horse to face the column and stood up in his stirrups so he could be heard.

'You have your orders,' he shouted, 'and know what is at risk. There will be no quarter shown, and no turning back. Our target is not the men to our front, but those ten leagues to the north so do not be drawn into close-quarter conflict. We smash through them and we drive on. Understood?'

'Aye,' roared the men.

'Leave the wounded where they fall,' continued Raynald, 'our rear echelons will care for them as they pass.' He paused before raising his voice even higher to reach the far ends of the column. 'Make no mistake, to falter is to fail. Ride hard and strike with every fibre of your being, for one thing is for sure, *God is with us.*'

'God is with us,' roared his men.

Raynald drew his sword, holding it high into the air as he turned to face the Saracens.

'Men of Jerusalem,' he roared, *'for God, for king and for Jerusalem...advance!'*

The sounds of horns rent through the air and as Raynald drew down the faceplate of his helmet, the army headed northward. The struggle for Jerusalem had begun.

Further north, on the slopes of Montgisard, Saladin and his generals stood on a ridge, watching their forces making ready for the push to Jerusalem, all attempts at subterfuge now abandoned as the time for battle neared.

The numbers were impressive, almost twenty-five thousand horsemen and infantry, all recruited from many different tribes to finally wrest Jerusalem from the hands of the Christians, yet Saladin's brow was creased with concern.

'Shirkuh,' he said to the man at his side. 'We should be ready to move by now. What is the delay?'

'My lord,' said the general, 'the arrival of Taqi ad-Din's men in the night along with those who have ridden from Ashkelon, has put a strain on our resources. Many need food and water and cannot be expected to ride until their horses have been refreshed.'

'I was told our supply lines are healthy,' said Saladin, 'why do we struggle with such a basic task?'

'The rains have swollen the river,' said Shirkuh, 'and so many men using the ford has turned the area into mud slowing the supply columns down. The majority will be across by dusk.'

Saladin turned to his general, the look on his face barely concealing his anger.

'We have come all this way,' he growled, 'and amassed an army capable of tearing down the walls of Jerusalem and yet you tell me I am to wait another day just because a stream has become swollen?'

'My lord,' said Shirkuh, 'with respect, it was unforeseen, and our supply caravans struggle in the mire. There is little to be done unless we build a bridge.'

'We have scouted these hills and plains for months,' said Saladin. 'All such obstacles should have been foreseen and allowed for.' He stared down again into the valley. Most of his army was already on the northern banks and ready to ride while the southern bank was a picture of disorganisation and confusion as the supply columns struggled to negotiate the muddy fields. He knew he needed the food and the barrels of water if he was to sustain his push northward, but he was also painfully aware that time was not on his side. If Baldwin found out about the subterfuge he would make every effort to chase him down.

'There is no time for bridges or alternative routes,' he said eventually. 'Leave the carts on the far side and load up every spare horse and camel on this bank with water skins. Every tenth horse to carry dried meat and biscuit.'

'It will not be enough,' said Shirkuh.

'It will be enough for us to reach Jerusalem,' snapped Saladin.' The rest of the caravan can follow on as soon as they are across. I will give you until dawn to sort this out and then we march north with whatever forces we have at hand.'

Without waiting for an answer, he turned and marched away, furious at the unforeseen delay.

Back on the Ashkelon plain, Raynald felt the blood coursing through his veins as he led the vanguard thundering into contact. To his front, the Saracens had closed ranks to form a wall of infantry, each presenting their spears against the Christians, but the Regent's men and horses were fully armoured, and it would take a very disciplined defensive line to maintain its formation against such an attack.

The stale smell of sweat and his own breath filled his helmet and his heart raced at the familiar stench of war as the enemy grew larger through the narrow slit in his visor. Saracen arrows fell all about them, but the knights' heavy chainmail combined with the quilted caparisons protecting their horses meant few did any serious damage and only one knight fell, suffering a broken neck when his mount tripped on the uneven ground.

Raynald's hand gripped his lance and he lowered it into the charge position, bending low over his horse to present a smaller target. All around him the rest of his men did the same and as they kicked their heels into their horses' flanks, the effect of such a formidable attacking force took its toll and many of the Saracens broke ranks to run from their path.

Instinctively the attacking knights turned slightly to take advantage of the weakened lines, causing more of the enemy to break and Raynald knew, before a single blow had been struck, the advantage was already his.

Within seconds the wedge of knights smashed into the front lines of the enemy infantry at full gallop, scattering defenders on all sides. Saracen lances shattered on the steel breast plates sewn into the horses' caparisons, and the knights drove deep into the heart of the defenders. The impetus was overwhelming, and those Saracens brave enough to face down the charge were cut down with impunity, victims of heavy broadswords wielded by strong men toughened by a lifetime of warfare and training.

Despite the bravery of the Saracen infantry, the vanguard broke through and as ordered, continued pushing onto the plain beyond. Behind them, the rest of the army poured into the breach, causing confusion throughout the defenders' position and even though the Saracens tried to counter the attack, the flanking Christian lancers fell upon them, cutting men down in their hundreds.

'The breach is formed,' roared one of the king's bodyguard, *'advance.'*

Immediately the core of the army spurred their horses forward, following the knights through the Ayyubid position. In the centre, the king, closely surrounded by his heavily armoured body guard, urged his own horse forward, followed by the clergy and the wagon bearing the carefully wrapped true cross. Behind them, the infantry fanned out and marched towards the panicking Saracen lines, while out on the flanks, the turcopoles caused mayhem with their arrows, cutting down any of the enemy trying to escape.

'Faster,' roared the king, seeing the enemy beginning to rally, 'we need to get through.'

The makeshift army surged forward and soon the Saracen position was cleaved completely in two, divided by the Christian column as they drove onward to the plains beyond.

The Ayyubid commander tried desperately to rally his command but the damage had been done and as he watched, many of his infantry turned away from the fight to try to escape with their lives. Baldwin's Turcopoles were causing terrible casualties on the flanks and he knew that it was foolish to continue with no hope of victory. He turned to the man at his side.

'Recall our cavalry,' he said, 'they are fighting a lost cause.'

'Why?' asked his fellow officer. 'This fight is not yet lost.'

'Our orders were to contain Baldwin,' came the reply, 'not engage in a meaningless battle with little depending on the outcome. His vanguard has already broken through our lines and the Christians pour through like blood from a slit throat. Saladin's cause will be better served if we withdraw while our men are still fresh and then delay their advance as much as we can as they ride north. Hopefully, he is already on his way to Jerusalem, but we cannot take that chance. Sound the retreat, there is still much to do.'

'They are falling back,' shouted William back in the Christian lines,' we've done it.'

'It was too easy,' said Baldwin, as the sound of Saracen horns filled the air, 'and I suspect it is a tactic only. Harden your resolve, my friend, and pray for God's speed. This race has just begun.'

On the seaward defensive walls of Gaza city, a sentry got to his feet and walked over to peer at a small fishing boat approaching the defensive chain stretching across the dock. It was not marked with the crests of the city and he did not recognise the two men standing in the bow.

'Hold there,' called the sentry, as the vessel neared, 'state your business.'

'My name is Assir,' said the first man, 'and this is my boat. I operate out of Ashkelon and seek a berth.'

'What is your cargo' asked the sentry.

'Nothing more than this man,' said the sailor, indicating the bedraggled soldier wrapped in a blanket at his side, 'he seeks audience with the master of the castle.'

The sentry turned towards the second man.

'And you are?'

'I am a scout in King Baldwin's army,' said Hunter, 'and I have an urgent message for the Grand Master of the Templars from the king himself.'

'And the message?'

'Is for his ears only but I will say this, the longer you delay my audience, the better the chance that every one of us could lay rotting upon the desert sands within weeks. Now, do you allow us to land or not?'

The sentry hesitated for a few moments for his orders were to let no ships through without authorisation from his commanders, but this was just one man, and a westerner at that.

'I will seek authorisation,' he said eventually and turned away.

'Wait,' shouted Hunter, 'there is no time. Jerusalem itself is under attack and unless I can get to the Templars urgently, we may be too late. You have to let me through.'

Again the sentry hesitated. If what the man said was true then every second counted, yet if the man was no more than a braggard, then he, and every one of his own comrades on duty that day could be punished.

'*You* may land,' he said eventually pointing at Hunter, 'but as soon as your boots hit the dock, the boat must leave without a berth.'

'Understood,' said Hunter.

'And I swear to you,' shouted the sentry again, 'if this is some sort of ruse, then I will see you hung by your balls from the highest tower in Gaza.'

'It is no ruse, my friend,' said Hunter, 'and by this action alone, you may just have saved us all.'

The sentry grunted and turned towards the port tower a hundred paces away.

'*Let her through,*' he shouted, '*lower the chains.*'

To the south of Blancheguarde castle, a group of ten knights rode their horses carefully along a mountain ledge, returning from a patrol amongst the hills. They were tired and hot from the trek but knew the safety and relative comfort of the Blancheguarde castle lay only a few hours away.

The patrol had been uneventful, yet their senses were ever alert, knowing that danger often lay only moments away.

The echoing of the horses' hooves in the silent rocky valley was hypnotic, almost lulling the riders into a false sense of security but the sound of a distant call made everyone sit upright in their saddles, their hands instinctively reaching for their shields and swords. The lead rider held up his hand, bringing the patrol to a halt.

'Did you hear that?' he asked.

'Aye, I did,' said the second knight.

The call came again, and all heads turned to stare toward the ridge on the opposite side of the valley.

'There,' said the second knight, pointing to a group of sprawling trees near the top, there's someone in the shade.'

As they watched, several men crawled from beneath the trees and struggled to their feet, waving their arms and calling out in a desperate attempt to gain the riders' attention.

'Seven men and what looks like an Arab boy,' said one of the knights, 'yet I see no horses.' They stared at the pathetic group. Even from across the small valley, the knights could see the travellers were in a terrible state and in dire need of help.

'My lords,' shouted one of the men across the valley, 'please, in the name of God, we need your aid.'

'Who are you,' shouted the knight, 'and what circumstances have brought you to this place?'

'The story is a long one,' shouted the man, 'and I will recount every word I swear, but there is no time. We have to get to Blancheguarde as soon as possible.'

'To what end?'

'To warn of a Saracen army not half a day's march from here,' shouted the man, 'Jerusalem is at risk, and we have to warn the castle.'

'The castle is garrisoned by Templars,' shouted the knight, 'and we are based there under their command. Why would they believe such a tale from someone such as you?'

'Because,' said the man, 'my name is Tom Cronin and I am a brother sergeant of the Templar order. Now please, you must take us to Blancheguarde before it is too late.'

Chapter Thirty-Two

Blancheguarde
November 22nd
AD 1177

Sir Redwood watched patiently as the seven men brought in by the patrol drank from the water skins provided by his steward. The eighth, a young boy, walked over and dipped his head into a water trough, immersing it completely before rising again, gasping as his long black hair fell sodden down his back.

All around the bailey, the men tasked with defending Blancheguarde stared down at the ragged remains of Sir Gerald's patrol. The rumours had already circulated about what had happened and the feeling of anger at the loss of so many good men was tempered with respect for those that had survived the hardships of the desert.

Cronin poured the last of the water over his head before turning to seek the Castellan.

'Up there,' said one of the knights, pointing up at the keep. 'He is expecting you.'

Cronin threw the water skin to one side and marched up the steps to the guarded entrance, closely followed by Hassan. The two sentries on duty stepped aside to allow the sergeant through yet lowered their spears to prevent the Bedouin boy from following.

'He is with me,' snapped Cronin, 'let him through.'

'Christians only,' snarled one of the guards, 'there's a dungeon for the likes of him.'

'He is as Christian as you or me,' said Cronin, 'now lower your spears.'

'Sorry,' said the guard without moving, 'can't do it. Orders you see.'

'Master Cronin,' said Hassan, from behind the sergeant, 'worry not, I will wait in the bailey. Go about your business.'

Cronin paused before walking into the keep and following the servant sent down to show him the way. Moments later he emerged onto the top of the tower, breathing heavily after climbing the particularly steep and winding staircase. As he emerged into the bright sunlight, he saw three Templar knights at the parapet, each fully clad in their white surcoats and chainmail despite the searing heat of the midday sun.

'Tom Cronin,' said one of the knights turning around, 'we thought you were long dead.'

Cronin stared in confusion. He had never seen the man before, yet he was being addressed directly by name.

'You know me?' he asked as the other two knights also turned.

'We know *of* you,' said the knight. 'Do not be surprised. We received a message from the Seneschal telling us of your task and asking us to take you in upon your return from Jerusalem, but since the king passed this way only a few days ago and had no idea who I was talking about, we assumed you had been killed.'

'My lord,' said Cronin, 'you have me at a disadvantage. May I ask who it is I am addressing?'

'I am Sir Redwood, castellan of this place and these are fellow brothers, Sir Mortimer and Sir Barnard.'

Both men nodded a greeting toward Cronin.

'So,' continued Sir Redwood, 'I am told you come with grave news.'

'I do,' said Cronin, 'Jerusalem is at great risk and I fear the king has no way of knowing the peril the city faces.'

'On the contrary,' said Redwood, 'I spent several evenings with him recently and he is doing everything in his power to defend Jerusalem. Even as we speak he gathers an army at Ashkelon to defend against the Ayyubid advance.'

'You don't understand,' said Cronin, 'Ashkelon is a feint and Saladin's army is already on its way to Jerusalem.'

'Where?'

'I don't know exactly but they must be forming up somewhere south of this place. They mustered east of the mountains in a place called the Maktesh Ramon and now pour down from the hills between the king and Jerusalem. Only Blancheguarde lies in Saladin's path.'

'And you sure of this?' asked Redwood walking briskly towards the sergeant.

'I have seen them with my own eyes,' said Cronin. 'The enemy camp spread as far as the eye could see, thousands of men hiding in a desert valley while waiting to mobilise against us. Even as we left there were signs they were breaking camp and were headed west.'

'Yet you escaped?'

'Only because of a Bedouin boy. Since we left we have seen the Saracens on the move, mainly headed down toward the plains below Montgisard.'

'But the king is garrisoned further south in Ashkelon, expecting an attack there. He has even fortified Gaza as a precaution.'

'I have no knowledge of the king's whereabouts and even less about his tactics,' replied Cronin, 'but I assure you, Saladin has bypassed both cities and is probably on his way here even as we speak.'

Redwood stared at the sergeant, shocked at the revelation. He looked out across the castle at the men at their stations along the castle walls, knowing they would not be found wanting in any fight, but if Cronin was right, they would be cast aside like driftwood on a flood should an attack come.

'Brother Mortimer,' he said turning to his fellow knights, 'stand to the garrison. Arm every man from knight to slave and fortify the battlements.'

'Yes, my lord,' said Mortimer and left the tower as Sir Redwood turned to the second knight.

'Brother Barnard, send out a patrol and find out what is happening to the south. Use our best men but do not engage any Saracens you find. It is imperative we find out what is the truth of the matter before we commit what resources we have.'

'Aye, my lord,' answered Barnard and followed Mortimer down the narrow spiral stairway to the keep below.

Redwood turned back to Cronin.

'You look exhausted,' he said, 'when was the last time you ate?'

'I don't recall,' said Cronin.

'We will get you and your men fed but while you eat, you will recount every single moment since you left the main patrol. You will leave nothing out, is that clear?'

'Aye, my lord.'

'Then come. There is much to be discussed.'

In Gaza, Hunter had spent two hours with the Grand Master and his officers, convincing them of what was happening north of Ashkelon. At first, they had been sceptical but soon realised they had been duped by Saladin and needed to join the king as soon as possible. Since then, the castle had been a hive of activity and by nightfall, fifty Templar knights, a hundred sergeants and two hundred lancers waited patiently alongside their horse in the narrow streets of the city, waiting for darkness to fall.

The plan was simple. At last light, the northern gates would open and the column would ride out to pierce the besieging line straddling the coastal road. The mission was to break through and ride towards Ashkelon as hard as they could, using surprise and the cover of darkness to gain as much advantage as possible. They were not worried about fighting the enemy, but it was a distraction they could do without. The greater need was to join the king's army before it was too late. Gaza would be left in the hands of the infantry for there was no way they would be able to keep up with the horses.

With every gate of the city locked and guarded, there was no way the Saracen army outside could possibly know what was being planned and the battlements swarmed with infantry, determined to stop any of the many spies within Gaza signalling the enemy positions outside.

The Grand Master walked slowly along the lines, talking quietly to each man as he passed. Behind him, dozens of young boys wormed their way amongst the column, bearing water buckets and arms full of hay for the horses while others serviced the waiting men with flagons of watered wine and chunks of boiled goat.

'Drink and eat you fill before we go,' said Amand as he walked, 'for there will be no pause for rest or sustenance before we reach Ashkelon. Once there we will pause only long enough to change our mounts and then plough on in Baldwin's footprints. We can only pray to God that we will be in time.' He reached the back of the fifty Templars and paused as he saw an unknown figure standing alongside a horse half hidden in the lengthening shadows.

'You,' he said, stopping in his tracks. 'Show yourself.'

For a moment the man didn't move but realising there was no other option, slowly stepped forward and pulled back his hood before staring at the Grand Master.

'James Hunter,' said Amand. 'You have done more than enough for our cause these past few days. There is no need for you to leave the safety of these walls.'

'With respect, my lord,' said Hunter, 'I request that I am allowed to join you in your quest to find the king and fight in the shadow of the true cross.'

'You are not strong enough,' said Amand. 'We will be riding hard with no rest.'

'I am no stranger to hardship and seek no preferential treatment. Let me follow and if I fall by the wayside then so be it.'

'And if I say no?'

'Then once you have gone I will find a way out of this castle and ride northward alone.'

'You would be dead within moments.'

'Perhaps so, but there are scores to settle and I will not be found wanting.'

'You are sure about this?'

'Aye, my lord. These past few days I have seen many I called friend die at the hands of the Saracens or from the injuries they sustained while doing the king's business. I would have retribution in their name.'

'You are a stubborn man,' said Amand eventually, 'and I think you are wrong to try, but as long as you know I will not pause for stragglers, then your fate is in your own hands.'

'That is all I ask,' said Hunter.

'In that case,' said the Grand Master, 'discard the disguise and take your place amongst us.'

Hunter threw away the cloak and led his horse to join the sergeants at the rear of the Templar knights.

Amand walked back to the head of the column and looked up at the sky. It was getting dark fast, but he knew he still needed some light to reach the northern road.

'Mount up,' he said quietly, and the word rippled back along the column.

Amand looked around. It was no time for rousing calls to action for their mission had been made painfully clear to every man.

'Ready?' he asked turning to the two men behind him.

'Aye,' came the reply from both the Seneschal and the Marshal.

'Then let's get this done, he said,' and turned his horse to face the sentries. 'Open the gates.'

Chapter Thirty-Three

The Cristian Column
November 24th
AD 1177

Baldwin sat on the tailgate of a cart in the centre of the makeshift camp, having the dressings on his hands changed. For two days they had marched north towards the city of Ibelin, desperate to use the good ground to their advantage before swinging inland towards Jerusalem. Now the column rested, using the cover of darkness to gather their strength and see to the horses. Many of the men were exhausted after the forced march, not least because of the constant harrying by the Saracens, but few had fallen and the Turcopoles had kept the worst away as they protected the army's flanks.

The physician carefully removed one of the bandages from the king's arm, causing Baldwin to gasp and grit his teeth against the pain.

'My apologies, your grace,' said the physician, 'your sores have deteriorated rapidly and need attention. I shall have the poultices made up as quickly as I can and have the servants boil water to wash you down.'

'Just clean the wounds,' said the king, 'and apply the new binds. We have no time for such niceties.'

'Your grace…' said the physician.

'Do as you are told,' said Baldwin, wincing again as the last of the dressings were removed. 'We could be attacked at any moment and I will not be found unready.'

The physician nodded and walked away to bring fresh bandages as Sir Raynald appeared from the gloom and walked over to talk with the king.

'Any news?' asked Baldwin.

'Indeed,' said Raynald, 'our scouts have returned with valuable information.'

'Tell me.'

'Saladin's has become bogged down not far from here and though he still has a vast army at his command, it is spread across a wide area and disorganised.'

'How far away?'

'About three leagues,' said Raynald, 'at the base of the hill known as Montgisard.'

'I know of it,' said Baldwin. 'There is a good ford there.'

'There is, and it is there that Saladin has stalled.'

Baldwin thought furiously. If this was true it was truly a gift that needed to be exploited.

'Bring me a map,' he snapped and jumped from the cart as one of his staff rolled out a parchment on the tailgate. Two servants brought candles as Raynald and the king pored over the document.

'We are here,' said the king marking the map with a piece of charcoal, 'and Jerusalem is here.' He pointed at the image of a city on the parchment. 'Show me Montgisard.'

'Here,' said Raynald making a mark slightly southeast of their position. By sticking to the road, we have advanced far enough north but must go inland tomorrow to cut off the route to Jerusalem.

'But if Saladin mobilises first, we will be eating the dust from his cavalry's hooves.'

'Your Grace,' said Raynald, 'like I said, he has become bogged down in the mire, giving us time to react.'

'But for how long?'

'There is no way of knowing but if we were to strike camp now and march north east we can block his way before dawn.'

'March an army across country in the dark?'

'Why not? We have done it before.'

'Yes, but not one of this size.'

'Whether it be a hundred men or ten thousand, the route is the same and besides, at least we will not be hounded by those Saracen archers.'

Baldwin stared at the map again. Ordinarily, it would take no more than an hour or so to cover the three leagues but in the dark, and with so many men on the move, the time would be tripled and contain many risks, not least the chance of being discovered and attacked while the column was strung out over rough ground.

'It is a dangerous ploy,' he said eventually, 'but to delay could see us fall too far behind. Rouse the men and make ready to move, it is time to stop Saladin once and for all.'

Three leagues away, Saladin too was looking over a map with his generals, but the mood was grim and the silence, tense.

'You promised me the rest of our men would be over by nightfall,' said Saladin eventually, his voice laden with threat.

'My lord,' said Taqi ad-Din, 'we have done everything possible to bring our caravans across but the more horses we move, the worse the quagmire becomes. We have men laying rushes and have stripped the surrounding land of all the trees to lay a path, but we need more time.'

'We have no more time,' said Saladin, 'Our scouts report that Baldwin stalks us like a lion. To wait invites disaster.'

'With respect, my lord,' said Shirkuh, 'even if we were to meet the Christian army, we outnumber them two to one. I fear nothing they may bring to the field.'

'Yet again you take your eyes off the true prize,' said Saladin. 'Have I not told you we do not seek to spill the blood of the Christians simply to redden our blades? It is Jerusalem itself that that is our goal and any time spent fighting Baldwin's mercenary army holds us from that task. How many men do we have this side of the river?'

'Almost twenty-five thousand,' said Shirkuh. 'We have enough rations for two days and only await your command.'

'And the rest of the supply caravans?'

'Will be across by no later than tomorrow night.'

'You are sure of this?'

'I will take full responsibility and swear that if they are not, I will fall upon my own blade.'

Saladin stared at his best general in admiration. His loyalty and abilities were second to none.

'Give the responsibility to another,' he said eventually, 'your skills will be put to better use elsewhere.'

'Understood,' said Shirkuh.

Saladin turned to the second general.

'Taqi ad-Din,' he said, 'these past few days your forces have ranged freely along the coastal road and enjoyed the spoils of war. They have earned much respect at the victories achieved. Tomorrow morning at dawn, you and your men will lead our army north as a reward. To you will fall the duty of besieging the castle they call Blancheguarde. Fall upon it with all your might and though our siege engines are mired, your task is to ensure the Templar garrison there is contained.'

'It will be our honour,' said Taqi ad-Din as he bowed, touching his fingers to his heart lips and head.

'Shirkuh, you will command the eastern tribes in my name,' continued Saladin, 'as soon as Blancheguarde is isolated, ride hard for Jerusalem. I will follow behind with the Ayyubid and the Mamluks. When you see the walls of Jerusalem, surround the city and secure the perimeter. We will ride through and take their walls from beneath the Christian noses.'

'You too will have no siege engines, my lord,' said Shirkuh.

'We have two thousand ladders already across the river,' said Saladin, 'and with Baldwin wasting time in the west, the city will be poorly defended. By the time they catch us up, we will already be on the mount and giving thanks to Allah for our victory.'

'It is a brave plan,' said Shirkuh, 'but I would advise waiting for the rest of our army to cross the river.'

'There is no more time,' said Saladin, 'and this may be our only opportunity. Prepare the men, we march at dawn.'

Chapter Thirty-Four

The Plains of Montgisard
November 25th
AD 1177

Taqi ad-Din rode his horse slowly along the front line of the Saracen army, over twenty thousand horsemen and infantry formed up and ready to make the final advance. Each wore quilted jackets or chain mail shirts, some reinforced with plates of iron hanging upon their chests. Every man, mounted or on foot, carried a round shield and a sword. Some wore turbans while most had chainmail coifs hanging from plumed, iron helmets to protect their heads and necks. It was an impressive sight and Taqi knew it was a formidable army.

The first glimmers of dawn appeared over the mountains in the east and a mood of expectation rippled through the lines. If everything went to plan, within hours the first five thousand warriors would fall upon the Templar castle like a desert storm, forcing the garrison there to fight for their lives. Since the briefing the previous night, they had managed to get a dozen ballistae across the river and the heavy timber catapults would be a major factor in subduing the fortress.

They had also managed to get one of the two massive battering rams through the mire along with several carts of timber to make covering shields while assaulting Jerusalem's gates. Overall, they were in a far better position than they had hoped, and the general's heart soared at the thought of the imminent battle.

Taqi had never seen such a fine sight in his lifetime. At long last the many tribes had answered the call and had joined forces to cast the Christian devils from the holiest of cities once and for all. His heart pounded with pride and with joy, and the fact that he was to lead the first attack made the blood race through his veins like the heaviest of torrents.

Behind Taqi's men came the next force, ten thousand men and horses commanded by Shirkuh. He too had received Ballistae during the night and if everything went to plan, the sky above Jerusalem would be alight with flaming fireballs by the time the sun set.

Shirkuh looked further back to the remaining ten thousand men. Amongst them was a thousand Mamluk warriors mounted on the best and strongest steeds, each man handpicked from the slave army due to their prowess in battle. The Mamluks also wore heavy plate and mail armour, with chainmail coifs hanging from their iron helmets. Each warrior bore a heavy lance along with a sword and a spiked mace for close quarter fighting. They were the Sultan's bodyguard, sworn to defend him with their lives.

In the centre was Saladin himself, dressed in lightweight leather armour covered with a decorated white cloak. He sat upon his pure black stallion and peered out over the front ranks of his army, hoping that within the next few hours he would finally see the results of many years planning come to fruition. In a few moments he would give the command to advance, and when he did, there would be no turning back.

'My lord,' said one of Saladin's Generals, riding up to the Sultan, 'your army is ready. We await your command.'

Saladin looked up at the morning sun cresting the mountains to the east. The time had finally come, and he turned to the signaller at his side.

'It is time to reclaim Jerusalem,' he said, 'sound the advance.'

The man took a few deep breaths and raised the curved horn to his lips, but as he braced to empty his lungs, Saladin's hand raised sharply up, stopping the signal.

'Wait,' he said, staring northward, *'what is that'*

As he and his men stared up the slope, the morning sun glinted off a giant golden crucifix appearing over a ridge. For a few moments they were transfixed as it rose higher above the ground until a few seconds later, the men bearing the true cross appeared beneath it. The first ranks of the Christian army had arrived.

Raynald urged his horse up the final slope. Beyond it lay the plains below Montgisard, the place where Saladin's army was reported to be assembling.

He looked to his own men on either side as they each rode slowly behind the true cross, knowing that the next few hours could be their last in this life. Behind them came the rest of the sprawling army, over ten thousand men including lancers, archers, infantry and even some civilians, each determined to deny Jerusalem to the Saracens.

The going had been hard through the night and it had taken far longer than anticipated due to the need to keep the army as tight as possible but they had finally arrived and as the sun appeared in the morning sky, they crested the last rolling hill to stare down onto the plain below... and what they saw, filled their hearts with dread.

Saladin stared up at the hill with barely concealed fury. He had been moments away from carrying out the will of Allah but even as he watched, the Christian army poured over the crest and began to form up on the forward slope. At the fore were rank after rank of mounted knights, each bedecked in the colours of the king or bearing their own crests upon their shields and tabards. Above them, hundreds of banners fluttered in the morning breeze, visible through the dust raised by the hooves of so many horses.

Behind them came the lighter cavalry, the lancers and Turcopoles, fanning out beside the heavy knights to provide a wider front, while others joined the central ranks, creating the depth needed should the army advance to contact.

'I was told Baldwin was encamped on the coastal road,' shouted Saladin, 'where have these men come from?'

'They must have marched through the night,' said a general beside him, 'and used the shield of darkness to block our path.'

As they both watched, the massed ranks of Christian infantry followed the cavalry over the ridge to join their comrades on the forward slope and amongst them, the many impressive banners of the king, flying proudly in the morning breeze as their bearers took their place at the head of the army.

'There,' said the general, pointing, 'it is the Christian king himself.'

Saladin stared at his adversary. Baldwin was well known to be a leper and it was impressive to see that despite his affliction, he still led his army on campaign.

'Whatever this day brings,' said Saladin, 'the king of the Christians deserves respect.' A horseman rode through the Saracen ranks and approached the Sultan.

'My lord,' said Shirkuh as he neared, 'what are your orders?'

Saladin took a deep breath and looked around at his gathered forces. The numbers of Christians now assembling on the slopes seemed impressive, but his own army still outweighed them two to one and he was confident of victory should it come to battle. Despite this, he knew the fight would be horrific but to come so far just to turn away now was unthinkable.

'My thoughts are these,' he said eventually. 'Shirkuh, you will take two men and ride to King Baldwin to offer terms. Tell him that if he stands aside and cedes Jerusalem, we will share access to the city with the Christians. We can live alongside each other, brothers in piety, yet each serving a different master. Do this and no man needs to die this day.'

A murmur of surprise rippled through the men closest to Saladin, shocked at the generosity of the offer.

'And if he declines?' asked Shirkuh.

'Then he must accept responsibility for the consequences,' said Saladin, 'and these sands will be stained with Christian blood.'

'So be it,' said Shirkuh and turned his horse away to do his Sultan's bidding.

Up on the slope, Baldwin dismounted from his own horse and accepted a gourd of water from one of his servants, drinking deeply before pouring the remainder over his face. The air was heavy with dust from the movement of so many men and horses and he coughed heavily, desperate to clear his lungs. William of Tyre joined him with his own flask and both men stared down onto the plain.

'So, the stories were true,' said Baldwin eventually, 'the Sultan has been playing us as fools. For weeks we were tempted by his lures yet all along, he mustered a great army under our very noses. It is only by the good fortune of lesser men that we now have a chance to foil his plans.'

'That and the grace of god,' said the prelate.

The king nodded but did not turn from the impressive sight below him. Thousands of Saracens stood waiting in columns, anticipating an advance to Jerusalem. In the distance, even more were frantically trying to cross the muddy fields caused by the swollen river. The Saracen forces were remarkable and though he would never admit it aloud, Baldwin silently doubted the ability of his hastily assembled army to emerge victorious.

'Where is Raynald?' he asked eventually.

'Down there,' said William pointing further down the slope, 'at the head of the vanguard.'

'Come,' said the king, 'we should join him.'

To the sounds of the many sergeants organising the army into formation, Baldwin and the prelate made their way through the throng to join the Regent at the forefront of the massed army. As they walked the assembled knights pulled aside their mounts to make a path and the two emerged besides Sir Raynald with unobstructed views of the Saracen lines.

'My king,' said Raynald with a slight bow, 'it seems we arrived not a minute too soon. It looks like Saladin was preparing to move his army northward.'

'And an impressive army it is,' said the king. 'Did you suspect such strength?'

'To be truthful, I did not but numbers do not always win wars.'

'They are twice as strong as us,' said the king. 'What is it that makes you so confident?'

'Our men are far better than theirs in close quarter battle,' said Raynald, 'and we have the advantage of this slope. To reach Jerusalem they have to pass this way and to defend from height is an easier task.'

'Do you think they will attack us?'

'If they want Jerusalem, then there is no other option.'

Baldwin stared past the army to the far distance.

'Is that their supply caravan?'

'I think so,' said Raynald, 'they have become bogged down, but it is only a matter of time before they are across and Saladin will have all the supplies he will need.'

'So time is of the essence.'

'It is, your grace. Our own supply caravan is delayed, and we can last a day, two at most but whatever our tactics, we must act soon.'

'Our men are tired, and the horses need rest.'

'I have arranged water and food to be distributed as quickly as possible,' said Raynald. Give me an hour and we are yours to command.'

William pointed down onto the plain.

'Look, they are sending riders.'

'He wants to parley,' said Raynald. 'Perhaps the sight of so many Christian men willing to fight and die in the name of God has forced the Sultan to have a change of heart.'

'We will see,' said the king. 'Tell your men to let them through.'

A few moments later, Shirkuh and the two riders at his side reined in their horses in front of the Christian army, staring around at the thousands of hostile faces.

'We would speak to your king,' he announced loudly, 'tell him we are here with Saladin's words and seek audience.'

'I am here,' said a voice and the front ranks parted to reveal Baldwin sitting on a rock, flanked by William and Raynald.

Shirkuh dismounted and walked between the walls of men to stand before the young king, bowing his head slightly in recognition of Baldwin's station.

'King Baldwin,' he said, staring at the king's uncomfortable perch, 'I did not expect to find you on so humble a throne.'

'A simple rock formed by God's hand is greater than the most spectacular of bejewelled seats made by the hand of man. Would you not agree?'

Again, Shirkuh inclined his head, impressed at the way the king had already bettered him with nothing more than words.

'I do,' he said. 'My name is Shirkuh ad-Din and I am a General in the Sultan's army. I am here at the behest of my Sultan.'

'Why did he not come himself? His safety would have been guaranteed.'

'Perhaps so,' said Shirkuh, 'and there may well be a time when you both share wine in an air of peace, but perhaps it is too soon to engage in such things.'

'If it is peace you want,' said the king, 'I assume you are going to return whence you came.'

'Alas we cannot do that,' said Shirkuh, 'and our claim to the holy city is well documented. However, the great An-Nasir, Salah ad-Din, Yusuf ibn Ayyub, exalted sultan of Syria and Egypt, has generously offered you terms which, if agreed, sends every man on both sides back home to their wives and children without a drop of blood having been spilled.'

'And these terms are?'

'Cede the road and open the gates of Jerusalem. Do this and the Sultan will ride through alongside you as an equal, accompanied with no more men than those that ride at your side. Equals in strength and role.'

Baldwin stared at Shirkuh with shock. He was not sure what he had expected but it certainly was not this.

'You want us to give Jerusalem to you?' he asked with incredulity.

'No,' said Shirkuh, 'simply to accept that the city belongs to men of all faiths and should be shared as such. If the gates are open to all, then all blades can remain sheathed. Of course, you will remain king of Jerusalem but will allow access to any pilgrims irrespective of nationality or religion.'

Baldwin glanced at William and saw the Prelate's face contorted with barely concealed rage. Raynald too was seething with anger and a murmur of unease rippled through those men near enough to hear the offer. Raynald made to step forward, his hand on the hilt of his sword but Baldwin's arm shot out to block his way.

'General Shirkuh,' he said standing up from the rock. 'Your offer was unexpected and needs consideration. I request that you now withdraw and give us time to discuss it amongst ourselves.'

'I understand.' said Shirkuh, 'but before I leave, know this. Before this month ends, Saladin will ride through the gates of Jerusalem. Hopefully it will be at your side but either way, there will be no withdrawal from this place. The choice is simple, peace or war. We will return at dusk for your answer.' He nodded again and turned abruptly to march away to his waiting horse.

The king watched him go before turning to walk back up the hill alone.

'Your grace, where are you going?' asked William.

'To consider the offer,' said the king.

An hour later, Baldwin sat in the shade of a canopy raised against the increasing heat of the mid-morning sun. William paced nervously while Raynald stood staring out over the army towards the Saracen positions. They had been discussing the options and the mood was strained.

'With respect,' snapped the prelate, 'you cannot seriously be considering the offer. To open the gates would invite the unbelievers into the heart of Christianity itself. Within years we would be back where we were before we first wrest Jerusalem from the Saracens. Seventy-seven years of bloodshed and sacrifice for what? Nothing more than to hand it back like a scared child.'

'I suggest you curb your manner,' said the king. 'I welcome your counsel, but rudeness does not become you, nor is it necessary.'

'My apologies,' said the prelate, 'my heart advanced my feelings before my thoughts. It will not happen again.'

'Good,' said the king. 'I understand your concern but as a man of God, does not the prospect of peace excite you? Would you not prefer that thousands of Christian children see their fathers again and wives embrace their husbands? Surely that in itself is a godly aim and deserves consideration?'

'Not at the expense of the holy city,' said the prelate. 'I will take up the sword myself and fight in God's name if I thought for one second that the walls will fall to the Saracens.'

'Your words surprise me,' said the king. 'I expected the opposite.' He turned to the Regent, still staring out over the Saracen army. 'And what of you, Sir Raynald. Am I to be just as surprised and hear you change your argument to one that pursues peace?'

'No, my king,' said Raynald, 'you will not. I agree with the prelate and advocate driving these people back whence they came. Jerusalem is ours and must remain so at all costs.'

'So you think we should engage them in battle?'

'I do.'

'And you are confident of victory?'

'I am, but to achieve this, we must act immediately. His supply caravans will soon be across the river along with many more men. We cannot afford to wait any longer.'

'I thought you said we were in the stronger position and enjoyed the territorial advantage?'

'We do, but don't forget, our own supply lines are weak, and we will last only so long without fresh food and water. Saladin will know this and can afford to wait.'

'So what do you suggest?'

'I think we should do the opposite of what he expects.'

'And that is?'

Raynald turned to stare at the king.

'The only thing we *can* do, your grace, and that is to immediately attack with everything we have at our disposal.'

Chapter Thirty-Five

The Saracen Positions
November 25th
AD 1177

Saladin sat in his campaign tent, picking on a platter of cold meat and dates. It had been several hours since Shirkuh had returned and they were still no closer to knowing whether the terms had been accepted. Most of the men in his army had taken the time to rest their horses while others had left their positions to eat from the communal pots provided by the few supply wagons already through the mire. Despite the enemy position looming above them, Saladin knew that Baldwin was an honourable man and would not attack whilst terms were being discussed. Besides, the Christians would be foolish to try such a thing and would be slaughtered out of hand.

'My lord Saladin,' said a voice outside the tent, 'we have received a message from the Christian King.'

The Sultan got to his feet, leaving his platter on one of the silken cushions. He ducked out through the flap and saw one of his men bearing a parchment sealed with the wax seal of Baldwin. He turned and nodded to one of his advisors who could speak the king's language.

'Read it,' he said.

The advisor broke the seal and unfurled the document.

'My lord,' he said, 'it says the following.'

'To Sultan Salah ad-Din, leader of the Ayyubid Empire and Sultan of Egypt and Syria. I thank you for your offer of a truce but regret that the terms are unacceptable to me and my people. Jerusalem is the place where our Lord Jesus Christ took his last breath and has been reclaimed in the name of God.

In addition, we see your foray into our lands as an insult and demand you leave immediately. If you do not, then you must face your own God with the deaths of thousands upon your conscience.

Jerusalem is in Christian hands and will remain so as long as I have a single breath left in my body.

We do not recognise your counter claim and reject your offer forthwith.

The messenger looked up, his face ashen at the implications.

'My lord, it is signed by the king himself.'

'It may be signed by the king,' said Saladin, 'but the words are from the mouth of his Regent. Baldwin has allowed himself to be seduced by the warmonger Raynald, and now there will be blood on his hands. Summon my generals, we are about to wage war.'

Baldwin IV walked through the ranks of soldiers to where William of Tyre and the Bishop of Bethlehem were waiting beneath the true cross. The king wore his full battle chainmail covered with a surcoat bearing the emblem of Jerusalem. His sword hung in a scabbard from his belt and on his head, he wore a full battle helmet with a copy of the crown fixed upon it.

He came to a stop beneath the relic and raised his bandaged arms to remove his helmet, handing it to one of the men at his side. Looking up he saw the magnificent golden cross silhouetted against the morning sky and he fell to his knees, knowing that at its heart was the sliver of wood that had once touched the flesh of Jesus Christ himself. All around him, many more men removed their helmets and knelt to join the king in prayer.

'*Almighty father,*' said Baldwin, '*hear our prayer. This day you have set us a task against a formidable army, yet our burden is as nothing when compared to that borne by your son, our lord Jesus Christ. Grant us this day his strength that we may do your will and the humility to know that when we strike our foes, we do so in your name only, for Jerusalem and to your glory. Amen.*'

'Amen,' replied the men surrounding the king and everyone got to their feet.

Baldwin climbed up onto the boulder where he had sat earlier that day and turned to face the army.

'Men of Jerusalem,' he called, his voice raised to reach as far as he could, 'it has been a long campaign against a cunning foe, but at last our own fate and the fate of Jerusalem is in our own hands. We were offered terms by Saladin this very morn, but it was a sacrifice too far and meant relinquishing access to Jerusalem to any vagrant who wished to enter the city. You will know by now that we rejected his terms and as such, now face conflict to decide who rides through the gates of Jerusalem as victors, Christians or Saracens.'

He looked around the faces of the men and knew every single one of them would die before seeing the holy city fall.

'In a few moments,' continued the king, 'we will ride down and show this Saracen army what it is like when God is on your side. Do not be afraid. Their numbers seem like ants upon the ground but like ants, they can be crushed beneath the foot of a stronger beast.' He looked around again and raised his voice higher. '*Today, we are that beast.*'

The men roared back in agreement.

'And today,' continued the king, 'Saladin will be crushed beneath men guided by the hand of God himself.'

Again the men roared their approval but before the Baldwin could continue, a commotion at the back of the lines caused him to pause and stare back up the hill.

'Clear a path,' shouted a voice and as the lines parted, Baldwin could see an enormous knight, wearing a white surcoat adorned with a blood red cross ride through the lines to join him at the front of the army. The king stared in astonishment as the man dismounted and took a knee.

'My king,' said the knight eventually, 'the Poor Fellow-Soldiers of Christ and of the Temple of Solomon are at your service.'

'Grand Master Amand,' said Baldwin, taken aback at the Templar knight's unexpected arrival, 'You got our message.'

'We did,' said Amand, 'We breached the Saracen lines before riding as hard as we dared to be at your side.'

'Stand, Grand Master,' said the king, 'for on this field we are all equals before God.'

The Templar got to his feet and stared into the eyes of the king.

'How many men have you brought?' asked Baldwin.

'Fifty knights supported by a hundred sergeants and three hundred lancers. They are watering their horses as we speak.'

'And your brother knights, are they fit and able to fight?'

'With all our hearts,' said Amand, 'and if it pleases the king, we beg leave to lead the charge. We are filled with God's strength and know our mounts well. They are strong, and we have ridden them sparingly during the darkness to ensure they remain ready for the fray.'

'Fifty men will not be a wide enough front,' said Raynald next to the king.

'Then let it be eighty,' shouted a voice and again the crowd split to let a man through, another Templar knight adorned in exactly the same garments as the Grand Master.

'Sir Redwood,' said Amand, recognising the castellan of Blancheguarde, 'well met. '

The king stared again, surprised at yet another unexpected addition to his forces.

'Sir Redwood,' he said, 'I thought I told you to remain at Blancheguarde.'

'You did, my king,' replied Redwood, 'but I too received a message, borne by one of our own sergeants by the name of Thomas Cronin. He had seen Saladin's camp for himself and risked his life to bring us the warnings.'

'I know of this man,' said the king, 'for it was he who is responsible for us understanding Saladin's true focus. When this is over, God willing, I will give him audience to bestow my personal thanks.'

'He is a good man,' said Sir Redwood, 'and when he told us of the risk, I sent out my own scouts to find out if it was true. Upon their return they reported the strength of the army facing you I judged we would be better utilised here. If I was wrong, I will accept your judgement.'

'How many men do you have?'

'Thirty brother knights and another hundred lancers. With these, I suspect the vanguard will more than meet your needs.'

Silence fell as the king looked between the two Templar knights. Their reputation in battle was second to none and he knew that if he was to succeed in defeating Saladin, then every sword arm would be desperately needed.

'Assuming I agree,' said the king, 'what would be your strategy?'

'We would do what we do best,' replied Grand Master Amand, 'and lead a charge directly into the heart of the enemy forces. While Sir Raynald here keeps the rest of the Saracen army busy, we will strike at its very heart.'

'You will go after Saladin himself?'

'Why not? Rip out the heart and the beast falls.'

The king turned to Raynald.

'What are your thoughts?'

'I am the regent,' said Raynald, 'so the glory for the first assault should fall on me and my men.'

'With respect, lord Raynald,' interjected Amand, 'the chances of you falling in the vanguard are very high and the king will need your military skill to guide his hand in the battle that follows. Let it be us brothers to force the breach while you follow up with the army.'

'The Grand Master makes sense,' said Baldwin. 'Your offer of leading the vanguard is noted but your skills will be far better utilised commanding our army. The Templars will form the spearhead while we will lead our own ranks.' He turned back to the Grand Master. 'You and your brother Templars will lead the charge. Get yourselves ready for there is no time to waste.'

'Thank you, my king,' said Amand and turned to walk away, closely followed by Sir Redwood.

'Do you think they can do it?' asked William at the king's side.

'I have no idea,' said Baldwin, 'but if anyone can, then it is the Templars.'

Half an hour later the whole army assembled into their formations and to the sound of beating drums walked slowly down the hill to the flat plain below. A few hundred paces away, the Saracen army stood motionless, vast swathes of Ayyubid knights and infantry, confident that they had the numbers to defeat the Christians. At their head was Taqi ad-Din and Shirkuh ad-Din, their roles now to face the Christian army head on with the entire might of the Saracen forces.

'It is a pretty thing they fight for,' said Taqi, looking up at the true cross still positioned on the hill, 'and when we take it from their dead hands I will melt it down to make a golden saddle for my best camel.'

'They lay great store in such things,' said Shirkuh, 'and will not give it up easily. Concentrate on the battle, not the spoils.' Both men fell silent as the Christian army reached the level plain and waited for everything to settle down. Finally, the dust cleared, and they stared across at the men they would soon meet at the end of a blade.

'They already look defeated,' said Taqi ad-Din, drawing his sword. 'Just say the word and my men will finish them off.'

'Wait,' said Shirkuh, 'something is happening.'

As they watched, the Christian lines parted, and a column of large, heavily bearded mounted knights emerged to form a defensive line several paces in front of the main army. Each wore a white surcoat emblazoned with the blood red cross and rode a huge, heavily armoured war horse. Every knight bore an upright lance in one hand, adorned at the top with the fluttering pennants of the Templars.

'I know of these men,' said Shirkuh, 'fearless warriors who do not know how to retreat or surrender.'

'As long as they know how to die,' said Taqi, 'then their purpose will be fulfilled.'

As they watched, the Templars formed a single line abreast and closed ranks until each knight was tight to the one on either side.

'An impressive sight,' said Taqi, 'but they will not survive an attack by our massed cavalry. I will prepare the men.'

Up on the hill, Sir Gerald stood alongside William of Tyre beneath the true cross, his left arm still in a sling from the injuries he sustained back on the Ashkelon plains. Alongside them stood Cronin and Hassan, each watching the events unfold as the two armies manoeuvred into position.

'It is a momentous day,' said Sir Gerald, 'and one way or the other the future of Jerusalem will be settled by sunset.'

'It is just as well you arrived at Ashkelon when you did,' said William, 'else we would still be crouched behind the city walls waiting for an attack that would never come.'

'It is not me who should bear your praise,' said Gerald, 'but the men at my side. It is they who found Saladin's camp and found their way back to warn the king.'

'You have the gratitude of every man in Christendom,' said William, turning to face Cronin.

'Don't forget James Hunter,' said Cronin, 'for he is the one who bore the message to the Templars at Gaza.'

'Where is he now?' asked William.

'He has joined his comrades ready for the fight,' said Gerald, 'a role that I envy with all my heart.'

'Why?'

'Because he will avenge the deaths of his fellows while we stay up here doing nothing. We should be down there amongst our comrades.'

'You would fight?'

'Aye, I still have one good arm, but the king has ordered me to remain.'

'The king is a good man,' said William, 'and thinks you have all done enough. But if there is fire in your soul and you truly believe God is summoning you to the fight, then who are we to deny his calling?'

'To deny my king goes against every vow I have taken.'

'God's service outranks even the highest of kings,' said William, 'and I believe that today, Christianity has need of men like you. The battle is about to commence, so I suggest that whatever the outcome, by its end the king will have other things on his mind.'

Sir Gerald paused momentarily before drawing his sword with his good arm and turning to the men at his side.

'Well,' he said, 'are you coming?'

Cronin turned to Hassan.

'What of it, Hassan,' he said, 'are you ready to ride into your first battle?'

The Bedouin boy reached beneath his thawb and produced the blade he had carried all the way from Acre.

'I am ready to do God's work, my lord,' he replied, 'whatever that may be.'

Without further ado, Sir Gerald started to walk down the hill towards the rear of the army, closely followed by Hassan and Tom Cronin.

Eudes St Amand sat astride his warhorse in the centre of the Templar line. Alongside him on his right was Brother Tristan, Jakelin de Mailly and Benedict of York. On the other side were Brother Valmont, Brother Redwood, and Richard of Kent.

The rest of the Templar line stretched away on both sides, every man waiting silently for the signal to advance. They were an impressive sight to men on both sides of the battlefield, eighty heavily armed warriors, strong in both faith and stature. Their heavy surcoats atop chainmail hauberks and quilted gambesons meant their bodies were well protected against the light arrows of the enemy archers and the full-faced heavy helmets over chainmail coifs protected their heads and necks. Most wore chainmail leggings strengthened with metal plates, along with studded gauntlets to protect their hands during battle.

The horses too were heavily protected, each draped with heavy, quilted caparisons hanging low past their fetlocks, protecting them from enemy arrows and all but the strongest of sword blows.

Wherever there was space on their customary white garb, the blood red cross was clearly emblazoned, pronouncing to the world, whether friend or foe that these were the Templars, and were to be feared.

'So, at last you face the battle you so desperately desired,' said De-Mailly to the man at his side. 'I hope it does not disappoint.'

'It is what I have prayed and trained for,' said Sir Benedict, 'and I swear I will not be found wanting.'

'I'm sure you will not,' said De-Mailly, 'but I have one piece of advice if you want to survive this fight. Shelve any humanity you have and embrace the cruelty that all men hide deep within their hearts. Strike hard and fast without thought for those beneath your blade for to pause is to die. If you are lucky and God is with us, there will be time to repent later.'

'Thank you, my friend,' said Benedict. 'Your advice is well received.'

Before they could continue, the Grand Master broke ranks and rode his horse out a few paces before turning to face his men.

'Fellow knights,' he called looking along the closely packed line, 'brother Templars. Today we have been brought together by God's grace and assemble in his name to prevent a great injustice.' He started to walk his horse down the line, addressing his men as he went. 'The enemy before you,' he shouted pointing towards the Saracens, 'those unbelievers, those defilers of women and killers of Christian children, would have us believe they are our equals and claim Jerusalem for their own God. Well we are here to deny them that privilege and send a message across the Outremer that Jerusalem is, and always will be a Christian city.' He reined in his horse and looked along the lines before raising his voice, demanding a response. *'And why are we doing this?'*

'God wills it,' shouted his command in reply.

'Yes, God wills it,' shouted Amand, turning his horse to head back the other way. 'That army before you may look numerous, but they are nothing before the hooves of our chargers because never forget, you are God's chosen warriors and when we ride, they will fall to his wrath. Again he stopped and looked towards the waiting Templar line. *'Why will they fall?'*

'God wills it,' roared his men again, the response even louder than before.

'Yes, God wills it,' shouted Amand, 'and I will tell you why.' He turned to point at the Saracen army again. 'At the heart of the beast is the one man responsible for all the pain and fear felt by the innocents of these lands. Kill him and not just Jerusalem but the whole of the Outremer will sleep easy at night. Cut him down and we end the Saracen's claim to Jerusalem once and for all and if you fall, let it be with God's name on your lips. So tell me again and this time, let the angels themselves hear you retort. *Why will we fight and die for Jerusalem?'*

'God wills it,' roared the men again at the top of their voices.

'Yes,' shouted Amand, *'God ...wills... it.'*

He turned his horse one more time and resumed his place in the line.

'Make ready,' he shouted, and every knight donned their helmets as they waited for the final command. Even the horses pawed the ground in anticipation as the Grand Master lifted the face plate on his own helmet and drew his sword.

'Brother Templars,' he shouted, raising the sword high above his head, 'for God, Jerusalem and for the king… advaaance!'

Chapter Thirty-Six

The Battle for Montgisard
November 25th
AD 1177

'What are they doing?' gasped Taqi at the front of the Saracen lines, 'they are no more than a hundred and we have twenty thousand at our call. They ride to their certain deaths.'

'Do not be so quick to dismiss them,' shouted Shirkuh, struggling to control his own horse, 'I have seen these men fight and they have no equal.' He turned to his own lines. *'Present shields,'* he roared, *'prepare to defend the lines.'*

The single rank of Templar Cavalry trotted toward the vast Saracen army, each keeping their place in the tightly packed line.

'Present lances,' shouted Amand and as every knight removed their heavy weapons from their sockets to couch them beneath their arms, the pace automatically increased to a canter.

With only a few hundred paces to go, the Grand Master said a silent prayer before giving gave the last order.

'Hold the line,' he roared, as the pace increased, 'present shields. Brother Templars, in the name of God almighty…*chaaarge!'*

The line of Templars spurred their horses to a gallop and within moments, eighty of the best, heavily armoured knights in the Holy land thundered towards the vast Saracen army.

'Prepare to advance,' shouted Raynald from the front rank of the main army a few hundred paces behind the Templars, 'men of Jerusalem, *forward.'*

Almost five thousand horsemen, knights, lancers and turcopoles spurred their horses to follow the Templars into battle. Behind them came the heavily armed infantry, another five thousand foot-soldiers bearing a vast array of weapons designed for mutilation and slaughter. Each man roared their battle cries as they ran, their whole being focused on one thing only, the killing of the men facing them across the battlefield. And as they raced towards death or glory, each knew there would be no quarter asked or given…*not this day.*

It was a charge, the likes of which had never seen before with little thought for position or detailed tactics, eighty Christian warriors, hell bent on driving a human wedge through the heart of the enemy.

Behind them, the army split into two distinct halves, led by Raynald and the king. The only plan was to follow the Templars into the breach before branching off towards the flanks to split the enemy position apart. It was a gamble like no other, but bearing in mind the strength of the enemy, it was the only way that Baldwin would have any chance of victory.

At the front, the disciplined line of Templar knights drove their horses as hard as they could, reaching full gallop just before they smashed into the enemy lines in a storm of flashing steel and screams of pain.

Saracens who, only moments earlier had stood resolute in their defence, were trampled mercilessly underfoot, their lightweight spears useless against the attackers' heavy armour and their bodies breaking like twigs beneath the thundering hooves of the war horses. Templar lances impaled men, sometimes more than one, such was the impact, before snapping or being wrenched from the bearer's hands due to the momentum of the charge.

Screams of agony and fear filled the air as hands that had borne lances only seconds earlier, seamlessly drew the heavy swords to lash out at their lightly armoured victims, cleaving flesh from bone and sending fountains of blood high into the air. The Templars ploughed on, forcing their mounts over and through whoever laid before them, their swords cutting down men with impunity, and though the charge slowed, the advance did not. Many of the horses, trained to a life of battle, trampled the enemy beneath their hooves, lashing out at anything in reach with their teeth, their nostrils flaring and eyes wide with fear as they ploughed onward over the sea of dead bodies.

Within moments the brutal charge had reached over halfway towards Saladin's position and though there were almost ten thousand enemy warriors to either side, most were powerless to react due to lack of room to manoeuvre.

Behind the Templars the shattered enemy lines struggled to reform, their commanders screaming for flanking soldiers to fill the gaping hole but there was no time. Only seconds after the vanguard had forced the breach, King Baldwin and Raynald of

Chatillon led the rest of the Christian army pouring through before each flanked off in different directions, one to the left, the other to the right, effectively splitting the Ayyubid forces into four. Their numbers were far larger than the Templars with over four hundred knights in the vanguard of each back-up force along with thousands of lancers and Turcopoles, and with the defending lines already in disarray from the shock tactics of the Templars, the Saracens struggled to organise any sort of unified defence. Suddenly the well packed lines favoured by Shirkuh and Taqi ad-Din changed from an impressively organised formation to a deadly hinderance, preventing any sort of counter attack.

Within minutes the Saracen position was in danger of falling apart and Saladin stared in horror from his horse several hundred paces to the rear of his army.

'*Where is Taqi?*' he roared, '*why do we sit back and die like sheep? Sound the attack.*'

The sound of horns rent the air and down at the front of the Saracen army, the panicking Taqi ad-Din realised the command was aimed directly at him. He drew his sword and holding it high in the air, led the counter charge from the right flank.

'*Allahu Akbar*' he roared and spurred his horse forward, charging towards the flanks of the penetrating enemy army. Most of his men followed but many, shocked at the brutality and impact of the Christian attack, swerved their horses away to head away from the battle field, leaving the Saracen general dangerously under strength.

Despite this, his men hardened to the task before them and crouched low in their saddles, determined to sever the deadly snake of horsemen penetrating the Saracen position but had covered only half the ground when a hail of arrows smashed into their flanks, cutting down men and horses alike. Taqi looked over and saw another line of Turcopole horsemen, hundreds strong, bearing down upon them from the hills, with bow skills second to none.

'*Keep going,*' he screamed as his men fell about him, 'we need to break their line.' Harder they galloped and though their numbers were vastly fewer than they had been only moments earlier, they smashed into the main body of Baldwin's men, having an instant impact.

Lancers who had been focussed on driving the charge forward were now forced to turn and defend themselves, and for a few moments, the king's advance faltered beneath the impact of the attack, but no sooner did the side battle commence than the Turcopoles caught up and fell on Taqi's men with their own blades. Within moments, any structure on both sides fell apart and the fight opened up across a wide front, each man for himself as any sort of communication became useless. Horses were cut down left right and centre, their own screams of pain merging with those of the many men cut asunder by Christian and Saracen blade alike and soon the fight became one between thousands of men afoot, each equally desperate to stay alive amongst the carnage.

At the battle's heart, Sir Gerald fought viciously, all thoughts of pain from his injuries forgotten in the heat of conflict, each swing of his sword accompanied by a roar of anger as he slaughtered any Saracen within reach. A few paces away was Cronin, no less lethal with his own blade and together they led by example, driving deep into the heart of the Saracen lines.

The sound of metal clashing against metal rang through the air as men fought and died in the name of their own Gods and screams of fear merged with those of victory as many suffered the brutal reality of war in their own desperate battles to survive.

Cronin dragged his sword from a Saracen's chest, turning his head away from the spray of blood erupting from the man's heart before spinning around to parry the thrust of another enemy blade. Desperately he fought and though his body was still weak from his time in the desert, the battle lust was upon him and he fought like a demon.

Hassan followed him through the throng, ensuring Cronin's victims posed no more threat by slitting their throats with his skinning knife but the enemy's numbers meant the pressure was unrelenting and no sooner had they killed one than another took his place. Over and over again, Cronin's sword flew through the air to end a fellow man's life, but even as the bodies fell about him, he slowly became aware that his strength was ebbing with every blow.

'My lord,' shouted Hassan suddenly, *'behind you!'*

Cronin spun around to see a Saracen swinging a blade towards his neck. With little time to parry the blow, he ducked and charged into his attacker's body, driving him to the ground. The two men fought desperately but the strength of the Saracen soon became apparent and he pinned Cronin to the floor, his hands tight around the sergeant's throat. Cronin struggled but he knew he was beaten but as the last of his strength left his body, the grip around his neck loosened and he looked up to see a narrow blade sticking out of the Saracen's throat.

Slowly his attacker fell aside, his spine severed by the blade and Cronin could see Hassan standing in his place, his face shocked at how close his master had come to death.

'Hassan,' croaked Cronin, struggling to his feet. 'You saved my life.'

'I did my duty,' said Hassan leaning down to retrieve his blade, 'nothing more.'

'Are you wounded?' shouted a voice and Cronin turned to see Hunter scrambling across a sea of dead bodies towards him.

'Scratches only,' said Cronin. 'It is good to see you again my friend.'

'And you,' said Hunter, 'but there is no time to talk. Have you seen Sir Gerald?'

'He was here a few moments ago,' said Cronin, 'and headed in that direction.' He pointed deeper into the heart of the battle.'

'Then I must go and join him,' said Hunter. He paused and stared at Cronin. 'You look spent,' he continued, 'leave the rest to the army and retire while you can.'

'I will gather my strength,' said Cronin, 'and then resume the fight. Every blade counts.'

'In that case, I wish you well,' said Hunter, 'and may God go with you.' Without another word he turned to follow Gerald.

'Here,' said Hassan, giving Cronin his water bottle, 'and catch your breath, my lord. Death was almost a bedfellow.'

'A few moments only,' said Cronin watching as another advance of Christian soldiers marched past to engage the enemy, 'and then we advance again. This fight is not yet over.'

'Kill the Kafirs,' screamed Taqi, his face splattered with rivulets of Christian blood, and he swung his sword mercilessly, a fearless warrior in the service of his sultan. All around him his men did the same, their victims piling up and as their counter charge started to take effect, Taqi, at last, saw his counter attack not been in vain. The king's line was breaking, giving a surge of extra strength to all the bloodied Saracens still fighting.

'Keep going,' screamed Taqi, *'do not falter!'* But even as his men pushed harder, one of his commanders caught sight of

something that made his blood run cold. To the rear of the Turcopoles came another body of men, and this time, he knew it was one that could not be bettered. It was the Christian foot soldiers...*thousands of them.*

In the vanguard, the Templars ploughed onward, fighting furiously against overwhelming odds. Behind them came their mounted sergeants, tasked with defending the knight's backs and keeping open the breach. They too fought furiously, and hundreds of Saracens died at their hands, completely overwhelmed by the brutality of the advance and the undoubted skills of their attackers.

The ferocious charge sent rivers of fear down the spines of the defenders and many in the Templars' path broke ranks, turning to run, terrified at the perceived invincibility of the giant men on brutes of horses. The Grand Master saw the cracks and seized the opportunity.

'Keep going,' he roared, forcing his horse even harder, and though it was unlikely that any man more than a few paces away heard him, the sight of Amand's huge horse surging forward urged the well-trained Templars to follow suit and they ploughed into the fray with renewed energy, determined to reach Saladin himself at the rear of the army.

Across the battlefield, the Christian advance cut through the enemy position like a knife through butter, splitting the Saracens apart. The effect was devastating and as the vicious battles continued on three fronts, those Saracens on the outer edges started to doubt the outcome and turned their hoses away to flee the scene. The trickle soon became a flood and soon, hundreds of men were galloping from Montgisard, knowing that they could not win.

'Where are they going?' screamed Saladin, 'order them back.'

Again, horns echoed through the air, but it was no use and as the Sultan watched, almost half of his army fled the scene, leaving the rest in disarray. Shirkuh ad-Din galloped up to him, forcing men to jump from his path.

'My lord,' said Shirkuh, 'you must leave this place.'

'No,' roared Saladin, 'we can still do this. We still outnumber them.'

'My lord,' shouted Shirkuh again, 'please listen to me. The Christians are driving through in three columns with no intent on engaging us on a wider front. This renders most of our army useless and we can only watch from the flanks as our men fall like autumn leaves. Already Raynald of Chatillon's column is in reach of our rear lines and if he breaks through, your escape route will be cut off.'

'Escape,' gasped Saladin incredulously, 'why do we need to do such a thing when we have the stronger force? It is they who should be seeking escape.'

'My lord,' said Shirkuh, 'Taqi ad-Din and his men are surrounded, half of the tribes already ride away to save their own skins and Raynald is about to cut us off from our caravans. On top of this, the Templars race like an arrow towards this position and my men can't hold them much longer. Leave this place while you still can and live to fight another day.'

Saladin was furious. Only a day ago he had an army capable of taking Jerusalem but the combination of the Christian's resolve, the unexpected charge of the Templars and the cowardice of some of the lesser tribes had seen him hamstrung. If he continued there was a possibility that his army could rally but even so, they would be in no state to besiege Jerusalem, the only thing that was important.

'Shirkuh,' he said eventually. 'As usual, your words are unwelcome yet wise. I will leave with my bodyguard and ride for the desert but there I will rally our men to see what options remain.'

'There are no options,' replied Shirkuh, 'except heading for Egypt. I will hold the Christians back as long as possible, but they have us on the retreat. Head east to the mountains as fast as you can. We have a corral of racing camels on the edge of the Negev, waiting in case this sort of thing happened.'

Saladin stared at Shirkuh, confused.

'How is this possible?' he asked eventually. 'Did you not believe that victory was achievable?'

'I believe in you, my lord, but no matter how sure I may be regarding your guidance, I will always ensure your safety is at the forefront of my thoughts. The camels are waiting, as are the guides to take you there. Now, I implore you, leave this place while you still can.'

Saladin turned and stared at the battle unfolding before him. As far as he could see, his defensive lines were breaking apart as men fought desperately for their lives, the screams of the wounded and dying echoing through the air alongside the terrible battle cries of their tormentors. Many of the enemy horsemen had now dismounted and fought afoot, their huge swords cleaving through the lighter armour of their opponents in a frenzy of aggression and brutality, and Saladin knew that when it came to close quarter battle, his own forces were no match for Christian knights.

'I do not understand,' he said eventually. 'This cannot be. Everything was in our favour, yet our men are being slaughtered like lambs. What have I done so wrong that incurs the wrath of Allah?'

'Now is not the time for self-doubt,' said Shirkuh, 'all that is important is that you escape to raise another army. Jerusalem will still be ours, my lord, but not this day.'

Saladin paused a moment longer before finally accepting the guidance of his most respected General.

'My heart is heavy,' he said, 'but I will do as you ask. '

'Thank you, my lord,' said Shirkuh and turned to the commander of the Saladin's bodyguard. 'Take the Sultan from this place,' he barked, 'and ensure you protect him with your lives. If a single hair on his head is harmed, I will have every man here skinned alive and his flesh rubbed with salt. Understood?'

'It will be done,' said the commander and turned to rally his men.

Shirkuh turned to Saladin.

'Waste no more time, my lord,' he said. 'Be gone from this place and one day return with an army ten times the size. Jerusalem will indeed be ours, I feel it in my heart.'

'You are a good man, Shirkuh,' said Saladin, 'do not die in this place.'

'I will do what needs to be done,' said Shirkuh, 'and if it is Allah's will I die here then I embrace his judgement.'

'*Allahu Akbar*,' said Saladin.

'*Allahu Akbar*,' replied Shirkuh and watched as his Sultan galloped from the field, surrounded by a thousand Mamluk warriors.

'My lord,' shouted a voice, 'the men of the red cross, they are almost through. What are we to do?'

Shirkuh dismounted and drew his sword.

'I'll tell you what we are going to do,' he shouted, 'we are going to fight until they are defeated or every last one of us lies dead in the dust.' He lifted his sword, rallying the men around him, '*death to the Kafirs,*' he called, '*Allahu Akbar.*'

'*Allahu Akbar,*' they roared in return and as Saladin and his bodyguard disappeared into the distance, the remains of his army turned back to face the rampaging Christians, determined to gain him as much time as possible.

King Baldwin waded through the bodies of dead men, his face pouring with sweat beneath his helmet. His personal bodyguard fought frantically all around him but still some Saracens got through and he was forced to defend himself as best he could. His bandaged arms felt leaden and his armour weighed him down like a horse upon his back, but he was determined to battle on, knowing that any king worth his salt should fight amongst his own men.

Those under his command had fought hard and for a while, the outcome had been under threat, especially when Taqi ad-Din's army had charged in from the flanks, but with discipline and the timely intervention of the Turcopoles, the Christians had endured and now marched forward, mopping up any of the enemy too stubborn to surrender.

A momentary lull in the battle allowed Baldwin to pause and he raised his helmet to get some fresh air. All around him there was a sea of dead bodies and though men still fought in all directions, it seemed to him that the tide was turning, and his army was getting the upper hand. As he watched, a voice cried out and he saw Gerald of Jerusalem running towards him.

At first, the king was confused as he had ordered Gerald to stay away from the fight but within moments realised that the knight was screaming a warning. Slowly he turned to see a lone Saracen horseman had breached the Christian lines and was riding hard towards him, guiding his mount with his knees as he pulled back the drawstring on his bow.

Without a shield there was little the Baldwin could do but just as the arrow was loosed, Sir Gerald reached the king and knocked him to the ground. Baldwin's knights fell upon the Saracen and cut him apart as others ran over to check the two men were okay.

Sir Gerald got to his knees and helped the king to sit up.

'Your grace,' he said, 'are you hurt?'

'Only my pride,' said the king, brushing the dust from his arms, 'you?'

'I think...' said the knight, but before he could continue, a single line of blood ran from the side of his mouth.

'Sir Gerald,' gasped the king, 'you are wounded.' He jumped to his feet and immediately saw the Saracen arrow sticking out of Gerald's back.

'Get some help here,' roared the king, but as he called, the knight fell forward into the dust, frothing at the mouth as his pierced lung filled with blood.

'Sir Gerald,' said the king again, falling to his knees and lifting the knight's head, 'don't you dare die. That arrow was meant for me. This not your time. *I order you to survive.'*

Sir Gerald looked up weakly and tried to speak, but it was no use and as men rallied to help, he choked to death in his king's arms.

Chapter Thirty-Seven

**Montgisard
November 25th
AD 1177**

On the far flank, Raynald had enjoyed spectacular success and had swept straight through the Saracens to burst out the back and circle around to attack their rear. It had been a remarkable result and the three-pronged attack had finally resulted in the rout of the far larger Saracen army. Men fled everywhere, pursued by Baldwin's army, emboldened by their unlikely victory.

Several hundred paces away, Eudes de St Amand, reined in his horse and removed his helmet. As far as he could see were hundreds of dead, the far majority being Saracens. The shock tactic of charging line abreast straight at the enemy had achieved the desired outcome and as he watched, those following up behind took over the task, leapfrogging the Templars to pursue the fleeing Ayyubid. Amand dismounted and looked around, his chest heaving as he drew in desperately needed lungsful of air.

The rest of his men were equally exhausted, and all soaked with the blood of their enemies. Some carried wounds, many serious but all had continued the fight for as long as they could. The toll had been heavy but not unexpected. One of his knights walked over to join him, removing his own helmet as he came.

'Brother Tristan,' said Amand as the Marshal neared, 'I bore witness to your bravery in the fight and you have my admiration.'

'Our brothers were true to their oaths,' said Tristan, 'and fought with God's strength.'

'Let us pray it will be enough. Do we know the count of those who paid the ultimate price?'

'The Seneschal is organising a muster, my lord, but we estimate about fourty. Everyone else carries wounds of some sort and almost all our horses are dead or will need to be killed such are their injuries. Sir Raynald has rolled up the right flank and the king has defeated the army on the left. The rest of Saladin's men flee like birds from a fire.'

'It is an outstanding victory,' said Amand, 'yet I feel we have failed in our own task.'

'In what way?'

'Saladin has escaped. We almost got to him, but he lives to fight another day and that lies heavy upon my heart.'

'Do not berate yourself, my lord,' said the Marshal. 'Our tactics enabled the rout of an army more than twice our size, a holy victory that secures our claim on Jerusalem. We should give thanks to God if only for that fact alone.'

'Saladin is a powerful man,' said Amand as fresh riders raced past them to pursue the fleeing Saracens, 'and he will not take this lying down.'

'With respect, my lord,' said the Marshal, 'perhaps we should let Saladin decide what he will or will not do. For now, we must look after our own men while the king's army clears the field. The rest is up to God.'

'Agreed,' said Amand, 'come, let us look to our brothers and help ease the passing of those who are beyond help.'

'My lord,' said the Marshal as Amand turned to walk away, 'there is something else you should know.'

'And that is?' asked the Grand Master.

'My lord, I am sorry to report that during the fight, Brother Jakelin broke ranks and rode from the field.'

'Brother Jakelin? Why would he do such a thing?'

'I have no idea. One minute he was at my side and the next he was riding away as if the devil himself was at his heels.'

'Do you suspect cowardice?'

'No, my lord, he is an excellent fighter but whatever the motive, his actions weakened our line. When we find him, as we surely will, he must be punished according to the rules of our temple.'

'That's if he still lives.'

'Of course,' said the Marshal.

The Grand Master stared at the Marshal for a few moments before continuing.

'You head back to help with the wounded, I have to report to the king. I'll join you as soon as I can.'

'Yes, my lord,' said the Marshal and watched as the Grand Master walked his horse towards the rear of the lines.

As the last of the fighting fell away, Baldwin's servants joined him from the rear lines, bringing water and ointments for his affliction. Still shaken by Gerald's death and hardly able to stand, he waited as they divested him of his armour before gently washing down his filthy body and donning him with a lightweight tunic. When done, he sat exhausted on a stool, sipping on watered wine while his generals reported in regarding their successes on the field.

Baldwin glanced to one side, seeing the Grand Master walking towards him, bloody but upright and undefeated.

'My king,' said Amand as he approached, 'this is truly a great day. Glory be to God for the victory.'

'And to the men who had the courage and heart to make it happen,' replied Baldwin.

Amand dropped to one knee and kissed the king's hand before getting back to his feet.

'Did you get Saladin?' asked Baldwin.

'Alas no, but thousands of Saracens lie dead upon the field while the rest flee or have been taken prisoner. Lord Raynald has sent what cavalry he could spare to pursue the Ayyubid, but the day is yours, my king. Jerusalem is saved.'

'Indeed,' said the king, 'and your men are to be thanked for the part they played. Your charge was truly guided by the hand of God.'

Before Amand could answer, one of the servants spoke up.

'Your grace, look.'

All heads turned to see a blood sodden Templar knight approaching the king. His pace was unsteady due to a heavy wound in his leg and in his hands, he carried a rolled-up Saracen cloak. As Baldwin watched he came to a halt and dropped to one knee.

'Your grace,' he said, his head bowed, 'Lord Amand, please forgive my intrusion. I beg audience.'

Amand stared at the knight, his face barely hiding his anger.

'Please arise,' said the king before the Grand Master could speak, 'for today it is *I* who am honoured to be in *your* presence.'

'Be sparing in your praise, your grace,' said Amand, his voice cold as he continued to stare at the knight, 'for this man is Jakelin de Mailly and there is an explanation to be had.'

'I don't understand,' said the king, recognising the ire in Amand's voice, 'is this not one of your own men?'

'Indeed he is,' said Amand, 'one who placed his brothers in danger by breaking ranks.'

Sir Jakelin struggled to his feet and breathed deeply as he gathered his thoughts.

'Your grace,' he said eventually, 'my lord Amand. 'I confess I broke ranks and will accept any punishment you see fit to bestow, but I saw an opportunity too great to miss.'

'You broke ranks,' snapped Amand, 'an act that is unforgiveable in our order. What possible excuse could you have to do such a thing?'

Jakelin looked between the two men again as everyone fell silent around them.

'Well,' asked the king, 'we are waiting?'

Without saying a word, Jakelin unwrapped the cloak still in his hands and allowed the contents to fall at Baldwin's feet. For a few moments there was silence as everyone stared at the decapitated head of a Saracen warrior.

'Who is it?' asked the king, turning to the Grand Master, 'do you recognise him?'

'Aye, your grace, I do,' said Amand, looking back up at Jakelin de Mailly with renewed respect, 'it is Saladin's nephew… Taqi ad-Din.'

An hour later, Jakelin de Mailly walked slowly along the row of dead Templars, saying a silent prayer as he recognised each face. All the victims had been gathered together by their fellow knights and laid out with their hands cradling the hilts of the swords laying upon their chests. As he neared the end of the line, he stopped and stared down at the man before him, his heart sinking as he recognised his friend.

'Oh Brother Benedict,' he said quietly, 'you so desperately craved the glory of battle and it has been the undoing of you. God will surely have a place for a man with such a great heart and a true soul.'

'He fought well,' said a voice and Jakelin turned to see the Marshal standing behind him.

'Brother Tristan,' said Jakelin, 'you survived.'

'It was a hard fight,' said Tristan, 'with a terrible toll but because the sacrifice of Brother Benedict and the others, Jerusalem is now safe. We will hold a service in their names as soon as we return to Acre. What of you, are you wounded?'

'Nothing that will send me to my grave,' said Jakelin, 'though my heart is mortally wounded at the sight of so many of my brothers lying in the dirt.'

'It is time to think of the living,' said the Marshal. 'Come, let's see if we can do anything to help.'

Chapter Thirty-Eight

**Montgisard
November 26th
AD 1177**

It had been twenty-four hours since the battle ended. All of the Christian dead were laid out in straight rows, each covered by blankets taken from the abandoned Saracen caravan, and in the distance, hundreds of captives dug a huge ditch to bury those who had fallen, closely watched by Turcopole archers.

Above the rows of dead, loomed the true cross, the golden effigy so important to Jerusalem and the rest of the Outremer. Beneath it knelt King Baldwin, William of Tyre and Raynald of Chatillon.

The bishop of Bethlehem carried out a service dedicated to those that had fallen and as the rest of the men looked up at the golden cross in awe, the sun glistened off its surface as if reflecting the glory of God's heaven. Many men, hard of heart and strong in battle, fell to their knees, dazzled by the majesty and they knew in their hearts that God had been with them that day. When the service was over, King Baldwin got to his feet and turned to face the army.

'Men of Jerusalem,' he called eventually, 'we give thanks to God this day for delivering us from the evil of Saladin. You men, whether lord or knave, knight or foot soldier are all equal in his sight today and all will have an equal share in the spoils from the Ayyubid caravans.'

A murmur of approval swept through the army at the generosity of the young king.

'Yesterday,' continued Baldwin, 'was the feast day of St Catherine of Alexandria, and to honour our victory, we will build a great monastery on this very spot, dedicated to her and her memory.'

Again, the sound of approval rippled through the massed ranks.

'Take time to bury our dead,' continued the king. 'Tomorrow I will head back to Ashkelon along with my knights while those of you who answered the Arriere-ban will be paid from the royal treasuries. Take your reward and return to your wives and children carrying whatever bounty you are allocated with your heads held high and your backs as straight as an arrow. Do not be so humble as to forget to regale them with stories of the part you played in this battle for make no mistake, it will be remembered for all time. *You* made this happen, *you* are the victors, and Jerusalem is saved because of *you*. Bask in the glory for, without you, Jerusalem would now be in the hands of the Ayyubid.'

The army got to their feet and raised their swords in salute, the air reverberating with cheers as the royal party turned away.

'It is a good day, my lord,' said Raynald as they walked.

'It is,' said the king with a grimace, 'but now we have to leave.'

'Are you well, my lord?' asked Raynald with a look of concern.

'No, Sir Raynald, I am not,' said the king, 'my affliction catches up with me and I feel my strength fleeing as I speak. I need to get to Ashkelon, Raynald. I need to get there quickly.'

After the service, Cronin and Hassan walked towards the area of the field where the Templars had set up their own camp. Their pace was slow and considered and both knew that their fate would be decided in the next few hours. As they approached, Sir Richard of Kent recognised the sergeant and strode over to greet them.

'Tom Cronin,' he said offering his arm in greeting, 'are the rumours true? Was it truly you who warned the king of Saladin's plans?'

'Amongst others,' said Cronin, 'not least of whom is this young man.' He indicated Hassan at his side.

'Ah, the Bedouin who wants to be a squire,' said Richard, looking at Hassan, 'yes I remember him well. Where are you headed?'

'I have to report to the Seneschal,' said Cronin, 'it has been several weeks since I left the column, and much has happened.'

'Indeed it has,' said Richard, 'come, I will take you to the Grand Master. Your survival and astonishing tale is to be celebrated.'

They walked through the camp towards one of the few tents on the field.

'Wait here,' said Sir Richard, 'I'll let them know.' He ducked inside and found the Grand Master talking to the Seneschal and William of Tyre.

'My lords,'' said Sir Richard, 'please forgive the intrusion but the sergeant responsible for bringing the news about Saladin's true intentions begs audience.'

'Brother Cronin?' asked the Seneschal.

'Yes, my lord. Shall I bring him in?'

'Give us a few minutes,' said the Seneschal before anyone could reply, 'we will call when ready.'

'Of course,' said Sir Richard and ducked back through the flap of the tent.

'Why did you delay?' asked the Grand Master. 'We should welcome him with open arms.'

'There is something you should know,' said the Seneschal, 'especially as it affects our honoured guest here.' He nodded towards the prelate.

'Your manner intrigues me,' said William, 'what is it that causes you so much concern?'

Brother Valmont glanced at the Grand Master, receiving a nod of consent in return.

'My lords,' continued the Seneschal, 'before I left Acre to join our brothers on the march to Gaza, I received a package from Rome and was asked to have it delivered to the king himself. With war looming it became difficult to find the time to ride to Jerusalem, especially as all Templars had been ordered south. Subsequently, I sent Brother Cronin to the holy city on our behalf, tasked with delivering the package to the king. It was during this task that he managed to find out Saladin's true intentions.'

'After delivering the package?' asked the Grand Master.

'No, my lord, he did not actually get to Jerusalem, he was attacked and robbed on the way. The package was lost.'

'And who told you this?'

'Sir Redwood of Blancheguarde Castle. Cronin confessed all upon his rescue from the desert.'

'What was in the package?' asked William

'Documents mainly,' said Seneschal, 'but there was also an artefact of considerable value.'

'And that was?'

'A bejewelled cross.'

'What sort of cross?' asked Amand.

'I never saw the piece for it remained wrapped whilst in my possession, but I have now been told it was an elegant piece, made from gold and inset with the rarest of rubies. It was intended for the king.'

'But why would such a wonderous thing be sent in a mere satchel,' asked Amand, 'surely such a treasure would have been secured and have an armed guard?'

'Apparently, it did,' said the Seneschal, 'but the ship that sailed from Rome carrying them was beset with a contagion and many men died, including the guards. The satchel was eventually delivered to me by the ship's Captain.'

'Wait,' said Raynald, 'are you talking about the cross of Courtenay?'

'I have no knowledge of its name,' said the Seneschal, turning to the prelate, 'only the description relayed to me by Sir Redwood.'

'If it is the one I am thinking of,' said William, 'the cross is a valuable artefact and belonged to Baldwin's father, King Almaric. It has been in his family's possession for generations. When Almaric married Agnes of Courtenay, he presented it to her as a wedding gift and had it renamed in her honour. Last year she asked king Baldwin to have it blessed by the pope. If we are talking about the same thing, then this is a disaster for all concerned. The Courtenay Cross is her most valued possession and Baldwin will not take it lightly if it becomes known it was lost whilst in your possession.'

The Seneschal glanced towards the Grand Master, a look of concern upon his face.

'Do we know who has it now?' asked Amand eventually.

'Brother Cronin does,' replied the Seneschal.

'Then bring him in. We need to find out the facts from the man himself before we can even start to address the issue.'

The Seneschal left the tent before returning moments later, lifting the flap to allow the sergeant through.

'Brother Cronin,' he said as Amand got to his feet. 'This is the Grand Master of our order, Eudes de St Amand.'

'We met at Acre,' said Cronin with a nod of the head.

'And this is Father William of Tyre,' continued the Seneschal. 'He has the ear of the king himself and is well thought of throughout the Outremer. He is a good friend and you can speak freely in his presence.'

'Father William,' said Cronin with another acknowledging nod of respect.

'Brother Cronin,' said Amand, when the introductions were over. 'I hear you have had a busy time these past few weeks and were instrumental in supplying the information that led to our victory.'

'One amongst others,' said Cronin.

'Your modesty is most gracious,' said Amand, 'but our ranks are awash with rumours of your feats and we are grateful, not just for the part you played but for bringing such honour on the name of our order.'

'Any man would have done the same, my lord.'

'Brother Cronin,' said William, 'I'm sure the king himself will want to reward you when normality returns, but in the meantime, there is a certain matter we need to clear up.'

'I assume you refer to the package I was meant to deliver to Jerusalem?' suggested Cronin.

'I do. Do you know what the satchel contained?'

'I did not at first but while I was a captive at the hands of those that stole it, they opened the satchel and burned the documents.'

'Are you aware of anything else in the satchel?'

Cronin paused, knowing that what he was about to say would incriminate himself in the loss of the cross and he would probably face severe disciplinary action.

'I became aware of something only after I managed to escape,' he said eventually, 'a golden cross the likes of which I have never seen before.'

'And were there any other features?'

'Yes, it was embedded with rubies.'

The prelate and the two Templar knights looked between each other. It was the cross they had been discussing only moments earlier.

'Tell, me,' said the Seneschal, 'you said you was a captive yet here you are, as free as a bird. How did you escape?'

'I was aided by my squire, my lord. He cut me loose in the night.'

'You have no squire,' said the Seneschal, 'you are a sergeant, not a knight.'

'Forgive me, my lord,' said Cronin, 'it was a slip of the tongue. The boy you sent with me to find a route across country to

Jerusalem has designs on becoming a squire and after his exploits these past few weeks, I have come to think of him as one.'

'So, you are talking about the Bedouin spy you saved from the gallows in Acre by using a coin you should not have had?'

Cronin paused, realising the questioning was turning hostile.

'I am,' he said eventually, 'but like I have said before, it was a mistake and he is definitely no spy.'

'A conversation for a different time,' intervened the Grand Master. 'What happened after you escaped?'

'I pursued the thieves responsible and killed one but the other escaped.'

'And it was he who had the satchel?'

'It was, my lord. Again, I pursued him and cornered him in a brigand's lair.'

'Did you also put him to the sword?'

Cronin paused again, knowing the next few moments could decide his fate.

'I did not,' he said eventually.

'Why not?' asked Brother Valmont.

'Because there had already been too much killing and he had a family to support.'

'Did he still have the cross?'

'He did,' said Cronin.

'And did you take it from him?'

'I did not.'

'Why?'

'Because the women and children were kin to the boy who saved my life and I reckoned I owed him recompense.'

An audible gasp came from William as the two Templars stared in disbelief.

'Are you saying,' said the Seneschal, 'that you gave up a Christian artefact to a murdering brigand just to pay off an imagined debt to a suspected spy?'

Cronin stayed silent, knowing that nothing he could say could make it sound any better.

'That cross would ransom a king,' said William, 'and you are a mere sergeant. What made you put such a value on your own life?'

'I did not do it for me,' said Cronin, 'but for the mother and sister of the boy who had saved my life.'

'After you saved him in the hanging square,' snapped the Seneschal, 'so his actions in saving your life could be seen as just repayment for your original act?'

'Possibly, but that did not occur to me at the time.'

'There is no possibility about it. There was no debt to be repaid and you have gifted a holy relic to an unbeliever for no reason.'

'My lords,' said Cronin. 'At the time I saw only the face of suffering. The women had been kept as captives and abused at the hands of brigands. I judged that our role as Christians was to look after the fate of innocents and as I had no other way to help, I used the only thing I had to ease their suffering.'

'*We look after Christian innocents,*' shouted the prelate, 'not unbelievers.'

'Are we all not the same in the sight of God?' asked Cronin calmly.

The Prelate's face reddened with rage but before he could respond, the Grand Master held up his hand.

'Enough,' he said. 'We need to think this through. Brother Cronin, please leave us and seek food and water at the camp kitchen. Return here within the hour.'

'Of course, my lord,' said Cronin and left the tent.

When he had gone the Grand Master turned to the prelate.

'Father William, please sit down and have a drink. I have never seen you in such a state.'

'Do you not think I have good reason?' asked the prelate. 'The man is an imbecile.'

'He comes highly recommended,' said Amand, 'and don't forget, is solely responsible for our victory here.'

'God is responsible,' snapped the prelate, 'it was he who guided his steps and indeed every man on this field of battle. Do not presume to claim it for yourselves or any other individual.'

'Of course,' said Amand calmly. 'Nevertheless, we have some things to discuss and decisions to make. First of all, are you confident it is the same cross?'

'Of course it is,' said William. 'There is no other like it.'

'And is the king expecting it to be returned any time soon?'

'All I know is that his mother wants to use it as a centrepiece in a service dedicated to Almaric next year.'

'When?'

'On the feast of Christ's Mass.'

'Over a year away,' said Amand, walking around the tent. 'So we have plenty of time to get it back.'

'How do we do that? We do not even know where it is or who has it.'

'Cronin does,' said Amand.

'He may know the name of the brigand, but he could be anywhere by now. Cronin would never find him before he sold it on.'

'Did he not say that the women were the boy's family?'

'He did,' said William.

'In that case, the boy will know all the likely places where they could go and don't forget, something of such value will not be sold easily, at least not for the sort of price the thief would expect. No, I suspect that the brigand responsible is probably still in possession and headed for the best market.'

'And where would that be?'

'Well certainly not east or south, as such an item would only be valued for its weight in gold but in Christian quarters it would be seen as a treasure beyond imagination and demand a far higher price.'

'A Christian city perhaps?' said the Seneschal.

'But which one,' intervened William, 'he could go anywhere in the Outremer.'

'He could,' said Amand, 'but wherever he may be headed, I reckon the boy will be able to find out. Don't forget he too is Bedouin and his family would have used the same trading trails for generations. He knows how his people think and I reckon if he was tasked with retrieving the cross, then he would have a very good chance of finding out where it was.'

'So we send the boy after the brigand?'

'Aye, we do, but if this is to work, then I think we need to send them both.'

'A sergeant and a native boy tasked with such an important task will not be enough,' said the Seneschal. 'We should send someone else along with them.'

'Who?'

'Someone who has a penance to pay,' said the Seneschal looking up at the Grand Master, 'and is second to none with sword in hand.'

An hour later, Cronin again stood in the command tent in front of the three men. This time, Hassan stood alongside him, his face a picture of nerves and not a little fear.

'First of all,' said the Grand Master, 'I would like to congratulate you both again on your contribution to this campaign. Your actions are to be commended and will not go unrewarded. Like Father William said a while ago, the king himself will want to bestow honours upon you and that will come in due course. In the meantime, we have arranged our own reward for each of you as a sign of our gratitude.' He looked directly at the sergeant. 'Brother Cronin,' he continued, 'you are of lowly stock, yet you have exhibited courage worthy of any knight. You have brought honour on the name of this order and undoubtedly saved the lives of many men. It is within my power to request a knighthood from the king and will do so at the earliest opportunity.'

Cronin's eyes widened, and he started to say something but was cut short when the Grand Master held up his hand.

'I have not finished,' said Amand. 'As you do not have the resources to sustain such a position, in recognition of your service to our order, we will award you a parcel of land anywhere you desire as long as we hold suitable assets there. Even England should you so desire. It will be big enough for you to maintain the position going forward and we will also provide a modest income for the rest of your life. Once settled, if you so wish, you may then apply to join the Poor Fellow-Soldiers of Christ and of the Temple of Solomon, as a brother knight, assuming of course that you have undertaken the necessary holy orders and are willing to meet the commitment. That decision will be up to you, but the offer will remain open for one year.'

He turned to Hassan.

'You, young man, will be welcomed into our order as a squire and be trained alongside others of the same calling. When your basic training has been done, you may stay with us and be placed alongside one of the brother knights in a paid position or take your leave and serve master Cronin, whichever path he may choose.'

Both Cronin and Hassan stared in silence, shocked at the generosity. Both had been prepared to be punished but the offers were beyond their wildest dreams.

'Well,' asked the Seneschal, 'are these actions agreeable to you both?'

'Of course,' said Cronin as Hassan nodded enthusiastically, 'but I do not understand. Only an hour ago there was anger at my actions and now I am being rewarded. How can this be?'

'Ah,' said Amand, 'the matter of the cross. Yes, we are upset at your actions and indeed, there may be severe repercussions from the king when he finds out what has happened. But that need not be for several months which gives us time to rectify the situation. To that end, the rewards we just mentioned, although made as a solemn vow, are made on one condition.'

'And that is?'

'You return the cross to our possession by the end of November next year.'

Cronin stared in disbelief as silence fell in the tent.

'But how am I supposed to do that?' he asked eventually. 'I have no idea where it is.'

'How you go about it is your concern,' said the Grand Master, 'but I suspect with the aid of your squire here, you will have a better idea than most where it could be.'

Cronin glanced at Hassan who stared blankly back, not sure what to say.

'So,' said the Seneschal as Cronin turned back to face the knights, 'the rewards are generous, and we believe that bearing in mind your exploits over the past few weeks, you are more than capable of achieving the desired outcome. All we need now is to learn if you accept the quest.'

'I'm not sure,' stuttered Cronin, 'even if it was possible, it would mean going back on my word with the boy's mother and sister.'

'We've thought about that,' said Amand. 'Once you return with the cross, the boy's family will be granted a generous purse to settle anywhere in the Outremer. If necessary, they will also be placed under our protection providing they are near one of our castles or outposts.'

'And Mehedi?'

'He is a brigand and will garner no sympathy.'

'What about support?' asked Cronin, 'are we to do this alone?'

'We feel that the smaller your group, the less attention you will attract.' He removed a ring from his finger and placed it on the table. 'This seal carries my authority and will guarantee you aid from any Templar outpost. 'In addition, we will furnish you with promissory notes for supplies and bribes as well as a purse of coins. If and when you find the cross, you are authorised to pay whatever the price demanded.'

'Anything?'

'The king's favour is of far greater value than a cart full of gold. Do what has to be done.'

'But…' started Cronin.

'This is not up for discussion,' interrupted Amand, 'the offer is clear. Do this and your lives change for the better.'

'And if we fail?'

'Then I will have no option but to declare you outlawed and will send messages throughout Christendom placing a reward on both of your heads.'

'On what charge?'

'Brigandry.'

'Why?'

'You gave the king's cross to a Bedouin thief of your own free will. That means you stole it and theft is brigandry.'

'So we have no choice?'

'On the contrary, the choices are clear. There is one more thing, however. You will take someone else with you on our behalf, someone who will be our eyes and ears. He looked towards the flap of a tent as another man ducked through to join them. He was dressed in a simple brown tunic unadorned with any symbols or colours yet had the bearing of a knight. 'This man is a brother Templar,' continued Amand, 'and will accompany you until the quest is over. His name is Jakelin de Mailly.'

Chapter Thirty-Nine

Montgisard
November 28th
AD 1177

Thomas Cronin and Hassan urged their horses and pack mules up the slope, reining them in when they reached the ridge before turning to stare back the way they had come. Far below was the plain of Montgisard, the place where only days earlier, men had died in their thousands over the perceived ownership of an ancient city.

Several columns of men could be seen in the distance heading homeward, slowed by the heavy carts bearing the wounded, yet despite their burdens, both physical and mental, everyone was just grateful that they had survived the carnage.

The plain was still littered with the corpses of horses and camels, the innocent victims of all such wars but there were far too many to burn and already the scavengers were circling, ready to feast on dead flesh for weeks, such was the bounty.

Further along the ridge, Jakelin de Mailly also stared down at the battlefield, alone with his own thoughts. He had hardly said a thing since leaving the camp and seemed keen to keep his own company.

'Will you ever return here?' asked Hassan to Cronin, breaking the silence.

'Possibly,' said the sergeant. 'It would be good to see the monastery once it has been built and regale the monks with stories about how it came to be. But that is in God's hands, not mine.'

'Perhaps you will be back in England by then,' said Hassan, 'farming your own lands.'

'Let's not get ahead of ourselves, Hassan,' said Cronin. 'The task before us is higher than the steepest mountain. That cross could be anywhere, and we don't even know where to start.'

'Actually,' said Hassan. 'There is an old man who may be able to help. '

'And who is he?'

'I don't recall his name, but I remember my father would always go there when he had something to sell. I believe Mehedi will go there also for the old man knows everything about such things.'

'And where is this place?'

Before Hassan could answer, someone called out and they turned to see another rider coming up the hill, leading a packhorse loaded with provisions.

'It's James Hunter,' said Cronin, 'I wonder what he wants.'

A few moments later, the scout reined in his horse alongside that of the sergeant.

'Tom Cronin,' he said, 'I was told I would find you out here.'

'Our departure was supposed to be known to only a selected few,' said Cronin. 'How did you know where we were?'

'I have my contacts,' said Hunter. 'I understand you are seeking a bejewelled cross belonging to the king?'

'We are, though I suspect it may be a hopeless task.'

'Then perhaps you could use another set of eyes.'

'You wish to come with us?'

'I don't see why not. All my comrades are dead, and I have been granted release from service by the king in recognition of what we went through back there.'

'But I thought you wanted to return to England?'

'One day, perhaps,' said Hunter. 'In the meantime, I thought I would ride alongside you, if you will have me.'

Cronin turned to call out to Jakelin de Mailly.

'My lord,' he shouted, 'this is James Hunter, the scout responsible for alerting you in Gaza. He wishes to join us.'

'I know who he is,' said Jakelin. 'Why would a free man wish to risk his life in the lands of the Saracens?'

'I feel I can be of use, my lord.' said Hunter, 'and besides, at this moment, I have nowhere else to go.'

De Mailly stared for a few moments before nodding and turning his horse away to head east.

'He is a man of few words,' said Cronin, 'but I think that was a yes.'

'Who is he?' asked Hunter.

'One of the brother knights.'

'A Templar?'

'Aye.'

'But why does he wear the garb of a mercenary.'

'I know not,' said Cronin, 'but the road before us is long so I expect we will learn soon enough.'

'So where does this road lead?'

'Only God knows the eventual destination.'

'Then that is all the more reason to have a scout.'

The two men grasped each other's forearms in friendship before Hunter turned to Hassan.

'Well, young squire,' he said, 'do you have any idea where to start?'

'Aye, I do,' said Hassan. 'A place called Segor on the southern edge of the salt sea, but worry not, I know a shortcut.'

Cronin turned to look at the battlefield one more time, pausing to reflect on how many had died.

'Leave it behind you, my friend,' said Hunter, seeing the look in Cronin's eyes, 'for it is a burden no man will ever bear well. Come, unless I am mistaken, there is a cross to retrieve and very little time to find it.'

Both men turned their horses away from Montgisard, and as they followed De Mailly and Hassan further into the hills, the weight of the quest burned deep into Cronin's thoughts.

The task before them was almost impossible, and the available time far too short, but with God on their side, he had to believe there was just the slightest chance they would find the Cross of Courtney. He had to believe it.

His and Hassan's lives depended on it!

The End

Author's notes

As is usual in this sort of book, the storyline is fictional but based around actual events at the time. On occasion, poetic license may have been applied to make the story work. If this has happened, I hope you will forgive the transgression to accommodate the tale but don't forget, it is a work of historical fiction. Any mistakes within are mine and mine alone.

Terminology

The term *'Saracen,'* was a general derogatory name often used for any Arab person at the time. It did not refer to any one tribe or religion and was considered offensive by many of the indigenous cultures of the Holy Land.

Similarly, the term *'Crusader,'* was never used in the twelfth century as a reference to the Christian forces. They were usually referred to as the Franks or Kafirs by the Saracens.

The *'Outremer,'* was a general name used for the Crusader states, especially the County of Edessa, the Principality of Antioch, the County of Tripoli, and the Kingdom of Jerusalem.

Templar Ranks Used in This Book

The Grand Master was head of the Templars and in charge of the entire order, worldwide. Odo de St. Amand (often known as Eudes) was the Grand Master of the Templars between AD 1171 and AD 1179. He was a powerful leader and fought in several campaigns but was most prominent in the Battle of Montgisard where he and a relatively small number of Templar knights led the charge that ultimately defeated a far superior Saracen army led by Saladin himself.

During times of war, the Seneschal organised the movement of the men, the pack trains, the food procurement, and any other issues involved in moving an army.

The Marshal, on the other hand, was very much a military man, and the Master would usually consult with him, as well as the Seneschal before making any final decisions on tactics.

The Leper King

King Baldwin IV was indeed a leper and it was William of Tyre who first noticed he suffered no pain when his arm was scratched while playing with other children when he was a child. This was a usually seen as a symptom of Leprosy.

Despite his young age, Baldwin went on to be a powerful and respected king, winning several battles against the Saracens. His biggest victory was at Montgisard when he was only sixteen years old. Toward the end of his life, he was often carried into battle on a stretcher, such was his deformity, to show his men he was with them both in spirit and body.

The Knights Templar

The Order of the Poor Fellow Soldiers of Christ and of the Temple of Solomon was formed in or around AD 1119 in Jerusalem by a French knight, Hugues de Payens. They were granted a headquarters in a captured Mosque on the Temple mount in Jerusalem by King Baldwin II.

At first, they were impoverished, focussing only on protecting the weak on the road to Jerusalem but after being supported by a powerful French Abbot, Bernard of Clairvaux, the order was officially recognised by the church at the Council of Troyes in AD 1129. From there they went from strength to strength and soon became the main monastic order of knights in the Holy Land. Their influence grew across the known world, not just for their deeds of bravery but because of their business acumen and the order went on to become very wealthy and very powerful.

The Emblems of the Templars

The Templar seal was a picture of two men riding a single horse. This is thought to depict the order's initial poverty when it was first formed though conversely, one of the rules of the order was that two knights could not ride one horse. When travelling or going to war, they often rode under a white flag emblazoned with a red cross. Some historians believe it was in honour of St George, who's spirit many soldiers believed was seen at the battle of Antioch in AD 1098 during the first crusade. Other flags were also used with one of the most common being the Baucent, a black and white war flag with the black half being at the top.

The image of the cross was also used on other items of clothing and equipment by the Templars, and indeed other orders of warrior monks (though not in red.) However, research shows that the red cross was not officially adopted until it was awarded by Pope Eugene III in AD 1147. Before this time the knights wore only a plain white coat.

Raynald of Châtillon

Raynald was the son a French noble who joined the third crusade in AD 1146. He served as a mercenary in Jerusalem before marrying the princess of Antioch, Constance of Hauteville in AD 1153. This made him prince of Antioch and he soon became known for his brutality and warlike tendencies. Always in need of funds, his reign was cut short in AD 1161 when he was captured by the Muslim governor of Aleppo after a raid in the Euphrates valley against the local peasants. He spent the next fifteen years in jail before finally being ransomed and set free.

King Baldwin made him *'Regent of the kingdom and of the armies,'* in AD 1177 and he was one of the leaders at the famous battle of Montgisard.

William of Tyre

William was the archbishop of Tyre and a renown chronicler. He was also King Baldwin's tutor and it was he that first saw the symptoms of leprosy when the king was only thirteen years old. He is the only known person living in Jerusalem who recorded events at that time.

The Battle of Montgisard

In November 1177, the sixteen-year-old Leper king, Baldwin IV, led a makeshift Christian army south from Jerusalem in a rushed effort to delay Saladin in his advance northward from Egypt.

In an attempt to cut off the Sultan's advance, Baldwin occupied the city of Ashkelon and ordered the Templars to hold Gaza, hoping to use both cities as the base from which he could launch his campaign of defence. In addition, as his main army was still in the north, he issued an Arriere-ban, a general call to arms that obligated every Christian to rally to his banner in defence of the realm.

Saladin responded by placing both cities under siege while his main army laid waste to the surrounding region including the towns of Ramla, Lydda and Arsuf. With the king contained within the city of Ashkelon, the sultan became complacent and allowed his men to rampage freely.

During this time, Baldwin became aware of the threat to Jerusalem itself and burst through the siege at Ashkelon before heading north to intercept the Ayyubid army. Some reports also say that the Templars did the same at Gaza and rendezvoused with the king at Montgisard. The Christian forces were heavily outnumbered with some records suggesting that Saladin had upward of twenty-six thousand men in the field while Baldwin's army was probably no more than ten thousand including just over four hundred knights.

However, by now Saladin was experiencing difficulties and his supply caravan had become bogged down at a nearby river. Baldwin took advantage of the confusion and decided to attack immediately but first, he prayed at the foot of the true cross, the giant Christian relic they had taken into battle.

The vanguard was led by the Templars, approximately eighty heavily armed knights who charged line abreast into the disorganised Saracen army. Their impact was overwhelming, and they pierced the position almost up to the Sultan himself. The rest of Saladin's army panicked and with the Templar's assault being followed up by Baldwin and the rest of the army, their lines soon disintegrated with many warriors fleeing the scene. Saladin's nephew and main commander, Taqi ad-Din was killed at the battle.

Saladin realised the day was lost and only escaped by riding a racing camel as fast as he could back towards Egypt. Behind him, many of his forces were slaughtered on the battlefield and most of the others killed as they fled southward. Very few made it home.

The Christian army did not have it all their own way though and some reports say that over a thousand died with almost the same number wounded. It was indeed, a very bloody day.

Baldwin celebrated the victory by erecting a monastery dedicated to Saint Catherine of Alexandria as the battle had fallen on the day of her feast.

The Templar Order

To finish off the book I was going to try and describe the order by reproducing a list of the many strict rules that the Templars had to obey. However, I eventually realised that the following chapter from a book written in the early 12th century, praising the fledgling order puts it far better than I ever could. I hope you enjoy.

From Saint Bernard of Clairvaux from his 12th century book - In praise of the new knighthood

Chapter 4 - On the life style of the knights of the temple

And now as a model, or at least for the shame of those knights of ours who are fighting for the devil rather than for God, we will briefly set forth the life and virtues of these cavaliers of Christ. Let us see how they conduct themselves at home as well as in battle, how they appear in public, and in what way the knight of God differs from the knight of the world.

In the first place, discipline is in no way lacking and obedience is never despised. As Scripture testifies, the undisciplined son shall perish and rebellion is as the sin of witchcraft, to refuse obedience is like the crime of idolatry. Therefore they come and go at the bidding of their superior. They wear what he gives them, and do not presume to wear or to eat anything from another source. Thus they shun every excess in clothing and food and content themselves with what is necessary. They live as brothers in joyful and sober company, without wives or children. So that their evangelical perfection will lack nothing, they dwell united in one family with no personal property whatever, careful to keep the unity of the Spirit in the bond of peace. You may say that the whole multitude has but one heart and one soul to the point that nobody follows his own will, but rather seeks to follow the commander.

They never sit in idleness or wander about aimlessly, but on the rare occasions when they are not on duty, they are always careful to earn their bread by repairing their worn armour and torn clothing, or simply by setting things to order. For the rest, they are guided by the common needs and by the orders of their master.

There is no distinction of persons among them, and deference is shown to merit rather than to noble blood. They rival one another in mutual consideration, and they carry one another's burdens, thus fulfilling the law of Christ. No inappropriate word, idle deed, unrestrained laugh, not even the slightest whisper or murmur is left uncorrected once it has been detected. They foreswear dice and chess, and abhor the chase; they take no delight in the ridiculous cruelty of falconry, as is the custom. As for jesters, magicians, bards, troubadours and jousters, they despise and reject them as so many vanities and unsound deceptions. Their hair is worn short, in conformity with the Apostle's saying, that it is shameful for a man to cultivate flowing locks. Indeed, they seldom wash and never set their hair – content to appear tousled and dusty, bearing the marks of the sun and of their armour.

When the battle is at hand, they arm themselves interiorly with faith and exteriorly with steel rather than decorate themselves with gold, since their business is to strike fear in the enemy rather than to incite his cupidity. They seek out horses which are strong and swift, rather than those which are brilliant and well-plumed, they set their minds on fighting to win rather than on parading for show. They think not of glory and seek to be formidable rather than flamboyant. At the same time, they are not quarrelsome, rash, or unduly hasty, but soberly, prudently and providently drawn up into orderly ranks, as we read of the fathers. Indeed, the true Israelite is a man of peace, even when he goes forth to battle.

Once he finds himself in the thick of battle, this knight sets aside his previous gentleness, as if to say, "Do I not hate those who hate you, O Lord; am I not disgusted with your enemies?" These men at once fall violently upon the foe, regarding them as so many sheep. No matter how outnumbered they are, they never regard these as fierce barbarians or as awe-inspiring hordes. Nor do they presume on their own strength, but trust in the Lord of armies to grant them the victory. They are mindful of the words of Maccabees, "It is simple enough for a multitude to be vanquished by a handful. It makes no difference to the God of heaven whether he grants deliverance by the hands of few or many; for victory in war is not dependent on a big army, and bravery is the gift of heaven." On numerous occasions they had seen one man pursue a thousand, and two put ten thousand to flight.

Thus in a wondrous and unique manner they appear gentler than lambs, yet fiercer than lions. I do not know if it would be more appropriate to refer to them as monks or as soldiers, unless perhaps it would be better to recognize them as being both. Indeed they lack neither monastic meekness nor military might. What can we say of this, except that this has been done by the Lord, and it is marvellous in our eyes. These are the picked troops of God, whom he has recruited from the ends of the earth; the valiant men of Israel chosen to guard well and faithfully that tomb which is the bed of the true Solomon, each man sword in hand, and superbly trained to war.

        I think that says it all.

        K.M.Ashman

        KMAshman.com

Printed in Great Britain
by Amazon